The Perfect Match

RENÉE ARONIS

To request permissions, contact the publisher at reneearonisauthor.com.

Paperback: 978-1-7367983-8-6
Ebook: 978-1-7367983-9-3

First edition June 2023.

Edited by Marni MacRae
Cover design by Rehman

Excerpt from "The Little House Series"
by Laura Ingalls Wilder

Printed in the USA.

Published by L. Boede

reneearonisauthor.com

To my best friend, Scott.
Thank you for everything you do for me
and for loving me as much as you do!

And, to my mommy, who always loved me
and took good care of me.
I'm sorry your dream of publishing
a masterpiece didn't happen,
but thank you for being
proud of my little stories.

Other Books in this Series:

Meet Your Match

Striking of the Match

Broken Match

CONTENTS

Chapter One

CLIVE MAKES HIS MOVE

On the first Friday in July, David Elliott had an interview with *Impressive Male* magazine. He'd been forced to cancel it after the fire at his cottage in the Scottish Highlands. His personal assistant, Tina, had rescheduled it for him, and he would be gone for the day. The housekeeper, Kitty, was upstairs, helping the children sort through their closets and dressers for clothes they'd outgrown. Erin March, his fiancée, Fertilis Defect match, and soon-to-be mother of his fifth child, was sitting in the kitchen with the cook, Francie, deciding on the menus for the week when the doorbell rang.

"I'll get it," Erin said and jumped up to answer the door. A quick look through the peephole revealed a cluster of police officers standing on the front stoop. She opened the door and froze. The man closest to her was sizeable, both in stature and bulk, his appearance solid, impenetrable. The hand holding up his photo name card and badge was massive and thick, his thumb and first two fingers scarred and bent. It was plain to see he was a violent man.

"I am Detective Chief Superintendent Dawson," he said. "We've had a report suggesting there may be illegal substances and/or activities inside this residence. We are prepared to do a search and seizure. Please move aside and allow us entry."

Erin was stunned and didn't know what to do. "The owner isn't home right now. He'll be back this evening, and I'd feel better if you came back when he's here," she said politely. "Also, do you have a warrant to search the house?" she asked, trying to sound respectful and yet stand her ground.

1

"A warrant is not required if there is sufficient reason to believe there is—"

"I'm sorry to interrupt you, sir, and I don't mean to be disrespectful, but I believe that you *do* need a warrant to enter this house," she said, aware he was lying to her. "I'm going to call David." She took out her phone and started to make the call, but DCS Dawson pushed past her, nonetheless. "Hey! You can't do that!"

"Erin? What's the matter?" David said when he answered his mobile, evidently hearing the distress in her voice.

"Detective *Clive Dawson* is here with a few other officers. They came in without a warrant to search the house for something he believes we are hiding. Please come home, and maybe call your law—umm, solicitor, too," she said quietly.

"A'right, love, don't worry. I'll be home in a bit," he said.

"Please hurry," she said and ended the call.

———

A week after finding the two hidden envelopes full of money, David took the currency out of the house without telling anyone. Fearing it might be traceable, he destroyed all of it, though he kept how he did it to himself. He didn't want them to have to lie about it if it came to that. The money in Susannah's bank book, over a million pounds, was donated anonymously to several charities. After that, David, Erin, and Kitty discussed what to do if the police ever came to the door. They agreed that standing back and allowing them to do their search unhindered would be the best course of action.

———

Erin tried to follow the officers as they searched the house, while poor Francie, scared out of her wits, sat frozen to her seat at the breakfast table. Kitty stood on the stairs, watching the officers essentially trashing the place, and kept her cool until the children joined her, looking frightened. Erin suggested that Kitty take them to the park until the coast was clear.

"I'll not leave you—" Peter protested.

"I'll be fine. Your father is on his way home now. I need you to help Kitty calm the others. There's nothing illegal in this house, darling, so there isn't anything to worry about, alright?" she said, and he nodded reluctantly.

It was nearly an hour later when David arrived home. The police were still searching the house, and Erin hugged him when he came in the door. "Are yeh a'right?" he asked, knowing full well who Clive Dawson was. He'd read all his love letters to his former wife, Susannah, telling her how he longed to have her for his own and couldn't wait to run away with her. Unfortunately for Mr. Dawson, she'd died before they could execute whatever plans they'd put in place to get him out of the way.

David had already stashed the love letters in a safe deposit box and destroyed the photos of what appeared to be him and several prominent members of society in crude, obscene, and pornographic poses. He'd learned later, after much heartache, that they were not of him but of his cousin, Bran Elliott, who looked very much like him. "He didn't hurt yeh, or anathin', did he?"

"No, nothing like that, but he tried to tell me that he didn't need a warrant," she said.

When the officers were finished, DCS Dawson told his men to wait outside and stood eye-to-eye with David. "I'll uncover it, Elliott. I know it's here, and I'll see you at His Majesty's pleasure for what we find," he hissed, spitting in David's face as he spoke. He glared at Erin and then left, slamming the door behind him.

David and Erin stared at each other. They weren't about to say anything incriminating, just in case listening devices had been planted in the house, no matter how improbable that was. He went to her and held her. "There's nothin' tae find, so we shouldn't worry," he said.

"But who's to say he won't… or hasn't, just now… planted something in order to find it later?" Erin said. "I don't understand what this guy has against you."

"Well, his letters were quite clear as tae how he felt for Susannah. I reckon he's angry their plan didn't work, and he didn't get what he wanted with her, so he's meanin' tae take et out on me. I only hope he cools down or finds somethin' else tae occupy him soon."

"What does 'His Majesty's pleasure' mean?"

"Humph, et means prison."

"That's what I thought. David—"

"Dinnae fash, love. He'll not find anathin', so put et out of your mind."

Later that day, after the children had returned and were in the basement media room watching a film, Erin remembered to ask David how the interview went. They were in the study, checking emails, and David was answering fan mail. He shook his head and said, "Humph, et wasn't bad at the start, but when… well, when his questions became insulting, I cut et short."

"Insulting? Oh, right, about me being fat? I'm sorry," she said, knowing if she were thinner, they wouldn't ask him that kind of thing.

"Dinnae apologize, Erin. He was wrong, not you. Yer sae bonnie tae me. He can fuck off!" he said. "I love yeh."

"I love yeh, as well," she parroted. "I'd love you more if you made love to me."

"Is that so? Well then, come here to me," he said and patted his lap.

Erin stood and went to him; she sat on his lap and put her head on his shoulder. She loved it when he held her like that; it made her feel safe and protected. It seemed like a primal thing, not something she sought but something she craved without realizing it. She put her hand up to his neck and pulled his head down, kissing him and longing for him to make love to her.

David rolled the two of them on his office chair to the door and turned the skeleton key, locking it with a gentle *clunk*. She started unbuckling his belt, but it was difficult with one hand, so he helped her. He also unbuttoned and unzipped his jeans for her. She was wearing a skirt, and he ran his hand down her leg, starting at her hip, then stopped at her knee-length hem. Their breathing became much more rapid as he began sliding her skirt up slowly, revealing her soft, pale leg and silky black panties.

When his hand reached her ass, he pulled her toward him, and she felt his hard-on against her other leg. She could also feel the zipper pull, so she tried to sit up, but he somehow managed to lift her. He then carried her to the sofa and laid her on the age-softened leather cushions.

She watched him remove his clothing and then reached for him, but he pulled away. "Wait," he said and knelt on the floor in front of her. "I want to touch yeh first." He lifted her top, kissed her pregnant stomach, though she wasn't showing yet, and made his way up to her sternum. He unfastened her bra, then pulled it and her top off over her head. Her right breast was now being explored by his mouth, and his hands began moving up and down her legs. Each time she thought he'd start fondling her, he'd move his hand back down her leg, driving her crazy.

"David… please!" she said out of desperation after the fifth time he did it.

"What is it, darling? What do yeh want?" he asked as he switched breasts.

"Touch me! Please!" she said breathlessly as she felt his hands get closer and closer to where she wanted them.

"I am touchin' yeh, am I not?" he teased, now using his index finger to trace the area around her vulva. She flexed her hips and tried to reach his hand to move it, but he started kissing her mouth and wouldn't allow her to reach it.

"Mmm, you're torturing me! Please!" she begged. As the last word left her mouth, he spread her lips apart with his fingers and touched her throbbing clitoris. When she began to climax, he entered her with his fingers.

"Ach, I love how et feels when yeh do that!" he said and began kissing her neck while his fingers gently slid in and out of her.

She'd had enough of him having all the control, and as he leaned in to kiss her, she surprised him by turning her head. When he leaned back, she took her opportunity to take control and sat up. He pulled his hand away. "What—" he began, but she shook her head and gently covered his mouth with her hand.

"My turn." She pointed to the floor, wanting him to lie on his back. "Knees up!" she said, and he did as he was told. She got on her hands and knees between his legs and kissed his erection.

He pushed her head down, lifting his hips. "Ach, Erin! Yeh drive me mental when yeh do that," he said and let go of her.

She smiled wickedly and started gently licking his shaft, tickling his head with the tip of her tongue until he let out a moan and pushed her head back. "Let me inside of yeh, please!" he begged.

She wasn't finished with him and took hold of his cock in her hand, stroking it, but only for a few moments. What she really wanted to do was take him into her mouth, so she licked her lips and covered his head with her soft, wet mouth, extracting from him a loud gasp.

The noises he began to make were too loud, so she put her hand over his mouth as she slid his hard-on all the way into her mouth. Then she pulled it almost all the way out again, but not quite. She continued like that until he pushed her head back down again. Though she wanted to keep teasing him, she longed for him to be inside her more, so she lifted her head and turned to face the couch, placing her elbows up on the cushions.

He was behind her in a flash, guiding himself into her. Grasping her hanging breasts, he pulled her upright with her back against his chest. He kissed her neck, then let her back down, thrusting deeply, his hands holding her hips. As their flesh slapped together, Erin held one of the throw pillows against her mouth to muffle the cries of pleasure she couldn't keep inside.

"Are yeh… ready?" he asked, and she somehow managed to nod her head. "Good, cuz I can't stop now." He released inside her, groaning and shuddering. Then she followed him, clenching and pulsing with her second climax.

"I thought I was too old for this kind of sex, but you make me feel young. I feel like I have superpowers when we make love, David. Nothing hurts, and no positions are off-limits; it's amazing! I wanna do this till we're ninety!" she said as she caught her breath, her chest lying flat on the seat of the sofa.

"Only ninety? Why set limits?" he said as he sat on the floor with his back against the couch, out of breath and smiling.

Chapter Two

MOMENTS

The weekend flew by and included several walks to the park that involved cricket and quoits with the children. They watched the film *Finding Neverland* while eating popcorn and ice cream in the media room, too. After that, Erin noticed David behaving more childlike every moment, full of imagination and even a bit of whimsy. It was as if the film had given him permission to see life through his children's eyes. The days were filled with laughter and games, and the nights ended by not falling into bed until way past everyone's bedtime.

On Monday morning, Erin kissed David goodbye before he left the house for another interview. After that, he was headed several blocks away to do a photo shoot for a high-end clothing company. At their last prenatal visit, Erin spoke to Dr. Jill about flying to America for a few weeks of vacation. Since she was no longer having symptoms, she was cleared on the condition that she followed her treatment schedule precisely.

They were leaving on Thursday, so it was decided that Erin would take each child shopping for summer clothes during the week. Peter was the first to be chosen, and it seemed as though he was excited. She was looking forward to spending some one-on-one time with him as well.

They went to several department stores and brand-name shops she'd never imagined stepping into, let alone being able to afford. Peter, though, was like a fish in water, choosing items that, when he tried them on, looked perfectly put together and stylish. They ate lunch at a restaurant he suggested and laughed a lot, completely comfortable in each other's company. The final stop was a shoe store, where he tried on so many shoes and sandals that Erin lost count. In the end, they left with three pairs for him and two for her.

Peter hailed a taxi, and Erin was beat as she got in and looked across the facing seats at the young man she cared so much about. He was changing into one of his new pairs of trainers and didn't know she was watching him. His look of concentration was so like David's that she couldn't help but laugh. He looked up and then out the windows as if trying to find out what she was laughing about, but that only made her laugh a bit harder.

"What's so funny?" he asked, holding a half-laced shoe in his hand.

"I'm not sure I could explain it. I've just had a really nice day with you and… I don't know, I'm happy. Well, and the way you were focused on lacing your shoe just so… the look on your face was priceless; so much like your dad… it amused me, that's all."

The teenager grinned and moved to sit on the seat next to her. He continued lacing his shoe as he spoke. "I've had a smashing time as well… Mum. I've never actually been clothes shopping before now."

"Never?"

"Well, we did for the funeral, but never for anything I've wanted to wear. Our mum would purchase whatever *she* thought most fashionable for how she wanted us to dress without asking what we wanted. Not that I'm complaining; she did well enough at it, but being allowed to choose whatever I fancied was brilliant." He put the shoe on his foot, tied it, then laid his head on Erin's shoulder and inhaled several times, making her think he was about to say something. Finally, he took her hand. "Thank you for this, Mum, I'll not forget it, truly," he said and gave her a light peck on the cheek.

He was so sincere that tears sprang up in her eyes, and she had to wipe them away. "Oh, Peter, you're so sweet. You're quite welcome, and thank you for just being an awesome kid… well, young man. I've met more boys your age than I can count over the many years I drove a school bus. None of them were as amazing as you. Sheesh, now I'm being sappy! Sorry, but it's true. I think we should try to have more days like this one. I'd like to get to know all of you better... on your own, you know?"

"I'd like that as well," he said just as the taxi turned onto their street. When the driver parked, Peter grabbed most of the shopping bags and set them on the sidewalk to help Erin out of the car. Before he could pick them up again, she hugged him and took one of the bags. She then scaled the five steps that led to their front door and opened it for him.

David entered the bedroom when he got home after the photo shoot that afternoon. He began undressing by loosening his tie and was about to take off his suit coat. "Wait!" Erin said, appearing from out of the bathroom. "Oh, David, you look so handsome in that suit! Let me look at you for a moment."

He'd gotten so used to Susannah ignoring him or nit-picking everything he wore that he smiled and put the jacket back over his shoulders. "A'right, you may have one moment," he said and looked at his watch as if timing her.

"Well, I might need two or three if you'd consider being that generous?" She stood before him and tightened his charcoal grey tie that had a small cream dot design on it, then she straightened the lapels of his dark grey suitcoat and buttoned the buttons. Next, she took a step back and looked him over, top to bottom. She walked around him, patting out wrinkles and picking off stray hairs and lint, then she faced him again and smiled. "I approve. You look amazing, stunning even, and I want to eat you up! You are just impossibly handsome wearing that, but you know what?"

"I've no clue, honestly," he said, enjoying her praise.

She unbuttoned his jacket and ran her hand over the front of his double-breasted, cornflower-blue waistcoat. Slowly, she began unbuttoning each small, dark-grey bespoke button from its hand-stitched buttonhole, then she started on his starched cream and blue striped dress shirt. She took off his pearl tie tack, put it in her pocket, and untied his beautiful silk tie.

Then, starting at his collar, she slipped each pale ivory disk through its buttonhole and groaned when his skin-tight, soft, cotton t-shirt was revealed. Her hands slid up under his dress shirt and over his shoulders, apparently wanting the whole thing to slide off at one time. He laughed when the long sleeves stayed tight on his wrists. "Cufflinks," they said in unison. A wily grin played on Erin's lips, and he realized that she had him in a precarious position, hands behind his back.

Next, she lifted his undershirt and began kissing his chest, working her way down, past his flat stomach, to his trousers. She unhooked and unzipped them, and they fell to the floor, then she knelt in front of him, her face so close to the front of his underpants. He wanted her to pull them down and wrap her warm mouth around his growing shaft.

Instead, she hovered there for a moment before beginning to untie his Italian, black leather, strait-laced shoes. Each one was pulled off slowly, along with each black sock, then each trouser leg was tugged by the hem off each leg, his left side first, then his right. "I'll tell you, then."

"Ach, I've forgotten the question," he said, panting in anticipation of what she might do next.

"Hmm, I said you were handsome in your suit and then said, but you know what?"

"Aye, what?"

"You're even more attractive with it off."

He closed his eyes as she gently pressed her face to the front of his underpants. Her breath was warm and urgent on his erection. "Ach, Erin, I like that," he said, wanting her to remove his pants and take him into her mouth, which is just what she did.

"You do?"

"Oh, yes, I do! Verra much!"

"So, you'd like me to continue, then?" she said after teasing him with her tongue.

"Yes, please! Don't stop."

"But now I'm feeling a bit overdressed. What can we do about that?"

"I'll tell you if you keep that up," he said and laughed when she sat back on her heels with her head cocked to one side. "A'right, stand up."

She looked once more at his cockstand and smiled at him. "Okay, one moment," she said and took his full length into her mouth.

"Ye're so good at that, Erin! Oh! I like that," he said when she started moving her tongue back and forth with each stroke. Then she gently cupped his balls in one hand, and he had to push her away. "Ach, stop, or I'll explode in your mouth."

She backed away and studied him as he stood at attention, then she blew small puffs of air on his head and gently kissed his shaft. "But I like to play with it," she said as she stood with his helping hand.

"And et likes tae be played with, verra much, but if yeh want et tae last, yeh must let et rest, yeh ken? Help me with ma cufflinks, woman." It wasn't easy to free his hands from their sleeve prison, but together they managed it, and he began undressing her by unbuttoning her dark green blouse.

"But I don't want it to go away," she said, pretending to be disappointed when she saw it was less hard than it had been a few moments earlier.

"Ach, et'll return soon enough." She kissed his chest as he unfastened her bra in the back and hugged him as he unbuttoned her skirt. All her clothing, except her bra, fell to the floor at the same time, revealing that she wasn't wearing underwear. He smiled as he pulled her bra off her, then bent over to take one of her breasts into his mouth while his hand began exploring between her legs. Their mutual energy was intoxicating, and he wanted her.

Maneuvering her toward their bed, he allowed her to step out of the pile of clothes at her feet. "Losh, yer lovely," he said as she sat on the mattress and laid back. He knelt before her, spread her legs apart, and began kissing the insides of her thighs, hearing her gasp in anticipation. Then, he commenced kissing her folds and licking her with his tongue.

She panted and moaned, tilting her hips and arching her back as she began to climax. "Please, David, make love to me now," she breathed. He kissed her belly and continued kissing up her chest as he crawled on top of her and entered her, sliding in easily.

The house was empty since it was Tuesday, Francie and Kitty's day off, and Peter had taken his siblings to the park. They weren't expected back for at least an hour, so taking advantage of that fact, they both let loose, neither of them caring how loud they were. They changed to the missionary position, and Erin climaxed again before things became quite intense.

He looked her in the eyes as he began moving more slowly, bringing himself to the brink of his release. Taking his time, he paid close attention to every feeling, and a warm tear rolled down his face as he climaxed inside her. At last, she managed one more small one as well. "I'm sorry," he whispered and rolled onto his back, embarrassed at his tears, though he didn't understand why; they'd both cried together many times before then.

"Sorry for what? That was incredible! No complaints from me," she said as she rolled over to lay her arm across his chest. After a few moments, speaking softly, she said, "Did I miss something?" He shook his head as a few more tears ran down his cheekbones and landed in his ears, then he sniffed without thinking about it. Her head shot up, and she looked at him anxiously. "David? What is it?"

"I'm not sure, exactly. I think et's just happiness. Ye're so verra much what I've always wanted and needed in ma life, and I think the fact of et just hit me suddenly."

Erin smiled and held him tighter. "I think that's a good reason to cry; you don't have to apologize to me. I love you, and I'm glad you're so happy. I hope you always are."

"Aye, and I hope you are as well, love. How was your day?"

"Long and lonely without you, though I had a lovely shopping trip with Peter. How was yours?"

"I'm glad tae hear et, love. Ma day was long and lonely but fulfilling, I reckon."

"Fulfilling?"

"Well, I did ma best, completed ma task, and you were here tae stroke ma ego, as well as other things, when I came home. I'd say et's been a good day so far," he said and took her hand, lacing his fingers with hers.

"Yeah, I'd say that part of my day was perfect; thank you. So, what's on the agenda for tonight?"

"We could watch some telly or go for a well-disguised walk with the children," he said.

"Perhaps both?"

"Perhaps."

"I look forward to it, but after a nap, okay?"

"Aye."

The next day, Erin decided to get Dan's shopping trip out of the way, sure he wouldn't want to do it and it would be a war. She saw Charlie ready to head up to his room and asked him to tell Dan to come down and speak with her. He gave her a smile that melted her heart and ran up the stairs.

A few minutes later, she watched as Daniel trudged down the stairs, acting like he was about to go before a firing squad. "What's the matter?" she asked, trying to hide her amusement over his dramatic performance.

"I didn't mean to do it! It was an accident, honestly," he said, and she saw his chin start to quiver.

"Well then, if it was an accident, what are you going to do about it, and how do you think you should be punished?" She had no idea what he'd done, but she wasn't going to let him know that.

The boy cocked his head to the side and knit his brows in concentration. "I reckon I'll apologize to Francie and tell her I'll never do it again; how's that?" he asked, his face a bit brighter than before.

"You should apologize, yes, but don't promise anything unless you plan to follow through, okay?"

He frowned again as if the idea was completely new to him. "Yeah, that's brilliant."

"And for your punishment?"

"Well, since I didn't *mean* to do it, the punishment shouldn't be too awful, I reckon. He scrunched up his mouth, then looked up and to the left, then down and to the right. "I know; I should be grounded for a... week?"

"Only a week?" It was difficult not to laugh at his seriousness mixed with the hope that she'd allow him to get off easier than he obviously knew he deserved.

His face fell, and he looked at the floor with a shrug of his small shoulders. "I reckon a month would make me learn my lesson, but I don't think I deserve any more than that, Erin," he said and gazed at her pleadingly.

"I'll tell you what; I'll make a deal with you. I will ease your sentence to one week *if* you come clothes shopping with me and have a good attitude."

He frowned and seemed to become agitated. "But what do you need me for? Can't you do your own clothes shopping?" he said with a bewildered, annoyed tone as if that would be more punishment than he deemed necessary.

Erin couldn't help herself and laughed out loud. She pulled him close and gave him a half hug. "Oh, Dan, not for me, silly, for you. You need new summer clothes and shoes, and I'd like to spend a bit of time with you... to get to know you better."

The boy's eyes lit up, and his dimples revealed themselves to her along with his smile. "Why didn't you say that in the first place? I've never been clothes shopping before... well, except for when Mum died, and we were forced to go then." His bright face grew a bit dim, but then, like magic, it lit back up again. "May we go to an arcade?"

"I don't think we'll have time for that today, but we can have lunch wherever you choose," she said.

"Alright, may we leave now?"

Erin shook her head in disbelief and smiled at him. "Yes, we can go now; let me tell your father, first."

Erin was astonished by how much fun they had together that day. They went to four shops before Daniel found the style he liked and then had to try almost everything on. He asked her opinion and seemed to take what she said to heart when deciding what to buy. He selected quite a few graphic t-shirts, board shorts, and a cool starched linen hat that suited his face perfectly. Finally, he chose two pairs of Converse high-tops, one pair of low-tops, and a pair of sandals that were adjustable by Velcro straps.

After lunch, he surprised her by asking to go to a barber to have his hair cut and wanted her opinion on which style to get. The thirty-something barber listened to him recount his whole day. Erin overheard Dan say that his dad's girlfriend was brilliant, and he couldn't wait until she was his new mum. The man smiled and looked at her with a nod.

On the way home in the taxi, Dan talked nonstop about how much fun he'd had and that he really liked the barber, saying he wanted to be one when he grew up. His smile and laughter filled Erin with joy, and when they got home, she followed him as he ran into the house and found his dad in the study.

"Dad! Look at my new hat and haircut! Erin is great fun! I think you should marry her tomorrow so I can call her mum! I really wanted to call her that, but she's not my mum yet, so I didn't, but if you marry her tomorrow, I can, so I think you should! I'm going to find Charlie and show him my new things now. I'm chuffed that Erin is going to be my new mum, and I love you," he said and ran out of the room, carrying the bags of clothing with him before David could say a thing.

"Well," David said and smiled at her. He was sitting in his desk chair and patted his lap.

"Well," she said and sat with him.

"I'd say that went well, eh?"

"Aye, it did. I really like him a lot. As he said, we had a great time. I also think you should marry me tomorrow; what do you say?"

"If only I could, love, I would in an instant," he said and kissed her.

"I know, darling, and I'd say I do tomorrow if only I could."

David held her for a few moments and then asked, "Who's next then? Charlie or Rosie?"

"Not sure. I only have tomorrow to do it, so I'll either have to start early or take them both at the same time."

"Perhaps you should ask them?" he said.

"Yes, that's what I plan to do at supper."

"May we go together, please?" Rosie asked, and Charlie nodded enthusiastically as they sat around the dining room table that night.

"If that's what you want, sure," Erin said.

"May I come, as well?" Daniel said.

"Sorry, kiddo, you've had your day out already. This one will be for—"

"Erin is loads of fun," he said to his brother and sister. "We had a banging time today!"

"Don't interrupt, Dan," David said.

"Did you apologize to Francie?" Erin asked the boy.

Daniel's eyes grew large, and his fork stopped mid-way to his mouth. "No, ma'am, I… forgot," he said and put his head down.

David eyed his son, raising his eyebrows. "And what was your transgression this time?" he asked.

"Dan tracked mud through the kitchen and then tried to say I'd done it," Charlie said. "Francie's much smarter than that, though. He also found her hidden box of Celebrations and ate nearly the whole carton."

"You told me that you didn't *mean* to do it, Dan," Erin said. "How—"

"But I didn't *mean* to track mud through the kitchen," he whined.

"And her chocolates?" David said.

"I… I couldn't help myself, Dad! I was empty, and Francie wouldn't feed me! It's not my fault she's daft at hiding things, is it?" he said.

"Oh, Dan, you must learn to—"

"But you told me that—"

"Don't interrupt!" David said, raising his voice.

"I will buy Francie a new box of chocolates tomorrow and you will apologize to her as soon as we're finished with our meal. You are grounded for one week, as we agreed, but you will offer to help Francie with her chores for the next two weeks," Erin said and then saw a slight grin cross the boy's face. "And don't think that just because we're leaving for America on Thursday, you'll get out of it. Your punishment will begin as soon as we return."

It was Charlie's turn to grin at his brother, and Dan stuck his tongue out at him. Erin could tell he wanted to argue, but he wisely seemed to change his mind. "Yes, ma'am," he said instead.

Erin was about halfway through *Anne of Green Gables* by then and read two more chapters to them that night at bedtime. David read Gilbert's lines when he was part of the story, which she loved. Routine wasn't something she enjoyed, but she looked forward to their nighttime ritual every day.

That night, Dan wanted to wear his new hat to bed, but she managed to convince him that it would be smashed and ruined if he did. He was allowed to keep it on his bedside table instead. She and David hugged and kissed the children goodnight and then headed to their room, where they both fell into bed, exhausted but happy.

Chapter Three

PROPER MANNERS

The next day, Rosie and Charlie were practically bouncing off the walls, excited about their turn to go shopping with Erin. They wrote out a list of places they wanted to go and even had ideas about where to have lunch. Breakfast was dizzying because of their chatter, to the point that David had to intervene, telling them to be quiet.

When the hired car pulled up to the house, Erin laughed as Charlie hurried outside and held the car door open for her. She sat in the front seat while he and Rosie sat in the back. "Tell the kind lady where you'd like to go," Erin said, looking back at him.

"Oh, right, uh, Harrods, please," he said, his voice squeaking a bit.

"Well done, Charlie," Erin said and nodded to the driver.

The car pulled up to the enormous department store, and as they all got out, Erin saw an ad on the end of a bus shelter. It was David, smiling and holding up a mobile phone with the caption, 'I do, so should you.' "Good night nurse!" she said, and Rosie hung her head. The car pulled away, and she asked Rosie what was wrong. "Was it the ad?"

The girl nodded. "It's so embarrassing! I wish I had a normal dad like my friends do."

"I do as well," Charlie said, his cheeks a bit pink.

"Your friends wish they had a famous dad, trust me! Let's go inside and not think about it, okay?"

"Okay, Mummy," Rosie said and took her hand.

A smartly dressed doorman opened the door for them and said, "Good morning, ma'am, children," then touched the brim of his cap.

"Good morning, thank you," Erin said and saw Rosie nudge Charlie. When the door was closed, she looked at them. "What was that about?" Rosie blushed, and Charlie shrugged, but Erin stayed put, waiting for an answer.

"Our mum never spoke to the doorman," Rosie said.

"She told us they are meant to be ignored, and only low, common people acknowledged them," Charlie continued.

"Is that so? Well then, I have half a mind to invite the man over for dinner!" The children looked at her, wide-eyed and unbelieving. "Don't be so shocked. I'd rather be your mum's idea of low and show kindness, love, and common courtesy to the most insignificant person I meet than to be so high and mighty. There's a scripture that says pride goes before the fall. It means to be humble, or you'll not be up on your high pedestal for very long."

"Is that why she died?" Rosie asked.

"No, baby girl, that isn't what I meant. She died because she didn't take care of herself. What I'm trying to say is that everyone deserves to be treated with respect and kindness, no matter how much money they make. Perhaps that man is a billionaire, but he loves being around people so much that as a retired person, he humbled himself and decided to take that job."

"I like the way you think, Erin," Charlie said. "I noticed that when I was with our dad, he would say hello and good morning to people like that man, and I liked it. Well, I was torn, actually—"

"Yes, I was as well!" Rosie cut in. "If only low people speak to people like him, then Daddy is low. I didn't like that feeling."

"Yes, exactly," Charlie said.

"Your dad is a very kind man, and I'm glad he's been a good example to you, even if your mum thought he was low for doing it. It's called integrity when you do a good thing even when people you are with think badly about you for doing it."

They had stood near the door as they spoke, but as they began to walk away, Erin felt a touch on her shoulder and turned around. The man who had opened the door for them was standing there with his hat in his hand. "Excuse me, ma'am, I don't mean to detain you for long. I apologize, but I overheard much of what you've said to your children," he said and looked at his hat self-consciously.

Erin's face was bright red, embarrassed that he'd heard her. "Oh, sir, I'm terribly sorry for speaking about you behind your back! I was—"

"Don't you worry about that, ma'am. The reason I stopped you was to thank you for your kindness and for trying to teach these lovely young people to do the same. I'm not meant to speak to the customers and may be in it deep for doing so, but I simply had to say something."

"Oh, I'm so glad you did… Toby," she said, reading his name badge.

"I'm no billionaire, but your mum is correct," he said, looking at the children. "My Hazel loved shopping at Harrods; it's where we met actually. I took this position so I could remember my darling, though she cannot remember me any longer. She suffers from dementia, you see, and is in a care facility."

"That's so sad!" Erin said.

"Yes, sir, it is," Charlie said, and Rosie nodded.

"Now, now; I've not told you my story to make you sad. I wanted you to know your mum was right on the nose, and I hope you can recall what she's said. Sadly, my rest break is over, so I must return to my post. I hope you have a lovely day."

"You too, Toby! May I… hug you?" Erin said.

"I'm afraid I'm not allowed to do that, ma'am, but I'll consider myself hugged if that'll do?" he said with a twinkle in his eye.

"That will do, and I'll consider myself the same. I'm so glad you stopped us." They waved as he stepped out the door, and Erin smiled at the children. "Well, I don't know about you, but that just made my day!"

"Me too," Rosie said, and then Charlie said the same.

"Now, let's find you some clothes," Erin said.

They stepped onto the escalator and headed upstairs to the children's wear department. At the first landing, they could see that the whole wall was a television screen, showing ads that changed every ten seconds or so. Halfway up, it became a clothing ad with David as the model. He was posed, leaning against a rustic fence, surrounded by fields, in a tweedy hunting suit. He looked amazingly handsome, and Erin's heart skipped a beat.

Suddenly, the children ran ahead of her. "Oh dear!" she said to herself and continued at a normal pace the rest of the way up. She found Rosie and Charlie, out of breath, on the fourth floor, waiting for her. She regarded their distressed faces and felt compassion for them. "I see your point, darling. I guess it would be embarrassing for you." *I'm just glad it wasn't an ad for underwear,* she thought.

"I hate that!" Charlie said, still out of breath.

"Me too! It's just everywhere! I don't want to stay here very long," Rosie said, and her brother nodded in agreement.

"Alright, but since we're here, let's at least have a look, okay?"

They entered the shopping area, and the kids wandered around, gathering things to try on. Erin was well aware of the store's high prices, so she tried not to look at tags, though it was difficult when trying to find the correct size. It didn't take long for her to feel overwhelmed, so she said, "When I was in London last month, I found some fun shops near the Ritz. The area was called Carnaby something."

"That's in Soho, I think," Rosie said. "Mummy never brought us there."

"Well then, I think it's about time someone did. Let's finish up, and we'll head over there," Erin said, so they made their purchases and took another way out, trying to avoid the dreaded advertisements.

Another doorman held the door for them when they left, and both children were courteous and friendly with him as they stepped outside. Erin hailed a taxi, and Rosie told the driver where they were headed. They were dropped off on the corner of Beak Street and Carnaby Street. "I didn't get this far when I was here before; let's see what we can find, shall we?" Erin said.

An hour later, they were hungry, so they ate at a casual hamburger restaurant. When they got their drinks, Erin carefully ripped only the top of the paper wrapping off her straw. When they weren't paying attention, she aimed it at Charlie and blew. The wrapper flew off the end of her straw and embedded itself in his wavey mop of light brown hair. Rosie's eyes grew large, and she gaped at her.

"Do close your mouth, Rosie; we are not a codfish," she said, trying to quote a line from *Mary Poppins*. The girl's mouth closed very slowly, as though it was taking genuine effort for her to do it. She looked at Charlie, who sat perfectly still, apparently unsure of what to do.

"Charlie, it's in your hair!" Rosie whispered.

"I know! Someone take a photo!" he said with an enormous grin.

Erin lifted her phone and snapped a few shots, then took a group selfie with the wrapper still sticking jauntily out of a nearly perfect ringlet curl. "You act like no one has ever done that in front of you before," she said.

"Mum would've been hacked off!" Charlie said and started laughing.

"Yes, she'd have been very upset!" Rosie agreed.

"Weren't you allowed to have any fun? What's the point of life if you can't laugh and have a good time… as long as you're not hurting anyone, that is. Did your father expect you to be so proper all the time, too?"

"Dad is much more fun, but I reckon he'd be Barney Rubble with Mum if she'd learned about something like this," Charlie said and pointed to the wrapper, still clinging to his head.

"Barney Rubble… oh, trouble!" Erin said, pleased she'd figured out the rhyming slang without help.

"Well done, you!" Charlie said.

"Okay, then, new rules… and they shall be enforced without fail! We… as a family, shall hereby, from this moment onward, uh, have loads of fun! Any sour-pussing or overly prim and proper behavior shall henceforth be punishable by, um, a *dreadful* tickling… until such time as the offender relaxes, which is nearly impossible whilst being tickled, or says uncle, or begins laughing, honestly, from the heart. Have I made myself clear?"

Rosie looked shocked, as though she'd been dropped in an alternate universe and couldn't make heads or tails of her surroundings. Charlie gave her a grin to rival Dan's. "As clear as the ice in my fizzy drink," he said and held out his hand to shake on it.

"Well said, Charlie!" Erin said and shook his hand. "How about you, Rosie? Don't you think life would be more… worth living with some fun thrown in?"

The nine-year-old girl furrowed her brow and nodded slowly, though she looked around the dining room warily. "Yes, Mummy, though our mum would—"

"Don't get into a two and eight, Rosie! Mum's dead! I'm sorry to say it like that, but it's true. She can't dictate our every move anymore. I say, if Erin wants us to have fun, we should be chuffed to do so."

"I'm not in a state! I agree with you, Charlie, except," she said and leaned in, "not in public, like this. Mum always said that we are David Elliott's children, so we should behave differently than other children. I don't want to… to be a disappointment."

Erin could see her genuine worry and realized that it might be difficult for her to relax, being so young and having been conditioned and trained to be proper at all times. It would take time, and expecting anything too far out of her comfort zone could alienate her. "Alright, Rosie, I understand. Charlie, please remove the wrapper now," she said.

Rosie leaned her head against Erin's arm. "I'm sorry, Mummy, I should do what you say. I didn't mean to make you upset."

Erin laid her head on the girl's and then turned to kiss her temple. "I'm not upset, baby girl. I'm sorry for making you uncomfortable. We have a lot to learn from each other, I guess."

They continued their meal with very few antics and when they were finished, resumed shopping. Charlie managed to convince Erin to try on quite a few items. She learned he had great taste and style sense. At the end of the day, she had several new outfits, too.

David was home when they returned, and Erin was ready for a nap. "I'd be happy not to go shopping again for at least a year or more!" she said to him when they got to their room. "The kids were brilliant, though there are a lot of things I need to remember about how they were raised." She explained what had happened at the restaurant, and he laughed.

"Ach, I wish I'd been there tae see their faces when yeh did et. Susannah wouldn't have allowed anathin' like that in public *or* private. I'm chuffed you're here tae bring a bit of levity into their... *our* lives."

"Me too, but poor Rosie was really distressed and worried that we would tarnish your, I don't know, reputation or status. That's just an odd thing for me to consider; I've never cared about that kind of thing."

"Aye, and I've not cared overly much maself, but their mother was verra strict about that. Et'll become easier over time, I reckon. Now, let's have a wee kip before supper, a'right?"

"Alright, I like kipping with you," Erin said.

The rest of the day was spent packing and preparing for their holiday. It was sheer madness, with everyone wanting Erin and David's attention whilst they were also trying to remember what to pack and what they'd already put into their suitcases.

They had a much-needed break for supper and then finished just before bedtime. Erin was so tired she didn't really want to read to them, but she soldiered on and read one chapter. Once they were all hugged, kissed, and tucked in, she and David trudged down the one flight of stairs and cloistered themselves in their bedroom, thankful for the peace and quiet.

Chapter Four

HOLIDAY IN THE USA

The family was up early in the morning. Because of the luggage and the number of people involved, David decided to hire a small minibus, or as Erin would call it, a large van. The driver pulled up to the house and between David, Kitty, Peter, and Erin, everything and everyone was loaded.

"'Ave a nice 'oliday!" Kitty said as Erin prepared to get into the passenger seat.

"You too!" Erin said and hugged her.

The driver pulled away from the house and into traffic, then dropped them off at Heathrow Airport, terminal three. Just past security, the duty-free shops, filled with booze, perfume, watches, and jewelry, greeted them. Erin heard Rosie groan when she saw David on one of the large screens, advertising a designer name cologne. She smiled at David then the ad was replaced with another one.

They'd been a bit worried about the paparazzi, but thankfully there were none. When they finally made it to the VIP lounge, they breathed a sigh of relief and were able to relax. Erin was glad that the children had behaved themselves and wondered what they would do once they had a baby to mind as well.

A few hours later, they were on the plane and settled into their business-class seats. Ten *long* hours later, they were boarding the connecting flight to Green Bay after a rather trying four-hour layover in Chicago. Everyone was exhausted as they walked through the arrivals gate, everyone, that is, except

Daniel, who had slept most of the way there. He was bouncing around, full of energy and excited to be in America for the first time. Erin was happy to see the children as excited as she'd been when she first visited England.

Her friends, Steve and Carrie Wilson, had invited them to their twenty-fifth wedding anniversary and vow renewal celebration. The event was in Manitowoc, about forty minutes south of Green Bay, two days later. Erin and David had decided to arrive early, hoping to get over the jet lag any of them might suffer, and Tina was asked to book a room in Green Bay.

After a long wait at the car rental counter and then waiting at the doors for their vehicle, the children commented about how strange it was to see Erin, who was driving, get in on the left side of the SUV. "Why are cars made wrong-way-round here?" Daniel asked.

"Because we drive on the opposite side of the road than you do in England," Erin replied.

The boy cocked his head to the side, apparently mulling over the foreign concept in his mind. "But why?" he asked, and everyone groaned.

"I don't know why, Dan, it's just how things are here," she said, hoping that would be the end of it, though she doubted it would be. He had done nothing but ask annoying questions the whole trip, and they were all tired of it.

"Be quiet, Dan! You're giving me a headache," Rosie snapped.

"Yes, Daniel, let's have a rest from your questions for a bit," David said.

They headed east on Hwy 172, and Erin took David's hand as she remembered his last visit, which wasn't actually that long ago, though it seemed like years. After crossing the Fox River, she took the Riverside Drive exit, just as she had before, and the memory of their excitement made them both smile.

"What's so funny?" Daniel said.

"What do you mean? We're not laughing," Erin said, and the boy frowned.

"You're smiling as though you have a secret. What is it?" he asked.

"Of all the times tae pay attention, Daniel, yeh choose this one? Never mind why we're smilin', just watch the river out the window and hush now." David said, squeezing Erin's hand.

"I'm glad Tina booked us at the Hotel Northland; it's supposed to be beautiful and had a lot of controversy surrounding it while it was being restored.

"That's not how you say that word!" Daniel piped up again. "It's not CON-troversy, it's con-TROV-ersy, Erin. Sometimes you just say things wrong, doesn't she, Dad?"

"Daniel, et's not polite tae say things like that. She's not saying et wrong. People in this part of the world say et that way. Now, mind yer own business and hu—"

"Are we almost there now? I'm tired of sitting," he interrupted.

"Yes, Dan, we're almost there," Erin said with a sigh.

"Don't interrupt, Dan. Et's not po—"

"But I had to say it or I'd forget!" the young boy whined.

"Daniel, will you please shut it? I'm knackered and sick of sitting as well. I'm also tired of your never-ending questions and comments!" Peter said, and the two others nodded their agreement.

They pulled up to the tall, grand, old building in downtown Green Bay and piled out of the SUV, everyone just wanting to sleep. Everyone, that is, except Daniel, who was still bouncing around, full of energy. David shot him a serious look, and he calmed down quite a bit, but Erin could tell it was a struggle. The bellboy, who, oddly, was wearing a fedora, came out to bring in their luggage, and the family trouped wearily into the building.

Erin gasped as she walked into the fully restored lobby. It was elegant and lush, with mosaic tiled floors, rich area rugs, and fine furniture surrounded by dark paneled walls and what appeared to be original chandeliers. They asked the children to sit on the couches while they checked in, and as they stepped up to the desk, the young man smiled. Erin smiled back and couldn't help herself. "Has anyone ever told you that you look just like a young Jimmy

Fallon? It's striking!" she said and then blushed, remembering that their waiter at St. Brendan's Inn had said almost the exact same thing to David when they were there a month and a half earlier.

"I have heard that before," he said and looked at David. "I could say the same—" he began.

"We have reservations for David Elliott," David said, making the man smile.

"Yes, sir," he said, and then they heard a noise that made Erin cringe. She whirled around and saw Daniel on the floor. Charlie and Rosie were sitting on one of the sofas, staring wide-eyed at their brother, and Peter was standing over him, clearly upset.

"Please excuse—" David began, but Erin was already standing beside the boy.

"Daniel Elliott, I swear… if you don't start behaving like a civilized human being, I'll… well, I'll take you over my knee and give you a spanking!" she said.

"But I didn't—" he began to protest, holding his arm in pain.

"He was standing on the sofa trying to reach the light fixtures. I tried to stop him without causing a scene, but then he fell. I'm sorry, Erin," Peter said, looking ashamed.

"Thank you for trying, Peter, but you shouldn't feel bad; it's all on Mr. Naughty Britches, here!" she said and then saw the shock and amusement on Rosie and Charlie's faces. She thought about what she'd just said, and between being overly tired and jet-lagged, she began to laugh. "Mr. Naughty Britches? Where did that even come from?" she said as the three of them laughed until it hurt.

David joined them and frowned. Daniel was sitting on one of the upholstered chairs with Peter guarding his every move. Erin was wiping tears from her eyes, with one arm wrapped around both Rosie and Charlie's shoulders. "I'm too tired tae deal with what happened just now, so we'll talk about et when we get tae our rooms. Daniel, come with me," he said and led the way to the elevators.

"Peter and I will take the next one, darling," Erin said and smiled at the young man who would soon be her stepson. He was already about two inches taller than her and just as handsome as his father. Once the doors had closed on David and the younger children and the elevator was moving, Peter touched the up button, and they waited. "You're so sweet, Peter; did you know that?"

"What do you mean?" he asked.

"You've been the eldest brother for a long time, and you seem to take your sibling's guilt onto yourself. You don't need to do that, you know. I'm not holding you accountable for their actions. It's so nice to have you there to help, but if they do something wrong, it's on them, not you," she said, and the door opened for them. Peter nodded slowly and furrowed his brow as they stepped inside. The doors closed, and Erin touched the eighth-floor button. "What is it?"

"It... wasn't that way with our mother. If Daniel had been allowed to do that whilst she was... with us, I'd have been scolded for not doing my job well enough," he said and lowered his head.

"*Your* job? But... it's not your job to mind your siblings, Peter; it's hers and your father's... well, and now mine. Did... your dad also scold you?" she asked, feeling horrified and not really wanting to know the answer.

"No, I doubt he knew about it, actually. She'd wait to discipline me until we returned home. That way, I had the whole trip to think about what I'd done and wonder what my punishment might be that time," he said quietly.

The sound of the bell when they reached their floor startled Erin, and she jumped. They stepped off the elevator, and she looked at him, so sweet and taken for granted. "Oh, Peter, that's so unfair! I'm sorry you were put through that. I promise I'll never do that to you, alright? You're such a good boy! I can't believe she'd treat you that way; it just... just makes me so angry," she said and felt hot tears welling up in her eyes.

He smiled at her and put his arm around her shoulders. "Don't cry, Mum. I reckon it's all over now, right?" he said and then stopped, waiting for her to tell him which direction to turn.

"Oh! He didn't tell me what rooms we were in! Now what? We can't knock on every door!" The thought of doing that struck her funny bone, and she started laughing again. "I guess I'll try to call him." She found his number and called him, though it took a long time for him to answer.

"Erin? Where are you?" he asked and heard her laughing.

"We're in the hallway. You didn't tell us which rooms we're in," she said and heard a door open at the end of the hall. Charlie stuck his head out and smiled at them as they began to walk in that direction.

"By the way, thank you," Peter said to her as they walked into the room.

Daniel was sitting on an armchair pouting, and Rosie was on her tiptoes, peering out the window at the city below them. "Is this where you grew up, Mummy?" she asked.

"No, I grew up about two hours south of here, darling. I'll tell you more about it later. Right now, I need to talk to your father," she said and turned to David. "I take it this is their room since there are two beds in here?"

"Aye," he said, sounding exasperated.

"Let's go to ours; I need to talk to you about Dan," she said. Charlie *tisked* at his brother, who stuck his tongue out at him. "Now, now, none of that; we'll be right back. Behave yourselves."

When they got to their room, David sat hard on the mattress and hung his head. "I'm seriously crap at this parenting thing, Erin. I don't even ken what to say or do tae him," he said miserably.

"What have you said so far?"

"I told him tae sit on the chair and not tae say anathin'."

"Alright, what should we do then? Let's think about it. Keep in mind that he's a young boy who's been relatively well-behaved all the way here. He may be dealing with a bit of his own form of jet lag."

"Right. Good point."

"I say we send him to bed early. I mean in his pajamas and on the bed while the others are allowed to move around the room. I can't think of anything else, can you?"

"No, I can't think of anathin'. I dinnae even ken what Susannah might do, either."

"Humph! I ken what she'd do, Peter told me, but I'll tell you later."

"What? Oh dear, that doesn't sound good," he said, and she shook her head.

"It's not. Now, let's go in there and lay down the law, Sheriff Elliott!"

Daniel was sent to bed, which meant that, in essence, everyone was sent to bed as well, which wasn't a big deal to them, as they were tired anyway. They were all yawning and droopy eyed as Erin and David tucked everyone in. "There used to be a mall that I loved going to, just kitty-corner to the hotel," Erin began.

"It's *catty-corner*, Erin," Dan said, but everyone shushed him, and she was allowed to continue her story.

That night, as she lay in bed with David, and the jetlag kicked in full force, she cried as she told him what Susannah had done to poor Peter. "I know I've said it so many times already, but how could anyone be so horrible and unfair? To ruin his holiday with the dread of what was to come! What an evil woman!"

"I... I didn't know anathin' about that. Where was I livin' this whole time, Mars? How did I end up so far removed from all aspects of ma family? What else did she do that we dinnae ken yet? Mebbe we need tae have a family meetin' and discuss some of et with them?" he said, sounding depressed.

Erin nodded; she was crying and longed to hold those beautiful children who'd been emotionally and most likely verbally abused most of their lives. She wanted to tell them they were safe and loved and that she would never treat them the way their mother had, no matter what.

"David?" she said, and somehow he seemed to know what she was going to say.

"Let's go in there and watch a film or just talk. I... need tae hold ma bairns," he said, and she hugged him tightly.

"That's exactly what I was going to suggest. I love you!"

They knocked on the adjoining door, and Peter opened it for them. Daniel was on the bed crying, and Rosie looked as though she was about to start as well.

"Oh, Daniel, what is it?" Erin asked and sat on the bed next to him.

"I'm sorry, Mummy. I'm old enough now to know how to behave myself. I made Daddy and you look bad, and it was wrong. Please don't stay mad at me!" he said and buried his face in his pillow.

31

Erin looked at David and nearly started crying again. "Daniel, my sweet boy, I understand that you're excited, and it's hard to be still and good with so many things going on. I'm not mad at you, Mr. Naughty Britches," she said, making them all laugh. "We'll just have to try harder tomorrow, alright?"

He looked up at her and smiled, showing off his adorable dimples. "Really? You're not disappointed in me and angry?" he said.

"I was upset at the time, but I'm not anymore. All's forgiven, okay?"

The children seemed stunned and looked at each other. "Our mum wouldn't have done that. She wasn't a forgiving type of person," Peter said.

"Well, good thing I'm not her then, right, Daniel?" Erin said, trying to fight the jet lag and not be emotional. "What do you say we order room service and watch a movie?"

"It's a film, not a—"

"Daniel!" David said, and he stopped talking.

"There's a lovely film I saw with a guy named Davis Arrigott… was that it? That doesn't sound right… Darfudd Emilott? Anyway, it was amazing! Oh, but I think it was rated PG13, so I guess that's out. Rats, and I really fancy Darfudd!" she said.

"Do you mean Daddy?" Rosie said, looking concerned, but then she got a twinkle in her eyes and smiled. "Did you forget his name?"

"No, sweety; I know his real name is Dingbat Elkhutt." Daniel and Charlie began to laugh hard at that one and nearly rolled out of bed. "Isn't that right, Dingbat?"

"How'd you know? I thought the records of that name were destroyed! Well, now that you know, do yeh still fancy me?" he asked.

"Of course! My favorite name is Dingbat!" she said.

"You're so much fun, Erin. I'm glad you're with us now," Peter said.

"Me too, darling boy, me too."

"It's 'I am as well,' Erin—" Dan began but stopped before anyone said anything.

"I'm glad you're not still upset at Dan," Charlie said. "Our mum would've been angry at us for the whole holiday."

"She'd also tell us that we'd ruined *her* holiday and make us feel guilty. I'm glad you're not angry, Mummy. It's not much fun to feel guilty for that long. Also, I don't really want to watch a fil—movie," Rosie said with an eyebrow raised at Daniel. "I'm too tired; may we lay here like this for a while longer, please? It's nice to have both our parents want to spend time with us. I've wanted that *all* my life."

David caught his breath and turned away. He sat on the far side of the bed, obviously trying to keep his composure. "I'm sorry, Daddy! I didn't mean to upset you." Rosie sounded worried, but after a few moments, he turned back and took her hand.

"I've wanted that all yer lives, as well, ma wee bairns."

Somewhere around midnight, Erin heard a knock on the door that separated the two bedrooms, so she got up, put her robe on, and turned on the bedside light. She unlocked the door and opened it, still a bit foggy, and saw a teary-eyed Rosie. Before she could say anything, the girl wrapped her arms around her and began crying in earnest. "What's the matter, darling?" she asked and heard David moving around behind her.

"What is it, Rosebud?" he asked and picked her up, bringing her to the bed. Erin closed the door after seeing that the boys were still asleep and got back into the king-sized bed.

"I had a dream that reminded me of something Mummy said when she was angry about one of us ruining her holiday," she said and buried her head in David's neck.

"What did she say, sweety?" Erin asked, not sure she wanted to hear the answer.

"She told us… me, Charlie, and Dan, that she hadn't wanted us at all but that she'd gotten pregnant so you'd stay married to her, Daddy. She said you'd had a row, and she thought you were going to leave her, so she got pregnant, though she didn't actually want us. Then she said that… that she still didn't want us and wished we'd just leave her alone." The poor girl bawled, gasping for breath between sobs.

33

Erin and David stared wide-eyed at each other, not believing their ears. Neither of them knew what to say, and after a while, she calmed down enough to speak again. "Did *you*... want us, Daddy?"

"Always, my Rosebud! I was chuffed beyond words when your mum told me she was pregnant with your brothers and you."

"Were you planning to leave her? Is it true?" she asked.

"I don't know... that was a long time ago. I don't remember havin' a row that serious."

"Wait, that wasn't the reason for all of us," she said. "The other was to keep you at home. She said that you wanted to go far away for a film, and she didn't want you to go, so she did it to make you stay, though I don't remember which of us it was."

"Yes, I remember that. I believe et was the twins. I was meant tae go tae Argentina, and she was unhappy about et. I never put the two events together," he said sadly.

Rosie suddenly turned and glared at Erin, narrowing her eyes suspiciously. "Is that what you've done, Erin? Did you get pregnant to make my daddy leave my mummy and stay with you? Did you?" she said, raising her voice.

"Rosie!" David scolded, but Erin looked at her sadly.

"It's okay, David. I understand why she'd ask me that question." She took Rosie's hand and pulled her closer to her. "I was told that I couldn't have babies, remember? So, we didn't think I'd get pregnant. I didn't do it to keep him with me or to trick or manipulate him or you or anyone. The treatments that help me with my disease also fixed the problem that kept me from getting pregnant. We didn't plan on having a baby, but we both want this one very much. It must feel horrible to know your mom didn't want you, but I do. I want you to be my daughter with all my heart; you and your brothers. You are so dear to me that I can't imagine my life without you. I hope you can believe me," she said and kissed her small hand.

Rosie looked at them both and then lowered her head. "I'm sorry, Mummy. I didn't really think you would do that, but something inside me had to ask," she said and crawled into her lap.

"It's okay, sweetheart. You'll learn that not everyone is like your mother. Actually, I don't think many people are."

"I feel much better now. You always make me feel better, Mummy and Daddy. I'm tired, so I'll go back to bed now."

"Do you need to sleep in here tonight?" David asked.

"No, Daddy. I don't like sleeping in the middle. I'll go back to our room now. I love you."

"I love you as well, Rosebud," he said while he hugged her.

"I love you too, darling girl. See you in the morning," Erin said, and they watched her walk away, disappearing through the door.

———

David followed her and locked it, then he took off his boxer shorts and got back onto the bed, sitting next to Erin. "Take your night clothes off and lay on your back, please," he said quietly. She seemed surprised by his request, but she did it anyway. He watched her undress, studying her body. She was only seven weeks pregnant, and he couldn't see any sign of it yet. He smiled at her as she lay next to him on her back, so trusting and amenable.

"What are you—" she began, but he shushed her gently and moved closer to her across the soft white sheets.

He touched the smooth, pale skin on her chest between her breasts with his pointer finger, eliciting a small gasp and then a quiet moan. He slid his finger slowly down her sternum to her belly button and stopped just above her pubic hair. He then laid his hand flat against her stomach, rubbing it gently. She smiled at him, and he smiled back as he bent his head to kiss her belly and the invisible life held within it.

"Hello, darling," he said to the place he'd just kissed. "Et's yer da'. I want you tae know I'm glad yer here and that I want yeh verra much. Ye're a blessin' tae yer mother and me, and we can't wait to meet yeh. Stay healthy, ma love." He kissed the spot again and then began making his way down her body, kissing her as he went. He got onto his hands and knees and straddled her so that his hard-on was over her face.

"Oh, David! I should wash—" she began to whisper, but he shushed her again.

"I dinnae care," he said and then used one hand to part her legs. He felt her take hold of his cock, and his knees grew weak. As he parted her lips and kissed her, she parted *her* lips and took him into her mouth. He began exploring her folds with his fingers and then used the tip of his tongue to stimulate her. She cupped his balls and took him all the way inside her wet mouth each time he thrust his hips forward.

It felt so good, and he began to suck gently on her clitoris, making it twitch as she moved her hips. Then he felt it; her whole vulva began to pulse with her first orgasm. He watched as the opening of her vagina throbbed, and he placed his mouth over it. He stuck his tongue inside her, wanting to taste her ejaculation. Finally, he felt it, hot and wet on his tongue, so he began to suck on her, drawing it out.

"What are you doing?" she gasped.

He'd never done that to her, never even thought of it until then. It must've felt good because she was thrusting her hips, causing his chin to rub against her clitoris. After only a few moments, he felt her body release again, and he needed to be inside her. He got up and stood at the side of the bed, pulling her legs toward him.

He could see how wet she was and touched her with his finger before he took hold of his cock. Watching intently, his head penetrated her slowly, then the rest of him slid easily into her. "Your body is so bonnie, Erin. I love tae watch you, especially when I'm inside you. I wish you could see it the way I do as I disappear and emerge again. Tae see how yeh take me intae you, and, ach, Erin, et feels so good! Does et feel good tae you as well?"

"It's like heaven, David! I crave the feeling of you inside me all the time. When you enter me and then pull almost all the way out… it feels like nothing I can describe, like I want to melt. Then, when you're all the way in me and you hit that spot, that sensitive spot deep inside… I want to explode. It's melting and exploding over and over each time you thrust, and there's nothing in the world like it. No one has ever come close to making me feel the way you do, and—Oh! Oh, yes! Just like that, please… don't… stop," she said and cried out a bit more loudly than she should've.

Her body was nearly shaking with a powerful orgasm he could feel pulsating around him. It reverberated through his balls as they lay against her, then he released. "Don't move, please. Just stay there, pressed against me. That feels so good! Each time your cock pulses, it sends a jolt through me, and I love it!"

He was still for several moments, then he bent over and kissed her, feeling her soft, plump body against his chest. He wanted to stay there, to live in that moment of satisfaction. "Alright, you should move now. I need to let my legs down," she said, and he pulled himself out of her gradually so that she moaned again. "I can't believe how long you stay hard enough for me to feel you! I like that a lot!"

"Erin, you have this way of makin' me feel like, well, like I'm good enough, or better than good enough. You never put me down or make me feel… less, yeh ken? I like *that* a lot," he said.

"You *are* more than good enough, David."

"I'm glad yeh feel that way, though—" he said as he went to the bathroom to get some tissues.

"Though?"

He returned with the box and sat on the side of the mattress. "Though sometimes I catch maself wonderin' if… et's not me yeh feel who's good enough, but someone yeh think I am, yeh ken? I've spent the last eighteen years feelin' less, verra much less, and et's hard tae believe anaone could find *me* anathin' more than that."

"Yes, I can see that now. The more I get to know Susannah posthumously, the more I don't understand how anyone could live with her. I met her twice and felt like less as well. That seemed to be her talent, making people feel inadequate, but she was the inadequate one, not us, and especially not you."

"Thank you, darling."

"Now, let's go to sleep. I'm tired of talking about her. I want to fall asleep hearing your heartbeat and feeling you breathing next to me, okay?"

"Aye."

Chapter Five

A DAY IN GREEN BAY

In the morning, Erin and the Elliott family ate breakfast in the Walnut Room. She was still in shock that there was a grand hotel like that one in Green Bay and couldn't help but study and explore every room she entered with her eyes. After another glance at the architecture, she looked at the people sitting around the table with her. Half the table was happy, the other half not so much. Jet lag had hit Peter, Charlie, and Rosie, making the boys grumpy and Rosie whiny. Dan was over his and was too full of energy for the others.

"Dan! Enough already!" Peter said.

"No, Dan, I don't want to! Leave me be!" Charlie added.

"I've got a headache! Can't you all be quiet? Daddy, tell them to be quiet, please?" Rosie said.

"Dan, come here," David said and asked Erin and Charlie to move over one seat so that Dan could sit between him and Erin.

"I was thinking we could go to Bay Beach and maybe the wildlife sanctuary today." When no one looked enthused, she said, "I guess we should plan for it later in the day."

"Aye, ma head's not feeling altogether well either, love. I wouldn't mind a bit of peace and quiet, maself," David said and rubbed his temples. The morning newspaper sat unread next to his plate.

"What's a Bay Beach? It doesn't sound interesting at all," Daniel said and blew a spitball at Peter through his straw.

"Dan! I'm going to give you a well-deserved thrashing!" Peter said and acted as though he were going to stand.

"That's enough!" David said quite loudly, causing several people at nearby tables to look up at them and then smile insincerely.

"Bay Beach is an amusement park with carnival rides and a roller coaster called the Zippin' Pippin. It's quite a lot of fun, but if you think it sounds boring, or if you continue to aggravate everyone, I can find a babysitter for you," Erin said and could almost hear the gears in the boy's head as he tried to decide if it was worth behaving himself.

"I reckon I'll go then," he said, trying to sound like he didn't care.

"Apologize to your siblings first," Erin said, and he rolled his eyes.

"Fine. Sorry. There, I did it," he said, then crossed his arms and slumped in his chair. It was woefully lacking any sincerity, and on any other day, she would've made him do better, but she decided not to poke the wasp nest that time.

"A real roller coaster?" Charlie said, beginning to perk up a bit. "Does it do loops?"

"No, no loops, but it's loads of fun. I've only been on it once, but I laughed until I almost peed myself.

Dan thought that was funny and snorted, which made Rosie smile. "Can we go now?" she asked.

"I'm not sure when they open, but we can go earlier if you're all up to it."

"It sounds like fun, "Peter said.

"Well then, let's finish our meal in peace," she said.

David opened the local paper and noticed an article on the second page about the Fertilis Defect, so he read it and then held it out to Erin. "You should read this, love," he said, and she took it from him.

Protesters March Against New
Fertilis Defect Treatments.

Tulsa: Demonstrators marched in front of the First Street Fertilis Defect Registry clinic in Tulsa this afternoon. They carried signs that read, *'Save Sex for*

Marriage,' and '*Stop Medical Prostitution.*' When asked why they were protesting, Nancy Smythe told us: "*This is but the next step towards making prostitution legal! Sex is sacred and calling it a medical treatment is an insult to our faith and intelligence. We know what they're up to, and we intend to stop it!*"

We also spoke with Barbara Gleeman, the director at the clinic, who didn't seem worried. "*These good people are misinformed and should do a bit more research before coming to false conclusions. The Registry is saving the lives of thousands of women all over the world, and we can back that up with scientific proof.*"

The demonstrators began by blocking the doors and harassing anyone in earshot. The police forced them to move away from the doors, though it's no surprise that the parking lot is empty. That means not as many men will register, so there will be fewer potential matches for FD sufferers.

"That's ridiculous!" she said and handed the page back to him. "Ignorant people should be—" She looked at the young, impressionable people sitting at the table and sighed. "They shouldn't be allowed to do that. It's none of their business, anyway!"

"Aye, but what is there to do about it? Not much, I reckon," David said.

"Aye, that's the cost of freedom of speech and the right to protest, but all they're doing is hurting innocent people. Ugg, I don't want to talk about it anymore. It's too depressing, and I want to have a nice holiday with you."

Chapter Six

BAY BEACH

E rin parked in front of the large, white pavilion at Bay Beach Amusement Park, and everyone piled out of the vehicle. The children had seen the rides from the road and were excited. "Let's go!" Dan said impatiently and began walking away from them.

"Hold up there! Did you get your ears and neck with sunscreen?" Erin asked. He shrugged and then nodded slowly. "Really? You're not convincing me; come here, please."

The preteen rolled his eyes and trudged back to the SUV, allowing her to smooth the cool, white cream over his skin. "There; you'll thank me later… okay, well, maybe you won't, but you'd be really sorry if I weren't so diligent— Never mind." She smiled at David, who was making sure Rosie was completely covered in sunscreen.

"Thank Erin for carin' about yeh so much, Daniel," he said, incurring another eye roll.

"Thank you, Erin. Now may I go?" Dan said, sounding quite testy.

"You may," she said, and he turned toward the park, "except—"

Dan stopped and his shoulders visibly dropped. "What now?" he said as he turned around.

"Well, my darling boy, you may run to the rides, but you won't be able to get on them without tickets." She looked at David, who was smiling at his son.

"Ye'll just have tae wait," he said.

"Fine," Dan said and leaned against the vehicle with his arms crossed, sulking.

Once everyone was ready, they walked through the shady parking lot and stood in line to buy tickets. Each goldenrod yellow ticket cost twenty-five cents and rides took between two and three tickets each. High school and college-age students were employed to operate the rides, ticket booths, concessions, and for cleaning up the park. They bought strings of tickets and handed them out, telling the children to come find them if they needed more.

Erin convinced David to join her on the Swings, a ride with individual seats that lifted and tilted as it swung in a large circle. It was her favorite ride at the park. When it finished, David helped her out of her seat, and they held hands as they exited the fenced-in area. "Mrs... wait, um... bus driver," they heard a male voice say.

Instinctively, Erin turned to see who it was. She saw a tall, young man of about eighteen smiling at her. "Patrick? Good night nurse! You're all grown up!" she said and put her hand over her mouth in surprise.

"I'm sorry... I forgot your... wait, Erin, that's it!" he said, clearly relieved.

"Well done, that was a long time ago," she said and then looked at David. "David, this is Patrick—"

"Hoks," the young man supplied.

"I've known him... well, he rode my bus starting at age six or seven, and now you're an adult!" she said, trying not to cry. "This is my fiancé, David," she said, and the boy shook his hand.

"Nice to meet you, Patrick," David said, using his received pronunciation accent.

"You too... nice accent! Erin was the best bus driver ever. My sister cried buckets when you stopped driving," he said and then blushed. "Okay, I might have shed one or two, but don't tell anyone."

"You always were the sweetest kid," she said and turned to David. "When Patrick got a bit older, he helped enforce my rules by reminding the younger kids to stay seated and not scream. He made my job so much easier." She beamed with pride over him. "How is Sophie?"

"She's here; she runs the Skat. I know she'd love to see you if you wanna follow me over there?" he said, then gave David a second look. "Were you a bus driver, too? You look really familiar."

"I'd be rubbish as a bus driver! Must be from something else."

Patrick shrugged and turned back to Erin. "I'd love to see her, of course," she said, glad David hadn't revealed his identity.

"Dad! Did you have more tickets? I gave all mine to Dan," Charlie said, running up to them.

"I'll meet you there, Erin," David said.

"Okay," she said and then followed Patrick to the Skat.

When they arrived, Sophie was loading the ride, making sure everyone was securely fastened in and not wearing anything that could fly off. Erin watched the young woman and had to bite her lip to keep from crying. As soon as Sophie saw her, she smiled brightly and put her finger up to ask for a minute.

"Erin! Oh my gosh!" she said once everything was running well and hugged her tightly.

Between Erin's jet lag and her tendency toward being sentimental anyway, she cried as she held the girl. "Look at you! You're so lovely! Both of you have grown up to be so... amazing!" she said and wiped her eyes with her hands. "Sorry for crying, but I'm going through jet lag, and this is what happens.

"That's okay, Miss Erin," she said. "I'm not supposed to talk to people while I'm manning the rides. I'm just covering for someone who knew they'd be late today, so I should be done in about twenty minutes if you'll still be here?"

"I will, and I'd love to talk to you. Meet you at the train station in half an hour or so?" Erin said.

"Perfect! Oh, and did you hear... someone saw *David Elliott* here with his kids and some woman?" she said excitedly.

"I think I did see him, actually. How cool, huh?" Erin said, smiling as she thought of the shock the girl was about to get. "If I see him, I'll ask him to meet us there as well."

"Yeah, you do that! I'm sure he'll be happy to!" Sophie said sarcastically and then laughed. "Though, knowing you, he'd probably agree." She waved as Erin and Patrick walked away from the ride together.

"Wait! Holy sh—Oops, sorry, but... that was him! That was him with you! You're engaged to David Elliott?" Patrick said, wide-eyed and in shock.

"You've figured it out! I'm glad you didn't know when we were with Sophie. She'll freak out, won't she?" Erin said and saw David near the Tilt-a-Whirl.

"I might freak out too," he said and hesitated.

"Aww, come on, Patrick, you were perfectly comfortable a few minutes ago. Don't worry, he doesn't bite, and he's really nice. I wouldn't marry someone who wasn't, would I?" she said and put her arm around his shoulders, pulling him with her.

"I hope not," he said cautiously as they stepped up to him.

"Sorry I didn't get to the... Skip, was it? Rosie wanted more tickets as well, and we were stood in the queue for a long while," David said and then noticed Patrick standing awkwardly about two paces away from them. "He's figured it out, has he?"

"His sister informed us that someone had seen... '*David Elliott, his kids, and some woman*' in the park. That's when it clicked for him. She couldn't talk, so we're gonna meet up when she's done. Will you please join us? She'll flip out," Erin said, laughing.

"Well, seeing I'm your prized poodle on a walkabout to show me off, I reckon I can't refuse," he said.

"Who's a good boy," Erin said and reached up to pat his head. "Patrick, come closer and be friendly. Go on and say whatever it is you're dying to say." The boy looked at her, opening his eyes wide. She shook her head and stood next to him, urging him closer. "I'll start. Let me think, what would I ask David Elliott if I got to meet him? Ooh, I know! Mr. Elliott? What's it like to be engaged to such a fantastic, brilliant, and amazing woman like Erin? You must fall to pieces every time you see her!" She laughed at the look on David's face.

He shook his head and smiled. "Aye, I do, actually," he said, making Erin blush and Patrick smile.

"Your turn, Patrick," she said.

"I don't know what to say except..." He looked at Erin and she nudged him. "Well, I want to be an actor, and I'd love to be in a movie with you someday, Mr. Elliott."

"Ach, well, I'd like that as well," David said, dropping the fake accent for his real one. "Though ye'd best hurry; who knows how long I'll be workin'. This business doesn't appreciate age, and I'm not gettin' any younger."

"Good night nurse, David. You're not *that* old!" Erin said, rolling her eyes. "We'd better head over to the train."

"I only say things like that tae get a rise out of her," David said to Patrick as they started following her.

"Daddy!" Rosie said and bounded toward them, her strawberry blonde ponytail bouncing behind her. "That was fun, may I—" She stopped talking and looked up at the tall, older boy. "I mean, what are you doing?"

"We're on our way tae meet someone who used tae ride Erin's bus. This is her brother, Patrick. Patrick, this is our daughter, Rosie," David said.

"Hi, Rosie, nice to meet you," he said, and Rosie blushed.

"Hi… Patrick," she said shyly and held David's hand.

They walked to the miniature train station and saw Sophie waiting for them. As soon as the girl saw them coming, her mouth dropped open and she took a step back, nearly stepping on a young boy's foot as he waited in line. "Well, Sophie, I saw David Elliott walking around, picking his nose. He clearly needed something to do, so I asked him to join me," Erin said. She saw the look on Sophie, Rosie, and David's faces and laughed heartily. "You should see the three of you! Priceless! I guess I'm the 'some woman' everyone's talking about. Sophie Hoks, I'd like you to meet my fiancé, David Elliott. David, this is Sophie. Oh, and this is Rosie Elliott, his… I mean, soon-to-be *our* daughter."

"Hello, Sophie; it's nice to meet you. I love your hair," Rosie said, looking up at her long, black curls that were pulled into a loose ponytail.

"Uh, thank you, Rosie. Um, I love yours too. I always wanted strawberry blonde hair. I thought it would be neat to have a hair color named after a fruit," Sophie said and blushed deep red.

"Your hair looks like dark chocolate. My mum… well, my *real* mum used to eat one bite of dark chocolate every day. She never allowed me to have any, though. She said it was her medicine, though it didn't work because she died, anyway." Rosie said and looked at the ground.

"That's so sad! I'm sorry your mom died. And Erin is going to be your stepmom soon?" Sophie said, crouching down to Rosie's height.

"Yes, and I'm very happy about it. I love her a lot," Rosie said and smiled at the older girl.

"I kinda wish she was gonna be my new mom, too! She was a really fun bus driver, and I cried when she told us she had to quit. She used to tell us jokes and play games with us. I think she'll be a good mom to you," Sophie said, forgetting David was standing next to her.

"I think she will, as well. Daddy? May I have more tickets, please? I'd like to go down the slide over there," Rosie said, pointing to the tall, light blue structure close to the water of the bay.

"Aye, ma love, would you like for me tae go with yeh?" he asked, also squatting to her level, and handed her a strip of yellow ride tickets.

"No, Daddy. Charlie and Dan are there, and so is Peter, but he's talking to a girl."

"A *girl?*" Erin said. "I think maybe we *should* head over there."

"She's wearing a shirt like yours," Rosie said, pointing to Sophie.

"Oh! That's Kendall. She's kind of a flirt. We should *definitely* go over there… if you don't mind me joining you?" she said as Erin helped David stand.

"Of course you can. Parenting rule number 249 states that you should *never* miss an opportunity to embarrass your teenage son," Erin said.

"Meet you there," Rosie said and ran ahead of them.

"Don't warn him!" Erin called after her.

———

"Well, Sophie, you certainly are good with children," David said as they walked through the park, dodging goose poop and dropped gum on the hot blacktop.

"Oh… uh, um, thank you, sir… Mr. Elliott, I mean." Her face was red, and she didn't look up at him.

"Thank you for tryin' tae comfort her. I didn't know about the chocolate, though she's correct; yer hair is just that color," he said.

"You're… welcome, Mr."

"Just call me David, okay?"

"Okay, um, and thanks. Erin's hair used to be almost the same color as mine, just a little bit lighter. I noticed it because there were a lot of blonde girls on my bus, but Erin's hair was dark and curly, like mine, so… I don't know… I just remember it," she said and shrugged.

"I've never seen et that dark. I imagine et was lovely, though I do like the streaks of silver et has now, don't you?" he asked, looking at Erin, who was walking in front of them, talking with Patrick.

"I like that too." Sophie was quiet for a few moments and then took a deep breath. "I… I'm sorry, but," she began.

"You dinnae need tae apologize for anathin'. Ye've not stepped on ma foot."

"Sorry… I mean, okay. I just want to say that… I love your accent. I… also loved you in *Future Explorations* and *Houlihan's Flat*. My *mom* absolutely *loves* you and watches your show *all* the time, so I have them memorized."

"Did yeh hear that, love?" he said to Erin. "Her mum loves me. Do yeh remember where they live?" he said and laughed until she turned and narrowed her eyes at him.

"Aye, I remember where they live. I'll take you there if you're tired of me already," she said, building tension as she stared him down for a few uncomfortable moments. "Well? Is that what you want, or not? Their mother is beautiful."

"I'm sure she is, though I reckon I'll stick with you. I can't imagine she'd ever compare, darling," he said with a grin.

"Wise decision, plus I doubt her husband would appreciate you hanging around." She laughed for a long time, slowing her pace to walk next to Sophie.

"Thank you for the compliment, Sophie. I appreciate et," David said, then joined Patrick ahead of them.

———

"You're so lucky, Erin! How on earth did you meet him? Oh! I'm sorry, that's probably not—"

"It's okay, hun; we met because of my disease. He's… well, my match, and I agree, I *am* really lucky."

"I heard that," David said, looking back at them.

They finally arrived at the Slide and saw Peter standing by the girl who was taking tickets at the top of the ride. They saw Dan coming down the wavy slide, sitting on a burlap sack and screaming at the top of his lungs. When he got to the bottom, he stood and was about to go right back up, but David caught his attention. The boy's shoulders slumped as he slowly made his way toward them.

"Yes, Dad?" he said glumly.

"Chin up, Dan, we're not leavin' quite yet," David said. Those were the magic words because Daniel smiled, his dimples and teeth revealing his relief. "Please tell Peter I'd like tae speak with him."

Dan cocked his head to the side as if deciding whether he would agree to do it or not. "But... I've run out of tickets, and the bird up there said we could go for free since she fancies Peter. If he leaves, she may change her mind."

"Take these and share them with the others, then do as I say, please," David said, handing him a stack of tickets.

"Thanks, Dad! Hi, Erin, this is the best ride ever, don't you agree?" he said and ran toward the tall set of stairs without waiting for an answer.

"Mind you share those tickets!" David called out. Dan waved and started climbing. It took quite a while for him to reach the top, carrying his brown sack at his side. They saw him say something to Peter and then scramble to the nearest open lane. Peter looked down at them and waved. Then he said something to the girl, who smiled up at him.

"She's not supposed to do that. If she gets caught, she'll get written up and could get fired," Sophie said as they watched Peter sit on a sack and slide down to them. As he got closer, smiling and looking so much like his dad, she whispered under her breath, "Wow, I don't blame her, though."

"What is it, Dad?" he asked and smiled at Sophie. Her cheeks turned pink, which Erin thought looked lovely with her sun-tanned skin.

"We have it on good authority that if you continue... distractin' that girl, she may get sacked, so et may be a good idea tae take a break from et... for a while," David said diplomatically.

Peter smiled at Sophie again and shrugged. "A'right, back in a tick." He returned to the ride and stopped Rosie as she ran by. He said something to her, gave her his tickets, and came back. "We were only talking anyway. She said she liked my accent and asked me to say things to her."

"I'm sure it wasn't just your accent," Sophie said under her breath again.

Erin heard her and smiled. "Sophie, this is my soon-to-be stepson, Peter. Peter, this is Sophie. I used to be her bus driver," she said.

"Hello, Sophie, it's a pleasure to meet you," Peter said, flashing his father's brilliant smile at the girl.

"Hello... uh, Peter," she said and looked at the ground. "Oh! I just remembered... not that I have to or anything, but I offered to stay late today. I'll be picking up garbage and stuff, so... I won't get in trouble for talking—"

"May I walk with you, then?" Peter asked her.

"Um, I'd like that, but only if you want to... I mean—"

"He wouldn't have asked if he didn't, Soph," Patrick said and rolled his eyes at his sister.

She shot him a look to kill but didn't say anything to him. "I need to get back to work now," she said. "It was really nice to see you again, Miss Erin, and to meet you... Mr., uh, David. I'm really happy for you both." She hugged Erin and then led Peter away.

"Well, he's popular with the girls," Erin said with a teasing smile at David.

"Of course he is! He looks like his dad! How can a man compete with that?" Patrick said under his breath.

"I don't think you need to worry about that, Patrick. I think Rosie was a bit smitten with you," Erin said.

"Rosie? But she's what, ten? Oh, I'm sorry, but—"

"Of course *she's* too young. What I meant was that you're an attractive young man, and the right girl for you will think you're a hundred times more good-looking than Peter Elliott, trust me!" she said and put her arm around his shoulders.

"Aye, and when you become an actor, ye'll have yer pick, as well," David said. "Are yeh in... what do yeh call et here?"

"Drama?" Erin supplied, looking at Patrick for a reply.

"I start my freshman year at Lawrence University next year. I'm nervous about it, though. What if I suck at acting?" he said.

"Well, yeh won't know until you get up there and do yer best. Ye're gonna suck sometimes, that's how et is, but yeh persevere until either yeh stop sucking or realize et's not somethin' yeh wannae do, after all," David said. "Yeh may discover you're better suited for directing or producing. Try yer hand at a variety of positions; there's far more to the industry than the actors."

"Wow, thanks, I'll remember that," Patrick said and smiled at Erin.

"Daddy! Please ride the Tilt-a-Whirl with me?" Rosie said, running up to them, out of breath.

"I'll go," Patrick said.

Rosie's eyes grew wide as she looked at her dad. "I'll go as well," he said, and Patrick turned to Erin.

"No way! Not unless you want to see what I ate for breakfast this morning! I'll take a few photos and then meet you in the pavilion. I need the loo, and I'm getting hungry," she said.

"A'right," David said and kissed her temple. "Do yeh need money or anathin?"

"No, I'm good." She stood back as they took their place in line.

The group of people in front of them didn't notice David until one of the kids turned around and said, "Mom! Mom! Isn't that John Thomas Fife?" He pointed at David, who smiled as Rosie rolled her eyes, and Patrick grinned.

"Oh, my God!" The woman said, far too loudly, "Oh! It's you! I can't believe it's really you! I just love you *sooo* much in *Future Explorations*! I can't believe you're here! Can I have a selfie?"

Erin shook her head and smiled at Rosie's long-suffering expression. Five more women worked their way back to him, also fawning over him and asking for selfies and autographs until the line started moving again. People in the vicinity of the loud women began gathering around the ride, making it impossible for him to be natural.

She felt bad, especially for Rosie, having to deal with all the attention, but once they were seated in their own red pod, she saw them relax a little bit. The young girl was seated between the men, presumably so she didn't get squished and hurt against the hard metal seat. She looked thrilled to be next to her daddy and a good-looking boy as she waved. Erin returned her wave and then lifted her phone to take a picture. David's smile shone out, and she couldn't help feeling a bit star-struck, too.

Once full, the operator, a nerdy boy with very long, pale legs sticking out of his khaki shorts, checked every seat, ensuring everyone was secure. Dozens of women, and a few men, circled the ride, all hoping to capture a photo of David Elliott. Soon the area was too crowded for Erin to get a good shot, so she made her way to the large, white pavilion built at the turn of the twentieth century. It had much-needed bathrooms, concessions, and a dining area for sitting, which she also craved.

After the bathroom stop, she stepped into the bright, open, cafeteria-like room and stood in line to order food. Not having children of her own, she didn't often go to Bay Beach, but she'd joined Lily a few times and had been there for other events before. She knew food there usually took a while, so she ordered a bit extra for when the others joined her.

As she stood waiting for her order, she gazed out the large windows at the bay of Green Bay. It was a bit cloudy over the water, but the sun shone brightly on the park. She saw Peter and Sophie near the picnic tables and the mini train tracks. He held a large, clear trash bag open while she used a grabber stick to pick up garbage. They were talking and would occasionally laugh together. She thought how bittersweet it was for them since they were from opposite sides of the world.

Finally, her number was called, and as she took the tray covered in food, she rethought her decision. "Allow me tae help," David's delicious voice said as he lifted the tray out of her hands. "Hungry, were yeh?" he teased.

"Where's Patrick and Rosie?" she asked, noticing their absence.

"They decided to have a go on the... Skip?"

"Skat," Erin corrected.

"Skat, right, but that seemed far more than I'd be able to stomach. The last ride was enough for me as et was," he said, and they found a table near the windows.

"I see. Well then, I got too much food. Oh well, I hope you're hungry."

"Famished. Blimey, is that Peter and—"

"Sophie—Yes, that's them. They *are* sweet together, aren't they?" Erin said, watching them walk side by side.

"Aye, but—"

"I know, it's sad. Poor Sophie, she'll be unhappy when we leave." She took a bite of a deep-fried cheese curd and moaned. "Mmm, I've missed these!" she said and handed one to David.

"And what might this be filled with?" he asked.

"Cheese, of course."

"Deep fried cheese? And I thought Scotland went overboard fryin' everathin'," he said, then popped the curd into his mouth. "Ach—'at's 'ot!" He opened his mouth and fanned it with his hand. People were now watching them, and many were taking pictures and videos.

"Sorry, I should've warned you to eat it in two bites, at least until they cool off. Here—" She handed him a napkin, "spit it out."

"No, et's a'right," he said with watering eyes. "I think et tastes good unless et's ma burnt tongue I'm tastin'. Aye, that's good, actually. I may brave another."

"Deep fried cheese curds along with creme brûlée are on my list of favorite things."

"You're on *my* list of favorite things," David said.

"As it should be," she said and laughed lightly. "After this, we should go on the Zippin' Pippin. It was Elvis's favorite roller coaster."

"Well, if et's good enough for Elvis, et's good enough for us, I reckon."

They ate as much as they could and binned the rest. It was nice holding hands as they walked all the way to the far side of the park. Some people stared, but most didn't even notice them. As they got closer to the ride, Erin squinted and shielded her eyes. "I know her," she said, pointing to a woman standing near a wheelchair. "Penny?"

"Erin! Oh, wow, it's good to see you!" the woman said.

"David, this is Lily's mom, Penny; she was also a bus driver. Penny, this is my fiancé, David," Erin said. As they greeted each other, she crouched down to speak with Ariana, Lily and Nick's daughter. "Hello, you! Look how you've grown!" The ten-year-old couldn't speak well, but she smiled and took Erin's hand, pulling her in for a hug.

"Hello, Ariana, et's good tae see yeh again," David said, using his John Thomas Fife accent, and crouched next to Erin.

The girl beamed and laughed. She took David's hand and pulled him into a hug, smiling so big that Erin thought it might be painful.

"She's glad to see *you*," Penny said. "Lily and Nick are in line for the Zippin' Pippin."

Erin saw Lily looking down at them from the halfway point on the staircase of the ride's entrance. She waved, said something to Nick, and started down the steps. "Erin! Oh my gosh! When did you get here? I mean to town, not *here*, exactly. Hello, David, it's good to see you again! I just can't believe you're here at the same time as us!" Lily said while David and Nick shook hands and greeted each other.

"We arrived yesterday evening. We're here for a friend's vow renewal and agreed that getting over any potential jet lag would be wise. I thought an adventure to the amusement park might be a good idea. The rest of clan Elliott is around here somewhere. I'll introduce you to them, but first, I wanna ride that," Erin said, pointing to the sizeable roller coaster. "Let's go together!"

"Dad! Wait," they heard as they were about to get in line. "May we join you?" Charlie said, walking next to Rosie.

"Aye, do yeh have tickets?" David asked, and they both shook their heads. "A'right, there's a booth over there; we'll wait for yeh." He handed them some money, and they ran off. Then they saw Peter and Sophie coming toward them, with Daniel lagging behind, looking mopey.

"What's wrong, Dan?" Erin asked.

"He's unhappy because he's out of tickets and can't ride the slide any longer," Peter supplied.

"I see... well, come with us on this one, Dan. I'm sure you'll like it even better. Also, I want you all to meet my best friend, but I'll wait until Rosie and Charlie come back. I hope they get enough tickets for everyone," Erin said.

"Oh, we just got here, so we have plenty of them," Lily said. "Our treat."

"That won't be—" David started to argue.

"Thank you, guys, that's so sweet," Erin said, cutting him off and giving him a look saying to go with it.

Charlie and Rosie returned with a thick stack of bright yellow tickets. "I'll take those; my friends are treating us this time," Erin said. "Everyone, this is my best friend Lily Graves, her husband Nick, her mother Penny, and daughter Ariana. Lily, Nick, this is my new family. There's Peter, Charlie, Dan, and Rosie Elliott."

"Pleased to meet you," the children said, in unison, making Lily and Erin laugh.

"Same here. Are you having fun? What's your favorite ride?" Lily asked.

"Oh, yes!" Charlie said. "I like—" He blushed, apparently reluctant to tell everyone his favorite.

"Go on," Erin said.

"The train. I like the scenery."

"I like it too," Erin said, earning a smile from the boy.

"Yes, ma'am! I'm having a fantastic time," Peter said. "I like the Ferris Wheel best."

"I'm having loads of fun!" Rosie said. "I really like the Tilt-a-Whirl."

"I wish we lived here!" Dan finished. "The slide is crackin'!"

"I like the slide, too, but climbing all those stairs is a lot of work! Makes me tired just thinking about it," Lily said.

"I usually have to push her up the last few steps," Nick said.

"You do not... well, okay, you do, *sometimes*," she admitted.

"Oh, I'm sorry, but this is Sophie... and where did Patrick go?" Erin asked.

"Here I am," he said. "Sorry, I had to talk to someone on my way here."

"Lily, this is—"

"Let's get in line. It isn't getting any shorter," Nick interrupted.

Erin finished the introductions as they climbed the many stairs to the platform. It took a while, but when they finally reached it, Sophie stepped up to the ride operator. She said something in his ear, and he nodded. "How many?" he asked.

"Ten, I think," she said and started pointing her finger at each person to count. The boy nodded again, and Sophie returned to the line.

"Oh, no!" Erin said and frowned. "This sign says that pregnant women shouldn't go on this ride. Oh, well, you guys go without me. I'll stay here and see if I can't get a photo or two."

"But, darling... I'll stay—" David began, but Erin interrupted him.

"No, go ahead and have this moment with your children, David. I'm fine, really," she said as the cars stopped in front of them and the previous riders exited on the other side of the platform. The ride operator began ushering them toward the empty cars, and Erin nudged him forward. Dan wanted to sit alone, so Charlie sat next to his dad, and everyone else paired up. Peter rode with Sophie, and Rosie got to ride with Patrick, which she was plainly happy about. When they were all seated, the young man stopped loading the cars, so they had the ride to themselves.

Soon they were climbing the first hill. Erin watched them and heard their screams as they raced down the steep decline. She took a few photos, but they were going too fast and were too far away for her to see anything. After only about two minutes, the ride came to a sudden, jarring halt, then moved slowly forward and stopped where they'd started. Everyone climbed out, laughing and talking, saying how much fun they'd had. "I couldn't stop laughing!" David said as they got back to Penny.

"And screaming," Charlie added.

"I'm hungry!" Dan said after informing them that the Slide was nothing compared to the Zippin' Pippin.

"I am as well," Charlie said.

David suggested they find food, and everyone agreed, so they said goodbye to Nick and Lily. Erin hugged her friend for a long time, telling David she'd catch up with them as they headed to the pavilion.

"They *are* amazing, Erin! I'm so glad I got to see you while you were here," Lily said, her eyes looking misty.

"Me too, Lil. I'm sorry I didn't tell you about our trip, but I didn't think we'd have enough time for a visit."

"It's okay, don't worry about it!" she said.

"Will you be my maid... Matron of Honor for the wedding? We'll fly you to... well, probably Scotland, but maybe London. Please say yes?"

"I don't know, Erin, I don't think we could bring Ariana—"

"I'll watch her," Penny said. "You need to be at your best friend's wedding!"

"Thanks, Mom! I guess that would be a yes, then. Oh, I can't wait!" Lily said.

"Me neither, and I'm so glad you'll be there! I hate to go, but I have a family waiting for me," Erin said and hugged her friends.

"Safe travels!" Lily said as Erin hurried away.

Erin stepped into the pavilion, expecting to find her family either lined up to order or waiting for their food. Instead, David was surrounded by fans asking for selfies and autographs. She heard one woman ask for a kiss, but he swiftly said no.

"Erin!" Charlie said from the far side of the room and rushed toward her.

"Where is everyone?" Erin asked, looking for the rest of the children.

"Over there," he said, pointing to a table in the corner of the cafeteria.

"Where are Patrick and Sophie?" she asked, not seeing them at the table.

"Patrick and Sophie had to go home; their mum was waiting for them in the car park. I think Sophie and Peter exchanged mobile numbers, and she told me to hug you for them," he said and hugged her.

"Have you ordered food yet?" Erin asked.

Dan yelled something that sounded like, 'Oi! Hurry up!' but it was hard to hear in the noisy, echoing building. "Hold on, you!" Charlie yelled back at him, then turned to Erin again. "We weren't able to queue up yet. They surrounded Dad before we could." He looked nervous and quite unhappy. All the children looked upset as she approached the table.

"I'm hungry!" Dan said pathetically.

"I know, honey. Let me see how much money I have," she said and dug her wallet out of her purse. "Okay, just order one thing, like a burger or hot dog, for now. I don't have much money on me, and I don't feel like fighting my way through the crowd."

"But I'm *very* hungry, Erin! One won't be enough," he whined.

"That's all I can do, Dan. Take it or go hungry. Let's get in line." They queued up and ordered, then waited for their number to be called. Erin kept a wary eye on the group of anxious women around David, somehow managing to keep her jealousy at bay. Then, just when she thought the ordeal was over, after they'd gotten their food and Daniel was starting to complain about still being hungry, it started all over again. Women seemed to come from everywhere. It was as if someone had made an announcement over the loudspeakers in the park saying that David Elliott was signing autographs in the pavilion and you'd better get yours right away.

Finally, she had enough. She mustered all her courage and pushed her way through the mob, hearing angry comments, such as, '*Wait your turn,*' '*I was here first,*' and, '*Bitch.*' She saw David frown, revealing that he'd heard it too.

He began moving toward her, and when he arrived, he surprised everyone, including her, by taking her into his arms and kissing her passionately. At first, she resisted, annoyed and still focused on the children, but then she understood what he was doing and began to enjoy it. The women were stunned into silence initially, but then the comments started. Erin heard everything from, '*Wow,*' and '*She's so lucky,*' to '*What the Fuck,*' and '*Get out of the way, I want my turn!*'

When he finally released her, he smiled at her and took her hand. "Sorry, everyone, but I'll be spending time with my family now. Thank you for saying hello, and have a pleasant day," he said and hurried to the table, still holding her hand, though she thought she felt his shaking a bit. "What do yeh need?" He listened while Daniel complained that he was still hungry.

"I didn't have enough money to get much. I'm sorry, David," Erin said, feeling really bad.

"Here," he said and gave Peter two twenty-dollar bills. "Please get everyone what they want. We'll be back soon."

"A'right, Dad," Peter said as David nearly pulled Erin out the back doors onto a narrow, concrete patio area that ran the whole length of the building. A few people were sitting at tables nearby, but it seemed he didn't notice.

She was confused, thinking he was upset or angry at her and began defending herself. "I said I was sorry, David. I don't know what—"

"Hush." He turned her to face him, and that's when she noticed how incredibly upset he appeared.

"What's—"

"Shh," he began, and she braced herself for an angry lecture, but then he took her hands in his trembling ones. "I'm so, so sorry, Erin. Yeh dinnae deserve that. I tried tae excuse maself several times, but they ignored me." He pulled her to him and held her, still shaking. "Please forgive me."

"Forgive you? What do you mean? Why—Did you do… something with… one of them? Did one of them do something to you that you… enjoyed? What am I missing here, and is that why you're shaking? Are you…

did you… change your mind about me… us?" she asked, completely taken off guard by his apology, and it was her turn to tremble in fear.

"What? Change my—Enjoyed? Are yeh mental? No, ma darling, ma love, none of that. I'm sorry for leavin' you tae tend to the children. Et's too much for you tae have tae do on yer own. Thank you for doin' everathin' yeh could for them."

The mental images that had gone through her head as to why he'd say he was sorry were almost enough to make her lose it. She was breathing heavily and trying, unsuccessfully, to keep from crying. In the span of a few moments, she had imagined everything, from some beautiful woman kissing him to the extreme of a public lap dance. She knew it was crazy, but her mind was far too imaginative. "O-kay—I mean… are you sure?"

"Am I sure of what?" he asked, frowning.

The jealousy she'd managed to push aside in the face of the children's needs was about to overwhelm her, and she buried her face in his chest, smelling his scent and feeling torn in two. "There were some really beautiful women in that crowd, David. Did one of them make you start to doubt your choice… of me?" She shook her head, not wanting to know the truth, which she was sure involved him changing his mind. "I mean… I wouldn't blame you if—"

———

"What?" David said far too loudly. "Erin… I'm shakin' because I'm furious with them and maself for that display. I should've been blunt and told them tae bugger off, but I… didn't. I didn't want tae disappoint anaone or bring us any more bad press. I wasn't attracted tae any of them."

He took a deep breath as he remembered what her doctor had told him about oxygen deprivation and what it could do to a person who'd been through it as many times and for as long as she had. "Darling," he said as gently as he could, "I love you and want tae be with you. I'm not gonna change ma mind, ever, a'right?"

Erin nodded slowly but didn't look up at him. "Alright, I'm sorry. I feel ridiculous, but I—I just get so afraid that… well, you know all about it. I didn't know what to do or… or how to react when I came in and saw them. I guess I went into autopilot mode."

"Aye, et must've been a shock for yeh, but you were brilliant. Ye're also an amazin' mum, darling, thank you."

"I'm a tired mum right now. I need a nap and then a good meal. I'd like... well—"

"*I'd* like tae give you a treatment; I'm sure yer overdue," he said and kissed her. He knew people were watching them, but he didn't care. He wanted them all to be envious of her.

They returned to the table, hoping to keep a low profile. "Good night nurse, you all look beat! Too much fresh air and jet lag, huh?" Erin said to the four Elliott children sitting at the table inside the pavilion.

"Oh, no you don't," Peter said unexpectedly and stood, still looking droopy-eyed. "He's not giving autographs or selfies right now, sorry." The three young women stood motionless for a moment, wide-eyed and mouths open. One of them stepped forward as though she planned to bypass the younger-looking David and speak to the elder one anyway, but then the other three children surrounded their father and shook their tired heads.

"Alright, guys, I think it's time to go now. Sorry, ladies, showtime's over, and he's ours now," Erin said. She placed her hand on Peter's shoulder and gently pushed him toward the door.

They were asleep standing up as they piled into the SUV. "I'm glad we're not far from the hotel. I'm not sure I can stay awake for very long," Erin said as she started the engine and pulled out of the parking lot.

When they got back to the hotel, they allowed the valet to park for them. They were just about to get into the elevator when the hotel manager stopped David.

"May I have a word, Mr. Elliott?" he asked.

"Of course," David said and turned to his family. "Go on without me. I'll be up shortly."

Erin wanted to intercede and tell the short, round, bald man that he'd have to wait until Mr. Elliott was rested, but she held her tongue. "Alright, but don't be too long, darling. We still need to… discuss our plans… for supper and… for tomorrow." She couldn't think of any other excuse to get the man to rush his discussion with him.

"Aye, love, I won't," he said, giving her his best smile, and then followed the manager toward the Walnut Room where they'd had breakfast that morning.

"Will you be alright in here?" she asked the children at the door to their room, just wanting to lay on the comfortable bed and sleep.

"Yes, Mum, we'll be fine, thanks," Peter said. He smiled sleepily at her and then joined his siblings, closing the door behind him.

Erin went to her room door and realized that David had the key. She'd left hers on the dresser. "Shit!" she said.

"Can I help you, ma'am?" A young woman said. She was wearing a black shirt with the hotel name and a name tag that read Sarai.

"Thank you, Sarai, I left my key in our room, and my fiancé got… waylaid by your manager."

"Yes, he's a talker," she said with a smile, her brown eyes crinkling at the corners. "I shouldn't have said that… I'm sorry. He's a good man, but… he has the gift of gab."

"I could tell just by looking at him. I made sure to tell David to hurry back and made up an excuse, but I don't think it'll work. Do you have a master key? We've spent the whole jet-lagged day at Bay Beach, and I'm exhausted."

"Oh, I understand that! I have two boys and they run me ragged when we go there! I wouldn't want to try it with jet lag! What's your name, please? I need to radio down to the desk before I can let people into their rooms."

"Erin March. I'm here with David Elliott, and I'm not sure they have my name on the list," she said, getting worried.

"Don't fret, Ms. March," she said and put her radio to her mouth. "Front desk, this is Sarai."

"What is it this time, Sarai? Did you see the ghost again?" The male voice said, and Erin thought she saw the tiny young woman's brown cheeks flush crimson.

"No, *Nathan*. I have a guest… who can hear you, by the way. She's locked out of her room. Please verify who's supposed to be in room 823."

"Well done, you!" Erin whispered.

"That's David Elliott's room," the man said, sounding much more professional.

"Yes, I know that, but is there anyone else listed?" she asked, rolling her eyes.

"Yes, it's a joint room with four youths."

"Is there anyone else? A woman?" she asked, frowning.

"That's what it says, Sarai. Wait—" There was silence for a long time, and the women looked at each other curiously.

"Dramatic pause—" Erin said with a smile.

"Let her in! Let her in, now!" came Nathan's harsh whisper.

"A'right," Sarai said with raised eyebrows. "I guess I'll let you in, then," she said to Erin as she pulled her key card, which was on a retractable wire, out of its fob on her belt buckle.

Just then, the elevator *dinged*, and the door opened. "Erin? What in the—" David began as he exited the elevator and walked briskly toward them.

"Don't be angry, David. This is Sarai, and she's helping me. I left my key in the room. She just had to verify—"

"But why was yer name not on the—"

"Darling, she doesn't have any control over that. She did her job and was completely pleasant and good company. That reminds me, Nathan mentioned a ghost. I'd like to hear more about that!" Erin said.

"I'm sorry, Ms. March, but I'm not allowed to talk about that with our guests," she said with a grin. "Whether I've seen it or not makes no difference. For instance, I *can't* tell you that I saw a shadowy figure one night."

"And that was on this floor?" Erin said, feeling goosebumps on her arms.

"I can't tell you that it was just over there," she said and pointed to the other end of the hallway."

"I'm glad you can't, as I'm not keen tae know about et. I'm gonna take a wee kip; care tae join me?" David asked Erin.

"I'd love to," she said. "Thanks, Sarai, for helping me. Oh, wait! We'll never use these, so you should have them and take your boys to Bay Beach." She handed her a thick pile of ride tickets and went straight into her room before the woman could refuse them.

"I dinnae understand why yer name wasn't in the computer," David said as he took his clothes off and got into bed.

"You'll have to ask Tina. Maybe she should be asked to include me from now on?"

"Aye, I'll do that. Now, come here so I can give you yer treatment," he said.

Chapter Seven

RENEWING THEIR VOWS

That afternoon, the Elliott family got dressed up for the vow renewal and then packed their belongings. They would be staying at a hotel in Manitowoc, where the event would take place. Everything, including the family, was back in the SUV, and they were ready to go when Erin realized she needed the bathroom. "I'll use the one in the lobby. Anyone else need to go before we leave?" she asked.

Everyone but Peter said they had better try, even David, so everyone piled out of the SUV again and headed back into the lobby. "You're her, aren't you?" a woman said as she approached them.

Erin turned to look over her shoulder before realizing she was talking to her. "I'm sorry, but—"

"You're the woman in the photo, right?" the lady said and then lowered her voice, "The naked photo in the newspapers?"

Erin's breath caught and blood rushed to her face, making her feel a bit lightheaded. She wanted to escape and didn't know what to say, so she slowly nodded.

The woman put her hand over her mouth and tears sprang to her eyes. "I'm sorry to bother you, but that photo is absolutely beautiful. My daughter is not… well, she's not a small girl, you see. She was in London when that story was in the tabloids, and she cut it out to take home with her. She's told me so many times that it makes her feel like there's hope for bigger women, you know, to be shown as desirable and sexy. Even though the article was printed to shame you, it didn't work, and I wanted you to know how much it means to her."

"Oh, well, thank you. I'm—I'm not sure what to say, but you can assure your daughter I'm proof that dreams can come true and that there's someone out there who'll love her for who she is on the inside and outside. It took a lot of heartache for me to find mine, and I hope she finds him… or her, I guess, really soon. I wish her the best, truly," Erin said and hugged the woman before rushing to the public restrooms.

"You handled that quite well, darling," David said once they were back in the vehicle.

"I was shaking like a leaf the whole time! It's like my adrenaline kicked into high gear," she said as she navigated the streets of downtown Green Bay. "I'm still a bit shaky."

"Aye, that often happened to me in the beginning. I'm proud of you; you managed it like a pro."

She looked quickly into the rearview mirror, and everyone nodded, though Peter looked uncomfortable. She knew he'd seen the newspaper that day as well. "Thanks. I guess I'll have to get used to it, won't I?"

"How many hours will it be until we're there, Erin?" Charlie asked.

"Oh, less than an hour," she replied, thankful for the change of subject, and merged onto highway 43, headed south.

Fifty minutes later, Erin pulled into the parking lot of their hotel. They got out of the SUV and stretched, then they unloaded their luggage and checked in. The place wasn't even close to what the Hotel Northland was, but it was a clean, comfortable place to sleep. Less than two hours later, they were ready to go again.

She was nervous as she parked across the street from the chapel and looked over at David, then at the kids in the rearview mirror. "Everyone ready?" she asked, and they smiled. " Now, if you have any trouble or hear someone saying something offensive to you, or about you, or us, please come to me, and I'll deal with it. My friends aren't always politically correct, and so—"

"Erin, I'm sure everathin' will be fine," David said reassuringly.

"All the same, I don't want you to think someone is trying to be rude; it's just that our sense of humor is a little bit... umm... out there sometimes," she said. She knew she was babbling, but she wanted everything to go well. They smiled and nodded again. "You all look so lovely tonight! Thank you for dressing up and coming to this thing where you won't know anyone. You're really good sports, all of you."

"Erin, this isn't exactly dressing up; it's no more than our school uniforms, except the kilts," Peter offered.

"Well, you'll look a hell of a lot better than the other kids... well, that might not be true tonight, being a dress-up affair—" she said.

"A'right, darling, now stop stalling," David said with a knowing grin.

She took a deep breath, and they piled out of the SUV. They walked up to the old church that had been converted into a wedding chapel and reception hall. She took David's hand as they stepped through the door and went up the short flight of stairs where Carrie and her husband Steve were greeting their guests as they arrived. Carrie was wearing a dark velvet dress, and her straight blonde hair was pulled back in a French twist. Steve was wearing a formal Highland jacket and a light blue and black kilt.

"Hi, Carrie," Erin said and hugged her friend, then she hugged Steve. "I'd like you to meet my fiancé David and his children. David, this is Steve and Carrie Wilson—"

She was interrupted by Carrie, who'd been standing with her mouth open, staring. "No! Way! *This* is your Mr. Miracle Man?"

Erin was surprised to find herself blushing and had an awful feeling come over her. It suddenly seemed like she was showing off her trophy or something. It felt wrong, but it was too late. "Yeah," she said, unexpectedly shy. "Umm, and these are his kids; Peter, Rosie, Dan, and Charlie."

They each shook her hand and said, "Congratulations, Mrs. Wilson." which melted both women's hearts.

"Oh, dear Lord, you are good-looking kids and so polite! It's nice to meet you." They all smiled and thanked her in unison. Erin imagined they were put through that sort of thing quite often and had been taught how to behave.

David smiled proudly at his children and then held out his hand to Steve, who stood nearly eye-to-eye with him. "David Elliott, congratulations; twenty-five years? Good on you," he said, using his RP accent.

Steve smiled. "David Elliott? Where have I heard that name before?"

Erin laughed, and Carrie rolled her eyes. They both knew perfectly well that Steve knew exactly who he was. Steve was the guy who went to all the conventions, standing in hour-long lines to get a photo and autograph with EVERYONE, probably even David at one time. "He was on *Future Explorations*, honey," Carrie said, playing along, but was interrupted by New Laura, who had just arrived with her husband, Scott, and was heading toward the group.

"Did someone say *Future Explorations*? I need to be involved in *that* conversation!" she said and staggered backward when Erin and David turned around. "Oh, my God! Oh, my God! Are you kidding me?" Everyone thought she was going to fall ass-over-feet down the stairs, so Scott and David caught her before she fell. She looked up at David and squeaked out, "Hi." David laughed and returned the greeting. Laura looked at Erin as though she'd never seen her before, but then she shook her head and composed herself. "I'm sorry, it was just a huge shock to see *you*... here. I'm Laura, and this is my husband Scott."

David shook Scott's hand. "Nice beard!" he said. Scott was a ginger with hair down past the middle of his back and a long red beard. "What do you think, Erin? Should I grow mine out? I've quite a lot of ginger in my beard."

"Do it!" Scott said, but Erin laughed and shook her head.

"On Scott, it's magnificent," she said, "I mean, look at that mane, but I'm not sure you could pull it off. Sorry, dear."

"How long did it take for you to grow your hair so long?" David asked.

Scott thought about it for a moment. "From your length? I'd say about five years, right, honey?" he said to Laura, who Erin could tell was trying very hard not to stare at David but failing miserably.

"What was that? Five years? Oh, yeah, about that long." She looked again at Erin and Carrie, then walked over to them. "Are you kidding me? Oh my God! He's *so* beautiful! Even better in person! How do you keep from staring at him all the time?" she said.

Erin saw Daniel roll his eyes, and she laughed. "Laura, these are David's kids."

She introduced her to them, and they were very polite, except when Rosie looked up at her and said, "Mummy! Daddy said you should say our kids, didn't he?"

"Yes, Rosebud, I forgot. I'll remember next time. Thank you for reminding me," she said.

"Well, you are the spitting image of your dad," Laura said to Peter. "You are all too lovely! It's so nice to meet you." The children smiled and thanked her, making Erin so proud. "They are so well-behaved, Erin!"

"They are now! You should've seen them before they met me!" Erin said and looked them over. "They were ugly and wild and couldn't even talk! All they did was grunt… ugg—hrugg—grugg—"

The children began to laugh. "You're so funny, Erin," Charlie said between bouts of the giggles. Daniel took his cue and continued talking in 'grunt' for a good five minutes until his father shot him a look that said to stop.

"So, what do you all think of Erin?" Laura asked the children. "Oh, maybe I shouldn't ask that in case you don't like her! That would be embarrassing!"

Rosie looked up and smiled. "We love her," she said, and the rest of them, even Daniel, nodded their agreement.

"She's the best thing to happen to our family," Peter said and then blushed scarlet.

"Oh! You guys are so sweet! Thank you, Peter; that means the world to me," Erin said and kissed the top of Rosie's head.

After a while, Erin noticed the children were getting bored, though they stood in a line, more well-behaved and patient than many adults would have been. "Children, you don't have to stand here. You may go and walk around if you'd like to. Your father and I will be done in a few minutes, and then we can find a table to sit at."

Daniel smiled and ran off, excited to have his freedom restored, but the rest of the children stayed put. Rosie held Erin's hand and smiled up at her. "I'd like to stay with you, Mummy," she said.

David joined the women, and Erin formally introduced him to Laura. "David, this is 'New Laura.' There are two of them, and she was the newest one to become part of our group of friends. I believe she might just be your biggest fan, well, next to me, that is," she said.

David raised his eyebrows and smiled, extending his hand in greeting. "Nice to meet you, New Laura," he said. He took her hand and kissed it in an endearing, old-fashioned way.

"I… just… can't believe you're here! It's a dream come true!" she said excitedly, her face red and splotchy.

"Thank you, Laura, I'm pleased to have been able to fulfill your dream," he said.

"I think we should find a table now," Erin said with a laugh at how Laura was gazing dreamily at him and took his hand.

"Please excuse us both. It was a pleasure speaking with you," he said so elegantly and formally that Erin had to laugh again. He looked at her as they walked away, and she shook her head. "What is et now?" he asked, rolling his eyes.

"You don't need to be so formal with these people. I mean, it's adorable and makes me want to eat you up, but it's not necessary."

"A'right, what would you have me do? Give them the finger and tell them they can kiss my arse?"

"Actually, most of them would be roaring with laughter at that. I dare you when you meet Marcia, Colleen, and Fucking Laura!" she said and then nudged his arm. "Well, speak of the devil." There was a commotion near the doors, and then three women were seen in the doorway to the hall, obviously searching the room for them.

His eyes grew wide, and he shook his head. "I'll not be taking yeh up on that dare!" he said.

Marcia saw them first and pulled Colleen and Laura close to say something. Then they made a beeline toward them. Erin held David's hand while they waited for her friends. "Erin! I've missed you so much!" Colleen said, staring at David.

"Hi, I've—"

"Erin March! How could you!" Marcia said over Erin's greeting to Colleen.

"What?"

"Yeah, what the fuck, Erin?" Fucking Laura said.

"This—this is your mystery miracle man? You should've told us!" Marcia said and then turned to David. "Hello, I'm Marcia."

David stood blinking for a moment, waiting to see if she was going to say anything else, then smiled and held out his hand. "It's a pleasure to meet you, Mar—"

"Marcia! You're embarrassing me!" Colleen whispered as she nudged her friend.

"Alright, girls, I'm sorry I didn't tell you, but I… didn't know how to, and, honestly, would you have believed me?"

"Hello, Mr. Elliott," Colleen said and accepted his handshake. "I'm Colleen."

David laughed good-naturedly and kissed the back of her hand. "It is a pleasure to meet you. I confess, Erin didn't tell me how lovely her friends were," he said and kissed the back of Marcia's outstretched hand.

"Oh, sit by us," Laura said, and Erin shook her head while David gave her the same greeting.

"I'm sorry, but our family will fill a whole table. We were just trying to find an empty one. We can talk later, though, okay?" Erin said.

"Okay, but we're gonna need details eventually, girl!" Marcia said, and the women walked away, giggling and nudging each other.

"I'm sorry about that," Erin said, but David pulled her close and kissed her hair.

"Dinnae fash, love. Your friends are funny; mystery miracle man, huh?"

"That's what they started calling you… well, my match, I mean… when I found out about… everything. I told them what the treatments were but not who you were. They never say it the same way, though. I kinda like it since you really are my Mr. Macho Miracle Manly Man."

"I am?"

"Aye, love, you are," she said, and he gave her a peck on the lips.

When they found a table with enough seats, they laid their things on the placemats or tipped the chairs to let people know the seats were taken. Everyone but Daniel, whom they couldn't see just then, joined them and sat watching as a line formed of people wanting to meet David. Erin felt bad; it was meant to be a party focused on Carrie and Steve, but it was starting to become David Elliott-centric. She stood and looked around the room, noticing that everyone was either in line, lining up, or standing in groups, pointing and whispering. She tapped David on the shoulder. "Will you be alright if I walk away for a few minutes?"

He looked up at her and smiled. "Of course I will, but thanks for askin'. If I need you, I'll holler," he said.

The thought of David hollering for her made her laugh out loud. She figured it probably wasn't much fun for the children, standing around while their dad was worshipped, so she beckoned them to come with her. "I'm going to find some of the younger people and introduce you to them," she said and saw the relief on their faces as they walked away from the spectacle that was their father.

They passed Carrie, and Erin asked if she'd seen their daughter, Jordan, lately.

"I think she's in the balcony," she said, and then whispered, "Well, he's popular, isn't he?"

Erin sighed. "I'm so sorry; I didn't think it through. I hope you're not upset!" she said, biting her bottom lip.

"Are you kidding! Upset? No, I'm thrilled! I'm sure all the fuss will die down in a little while," she assured her.

"Okay, good; I'm sure you're right. Oh! We forgot your gift in the rental! Don't let us leave without giving it to you! It's freaking awesome!

"Oh, trust me, I won't!" Carrie said and was called away by someone needing her attention.

Erin continued her mission; she searched for the stairs leading up to the balcony and found them easily enough. When they arrived at the top step, she saw Jordan sitting on a folding chair, looking at her cell phone. She was eighteen, but Erin couldn't see her as anything over sixteen. Erin loved her; she was really sweet and put up with her parents and their friends like a champ.

"Hi, Erin!" Jordan said, looking up from her phone. "How are you?" She stood to give Erin a hug and saw the group of kids behind her.

"Oh, it's so good to see you! It feels like forever!" Erin said to her. "I'm doing really good; better than ever, in fact. Thanks for asking. Jordan, I'd like you to meet—" she looked at Rosie, "*my* new family. The tall one is Peter, he's sixteen, and then there's Charlie; he, and his brother, Dan, who's running around here somewhere, are both ten, nearly eleven, and Rosie, she's nine."

Jordan put her hand up in a little wave to say 'hi,' and the kids, not knowing what to do, did the same. "You see, they don't know anyone… well, in this whole country, except me. Would you mind introducing them to some of the younger kids? It would be a real help to me and David."

"David? I haven't met him, have I?" she said.

Erin smiled and shook her head. "You'd know it if you had." She took her to the railing and pointed to the crowd gathered around the poor, lone man. Jordan squinted, trying to make out who he was, but his back was toward them. "David Elliott," Erin whispered, and Jordan's eyes popped open.

"Really! I love *Future Explorations*! My friends and I watch it all the time!" She looked at the three kids standing together and raised her eyebrows. And these are *his* kids?" she said.

"We're Erin's kids now as well," Rosie said bravely.

"So, how long have you known Erin?" Jordan asked them.

"I reckon it's been about a month," Peter answered in his impeccable Received Pronunciation accent.

Erin could see Jordan melt and knew it would be okay. She looked over the balcony edge again and saw the tables below her. David was now completely surrounded. "Oh dear, I think I need to go rescue your dad," she said to the children, and they all looked over the edge at their father.

"Hi, Daddy!" Rosie said, not realizing that her voice would carry so far. The entire room looked up, making her blush, but then David flashed her his brilliant smile and waved. He then looked at Erin and mouthed, 'I love you.'

Her heart melted as she mouthed, 'I love you, too,' and the whole room applauded. "Alright, enough spectacle! Do you mind helping them, Jordan?"

The young woman smiled at her and then looked at the kids. "Sure, no problem. I think you're right, though, you might want to rescue him."

"Thanks! Alright, kids, I'm not passing you off; I just don't want you to have to stand around while everyone gawks at your dad. You should have fun and make some friends, okay?" Erin said, and they nodded. "If you get bored or feel uncomfortable, you can come back to us—"

"It's fine, Mum," Peter said, so she ran down the stairs just in time to see the crowd pressing in on David.

She stood at the outer rim of people and put up her hands. "Alright now, let the man breathe," she said, then pressed through them and stood next to him. "I've come to save you, my darling."

He laughed and put his arm around her waist. "Sorry, everyone. I'm being rescued at the moment, so I must leave you," he said, and the crowd parted, making way for them.

"I'm sorry. I didn't think this through very well," she said, but David shook his head.

"I'm used to it, don't worry."

"Maybe so, but it's not fair to you or the kids. I want you and them to have a good time, not—"

David turned to her and put his finger to her lips. "Shh, dinnae fash, my love." He bent down and kissed her, making the crowd cheer.

Erin's eyes grew wide, and she felt really weird. "Let's go up to the balcony for a little while," she whispered.

"A'right, but I need a wee first," he said, then he kissed her again and walked away.

Erin saw Carrie heading toward her, looking upset about something, and met her halfway. "What's wrong?" she asked.

"Oh, Erin! There's a problem," Carrie said, sounding worried.

"Okay, how can I help?"

"It's not that kind of problem. It appears Steve told... Todd—" She didn't get to finish before they both heard a familiar voice.

"*Not you! Not here!*"

Erin flew to where she'd heard Todd's voice come from. Steve was standing between him and David, making sure nothing happened. "Alright, that's enough. This building is big enough for all of us. We'll just have to keep our distance. I'm sure you can be an adult for one night, Todd," Erin said, not caring if she insulted him, not after he'd broken David's nose one month earlier in a drunken, jealous fit. "Thank you, Steve, but I'm sure everything will be fine."

Peter and Rosie were now standing by David, while Dan and Charlie stood next to Erin. Rosie took her dad's hand. "Who is that man, Daddy? And why does he look angry with you?" she asked, sounding a bit frightened.

Erin saw David make eye contact with Todd. They seemed to come to a silent understanding that the children didn't need to witness their animosity. He crouched in front of her and said, "Don't worry, darling."

Steve led Todd to the bar while Erin, David, and the children went back into the main hall and sat at their table, waiting for the meal. Peter leaned over and asked Erin if that had been her husband.

"You're so astute, Peter. Yes, but we're divorced now," she said.

"He wanted to hit my dad, didn't he? Is he going to stay here?" he asked, looking toward the bar.

"I imagine he will; these are his friends too. We just need to keep an eye out so he and your father stay apart, alright?" she said, but Peter still looked worried. "He won't hurt you or your siblings. It's only your dad he's upset with if that's what you're afraid of." He nodded, still watching him.

It was announced that the meal was ready, and everyone was asked to bow their heads for a prayer. After that, each table was dismissed, one by one. Erin watched Todd, who was still sitting at the bar, and prayed he'd get up before he drank any more. In the whole time they'd been married, she'd only seen him drunk twice, and in just the last month, she'd seen him drunk at least three times. Here he was, working on the fourth. She had a feeling it was becoming a regular thing and wished she could talk to him. She felt guilty and wanted to help, but she knew there wasn't anything she could do anymore.

Jordan came up to the table, looking worried. "There you are! One minute we were standing together, and the next, they were gone."

Erin and David both looked at Peter, wanting an explanation.

"I'm sorry. We saw that man yelling at our dad and came to stand with him. We didn't mean to frighten you, Jordan," Peter said so maturely it was impossible to be upset.

Jordan shrugged and looked at David. Erin could tell she was fangirling and trying to hide it. "That's okay. I'm just glad you're alright," she said.

"Jordan, I'd like you to meet David; David, this is Steve and Carrie's daughter, Jordan. She's been introducing the children to some of the kids."

David stood and looked directly at her. "Well, thank you for that, Jordan. It's a pleasure to meet you," he said, sounding so dreamy, even Erin's heart fluttered. He took Jordan's hand and kissed it, making her blush, and Erin thought she might've seen a tear welling up in her eye.

"It's... well, it's nice to meet you too, Mr. Elliott. I just love *Future Explorations*, I really do! My friends and I watch it *all* the time. You're so perfect as John Thomas!" she said with a huge smile.

"You may call me David, and I'm so pleased to hear how much—"

Erin put her hand up. "Stop."

"What?" he said, looking confused.

"Enough with the RP English, David. These people don't need you to be posh, they need you to be you. Please, I know everyone will enjoy your natural accent much more than your fake one. Just look at all the kilts in this room. Now, if you don't mind, would you please repeat and finish what you were saying to Jordan?"

He looked at Jordan and shrugged. "Well then, Jordan, you may call me David, and I'm pleased yeh like the show so much. I'm glad you and yer friends are still watchin' et after all these years. Is that better?" he asked Erin, but Jordan responded.

"Oh yes! That was beautiful! I'm gonna sit here all night and listen to you talk if that's okay?" she said. "Just kidding, but it was much better."

"A'right, I surrender!" he said and held up his hands.

"We didn't actually get a chance to meet anyone before the hullabaloo," Charlie said and seemed proud of himself for the big word.

"Hullabaloo, huh? Well, that's an impressive word, isn't it?" Erin said. "I'm sure there will be plenty of time after the meal to meet people. Now that you know Jordan, you can find her when we're done."

"Yeah, I'll be at the head table," she said, clearly not excited about it. "I hate people staring at me!" she said. The whole table nodded, understanding completely what she meant.

It was finally their turn to get in line for food, so they stood and queued up with the people at the back. David put his hands on Erin's shoulders and massaged them, making her groan. "I'll give you exactly five hours to stop that," she said, making him laugh. She looked over her shoulder to make sure the kids were all in line and saw Todd sitting at the bar, watching them. He didn't look away when they made eye contact, and a shiver ran through her.

"What is et, hen?" David asked, and then glanced in the direction she'd been looking. "Ach, I see. Do yeh reckon he'll make trouble, then?"

"I don't know. I'm sure he wants to beat the pulp out of you, though I think he learned his lesson at the hotel and wouldn't actually do it. Having the kids here will keep him tame, at least until he gets too drunk, but I hope he'll leave before then," she said.

They reached the long tables laden with dinnerware, napkins, cutlery, and lots of food. She'd already started putting food on her plate when Erin remembered that everyone was watching them. She felt self-conscious about serving herself too much and having people think she was a pig.

Apparently, David noticed how little she was giving herself. "Darling, you should take what yeh want. No one's lookin' at yer plate, trust me, and if they are, then… fuck them," he said very uncharacteristically, which made Erin do a double take.

"Who is this beautiful man with the foul mouth standing beside me? What's come over you?" she asked, and David shrugged.

"I've heard the way you and yer friends speak when yeh think I'm not listenin', and ye've the most Scottish mouths… the lot of yeh! I thought we were bad at droppin' f-bombs, but ye've got us beat! Now, load up, and let's sit!" he said and put a large spoonful of mashed potatoes on her plate. When they were through, they made their way back to the table while people stared and whispered all over the room.

"Holy Moses, that's horrible!" Erin said.

"You get used to it," Peter said. "Ignore them and get on with your life. Right, Dad?"

"Right, Peter," he replied.

Chapter Eight

CORK WARS

In the center of each large, round, dining table was a small arrangement of wine corks and plastic bunches of grapes in green and purple, hot glued to mirrors. At one point during the meal, Erin saw a cork fly past Peter's head, then a purple grape landed next to Erin's coffee cup. *What in the world?* she thought and noticed that a few of the nearby tables were having a cork and grape war.

Not being one to miss out on throwing things, Erin took the grape and aimed it at one of her friends named Becky. She knew that if anyone had started that fight, it was either her, her husband Josh, or possibly New Laura's husband Scott. The grape bounced off Becky's green hair and landed on the floor. She looked behind her, and that was it; Erin was now being pelted with grapes and corks.

The children ducked, not knowing what to do. "Are yeh gonnae leave me defenseless here?" Erin called to them. "I need the Elliott clan as ma allies! Take up yer corks and fight!"

They looked at their dad, who was laughing. "Aye! Dinnae leave her hangin', mates!" David said and started throwing grapes and corks at people he didn't even know. Dan and Charlie began gathering the corks and grapes off the floor where they landed and laying them on the table for the others to throw. Peter was dismantling their bunches of grapes to use as ammunition.

A green grape bounced off Rosie's head and landed in Peter's hand. Rosie sat stunned, not knowing whether to laugh or get angry until Peter threw it back, and it landed in one of the enemy's drinks. Everyone at the other table stopped and stared at the floating grape. Erin could tell Peter was worried that someone would be upset, but then they erupted in laughter, congratulating him on his good aim.

———

David was laughing and having the time of his life. *Who are these people?* he thought. *They don't care if they act like children; life is fun for them! No wonder Erin is friends with them.* Erin whispered something into Peter's ear, and they both stood, taking much of their ammunition with them. After a minute, David saw a cork coming from above. He realized that Erin and Peter had gone to the balcony, so he and Rosie joined them to fight with the advantage of height.

The battle continued until the caterers began clearing the tables, then they stopped and went back to the dining area. The war was pretty much finished, except for a few strays that *accidentally* made their way down from the balcony every now and then. Erin held David's hand as they left their strategic sniper's nest and then approached the enemy's table, laughing. Becky gave her a big hug and said, "Scott started it!"

Scott heard her and pointed at himself. "You can't prove it!" he said.

"I've never had as much fun as that… at least not in public," David said and shook Scott's hand.

"David, this is my dear friend, Becky, and her husband Josh," Erin said.

"David Elliott, it's a true pleasure to meet you both," he said and shook their hands enthusiastically.

Becky turned toward Erin, speaking softly. "I'm so happy for you! I'm sad for Todd, but David is—" Someone said something at the same time, so he didn't hear what she said.

Erin laughed so hard she snorted. "Good night nurse, Becks! I'd forgotten all about that one! Yes, he is!"

David looked at her and raised his eyebrows. "Whom is what?" he asked. "Or do I want to know?"

"You, my love, are totally testicles," Erin said. She and Becky were laughing so hard they were holding each other up.

David looked at Josh, who shrugged. "Yeah, they were always making up things like that. You'll get used to it," he said. "There was also a thing about husbands, but I lost track of that."

"Holy Moses! You were my fifth husband because you wanted to be called Fives. Paul was number one, Liz was number two, Steve was number four... Who was three?" Erin said between snorts.

"You have more husbands—" David began.

"No, wait, Todd was number one... Umm, I mean—" Becky said and then turned bright red.

"Right, Paul was number two, and so on. I had to pick a number four, so you could be Fives. That's how Steve got on the list. Don't worry, Becky, it's okay," Erin said and put her arm around her friend's shoulders.

"We all love *Future Explorations*. I thought you should know," Becky said to David, and everyone began talking over each other.

"Yeah, the catacombs were great! Was it real or just a set?"

"The scene at the end, when you return to the farmhouse, broke my heart!"

"Is the old farmhouse a real place? I'd love to see it someday!"

"Me too! Do you live in Scotland now or London?"

"Do you still have the kilt—"

"Yeah, or the time travel device?"

"Do you ever pretend that you're John Thomas and Erin is... I don't know, one of the characters in the show? That would be so much fun!"

Erin laughed each time he began to answer, just for someone to begin the next question. She put her hands up and looked at him. "Catacombs?"

"Et was a set, sorry," he said.

"That scene at the end breaks me up too," she said and looked at him again.

"Aye, et wasn't easy to shoot. I had tae dig deep for et."

"I've got the rest... yes, and you'd love it; London; yes, yes, and none of your bee's wax!" she said to a lot of laughter.

"I wish I remembered the questions," he said and then had to get out of the way because people were moving the tables to make room for dancing.

Soon, the DJ came out to set up his equipment, and Erin nearly peed her pants when she saw him. She knew exactly who he was; Jeff Miller, the DJ at the country bar where she used to dance. They'd dated for a while, if you could really call it that, until another dancer caught his eye and he started paying attention to her instead. She was secretly glad that he looked older, balder, and much the worse for wear. Though she wasn't a size six any longer, she knew she looked good that night, and above all, she was with someone who truly loved her.

Jeff started the music with a set of fast songs, then he played a slow set. Before Erin could think, David was standing in front of her, asking her to dance. The song was "You Look Wonderful Tonight" by Eric Clapton, and the whole room watched as David led her to the tiny dance floor.

He was beaming, and as he took her into his arms, she felt like Eliza Doolittle, asked to dance by the Prince of Transylvania. She laughed, and when he looked at her questioningly, she stood on her tiptoes to whisper her thoughts into his ear. He laughed out loud and kissed her tenderly, which made the crowd sigh collectively. Erin rolled her eyes and then saw Todd walking, or more accurately, staggering toward them.

"Oh no!" she said to David, who looked behind him.

Before anyone could react, Todd was stopped by Peter and Charlie, of all people. Erin knew David was about to take action, but she saw something in Todd that made her stop him. "Wait, I think that might have been the best thing to do. He won't touch a child." She watched as Todd found a chair up against the wall and sat there staring at them.

The next song Jeff played was "I'm Not Supposed to Love You Anymore" by Bryan White. Erin had every intention of staying on the floor with David, but Rosie was waving at him, so they started to walk off the floor. Someone took hold of Erin's arm, and before she could do anything, Todd had her back on the dance floor, holding her just tight enough so she couldn't easily walk away. "Todd! I don't want—" she began and struggled.

"Erin, let me have one dance, please?" he said, and she stopped fighting him.

"Fine, but will you please leave afterward?" He didn't answer; he just held her against his chest and put his cheek against her ear, rocking back and forth to the beat of the music. Erin felt his tears fall on her shoulder and listened to the words of the song as Todd sang along.

"You requested this, didn't you?" she asked, aggravated.

"Shh," he said quietly. "I miss you so much, Erin. Please tell me you still love me."

———

David was trying to pay attention to Rosie, but all he could do was stand and watch Erin being moved side to side by Todd. He also listened to the words about a man whose wife left him and he can't move on. Growing tired of watching Todd hold her, he wanted to stop him.

She put her hand up, telling him not to, though he had a mind to intervene whether Erin liked it or not. When the song ended, Todd finally took his hands off her. He kept his head down, and David heard their conversation. "Please—Erin?" Todd said and waited for a reply.

She shook her head. "I can't," she said. "I'm sorry, but I don't." Todd nodded and glared at David, then he looked at Rosie standing next to him, watching them, and walked away. Erin went straight to David and hugged him. "I think he's going to leave now; at least I asked him to, anyway."

Rosie took hold of Erin's hand. "I was scared, Erin. I thought he might hurt you," she said, and Erin crouched down to hug her.

"No, sweetheart, he wasn't going to hurt me. He's just sad that I love your daddy now," Erin said.

"Did you love him before you met my daddy?" Rosie asked.

She looked up at her with large, serious eyes, and Erin sighed. "I did, but I don't anymore. Now I love your daddy and you and your brothers; you are my family."

Rosie nodded, and an odd expression fell over her face. "Erin? Is your mummy still alive?" Erin looked up at David, who hadn't been listening; he was watching an argument at the bar involving Todd and Steve.

"I'll be back shortly," David said to her as he walked away.

"Yes, Rosie, my mom is alive, and so is my dad."

The young girl's eyes sparkled. "So, I'll have more grandparents when you and Daddy get married? May I meet them? Do they live far away?" she asked as excitedly as Erin had ever seen her. She was about to answer when she heard Todd yelling.

Chapter Nine

HE OFFERED A CAB!

"Whahht do yhou care? Whouldn't you be happy if I d-ied?" Todd said and got up in David's face.

"I'll be right back, darling," Erin said to Rosie and rushed to David's side. "What's going on?" she asked when she got to them.

Todd looked disgusted. "Yhour boyfriend here jusst offered to call me—a cab," he slurred.

"Then say thank you! You're too drunk to drive. We'll figure out how to get your car back home in the morning. There's no reason why we can't be in the same building together for one lousy night, Todd, but you're causing scene upon scene and ruining Steve and Carrie's party. Please stop acting like a child and either sober up or accept the offer like a man," she said.

He scanned the room and turned away. "Fine, call the fucking cab! I'll wait outside," he said.

Erin put her hand on his arm and held out her hand. Todd handed his keys to her; she took off the one for the car and gave the rest back to him. "This might sound crazy, but have you considered signing up for the Registry? I mean, maybe you'll be matched with someone who can help you forget about me. I know you think you don't want to do that right now, but you can't live like this for the rest of your life. Plus, you'd be helping someone like me beat this horrible disease."

He narrowed his eyes at her. "What, and become someone else's nursemaid? I don't think so!" he spat.

"I'm sorry you had to be that for me," she said sadly and took a step back.

"Shit, I shouldn't have said that. I'll think about it, okay," he said and walked out the door.

It seemed like the whole room breathed a sigh of relief together. David used his phone to order a car for Todd, and Erin talked to some of her friends to see if any of them would mind bringing his car back for him. Colleen and her husband Brad said they'd do it, and it was settled.

David and Erin could finally relax again, except now there were even more whispers and stares from the crowd. They sat at their table and held hands while they listened to the music. David saw a cork lying near him, a remnant of the cork wars, and smiled. "Tell me again, how do yeh know these people?" he asked.

"We're all part of a Sci-Fi costuming group. We dress up for charities."

"Really? I dinnae think ye've mentioned that before."

Erin smiled and shrugged. "Well, I haven't done it in a while. There was drama in the leadership, and it wasn't fun anymore. Then my symptoms started getting worse, so I quit doing it."

"So, then—what was yer costume?" he said with an amused grin. "I'm imagining you in a bunny suit for some reason."

"I wasn't a Furry, silly; I was a Mando," she said, and he frowned.

"A what?" he said, sounding confused.

"*Star Wars*; just think Boba Fett—I'll show you a photo," she said and took out her phone. She had to go to Facebook and scroll years back, but she found one she liked and showed it to him.

"Ma Losh! That's fantastic! Where'd yeh find something like that?"

"We make them," she said.

"Blimey! That's brilliant! I think et would be fun and freein' with the helmets on."

She was about to reply when Charlie walked up and saw the photo on her phone. "Mandalorians? Cool!" he said.

Erin looked at him with her mouth open. "You know what a Mando is?" she asked.

"Sure, my friend, Sid, is into *Star Wars*. I've seen *Rebels* and *The Mandalorian*," Charlie said.

"Son, do yeh know who this is?" David asked, pointing to the Mando in the blue costume on the right of the screen.

"No idea; I don't remember their names, but I like the look of that one," he said.

David shook his head. "I meant the person in the costume," he clarified, and Charlie shrugged. "Et's our Erin."

Charlie's eyes grew large as he looked closer at Erin's phone. "Cor blimey!" he said, and Erin swiped to the next photo, which showed her with her helmet off. "That's wicked, Erin! I'd love to do something like that! Wait, isn't that the man you danced with earlier?" He pointed to the Mando standing next to her.

"Yeah, that's my ex-husband," she replied.

"That was your—He was here?" Charlie said, "Wow! I reckon that's why he glared at Dad as he did."

Erin nodded. "Yes, he's not a fan of your father," she said but didn't mean it in the famous person way.

They heard the theme song for *Future Explorations*, and Erin turned toward the small DJ booth, furious at Jeff for not asking first. Everyone in the room applauded, then he left the mixing board to approach David.

"It's great to meet you!" Jeff said as he shook his hand.

As charming as ever, Erin thought and rolled her eyes as David returned his greeting. "Since when do you like *Future Explorations*, Jeff?" she said, which made him give her a double take.

"Umm… I'm sorry, do I know you?" he said, clearly trying to place her.

Erin shook her head. "I guess not," she said and looked away.

"Wait! I'm sorry, what's your name?" he asked, and she frowned.

"You knew me as Erin Wallace."

His eyes grew large, but the song was about to end. "Oh, Erin! Please don't go anywhere," he said and ran back to his soundboard.

David took her hand, looking puzzled. "What was that about?" he asked.

"That was Jeff—" she began, but he was back and handed David a microphone.

"Would you like to say a few words to the happy couple, Mr. Elliott?" Jeff said, not actually giving him a choice.

Erin wanted to punch him. "No! Jeff! How dare you?" she hissed.

David smiled genuinely, as though he hadn't been put on the spot, and everyone in the room shut up. It was eerily quiet, and his voice sounded enormous. "Hello everyone. I'd like tae say congratulations tae Steve and Carrie on twenty-five years of marriage. I'm honored tae have been part of the celebration! I wish you much happiness in all yer future explorations," he said and handed the microphone back to John.

The room exploded in applause, and Erin thought David would want to retreat after that. Instead, he went to Steve and shook his hand, then he hugged Carrie, whose face turned a lovely shade of rose. Again, the crowd cheered and whistled, making a deafening noise.

Jeff put on a long song, and once David returned to Erin, he stepped up to them. "I'm so glad to see you, Erin! I've wanted to talk to you for years, but I didn't know how to get a hold of you," he said humbly.

"Oh, this ought to be good," she said sarcastically. "Go on then."

"Ach, Erin—" David began.

"No, she has every right to be upset. I was a real asshole to you; I know it," he said, and Erin nodded.

"Yeah, and?" she said, not letting him off the hook so easily.

"Yes, do continue," David said with his eyebrows raised.

"Uh, I don't have a good excuse, Erin, but I wanted to apologize to you. I was young and stupid, and you deserved so much better. Well, it seems like you've found that in him, and I'm happy for you," he said, nodding his head in David's direction.

Erin wasn't sure what to do, but it had been a long time ago, and with such a sincere apology, her anger melted. "Well, thanks for that, Jeff. I guess I can forgive you then," she said and gave him a slight smile.

"Thank you. It means a lot," Jeff said gratefully.

"Listen, could I make a request?" Erin asked, unexpectedly.

"Sure, what is it?"

Erin whispered into his ear, and he nodded. "I'll find it," he said, then shook David's hand again and walked away to start another song.

David looked at her. "I assume he was an ex-boyfriend, then?" he said.

"Yeah, he was the DJ at the country bar I used to dance at. It was before I met Todd, so, like, a million years ago. I thought he was the bee's knees at the time but look at him now! Time hasn't been kind." She watched David look at him with a slight frown on his handsome face. "Now you, on the other hand, look better now than you ever have!" she said and kissed him. "Especially in that kilt! All I want to do is reach underneath it and touch you. You may not be able to tell, but it's driving me crazy!"

———

David could imagine her doing it and was becoming aroused, which, even with a sporran, was dangerous in a kilt. "Ach, Erin!" he said. "Yeh shouldn't say things like that to me! She smiled at him, and a lightning bolt passed between them, making his condition even worse. "Ma Losh, woman! What am I gonna do with yeh?"

Erin glanced around the room. "I have an idea," she said, which he was immediately leery of. "Follow me."

He shook his head. "I can't walk around in this condition! Are yeh mental?" he said, looking around them and seeing everyone's eyes on him.

"You're wearing your sporran; isn't that what it's there for?" she asked. "I wouldn't mind seeing you without it, though, standing in front of me with your kilt tented in the front." She looked at him again, and the invisible bolt of lightning flashed between them once more. It was getting much worse, and he couldn't help but breathe harder.

"Bloody hell, I'll no' be standin' after that!"

She heard the song she'd requested and looked at him pleadingly. "Could I have this dance at least?" she asked. "It's the one I requested."

"Let me check my dance card, yeh wee kelpie," he said, trying to buy a little time. *Football! Think of bloody football!* he thought to himself. "Looks like I'm free." He took her hand, praying that his sporran would do its job. He heard the first few lines of the song and paused. "Wait, is this the one—" he said.

Erin nodded and smiled. "Yep."

"What's the name of et, again?"

"Whenever You Come Around."

He looked at her, remembering the day she'd sung that song in the shower in New Orleans when he was so torn and hurting. "This song broke ma heart when I heard yeh sing it, but now ye're mine, and I'm so happy." His eyes were wet, though no tears fell. "I love yeh," he said tenderly.

"I love you too, David," she said and laid her head on his chest.

When the song was over, she took him by the hand and led him down a small flight of stairs. "I noticed this when I was looking for Jordan earlier," she said. At the bottom of the stairs was a small bathroom. She pulled him into it and locked the door.

"What are yeh—" he said, trying to protest, but she reached her hand up under his kilt, and his knees grew weak. "Ma Losh, Erin!" he said in a hoarse whisper. He closed his eyes and opened his mouth as she ran her hand up the inside of his thigh, making him pant. She gently cupped his testicles, then her hand moved slowly upward until she was holding his cock. Suddenly, her mouth was over his, and he kissed her while she stroked him under his sporran and woolen tartan.

He could take no more and pushed her away. In an instant, he had her pinned against the sink and studied her face in the mirror. The electricity was being reflected back at them and seemed to intensify everything. He stepped back and pulled her hips toward him so she was bent forward. Then he lifted her skirt and moved her panties to the side, wanting to touch her. She was wet and warm, and he needed her so badly. He lifted his kilt, laid it over her back, and pressed himself against her, hearing her gasp quietly. Then he felt her yield and envelope him.

Wasting no time, he thrust into her, trying to remain silent, then they heard a group of people outside the door, talking and laughing. "Keep going! The door is locked, and I don't think they want to use the bathroom, anyway," she gasped, just above a whisper. He was so turned on as he watched her in the mirror, her backside covered in his family tartan. He felt her release, pulsing and clenching around him, then he climaxed, filling her up soundlessly. They stood like that for a moment to catch their breath, and then someone tried the door handle, so they knew they had to clean up quickly.

———

"One minute, please," Erin said.

"Erin?" Marcia said.

"Uh, yeah."

"You'd better hurry your ass up, girl! I'm sure your *macho manly miracle man* won't want to be away from you for too long!" she said, and they heard a group of women laugh. "Come out and share a drink with us!" she added in a loud whisper.

Erin looked at David. "We have to go out there; there isn't anything we can do about it," she whispered and shook her head.

David was smiling. "Macho manly miracle man, huh?" he whispered.

Erin rolled her eyes and laughed lightly. "Let me look you over and make sure you're all put together with nothing hanging out."

"Yeh look bonnie, ma love," he said, and she unlocked the deadbolt. A mini booze bottle was thrust in her face before the door was all the way open. She laughed with them until the door opened the rest of the way, and they saw David standing behind her.

"Holy shit! You were... in there?" Marcia said and took back the bottle of 100-proof butterscotch flavored vodka and downed it. "I need this more than you."

"Holy fuck!" Fucking Laura said and reached for another bottle of booze.

Erin and David were bright red, and they tried to get past them, but the girls wanted to talk to them. Marcia handed each of them a random mini bottle of alcohol, and after reading them, they switched bottles. Erin ended up with cherry McGillicuddy's, which is like Kool-Aid, and David got Fireball whiskey. Erin took a tiny sip and put the cover back on, not wanting anyone to know she was pregnant yet.

David downed his, and although he was Scottish and used to whisky, he coughed a bit. "Wow! That's powerful!" he said, looking at the bottle.

"We're not supposed to bring contraband in and could get kicked out for it, so be quiet," she said, handing them another bottle each. They both refused, using the excuse that it was getting late and Erin still had to drive them back to the hotel.

"So, what do you think of Erin's friends?" Fucking Laura asked David.

He raised his eyebrows. "Do yeh really want tae know?" he asked, and they all nodded. "I think ye're all pure radge! But I love et! I can see why she gets on with yeh as she does."

"Pure radge? What does that mean?" New Laura asked.

"Et means crazy, completely and utterly mental," he said. "Now, if ye'll excuse me, I'd better find ma children and make sure they're behavin' themselves." He looked at Erin, smiled his beautiful smile, and fled up the stairs.

"I can't believe you didn't tell us!" Colleen said when he was gone, and the rest of the women nodded.

"Sorry, I didn't tell anyone, really. I wanted it to be my little secret. I knew if I told you we wouldn't be able to talk about him at the girls' weekend, so I kept my mouth shut," Erin said.

"He is fucking delicious!" Fucking Laura said. "I can't believe you had a quickie with HIM in that bathroom! You're the ones who are pure radge!"

"Well, you're not wrong; radge and horny!" Erin said with a laugh and managed to escape up the stairs to find him.

John played a set of crowd favorites such as "Uptown Funk" and "YMCA". Erin danced with her friends and new brood of children, having a great time, while David sat and watched them. They returned to the table, exhausted but laughing.

A slow song started, and a woman Erin didn't know came up to David to ask for a dance. David smiled at her kindly and said, "Thank you for asking, but I'm afraid I'm only dancing with my fiancée this evening." She looked sad and slightly mortified as she walked away.

"Who was that?" he asked Erin after the woman left.

"No clue," she said. "Must be one of their family or something."

A few moments later, Carrie approached the table and leaned in. "The woman who asked you to dance, she's one of my cousins. It's her birthday today… she's on the spectrum and extremely shy. We were all astonished that she worked up the courage to come to your table, let alone ask you to dance. Would it be too much to ask you to make an exception for her?"

David looked at Erin.

"I don't mind," she said, and he smiled at Carrie.

"Aye, of course I will; I'm glad you told me." David leaned in to kiss Erin, then he stood and she, as well as everyone else in the room, watched as he walked over to the table where the woman was sitting. He approached her and said something that made her smile broadly, nod, and then stand.

Holy Moses, he looks good in that Kilt! Erin thought as he led the woman to the dance floor. She reminded her of Tilly, plain and small, not David's type.

David was smiling, and the woman was glowing. By the time they got to the dance floor, the song was mostly through, so, like the gentleman he was, he danced the next one with her. About a quarter of the way through the second song, the woman suddenly put her head on David's chest, startling both him and Erin. Then, when the song was over, she didn't want to let go.

Erin could see he was trying to be kind while pushing her gently away. She made eye contact with Carrie, who then went up to the woman and led her off the floor, thankfully away from David. Erin went to him for the next dance, and they talked about it. "Well, that was strange, wasn't it?"

"Aye, she didn't say anathin'. She either stared up at me or held me for dear life," he said with a chuckle.

"I feel like that's all I do with you as well," Erin said, smiling.

"Ach, yeh do a wee bit more than that!" he said. They finished the last slow dance, and the next song was a Cha Cha. Erin would have loved to dance it, but she wasn't sure about asking David. He'd told her he could dance, but they never actually tried it. She was about to walk away when he took hold of her hand.

"Where do you think ye're goin'?" he said and brought her up into position to start the dance.

She was out of practice and hoped she'd be able to follow him. Instead of worrying, she looked into his eyes and waited for his lead. He started moving her, keeping perfect time, and she had no trouble at all following. Before long, they realized they had a rapt audience. Erin was falling in love all over again and was determined to dance with him more often, even if it was in their living room. "You are an amazing dancer," she said, "You lead perfectly!"

"You follow like a dream, Erin. I'm surprised we're doin' so well, seeing we've not danced more than a few slow dances before now."

She felt like she was flying; she didn't have to think or anticipate. The room around her and the people staring at them faded away until it was only the two of them in perfect sync. "This is so nice, you, being here with me," Erin said. "I know this is a far cry from what you're used to, so thanks for being a good sport and for being so charming and wonderful. You really are the most amazing man."

The song ended and the whole room clapped and cheered once more.

"Before I forget, Rosie wants to meet my mom," Erin said when they returned to the table and waited for his reaction. David raised his eyebrows and she laughed. "I know, but the seer said to forgive her, right?"

"Oh, I've forgiven her, et's just hard tae forget, and seein' her again so soon is somethin' I'm not sure I wanna do."

"Okay, then I'll just have to tell poor little Rosie how her father is too much of a coward—" she said, sounding pathetic.

"Ach, yeh ken how tae hit a man where et hurts!"

"I know my parents would love to meet the children, and they can play outside, or we can go for a walk and explore the land."

He leaned over and kissed her cheek. "Aye, a'right; make the plans, and we'll do et."

"I'll send her a message now."

> Erin: *Hey, Mom. We're gonna be in the
> area for the next few days, and I have
> someone here who wants to meet you.
> Will you be home?*

A few minutes later, she got a reply.

> Liz: *Yes, we'll be home, but are you sure? I mean after last time.*

> E: *Just don't get drunk, for goodness' sake, and everything will be fine.*

> L: *Well, I won't tell you not to come, but...*

> E: *Thanks, Mom! There will be six of us, and it would be nice to stay there if you're ok with it?*

> L: *Six! Okay, I'll prepare the spare room then. When will you get here?*

> E: *Is tomorrow too soon? We need to be in Door County on Tuesday.*

> L: *Yes, that's fine.*

> E: *Mom... Don't worry! Just be yourself and pretend it didn't happen, or just make a joke out of it. It'll be fine, plus the kids will be there to help take the focus away.*

> L: *Okay, see you then. I have a lot to do.*

Erin shook her head and turned back to David. "I told her we'd be there tomorrow sometime."

He raised his eyebrows. "That soon?" he said, and she kissed his cheek.

"Yup. That soon." She saw Peter speaking to one of the men in the group. "Look at your boy, David. He looks so grown up and handsome."

He watched his eldest son and frowned. "Aye, and I've missed et all," he said sadly.

"Dinnae fash, my love, there's still plenty of time left. Just make these years count, and it'll be okay. I'm so glad I get to be part of your children's lives now!"

"And I thank God everaday they'll have you as their mum."

Chapter Ten

DON'T FORGET THE GIFT!

E rin saw Charlie and Rosie near their table, so she headed over to them. "I'm gonna go get the gift from the car now," she said.

"I'll go with you," Charlie volunteered.

"Okay, thanks."

They left the building together, headed out to the rented SUV, and Erin unlocked it with the key fob. The night sky was filled with stars, though the lights from the city dimmed them a bit. It was nice to step away from the crowd and noise, but the lake breeze made her shiver. "So, Charlie, have you had a good night?"

"Yes, I have. Your friends are a lot of fun, like you," he said.

"Oh, Charlie, you make my day… no, wait, I take that back, you make my life!" She hugged him, then opened the back hatch and grabbed the small, wrapped box and envelope. "I hope they open it while we're here!" she said.

Charlie tried to close the door, but he couldn't reach it, though he jumped a few times, trying. "I can't—"

"Let me help you," came a voice from behind them. Peter was standing there looking so handsome in his kilt and jacket. He really was the spitting image of his father.

"Thank you, Peter. You can open the church door for me instead, Charlie," she said. The threesome walked back inside and heard a child yelling. Erin knew right away it was Dan. "Oh, Peter, would you please find out what's wrong with Dan while I put this on the gift table? I'll be back in a few minutes."

"No problem, I'm used to it," he said and walked toward the sound of his brother's voice.

Erin set the box on the table and found David talking to Steve. "Sorry to interrupt, but Dan seems to be having an issue on the balcony." David rolled his eyes and headed off to find his son. She looked at Steve and said, "Please tell Carrie I brought in your gift. It's on the table."

He glanced at the overflowing table and raised his eyebrows. "Oh, I will! Let us know before you leave and we'll open it, okay?"

"Okay, I'd like that. It seems like we'll be leaving soon; I think Dan is ready to go." Just then, the boy let out a full-volume volley of insults, with a few curse words thrown out as well.

———

"Daniel! Haud yer wheesht!" David snapped at him and took him by the arm. "What's this about?"

"He said *Star Wars* is better than *Future Explorations*, Dad!" Dan said, his fists clenched and his face red. "It's not better, it's not!" he said, far more upset than it seemed he should've been.

Erin arrived, having heard what he said. "Dan! We've already been over this with Charlie's letter, right?" she said. "It's okay to think something is better than something else; everyone has their own taste. What's really the matter?"

Dan lowered his head but didn't say anything.

"He's angry because someone said I was pretty, and he didn't like it," Rosie said, blushing.

"I see," Erin said and looked at David.

"Is that true, Dan?" David asked.

Daniel struggled and tried to get away, but David didn't let go. "She's not pretty, she's my sister, and if he doesn't stay away from her, I'll give 'im a thrashing!" he yelled.

"She is so, pretty!" a boy who appeared to be only a year older than Dan said. Dan's face grew even darker red. He raised his fists and swung at the boy, only missing by a few millimeters.

"Dan! Stop it! Why is it so bad that he thinks your sister is pretty? Isn't that a good thing? I mean, wouldn't it have been worse if he'd said she was ugly? Why are you trying to hit him?" Erin said, but David knelt in front of him.

"Oh, Dan," he said and pulled him close. "I'm afraid you're gonna have tae get used to people saying Rosie is pretty. She's verra pretty, but yeh can't beat them up for et. I ken yeh wannae protect yer wee sister, but—"

"He'd better stay away from her," Dan said, aimed at the boy. David didn't know what else to say.

"Let me talk to him, Dad. I think I understand what he's feeling," Peter said and took Dan by the shoulders. David let go and Peter led him to a corner, away from the other kids.

"Okay, everyone, go find something else to do now," Erin said, and the kids went off in different directions. "Rosie and Charlie, please come with me. We're going to leave soon, and—"

"Please, Mum, may I say goodbye to the friends I've made here first?" Rosie interrupted.

"Yes, you may, but please don't interrupt next time. Be back here in about twenty minutes, okay?" They both nodded and ran off.

"I honestly have no idea what tae do with ma own children; I'm clueless!" David said as they walked down the stairs, and Erin kissed the hand she was holding.

"I disagree; I think you're brilliant, but it's a good thing we have Peter!" she said.

"Agreed!" He stopped at the bottom step. Erin was one step above him, which nearly made up for their height difference. "Thank you for havin' confidence in me."

"You're welcome, darling. You're too hard on yourself sometimes." Suddenly, a group of kids ran past them like a stampede. David held her close until the danger of being trampled was over. "My hero!" she said.

He kissed her tenderly, holding her in his arms until they heard people behind them whispering, then they smiled and broke away. "That's verra nice!"

"I agree. Steve said they'd open our gift before we leave. I can't wait to see his face!"

"Aye, neither can I. I need the loo, then I'll meet yeh by the gift table."

"Well, I think it's time to head back to the hotel," Erin said to Carrie when she returned to the festivities. "We've had a really nice time! Thanks for allowing me to bring my new family."

Carrie shook her head. "No, thank *you* for bringing them! I still can't believe it, but you two are perfect together," she said.

Erin smiled at her, blushing. "Yeah, I think so, too."

"Steve said he wanted to open your present before you left, so let me find him." A kid who appeared to be about six hurried past them, but Carrie caught her by the arm. "Please tell Steve I'm looking for him, okay?" she said. The girl nodded and ran off.

"Neat trick!" Erin said.

Carrie looked around, making sure no one would overhear them, and said, "You have to tell me what he's really like!"

"He's... he's sweet and thoughtful and tries so hard to be... I don't know, right. To do right... with me, with his—I mean *our* kids, and with the people he employs."

Carrie raised her eyebrows, "Employs? Like... servants?" she whispered.

"Oh, Carrie, you're funny. We have a housekeeper and a cook, that's all."

"That's all! What I wouldn't give! Keep going, though."

"Where was I? Right, Susannah made him feel small and insignificant like his ideas didn't matter. Like he wasn't smart enough to have a valid opinion. She was horrible to him... to them all, and she was wrong! He's so very smart and witty. I really enjoy just being with him, and his... *our* children," she said.

"I heard about his wife dying. How is everyone holding up? How is he managing with the kids now?" she asked.

"God, Carrie, he loves his kids so much! I won't go into too much detail, but Susannah did nothing but play mind games and manipulate him. She was the epitome of evil! She hid things from him, making him look like a horrible person to the poor wee babies, and never allowed him to spend time with them."

"How awful!"

"Yeah. He's doing everything he can to make it up to them, and now they know it was their mother's fault—Oh, Carrie, if you only knew! She was wicked to the core. I think that's why they have taken to me so quickly. I think they knew, deep down, that she was bad, but she was their mom, and you're supposed to believe good about your mom. Anyway, I think now that she's gone, they'll be able to heal."

———

David arrived just as Carrie sent the child to fetch Steve and unashamedly eavesdropped on the women's conversation. He couldn't believe what Erin was saying, it was as if she'd read his heart. She saw everything he strived to be and appreciated him for who he was. It made him love her even more, which was technically impossible. He saw Steve coming toward him, so he tried to appear as though he weren't guilty of listening in.

"Is it anything good?" Steve asked quietly, clearly knowing exactly what he was doing.

David looked at him and smiled sheepishly. "Aye, she… well, she really loves me, and I know she would do even without the fame and nonsense that goes with it," he said.

"Erin's a good egg, and so's Carrie. We're pretty lucky, I guess," Steve said and stepped out of their hiding place. David followed as they joined the women, then they all walked to the gift table.

———

"The envelope is for you, Carrie, and the box is for Steve," Erin said. Carrie lifted the envelope and raised her eyebrows. "Let me guess… an all-expenses paid trip to Scotland for two? How generous!" she said, and Erin laughed.

David shrugged. "Mebbe for yer next vow renewal," he said and gave her his best smile.

Erin could see Carrie melt and took her arm to make sure she didn't end up in a puddle on the floor at their feet. She opened the envelope and hugged Erin tightly before announcing what it was.

"It's a wine of the month subscription!" she said and squeed. "It's perfect! How'd you know?" she said jokingly; she was known for her love of wine and flamingos.

"Okay, Steve, open your gift now!" Erin said. "I'm dying to see your reaction." He smiled and ripped the paper off the box. His face grew bright as he saw a box set of all three seasons of *Future Explorations* and an unopened, original John Thomas of Fife collectible figure. "It's in mint condition, and I asked David to sign it for you."

Steve was like a little boy on Christmas morning, opening the one thing he'd asked Santa for. "Wow!" he said reverently, over and over. "This is great! I can't believe it! This completes my collection." He whirled around and gave Erin a bear hug, then he shook David's hand. "Thank you so much," he said.

"Erin said you'd appreciate one of them. She told me about all the charity work you do, goin' above and beyond tae do good and help people. And well, those were Joe's final words, right? I reckon you deserve et... though et seems a bit narcissistic on my part," David said.

"It means a lot to hear you say that. I can't thank you enough," he said. "Oh, and thank you for the movies, too!"

"My pleasure," David said. "Now I think we ought tae get goin'; where are our children, then?"

The first child to appear was Charlie, then Rosie, and then Peter walked up with Dan following close behind. He looked up and saw Rosie. "I'm sorry, Rosie," he said softly.

Rosie nodded. "I'm sorry as well," she said. The children stood a few feet away, waiting for the adults to stop talking. Erin held her arm out, inviting them to join them, and Rosie ran to her, putting her small arms around her. "Are we going to leave now, Mummy?" she asked, looking up at her adoringly.

"Yes, Rosebud, we are."

"I'm so glad you could come, and I'm really sorry about the Todd thing; I didn't know," Steve said.

"No worries, it's okay," Erin said and looked at David. "What's life without a little drama to make it a bit less comfortable?" They all laughed as Erin hugged Steve and then Carrie, and David said his farewells. They made their way to the table where Erin's friends were gathered and said goodbye, hugging them. She knew she might not see them for a very long time, so it was bittersweet.

"I'm gonna miss you all so much!" she said, getting emotional. "I'll be living in England now, so I won't get to hang out with you, but I'll try to visit when I can." They did a group hug, everyone smooshing everyone else, and David was surprised to be included in it, as well as the children.

"We wish you all the happiness in the world!" Becky said after the hug was finished and started crying. She was extremely empathetic and cried often.

Usually Erin shrugged it off, but this time it made her lose her composure completely. "Thanks, guys," she said, and then it was time to go.

Chapter Eleven

THE AFTER PARTY

The family headed out the door and back to the rental car feeling worn out, though they'd had a good time. Rosie and Dan fell asleep as Erin drove them back to the hotel. They had booked adjoining rooms, so David carried Dan to their room since Rosie was better at waking up than he was. He laid Dan on the bed, then helped him get his pajamas on. The boys' kilts were laid neatly on the desk at the end of their beds, and everyone was tucked in and kissed goodnight.

"Goodnight, everyone, sleep tight!" Erin said as she closed the door that separated the two rooms and locked it. When she turned, she noticed David was wearing only his kilt, so she took a step toward him.

"I've been longin' for yeh tae reach under ma kilt again for more than just a quick shag in the toilets all night! Please—" he began but didn't need to finish as she placed her hand on his leg and ran it down the woolen tartan fabric.

"Like this?" she said quietly as she reached the hem. She lifted it slowly with her wrist, ending up cupping his soft, warm balls in her hand. The quickie earlier had been nice, but she'd wanted to take her time under his kilt since the moment he'd walked out of the hotel bathroom that afternoon wearing it.

"Aye," he moaned.

His sporran was off, and the fabric was tented in the front, making her melt. She knelt before him, lifted the fabric over her head, and took his cock into her mouth. He staggered a bit, having to hold onto the footboard to steady himself, and began to pant. "Do you like that?" she asked, her head still buried under the tartan his family had used for generations, already knowing the answer.

"Aye, dinnae stop!" he pleaded, so she continued until he backed up and helped her to stand. He turned her away from him and slowly unzipped her long zipper, kissing the exposed flesh as he went.

She allowed the dress to slide off her body, revealing that she'd taken her underwear off. "I didn't want to be left out," she said and allowed him to unhook her bra. He began unfastening his kilt, but she turned and placed her hand over his. "Leave it on." She stepped toward him and felt his erection against her skin through the blue, brown, and red fabric. "I want you to cover me with your skirt."

"Turn around," he said, and she did as she was told. He stepped up behind her and ran his hand over her bare back, bending her over the king-sized bed. Then, he lifted the front of his kilt and laid it over her, positioning his cockstand between her legs. She inhaled sharply, then moaned, longing for him to enter her. Instead, he leaned over her, kissing each of her vertebrae, making her wait.

"Please—" she said, then felt him reach down to guide himself into her. She could feel the pressure of his cock against her, seeking entry, until his shaft filled her. As she reached her first orgasm, pulsing and tightening around him, she had to bite her lip to keep from crying out.

He began to thrust, slowly at first, then he built up his speed and intensity until she could hear their flesh slapping together, only muted by the heavy fabric. It was feeling so good, but then he stopped and pulled out of her. "Ach, this isn't much different than in the toilets," he said. "Lay on your back, love."

She crawled onto the bed and lay on her side, her top leg bent in front of her. He straddled the straight leg and entered her again, plunging deeply as he lifted the bent leg a bit. That time she did let out a deep moan, though it wasn't very loud. "Are yeh ready?" he asked.

"Just a little more, please," she said and felt another orgasm rock her body.

———

"Alright," she whispered, which was all he needed to hear. He pressed himself deep within her and felt the powerful release flow through him. He stood motionless, still pressing himself tightly against her, wanting to hold onto the feeling for a few extra seconds.

He unfastened his kilt and tossed it on the floor, Erin's back and rear end now visible. "Yer sae bonnie, my darling," he said, admiring her pale skin. As he pulled out of her, he placed his first finger over the small scar on her back that he'd seen so many times, then kissed it lightly. "How'd yeh get this scar?"

"I have a scar?" she said and rolled over, smiling up at him as he picked up his kilt and folded it neatly.

He laid it on his suitcase and turned to her. "Aye, where I kissed yeh. Et's just a wee thing, but I've wanted tae ask yeh about it for a while now," he said and then stepped into the bathroom. When he returned a few moments later, Erin was standing in front of the mirror over the small dressing table, trying to see it. He stepped up to her and touched it again, looking at her reflection. "Et's here."

"I didn't know I had it," she said. "It's probably from falling out of a tree or skidding out on my bike. I was a rough and tumble kid and always had bruises, scrapes, and cuts to prove it."

He stood behind her, watching their reflection as she straightened up. Then he took her hands and wrapped them around her waist, covering them with his as he laid them flat on her belly. He smiled at her, and they stood together in silence, each thinking of the life growing inside her. "I hope our bairn is a rough and tumble kid," he said, and she smiled.

"Me too."

Todd woke up the day after the vow renewal reception, hungover and miserable. He could remember bits and pieces of his behavior and was embarrassed at his display. Memories from the night before came and went during the day as he mowed the lawn, took a shower, and filled the dishwasher. He was drying his hands on the flour sack towel that had hung on the oven door since he and Erin had gotten married when he remembered something she'd said to him before he walked out of the building.

"...*This might sound crazy, but have you considered signing up for the Registry? I mean, maybe you'll be matched with someone who can help you forget about me. I know you think you don't want to do that right now, but you can't live like this for the rest of your life. Plus, you'd be helping someone like me beat this horrible disease.*"

Maybe she's right, he thought as he walked into the living room. He picked up his phone and searched 'Fertilis Defect Registry near me.' Several locations came up, one was just across the river, so he touched the link for the website, which said they accepted walk-ins. He decided to go right away before he chickened out and changed his mind.

Chapter Twelve

BACK HOME AGAIN

In the morning David, Erin, and the children packed up their things and ate the free continental breakfast provided by the hotel. When they were all in the SUV, Erin pulled out of the parking lot and headed southeast. She went the long way, down country roads edged by fields filled with waist-high corn.

She drove past the high school and middle school she'd attended and told them what American school was like. The children asked her loads of questions, and she enjoyed telling them stories about her childhood. They ate lunch in Port Washington and then headed west on Highway 33 to Erin's parent's home.

Erin drove down the long, gravel driveway, hearing the crunch of small stones under the tires, and tried to avoid the potholes. Rosie was beside herself, bouncing on the seat and smiling broadly. Erin wasn't sure what Rosie expected to see in her mother but was glad it meant so much to her.

Peter was staring out the window with his earbuds in, Charlie was reading, and Daniel was sound asleep. Erin parked in the same place she'd done the last time they'd visited and took a deep breath once the car was turned off. It was drizzling and overcast, but the forecast had lots of sunshine for the next day.

"Okay, guys, are you ready to meet my mum and dad?" Erin said into the back of the SUV. The children smiled and nodded, except for Dan, who was still rubbing his eyes, having just woken up.

"Where are we?" he said, still sounding sleepy.

"We're at my parent's house, Dan. Okay, let's go."

Peter and Charlie opened the back doors, and everyone piled out. They walked up the old concrete path, but as they reached the steps, the rain picked up, so they made a run for the shelter of the enclosed porch. Erin rang the doorbell and her mother answered the door.

As soon as she saw her, Erin let out a squeal of delight, "Oh, Mom! I love it! It suits you perfectly," she said as they entered the kitchen.

It was then that David saw what she'd been so excited about. Liz had gotten her hair cut short. It was cute and looked good on her, but he wasn't going to say anything about it. He figured it was best to stay neutral. He stepped up to her and held out his hand. "Good afternoon, Liz," he said congenially.

She blushed slightly but took his hand in hers and patted it in a warm handshake. "Hello, David. It's good to see you again; awkward, but good." She smiled and then laughed good-naturedly.

"Aye, my sentiments exactly," he said, his cheeks also slightly pink. "I'd like for you to meet our children."

The foursome had been standing perfectly still, waiting patiently to be introduced. Rosie was enraptured, looking up at Liz as though she were Captain Marvel. David introduced the boys, who all shook her hand and said, "Pleased to meet you, Mrs. Wallace," which had her grinning from ear to ear.

At last, Erin stood next to Rosie with her hands on her shoulders and introduced her. "Mom, this is Rosie. She's been on pins and needles waiting to meet you." Rosie stepped up to Liz and held out her hand, only to drop it. Then she stepped forward and gave her a huge bear hug. Liz, Erin, and David all exchanged glances of confusion. After a moment, Rosie let go, and they all noticed she was crying. "Oh, my darling girl, what's the matter?" Erin exclaimed.

Rosie looked up, stood on her tiptoes, and whispered into Erin's ear, "I'd like to say something to your mum, but in her ear, please."

Erin looked at her mother and relayed the message. Liz squatted down to Rosie's level, seemingly enchanted with the sweet little girl. Rosie approached her and put her hand up so no one could overhear what she was saying. Everyone waited, curious to hear what she'd said.

Liz put her hand up to her mouth, and Erin saw tears spring to her eyes. She looked at David, who appeared to be just as baffled as she was. When Rosie was done, Liz gave her a big hug and thanked her, having to wipe the tears away with her hand.

"What'd she say?" Dan said, which was what everyone wanted to know.

"That's between the two of us for now. She's given me permission to tell 'her parents' after she goes to bed, but not before." Rosie stood next to Erin and hugged her, making Liz cry again.

"Well, I can't wait tae hear et!" David said.

"Me too!" Erin said and stroked Rosie's hair. "Now, where's Dad? He's not still hiding in the basement, is he?"

"No, he went to get a few groceries; he'll be back soon," Liz said, wiping her eyes.

"Okay, then I'll show the kids where they'll be sleeping tonight. Do you have an estimate on when supper will be done?" Erin asked her mom.

"Not sure. I still need to start it, and there's lots to do with such a big crowd to feed. You can help me if you want to," Liz said to the children, who had all stood perfectly well-behaved the whole time.

"Oh, may I, Mummy, please?" Rosie asked, bouncing on the balls of her feet excitedly.

"Well, aren't you just the sweetest thing ever!" Liz said.

"Of course you may, Rosebud. Why don't we figure out the sleeping arrangements, and my mom can try to think of ways you lot can help her, okay?"

"Okay, thank you, Mummy. I've never been allowed to help with dinner before. Our mum—" The young girl looked down at her feet at the mention of her birth mother. "She never allowed us to do domestic things. She said it was for the staff to do and that we were better than them."

When she looked up, Erin saw that her little cheeks were red with embarrassment, so she gave her a big smile. "Never mind, sweetheart, that's all over now. Alright, troop, follow me," she said and led them through the living room and up the narrow staircase to the spare bedroom.

The room contained a full-sized bed, a nightstand with a lamp, and a tall dresser. Liz had set out two sleeping bags on the bed, still rolled up. One was an old green Coleman they'd used every time they had gone camping, and the other had Smurfs on it. It had been Erin's very first sleeping bag, and she couldn't believe her mother still had it.

———

From the bedroom window, Peter saw his dad leave the house and then noticed a car pull up, so he asked if he might help his father with their things. Really, he was curious to meet Erin's father, and that was his excuse. He entered the kitchen just as the two men walked in, and he took the brown paper grocery bags from the man he could tell was Erin's father, setting them on the large wooden table in the center of the room. "May I help with anything?" Peter asked.

"Aye, come with us," David said, and they all headed back outside. "Frank, this is my eldest son, Peter."

Frank held out his hand, and Peter shook it. "It's a pleasure to meet you, Mr. Wallace," he said with a smile. He could see the family resemblance; Frank had the same twinkle in his eyes as Erin did.

"How old are you, Peter?" Frank asked.

"Sixteen, sir," he said politely.

"Well, I'd say you're old enough to call me Frank," he said, and Peter smiled.

"Yes, sir, I mean Frank."

"Sixteen, huh? Are you learning to drive yet?"

Peter looked at him and then at his dad. "He must be seventeen to be issued a learner's permit in England," David explained. "Though he really wouldn't need one in London.

"I see," Frank said. "I began teaching Erin to drive when she was fourteen but only on the back roads. She passed her test on her sixteenth birthday, first try," he said, beaming with pride.

Peter smiled, imagining Erin at his age. Frank handed him a brown paper bag filled with groceries, and he took the last one. "I think we ought to move here, Dad," Peter said, which made both men laugh.

"Aye, son, et's temptin'," David said.

"I could… ahh… take him down a back road or two while you're here… with your permission, David."

———

David wasn't sure it was a good idea, but he saw the look on Peter's face and agreed. "I reckon yeh could," he said, trying to sound less nervous about it than he was. Both Frank and Peter looked excited as they got back to the kitchen. "Now, please help me bring the luggage upstairs."

Peter smiled his own smile back at him and lifted one of the heavier suitcases. "Okay, Dad," he said.

They took the first load up with Frank's help.

———

Erin was in the spare room, trying to get the children settled. When she saw her father, she squeed and nearly trampled everyone to get to him. "Hi, Daddy!" she said, sounding like a little girl. "I want you to meet—" she began and heard David clear his throat ever so softly, "*my* children."

"I've just met Peter, and he seems like a fine boy," Frank said.

"He is, Daddy. He should talk to mom! He loves all things plants, don't you?" she said excitedly.

"Yes, I do," Peter said as he put the suitcase he was carrying onto the bed.

She introduced Charlie and Dan, who each held out their hand as Peter had done and called him Mr. Wallace. "Dad, this is our Rosie; she'd been so excited to meet you and Mom," she said.

Rosie stepped forward, holding out her hand and shaking Frank's very formally. "Pleased to meet you—" she began but then stopped. She looked at her dad and then at Erin. Erin was just about to remind her of his name when she smiled and said, "Granddad." Frank put his other hand over hers and smiled.

"But he's not our granddad!" Dan said.

Rosie gave him a scornful look and shrugged. "Maybe he isn't yet, but he will be someday, and I'd like to start calling him that now, if it's alright?" she said, gazing hopefully up at the man who looked so much like Erin.

The adults looked at each other as Rosie motioned for Frank to get down to her level. She whispered something into his ear, just as she'd done with Liz, and Erin didn't know what to think of it.

109

When she was finished with her message, Frank stood with wet eyes and smiled at his daughter, then he stepped up to David and shook his hand. "You've done a fine job of raising this little girl, David. She's extraordinary."

———

David was startled, not knowing what to say. He knew it wasn't any of his doing, but he doubted it had anything to do with the nanny or the school either. "Ahh, thank you," he managed to say.

"And Rosie, you can call me granddad, or grandpa, if you want to; you can too, boys," he said and then put his arm around Erin. "You're already an amazing mom!"

"I think so too!" Charlie said and then blushed when everyone looked at him.

"Thank you, Charlie, and thanks, Dad, but I can't really take any credit. They are just naturally sweet kids," Erin said.

"You must be doing something right! Look at you; what a beautiful family you make together!" The wetness in his eyes was threatening to escape, so he decided to leave before it did. "I hate to hug and run, but I've got some... things to do. I'll see you later," he said and left the room.

"Well, that was interesting," Erin said, and David nodded in agreement. "Okay, let's put your things away. Peter, you get the top drawer, Charlie the next, and so on. Now, let me show you where the bathroom is."

She led the troop down the hall to the infamous room where Liz had walked in on David in the bath. "Hmm, I've had better memories," he whispered to Erin as they all squeezed into the room, and she smiled at him. She showed them how to work the fixtures and explained that they were limited on hot water, so it was best to take a short shower unless they wanted to finish with cold water. They all said they understood and piled out.

They made their way back to the kitchen, where Liz was waiting for them. "Look what I found!" she said and held out a small apron with Holly Hobby on it.

"Oh, Mom, I remember that! It was mine when I was small, though I only ever used it for Thanksgiving and Christmas," she explained to the crowd. Liz held it out to Rosie and put it around her little waist, tying it in a large bow behind her back.

"Perfect," Erin said.

Liz was making meatloaf with mashed potatoes and sweet corn and set them all to work. She had Daniel open the cans of corn and then dump them into a pot while Peter and Charlie got to peel potatoes with a vegetable peeler. Rosie got to pound on some crackers in a plastic zip-top bag to make breadcrumbs, and then she helped chop onions.

Erin was in charge of the apple crisp, and when he was done with the corn, she asked Daniel to pound on some graham crackers in a bag for her. They were all working hard, and no one was complaining. Liz and Erin exchanged more than one glance of amazement that afternoon.

While they worked on supper, Frank and David stole away to the basement to talk. "I want... I mean, *we* wanted to apologize for what happened at your last visit," Frank said, but David shook his head.

"That's really not necessary, but thank you. All's forgiven, now let's try tae forget about et, shall we?" he said with rosy cheeks.

Frank smiled, and they shook hands, as it seemed the thing to do. "Your daughter is an amazing young lady," he said.

"May... I ask what she said tae yeh? She did the same thing tae Liz earlier, and I'm verra curious," David said.

"Sorry, but I'm sworn to secrecy until after she and her brothers are all in bed tonight. I don't know why that is important to her, but it is."

"Well then," David said and returned his smile. He was surprised when Frank's grin turned into a slight frown.

"I... noticed a lovely ring on Erin's hand."

David nodded slowly. *Didn't Erin tell them about our engagement?* he thought. "Aye. I told yeh, I love her," he said.

The older man's eyes narrowed a bit. "But what about the wife you already have?"

"Did yeh not hear about Susannah's death?" he said, a bit stunned at the question.

"Her *death*? No, I didn't... I'm sorry, David," he said sincerely.

———

Peter started down the stairs, but his dad and new granddad didn't seem to notice. The boy had caught a bit of their conversation and couldn't help himself; he stood quietly in the shadows, listening to the adult's talk about his mother.

"Aye, she had an eating disorder, and her heart gave out. Your Erin helped with CPR, fighting at ma side tae keep her alive. She was brilliant, our Erin, and when the time is right, I intend tae tell the children what she did for their mum that terrible day."

"Erin helped you try to save your wife?" he said. "That must've been traumatic for you both."

"Aye, et was. But now we can move on, and as you can see, the children already love her. I mean, what's not tae love?"

"Yes, they do, and I don't think it will betray Rosie to say that was the subject of her comment to me."

"Really? That's amazin'!" David said and raised his eyebrows. "Et's somethin', seeing them together; ye'd think she was their birth mother. I truly do love her, Frank."

"I believe you do," Frank said.

Without thinking, Peter sniffed, feeling emotional about what he'd just learned. His dad must've heard him because he turned and peered up the stairs at him. "Peter? Were you eavesdropping?" he said, sounding shocked and angry. "How much of that did yeh hear?"

Peter slowly descended the stairs, blushing and sniffling. "Did Erin really help you try to save Mum?" he asked and hugged his father, not wanting to cry but unable to stop himself. Just then Erin called down the stairs, asking for help setting the table, so Frank left them to talk.

"Aye, son, but yeh weren't meant to hear about that yet," David said, holding his son who was nearly as tall as he was.

"But Dad, I'm glad I know about it. I think you should tell the rest of us as well. It's important, especially... well... after what the reporters said at the airport. They accused Erin of killing Mum, not that any of us believed it, but it would be comforting to... the smaller ones to know what she did," he said, finally able to get his emotions in check.

"Do yeh truly think so? I was going to wait till you were all a bit older and the newness of et had worn off a bit. But if you believe it will be helpful, I'll do et soon. I should talk to Erin about et first, though, I think," David said, marveling at his son's maturity and vulnerability. "Now—"

"But, Dad, if you talk to her, she'll likely say not to… or be too embarrassed, but I want to see her face when you say it. I want her parents to know it too. Would you do it tonight, Dad, please?"

David wasn't sure about that idea. He didn't want to put her on the spot, but he also knew Peter was most likely correct, and since it was only family, he agreed. "A'right, Peter, I'll do it tonight, but don't rush me. I must wait for the proper time," he said. Peter was beaming; David could see how excited he was and only hoped Erin would forgive him.

Everyone was laughing when David and Peter returned to the kitchen. Daniel had apple peels draped over his head and said he liked being ginger since the apple peels were red. David was shocked to see Rosie crying, though he noticed she was also laughing.

"What's the matter, Rosebud?" he asked, and she pointed to the cutting board.

"Onions, Dad. I didn't know they made you cry when you cut them! I've never cut an onion before, and I'm having fun." She finished her onion and carefully used the knife to scrape the cut bits into a bowl. Then she took the cutting board and knife to the sink and handed them to Liz, who was keeping up with the dirty dishes. "Grandma taught me to use a knife," she said excitedly.

"And she's done very well!" Liz said proudly. "Would you boys mind helping Frank set the table? Also, please take that stack of dishes out there with you."

Erin noticed Peter was watching her and smiling. He went to her and hugged her tightly. "I love you, Erin, thank you," he said and then turned, following his dad out of the room.

Erin looked at her mother and then at the other children. "Well! I wonder what that was about?" she said and shrugged. The rest of them shrugged, too, so she figured she'd find out eventually. "So, you're using the wedding dishes again, mom?" she asked.

"Yes, well, we might as well use them," she said.

"For meatloaf?" Erin said and then laughed.

"Somehow, I don't think they will be offended," Liz said, which made Erin laugh even harder. "And from the pretty ring on your hand, I think we should be celebrating, don't you, kids?" They looked at Erin's hand as Liz went to her daughter and took it in hers to examine it. "That's an exquisite antique ring, Erin. It fits you perfectly… I mean, the style and shape are stunning." The kids dropped what they were doing and came over to look at it.

"It was David's great-grandmother's wedding ring. That would be your great-great-grandmother," she said to the kids. "David's mother, your gran, wore it for a long time as well, but she has arthritis, so she took it off before she couldn't anymore. I just love it and never want to take it off… ever."

"So, my daddy asked you to marry him?" Rosie said. "I want to hear how he did it!"

"Yes, please tell us the story," Charlie said.

Erin found herself blushing and didn't know why. "Alright, how about I tell the story at supper?" she said, and the children agreed, so it was settled. She only hoped David would be okay with it.

"I think we should go for a walk. How much time do we have, Liz?" David asked her when he and Peter got back to the kitchen.

"But it's raining!" both Erin and Daniel said together before Liz could answer.

"I'd say you have about forty-five minutes," Liz said.

"It's stopped raining, and furthermore, we live in London. If we waited until it stopped raining, we'd never do anything," he said.

Erin helped Rosie off with her new apron, and they took themselves outside. The grass was soaking wet, but as long as they stayed on the walk and driveway, they would stay dry. Daniel didn't care about being dry. As soon as they cleared the side yard and reached the driveway, he went running through the grass and around the trees in the front of the house that Frank had planted so long ago.

"Daniel!" Erin and David called to him, but he had his selective hearing on and didn't listen. The rest of the clan stayed on the gravel driveway, and Erin told them about when she lived there as a teenager.

"When I was about fourteen, I decided to go sunbathing. It was spring, and the weather was starting to get warm in the middle of the day. I put on my swimming suit, grabbed a big beach towel, and lay myself right here," she said and pointed to a grassy spot in the center of the circle at the top of the driveway.

"I'd been there for about five minutes when I heard an odd hissing or screeching sort of noise." Rosie gasped, and Erin raised her eyebrows. "I sat up and nearly screamed! Right there," she pointed to an area with long, wild grass at the corner of the old building Frank used as a garage, "was a badger!" she said, and they all started talking at once.

"Oh, we like badgers!" Was the gist of what everyone was saying.

"English Badgers are nothing like the ones we have in Wisconsin. Ours are mean and vicious, and I was terrified."

"What did you do?" Rosie asked, looking suspiciously at the spot Erin had pointed to.

"I took up my towel and ran pell-mell back into the house, deciding never to do that again!" She could see that Rosie was scared now. "Don't worry, sweetheart," she said.

"Aye," David said. "There are too many of us for anathin' tae bother us, but keep that in mind, and dinnae go off on your own."

"It was also nearly twenty-six years ago, so I highly doubt it's still around. I'm sure we're safe now."

David held Erin's hand, and Erin held Rosie's as they walked to the end of the long driveway. It was warm, and a beautiful, yet eerie, mist was rising off the tall, wet grass on the wild, unmown side of the driveway. They were laughing about something when Dan ran up to them and jumped into a deep pothole, spraying them all with cold, muddy water.

"Daniel Lawrence Elliott!" David yelled. Everyone stopped, and no one made a sound. Erin had never heard him raise his voice to one of his children before. "Go back to the house this instant and ask Mrs. Wallace to help you change yer clothes. Then stay in the spare room until either Erin or I tell yeh tae come down."

Rosie moved closer to Erin and hugged her arm. She put her hand on the young girl's hair and smoothed it gently. "I guess we should head back, too, since we're all wet now," she said, and David sighed.

"I'm sorry, Erin, but that's something he needs to learn not to do," he said. "I'm sorry I lost my temper. I'm also sorry if I frightened you, children. I reckon I've a lot to learn as a parent."

"You're right, it was annoying, and I don't blame you for losing your temper and yelling at him. Just remember, he's a young boy, and sometimes it takes a while for boys to understand things like that," Erin said quietly to him as they walked back to the house.

"Aye."

As they entered the kitchen, a wonderful smell greeted them. "That smells fantastic!" David said, making Liz smile.

They all headed upstairs to wash the spattered mud off their legs. Daniel was sitting on the bed in the spare room, looking sad and upset. When she was cleaned up, Erin entered the room and sat on the bed next to him. "Dad has never lost his temper with any of us before now," he said quietly.

"Well, darling, can you understand why he did it today?" she asked.

He looked up at her and nodded. "Yes, ma'am. I was just trying to have some fun!" he whined, looking gloomy.

"None of us thought it was fun. You're going to have to learn to think things through before you do them, Dan," she said.

"Yes, ma'am," he said sadly.

Erin put her arm around his shoulders and kissed his hair. "It'll come to you, and someday it won't be so hard. Now, go apologize to the others, and then we can eat. I'm starving!"

David came into the room, and Daniel got up. He stood in front of his dad. "I'm sorry I splashed everyone, Dad. I will try to think things through before I do them in the future," he said, trying to say exactly what Erin had told him to.

"A'right, Dan, now apologize tae the others, and we'll meet yeh downstairs," he said gently. Dan walked out of the room with his head down. They heard him talking to his brothers and sister, and it seemed to go well. "Erin, ye're amazin'. You always know the right thing tae say and the right way tae say et," he said.

She raised her eyebrows and shook her head, "Not really! I just open my mouth and things fall out of it. Sometimes it's good and sometimes not so much," she said.

"Yeh dinnae give yourself enough credit," David countered.

Chapter Thirteen

AFTER DINNER SURPRISES

When supper was ready, those who assisted with the meal brought the thing they helped with to the table. Everyone took a seat, held hands for the prayer, then dug into the food. The children had never eaten home-cooked meatloaf before and commented on how good it was.

As the meal was wrapping up, Erin stood and cleared her throat. "I'd like to propose a toast and tell a story requested by my children," she said, beaming. "First, to family! I'm so blessed to have such a wonderful one!"

Everyone raised their glass. "To family! *Slàinte mhath* (Slange-eh vah)!" the adults said, and the children looked strangely at them. Erin explained that it was Scots Gaelic for good health.

"Next, the story," she said, building a bit of suspense. "One day, not long ago, there was a man by the name of David Elliott." She paused, nudged Charlie, and pointed to his father as if to reveal the person she was talking about. The whole table laughed and looked at her expectantly.

"He took me into his office and opened a *hidden* safe. From it, he took a small drawer and an old wooden box. Out of the drawer, he lifted a string of pearls and then showed me some fancy rings that had belonged to his father and grandparents. Next, he opened the wooden box. It was filled with old war medals for bravery and things like that, and they were beautiful! They had belonged to his great-grandfather, whose name was also David Elliott. I had seen a photo of him at your Gran's house, so I knew what he looked like.

"Finally, he took out a small, brown velvet box that looked very old. He got down on one knee and asked me if I would honor him by promising to be his wife. It was so lovely, and we both cried, *but don't tell him I told you!*" she said in a loud whisper. "Then, he kissed my belly and spoke to the baby, telling it—" She didn't get to finish, as Liz let out a cry, covered her mouth, and then Frank stood. Everyone at the table was stunned.

"The *baby?*" Liz said. Her eyes were wide, and she looked as though she were going to cry.

"I told you... I'm sure I... didn't I?" Erin looked at David, who raised his hands. "Oh, Mom, I'm sorry! Yes, we're going to have a baby. I'm only two and a half months along, so—" she began, but Liz had come to her and was holding her tightly. David and Frank were beaming and shook hands.

"Oh, my baby girl! I'm so happy! We'd given up on the hope of becoming grandparents, and now we'll have five!" She looked at Frank, and he went to them, joining the hug. Rosie got up, then Charlie, and before long, the whole lot of them, except for Daniel, who stayed in his chair, were hugging and crying and carrying on.

"That was a beautiful story," Rosie said, then Peter returned to his seat and cleared his throat.

"Erm, I'd like to propose a toast... to... uh... to Erin, the baby, and... new grandparents," he said.

The whole family went back to their seats to raise their glasses. "To Erin, the baby, and new grandparents! Slàinte mhath!" they all said. Peter nudged his dad and mouthed, "Go on, Dad!"

David shook his head, but Erin saw it and raised an eyebrow. "Okay, what's all that about?" she said, looking between the two eldest male Elliotts.

"Tell the story, Dad," Peter said.

David looked at his son and stood, shaking his head. "I'm not sure this is the best time, but since ye've asked... Our Peter overheard somethin' I was tellin' yer dad about, well, about when Susannah died," he said, and Erin frowned.

"Uh, maybe you're right—" she said, but Peter interrupted her.

"I think we all need to hear it, Erin. Please say it's okay."

She hesitated, but when Peter gave her a pleading look, she gave in. "I guess," she said and sat in her chair with a sigh.

"Well," David continued, "I thought everaone here knew that ma wife, Susannah, had died unexpectedly of a heart attack last month, but Frank hadn't heard the news, so I was tellin' him how Erin helped me tae give her CPR." The children were all looking at her, and she was red in the face.

"Let me start over. Susannah, yer mum, had come tae yer gran's house tae convince me tae come back tae her, but I told her et wasn't goin' tae happen. I had just gotten out of hospital after the fire—" he said, and the boys gasped, as they hadn't heard about that yet. "Oh dear, this is gonna be a long story. I'm afraid the cottage burned down, and old John pulled me out, saving ma life, but we'll talk about that later." The boys were frowning, obviously wanting to talk about it then, but they didn't say anything.

"Where was I?" he said. "Right, I'd inhaled quite a lot of smoke, so I couldn't breathe verra well for maself, let alone for CPR, so I asked Erin tae help me do the breathin'. I didn't realize what I was askin' her tae do, but she... did et. She breathed her own breath intae yer mum's lungs tae try tae keep her alive, so if anaone ever tries tae tell you that Erin killed yer mum, ye'll know they're lyin' to yeh," he said.

Liz looked at her daughter. "Oh, Erin, I'm so proud of you," she said.

Erin wanted to dismiss it and say it wasn't a big deal, but she knew that to the people at that table, it was a very big deal, so she kept her mouth shut.

"You tried to save my mummy's life?" Rosie said, and Erin shrugged.

"I... did but—"

"Thank you for doing that, but—" Rosie said. She didn't finish and put her head down, clearly not wanting to say what she was thinking.

"It's okay, baby girl, I understand," Erin said.

Dan just stared at her, and it seemed that Charlie wanted to say something, so he looked at his dad, who nodded. "Wow, Erin," the boy said. "I'm glad you allowed Dad to tell us, and I'm glad Peter overheard. I... I don't think Mum liked me very much. I... well, I'm not the eldest, like Peter, and I'm not the youngest, and a girl, like Rosie, so—I don't think... well, I know she didn't want me, so I don't think she cared overly much about me." Both David and Erin wanted to contradict him, but they knew he was right.

"Oh, Charlie!" Liz said. "I'm sure you're wrong! Every mother loves her children." She looked at Erin and then at David, who both furrowed their brows and just barely shook their heads, verifying Charlie's account.

"Well, I know she didn't like Erin! She told us all as much," Daniel said.

Peter's eyes grew wide, and Rosie opened her mouth in shock. "You weren't meant to tell anyone! Mum made us promise!" Charlie said.

"I don't care. She isn't here, so I'll say it if I want to. After the day we talked to Dad in his office, she started asking us things, things that made me feel bad. She wanted to know what Dad had told us about you, Erin, and she was quite brutal. She told us we weren't allowed to like you if we ever met you, and she called you rude names that I'm not allowed to say."

"She did," Charlie said. "Dan's right... Mum's not here, so I'll say it. She made it sound as though she knew you, Erin, and that you were a bad person, so when you were at Gran's house after she died, I just *had* to meet you." He looked at her and smiled. "I had a feeling she was lying. I knew, in my... well, in my heart, she was saying it to turn us against you, but Dad had told us how good you were, so I chose to believe him. As soon as I walked into Roger's flat and saw you, I knew she was completely wrong—"

"So did I!" Rosie interrupted. "I didn't know what to say, but I *knew* I'd like you. You were very kind to us."

Erin didn't want to cry and managed to hold back the tears, but it was getting more difficult by the minute.

"Anyway, I know our mum wasn't a nice person. She wasn't nice to us, and she was mean to Dad and Kitty. I'm sure if you met her, you knew it as well, so knowing you tried to save her life means a lot to me, but... I'm chuffed you're going to be our mum now," Charlie continued, then he stood and went to her. He sat on her lap and held her tightly.

It was no use trying to stop the tears at that point. "Such grown-up words for a young man. Thank you, Charlie. I love you so much. I love you too, Rosie, Dan, and Peter... thank you," she said once she'd gotten herself under control.

"I told you, Dad," Peter said to David. "We all needed to know. Mum made us feel as though Erin was... well, the devil, but she was wrong. I mean, we already knew she was wrong, but those reporters were really horrible, and well, this was good. Thank you."

Frank was beaming and looked at his daughter with pride. He stood, raising his glass. "A toast," he said and waited for everyone to get their glasses ready. "To new beginnings and a new mother's love!"

They all raised their glasses and repeated, "To new beginnings and a new mother's love! *Slàinte mhath!*"

"So, since it's still light out, what do you say to a quick driving lesson, Peter?" Frank said once the table was cleared.

"Ach, are yeh sure that's a good idea, I mean—" David began to protest.

"I'll be fine, Dad," Peter said, using his charming smile and puppy dog eyes to persuade him.

"Don't worry, David, I won't have him going fast," Frank said.

"Aye, thought I dinnae see how ye'd control that," David said.

Erin put her hand on his arm. "Dinnae fash, darling."

David sighed and shrugged his shoulders resignedly. "A'right, then."

Peter took Frank's hand and tugged, clearly wanting to get going before his dad changed his mind. The two excited men stepped outside into the mild summer evening and got into the car. Frank started his older grey Honda then drove slowly down the long driveway. "Oh no!" Peter exclaimed anxiously.

"What is it?" Frank asked.

"Your car and roads… the side you drive on… are opposite to ours! Maybe I shouldn't—"

"Aww, I don't think it'll matter much," Frank interrupted. "You'll only be driving for a little while and by the time you're old enough to get your temps… I mean learner's permit, you won't remember much of it, anyway."

Peter smiled at him. "Yeah… okay, that makes sense."

After a few minutes, Frank turned onto an old, country road with a sign that read DEAD END. "This is Blue Goose Road," he said as he pulled over and put the car in Park. "It's not busy, so you won't have to worry about being rushed. If someone pulls up behind us, I'll wave them around us, okay?"

"Uh, okay. I'm suddenly shook!"

Frank frowned and gave him a sideways look. "Shook? Give it to me in plain English," he said.

"Sorry, it means nervous. My palms are sweating!"

"Don't worry, Peter, just do what I say, and you'll be a pro in no time." Frank opened his door and Peter did the same. They got out and Frank led him around the car, checking for burned out bulbs and such. "If everything looks okay, then go ahead and get in." The boy tried to get into the driver's seat, but his legs were too long. "Just like your father," Frank said with a laugh and showed him how to adjust it. Then, he showed him how to adjust the mirrors and steering wheel. The older man patiently told the younger one where everything was, and after a few minutes, they were ready to go. "Now, put your foot on the break and use your directional to signal that you're going to pull onto the road, then check your mirrors."

Peter took a deep breath and did as he was told. "Okay, now what?"

"Now shift the car into drive, then let off the break and slowly push on the gas pedal."

The car began to move forward, and the boy couldn't hide his grin. "Cor blimey! Now what? How fast should I go?"

"Why don't you start at forty miles per hour? We can go faster after a few times up and down the road.

They spent over an hour traversing the old road. Frank taught him how to do a Y turn and the basics of parallel parking, amazed at how quickly he caught on. He wished they lived closer to the new members of his family and sighed. "What's wrong… Grandpa Frank?" Peter asked.

"Oh, I'm just sorry that I won't be able to give you any more lessons after you go back home, that's all," Frank said.

At the dead end, Peter shifted into Park and turned to Erin's dad with a smile. "I am too, but I'm really chuffed that you did this for me. I'll never forget it, thanks."

They had a nice long conversation, man to man, then it was time to switch sides and go back to the house.

David watched Frank's car turn onto the gravel drive and then stop. The doors opened simultaneously, and the two men switched places so that Peter could drive the rest of the way to the house. David went outside to meet them, arriving just as his son turned off the ignition. The men talked for a moment and were laughing as they got out and stood on the gravel, both smiling. "Well done, Peter," he said.

"I drove the car, Dad!" he said excitedly. "I *LOVE* driving! Thank you for allowing me to do it! Grandpa Frank is brills and a fantastic teacher!" Peter was talking a mile per minute in his excitement, then he stepped toward his dad and hugged him tightly.

"I'm—" David began, but Peter was already running toward the house.

"He's an excellent student, David," Frank said with a laugh as he joined him and stood watching the boy disappear through the kitchen door. "Did everything I said and remembered it all. He's also very polite and has a good head on his shoulders. You really have done a great job raising them. You should be proud."

David stared at the door and shook his head. "No, sir, I didn't," he said and turned to see the frown on Frank's face. "I had little to do with how they turned out, actually. Their mother wouldn't allow me tae do much with them when they were wee, then she sent them to a boarding school. I wasn't there for them verra much, so I can't take the credit."

"I think you've had more influence and impact on them than you think. Peter told me what you did with the hidden letters and that it's made him love and respect you more than he ever has before. He also told me how much he loves Erin, saying that even though he was upset about you and her at the beginning, he can now see how brilliant you are together. He said that she's a, quote, 'great stepmum,' end quote," Frank said, beaming.

"He said all of that?"

"Yessir, he did. He's very mature. I only wish you didn't live so far away, or that we lived closer. I know Erin isn't going to leave England, it's been her dream to live there for, well, for as long as I can remember."

"Aye, you're right about that! Ye're welcome to visit anatime, yeh know," David said as they walked side by side to the house.

"We'll just have to do that, then. Thanks for the invite."

At bedtime, the children made their way to the spare room. Dan and Charlie slept in the bed, while Peter and Rosie slept on the floor in the sleeping bags. David and Erin tucked them in, and she read the next chapter in *Anne of Green Gables* to them.

Once the children were tucked in, David and Erin rushed back downstairs to finally find out what Rosie had said to her new grandparents. They stood in front of Liz as she finished washing the dishes. "Well?" Erin said and raised her eyebrows expectantly.

"Whatever do you mean?" she said, feigning ignorance, then laughed when she saw the unamused looks on their faces. "Okay, okay." Her eyes suddenly filled with tears. "She told me she couldn't wait to meet me because… she needed to tell me how much she loves you, Erin, and that she was… glad I'd had you, so you could be her new mummy." Tears were now falling unchecked down Liz's cheeks, and Erin hugged her.

"I'm glad yeh did as well," David said tenderly.

"She must've said the same thing to Dad. It amazes me the way they think. They're so mature, well, except for Dan, he's the exception," Erin said, smiling at David. "I've never known kids to be able to express themselves so well."

"Well, they are *my* children, after all," David said, puffing out his chest dramatically.

"My point, exactly. Where did it come from?" Erin said and laughed along with Liz at his fake look of surprise.

"In all seriousness, they are delightful, David. You must be so proud," Liz said.

"Aye, verra proud, thank you."

Later that night, David and Erin climbed the stairs, feeling very tired. They had to pass the spare room to get to Erin's and overheard the kids talking and laughing about things that had happened that day. When they got to her room, they changed the sheets, remade the bed, put on their pajamas, and then got under the blankets, holding each other tightly.

"I imagine, with all the heartache and regret yer parents have felt about their decision tae use Fertilis, Rosie's words must have been a healing balm tae them," David said.

"I know it was. She has no idea what her sweet, innocent, heartfelt words have done to heal their hearts as well as mine."

"I'm verra glad ma kids love yeh so much."

"Me too!" Erin said. "It's not supposed to be like this. Usually, kids don't like their stepparent, or at least don't warm to them so quickly. Do you think it's because of our connection? That somehow they're affected by whatever it is we have together as well?"

"I reckon et's possible. Speaking of connection," he said and pulled her shoulder toward him. "I'd fancy makin' love tae you in here, without the fear of... well, of a drunken woman bargin' in on us," he said with a grin.

"I'd like that too," she said simply, and allowed him to pull her undies off her. She took off her nightgown, and he stared at her body. It was nearly a full moon, so the room was lit quite well.

"Ach, ye're bonnie, Erin. I love how the light reflects off your skin and glows in the moonlight." He gently grazed one of her breasts with the tips of his fingers.

"I'm so white, I glow... is that what you're saying?" she said and laughed.

He traced the shadow of the window sash, which fell across her stomach. "Aye, as white as a spoonful of creme brûlée... delicious," he said and lay on top of her.

Chapter Fourteen

GOOD MORNING

When Erin and David came downstairs in the morning, there was a stack of photo albums on the kitchen table. Liz was filling the coffee pot with water from the decanter and said, "Good morning," as they walked in.

"Aww, Mom! Not my baby pictures," Erin said with a slight whine.

"I found those—"

"You knew exactly where they were, Mom! Don't try the 'look what I just found' tactic on me," Erin interjected.

"Ach, I like old photos!" David said. "Especially the naked baby kind!" He laughed, and Erin rolled her eyes.

"Isn't the naked adult enough for you?" she said, clearly not thinking about her mother standing there.

"La-la-la-la—I don't want to hear this," Liz said and put her hands over her ears.

David stood in front of the pile of albums and flipped open the cover of the one on top. The first photo was of Liz wearing a hospital gown, holding a tiny infant. The second was of Frank, a hospital gown over his clothing, holding the same tiny bundle of blankets, which was wearing a pink knitted cap. They looked so happy, holding their newborn daughter. He didn't have a photo like that for any of his children and had to look away so he wouldn't get emotional about it.

Erin stepped up beside him and laughed. "Look how young they are!" she said, pointing to her dad's face. He had a horrible haircut, but his hair was blazing red.

David hadn't thought of it since he'd only ever seen him with white hair. "I reckon our child could be ginger, eh?" he said mainly to himself.

"Is that a bad thing?" Erin said and cocked her head to the side.

"What—" David began but was interrupted.

"Why would that be a bad thing?" Liz asked.

"Red-headed people are often looked down upon in England, so I'm just making sure that's not what he meant by his comment," Erin said with her eyes narrowed at David.

"Ach, woman! Et's not a bad thing, not tae me anaway. Et was only an observation."

"Good," she said, "because I have a real affinity for redheads." She lay her finger on her father's image and smiled.

"Did I hear something about an affinity for redheads?" Frank said as he entered the kitchen. He walked up to Erin, put his arm around her shoulders, and kissed her hair. "What's this?" He looked down at the opened album. "Look at him! What a handsome fella!" he said with a twinkle in his eyes.

———

"How old were you when I was born, Daddy?" Erin asked and turned the page.

"Oh, somewhere just over thirty, I think," he said and looked at Liz for confirmation.

"You were thirty-three, Frank," she said.

"I… feel too old to be pregnant," Erin said and sat on the chair next to her, the fear and dread coming back.

"Dinnae worry, love. Ye're gonna be an amazin' mum!" David said.

They heard what sounded like a herd of elephants coming down the stairs, along with a cacophony of voices. Peter was trying to calm Rosie, who was in tears. Liz was the first to respond when she saw the poor girl taking staggered breaths. "Oh, sweet Rosie! What happened?" she said and held out her arms. Rosie went to her and cried even harder.

"I don't know what he said, Dad, but it was Dan who made her cry," Peter said.

"Alright, Peter. Thank you," David said and took Dan into the next room.

Eventually, Rosie calmed down enough to tell Liz and Erin what he said. "Dan said the only reason you like us is because Dad is famous, and you wouldn't if he wasn't."

Erin and Liz exchanged looks. "Now, you must know that's not true, darling girl! I like you because you're sweet and thoughtful and... well, because of the person you are, not because of your father, or Erin, or anyone else," Liz said. "I'm so glad I get *you* for a grandchild, and Erin gets you for her baby girl."

"I'm not a baby," Rosie said and smiled knowingly at Erin.

Liz shook her head. "Doesn't matter. Erin will always be *my* baby girl, and I'm sure, even though she didn't know you when you were a baby, she'll probably still call you that." The two women looked at each other and smiled.

David returned with an unhappy Daniel, who walked over to Rosie and said, "Sorry."

"Is that what you really believe, Dan? Do you think people only like you because you're David Elliott's son?" Erin asked.

He shrugged, reluctantly shook his head, then nodded. "People are always saying, 'If you weren't David Elliott's son, I'd...'" he said, looking at the floor.

"Who's said that to yeh?" David asked, plainly shocked.

"Teachers, mainly. Headmaster Campbell has said it to me... and Charlie as well; I heard him!" he said defensively.

"Oh, you poor thing!" Liz said and held out her arms for a hug. Erin saw him roll his eyes as he allowed her to embrace him for all of three seconds and then wiggled free of her grasp. Charlie, on the other hand, wasn't going to miss out on a free hug, so he looked at Erin, who nodded her head toward her mom, indicating he should go for it. Liz smiled as the boy wrapped his arms around her neck and held on for a long time.

"Alright, Peter," Erin said, laughing, "you'd better get in there if you want one, too."

Peter smiled, and when Charlie's hug was done, he helped Liz stand to her feet since he was too tall for a crouched hug. Liz wrapped her arms around him for a quick squeeze. "I like being a grandma!" she said.

"Well, it's a good thing you won't have to go to that school any longer, right?" Erin said. She tousled Charlie's hair and put her arm around his shoulders. "Want to see pictures of me as a child?"

"Yes, please!" he said, and they all crowded around her.

"Okay, then sit at the table and look through the photo albums." The children rushed to the table and laughed as they flipped the pages, seeing Erin grow from a baby to a child, then a teenager, and finally a young woman.

———

David watched over everyone's shoulders, enjoying their reactions. The last album was full of Erin and Todd's wedding photos and fifteen years of Christmases and Thanksgivings. A sick, uncomfortable feeling made him look away at first, but something made him turn back. He saw Erin in her mid-twenties, looking radiant in her wedding gown, so young and happy. He also saw Liz and Frank at the age he was then.

Erin had gone to the bathroom about midway through the pile. When she returned, she must've noticed the quiet awkwardness at the table because she peeked over Rosie's shoulder. "Oh no! You guys don't want to see those!" She looked at David and frowned. "I'm sorry, David," she said and tried to take the book off the table, but he put his hand on hers.

"Dinnae worry, love, I'm a'right. Yeh look lovely in yer dress." He imagined an album filled with photos of their wedding. "And ye'll look even lovelier in the album we'll be in together."

"Aye, and you can put a tiny photo of us in your accordion... wait, do you still have it? Did it burn in the fire, David?" she asked, sounding upset at the prospect.

"Ach, they found a lump of plastic and paper in ma holdall. Et was in the box they sent. Et's a'right, darling, I'll get another one and fill it with the memories we make," he said and kissed her hair.

"I look forward to every minute of it."

Chapter Fifteen

DO YOU REMEMBER, MAMMA?

"How old was I when we moved here?" Erin asked after breakfast. "You were seven when we moved. We rented a house on Lakeland Road for a few years and then bought this old place when you were about… thirteen, I think.

"Why did we move here? I mean, didn't we live in the city when I was born?"

"Your father lost his high-paying job and found one in Grafton, so we had to move. It was a big change, but I'm glad it happened that way," Liz said.

"Really? I thought you'd just decided to move us to the country so I'd have a better life?"

"No, though I did choose a place with land so you could run and play instead of living in town, but honestly, it was all we could afford at the time. Times were tight," Liz said, blushing.

"I never felt poor. There were kids in my school who had more things, like name-brand clothes and all, but I always had plenty. I was never hungry, and I didn't need all that much. I had my bike, roller skates, and disk swing in the big tree. I had the freedom to go anywhere I wanted, and boy did I! You would freak out to know the things Mindy, Betsy, and I did in the summer! We were crazy!"

"Do tell, Erin. I'd like tae know the crazy things yeh did as a girl," David said, and suddenly the children were all ears.

"Yes, Mum, I'd like to know as well!" Charlie said.

131

Erin smiled at him and tousled his light brown hair. "I wish we could all go for a bike ride together or even a walk, so I could show you." She sat for a few moments, trying to come up with good stories to tell. "I don't know where to start. Oh wait... well, this isn't the best one, but it's a place to begin.

"I had my first sleepover not long after we moved. Mindy was turning seven, and I already was. I had never slept away from home before and was really excited. The invitation said to bring a sleeping bag, but I didn't have one, so my mom said she'd bring some rolled-up blankets for me to use. Of course, that wasn't what I really wanted, but it would work.

"I don't remember how I got there, I only remember walking into their house and having a wonderful time. They played games, sang *Happy Birthday*, and had cake. When it was time for bed, I asked Mindy's mother where my blankets were. She walked over to a brand-new sleeping bag, all rolled up on the floor. I told her that it wasn't mine since I didn't have one, but she told me that my mom had dropped it off before I got there and that it actually *was* mine.

"I was so excited! I picked it up and rolled it out onto the floor. It had blue Smurfs on it, and the white hats were the softest thing I'd ever felt. It's strange, I don't usually associate 'things' with love, but that night, I felt loved by my mom. She'd surprised me with something so wonderful that I felt like crying. I didn't cry, I just got into it and lay on the floor with the other little girls and ran my hand over the soft white fabric, knowing that my mom cared." Erin looked up and saw her mother wipe a tear from her cheek.

"Is that the same one I'm using?" Rosie asked.

"It is, darling. I was surprised to see it, and that it was still in one piece."

"I found it in your closet a long time ago. I have no clue why I didn't throw it away or donate it. I didn't think I'd have the joy of little ones in my house again," Liz said and wiped another tear away. Rosie stood and crawled onto her lap, giving her a hug.

"I think I ended up missing my mom that night and cried until she picked me up, so I don't think I actually used it for very long, but that's not what the story is about," Erin finished.

"Keep going! I want to hear something dangerous!" Dan said, smiling so that his dimples showed.

"Dangerous? Let me think. Well, there used to be a barn near the other house. It was really old, and my parents told me never to go in it. I probably wouldn't have, except Betsy had the idea to check it out, so I went along. I was a bit older then, about ten or eleven. It hadn't been used in many years, but it was dry and smelled of hay. In the center of the building there was an open space flanked on either side by hay lofts. We never found a ladder, but there was an enormous wooden wheel, for what purpose, I have no idea, maybe a pulley system? We would climb up that wheel and hoist ourselves up onto that hay loft to play up there.

"The dangerous part was that there was a light dusting of straw over the whole floor, hiding the fact that parts of it were rotted away. I could see the bigger areas, but we really didn't know if there were other parts that might give way. I looked into the biggest hole in the floor a few times and saw rusty, jagged farm machinery. If one of us had fallen in, we'd have been skewered!" she said, and her mother gasped.

"Erin! That's horrible! I'm glad I didn't know," Liz said.

"That's not even the worst thing," she continued, watching the smiles on everyone but her mother's face. "There was a small door at the end of the loft, and one day, Betsy decided it would be fun to pile up some hay on the ground beneath it and jump down. I helped pile up the hay, and she and Mindy jumped, landing hard, but didn't get hurt. I think I jumped out of it once, but I was too scared to do it again. Plus, we'd have to climb up that big wheel each time, and it wasn't easy to do, so I let them do it while I watched."

"I want to see the barn!" Dan said, and Erin could see the wheels of mischief turning in his mind. "I'd put a trampoline under the door and jump onto it! That would be great fun!"

"Last time I drove past the house, it wasn't there. It must've been torn down. Sorry, Dan. That was the house we stopped at, David."

"Aye, I didn't see a barn, Dan," he said.

"Another dangerous story that will have my mom cringing is that we used to have an old, yellow Ford truck with a cap on it. One summer, my mother drove us down to Six Flags, Great America, in Illinois. All us kids, including me, Mindy, Betsy, my aunt, Prestana, who is my mom's sister and only a little bit older than me, and her friend, Cathy, piled into the back of the truck. There were no seats or seat belts, mind you, and it's over an hour away! That was the most fun, though, we played games and sang songs all the way there!"

"We could do things like that back then," Liz said. "I wouldn't even think of it now!"

"Do you have more stories, Erin?" Peter asked and flashed his father's smile at her.

"Hmmm, then there was the night me, Mindy, Betsy, and their cousin, Brad, went sledding on the hill behind their dad's semi-truck repair shop, which was behind our house. Of course, my mom told me not to do that either, but I didn't think of that when I was doing it. We all went down the hill once, and it was fun, so Brad, who was a few years younger than me, got on his little red saucer sled, and we let him go, but this time he leaned so that he started veering off toward the semi-trailers sitting in the yard.

"We yelled at him to roll off and ran after him, but he must've panicked and slid right under one of them, hitting his forehead on the metal box that held the spare tire. I don't know who found my mom, but suddenly she was there. I remember it was dark and the only lights were tall streetlights illuminating the yard. Brad was bleeding everywhere and didn't start crying until he saw the blood, then he bawled and carried on like a baby. I guess it was really traumatic for him, but I'll never forget it!"

"I remember that! I was furious! Poor Brad had to have six stitches, and his mother was really upset with me, as though I had something to do with it. I'm the one who rushed him to the hospital, after all. She could've been a little bit thankful," Liz said, frowning, but then smiled at them all.

"One winter, my uncle, Kenneth, stayed with us for a few weeks. He was from Texas and only about ten years older than me. That year, he broke my favorite sled. He was about twenty and had a lot of meat on his bones, so to speak. He made a ramp on a hill, took my sled down it, and smashed it with his big old butt," Erin said, still sore about it thirty years later. "Then, he helped me build a snowman. It was a really great, fat snowman, and I thought it was wonderful. The next morning, when I went out to look at it, he'd... given it... breasts."

There was silence in the room for about fifteen seconds as everyone's imagination started visualizing it, then they started laughing. "I think there's a picture of it in one of the photo albums. I had to admit it was funny, but I was glad when he left.

"I think we all were. He was a bit… coarse. He only stayed for two weeks, but it seemed like much longer," Liz said.

"Tell us one that's funny, Mummy!" Rosie said.

"Okay, let me think. One time, in summer, when we were bored, we drew pictures on small pieces of paper and folded them up neatly. We rode our bikes to all the houses scattered around us and knocked on the doors. We didn't know any of the people, just so you know, this was completely crazy! When someone opened their door, we would ask them a ridiculous question, like, 'How old are you?' or 'How many appliances do you have in your kitchen?' Silly things like that. I think we had a clipboard and asked them to sign their names, then we gave them one of our pictures.

"One man was really funny. He came to the door, and we gave him our little spiel, but he said he didn't want to sign on our clipboard. We asked him why not, and he said that we might be aliens and his signature might give us permission to take him into outer space. We vowed and promised him that we weren't aliens and that he was safe, so he signed it.

"When we gave him his picture, he said, 'See! I told you! This says that I'm going to be taken by your people, doesn't it?' We told him it didn't, so he unfolded it and saw that it was only a drawing. He acted relieved, and it was really funny! Good times!"

"You were mad!" David said, laughing. "It would never have occurred to me to do something so odd, but I can absolutely visualize you doing it. I've got to meet these crazy friends of yours!"

Erin's face fell a bit. "Mindy lives in Sheboygan with her husband and two sons, but I'm not friends with Betsy. I think she married Doug and moved away," she said, putting on a smile.

David took her hand. "Ach, I'm sorry. I forgot about that," he said.

She shrugged and smiled at him. "It doesn't matter. Look who I'm with now! Doug could never compete with you." She leaned close and kissed him, making the twins groan and look away, but Rosie and Peter smiled at them.

Chapter Sixteen

A WALK IN THE WOODS

"Who wants to go on an adventure?" Erin asked after lunch. Each of the four children, David, and even Frank said they would. "Good! I thought we could take a walk in the wilds of the woods and land around the house. You can be our guide, Dad."

"Sounds like fun, but we need to be prepared," Frank said. There are ticks and mosquitoes out there, so we should all wear long pants." At that, the children giggled, and Frank looked around him, confused.

"Dad, in England, pants refer to underwear," Erin explained.

"Oh, oops," he said, laughing. "Well then, long—"

"Trousers," Charlie supplied helpfully.

"Trousers then," Frank said. "Also, long socks, and sturdy shoes."

"I will also spray you all down with bug repellent," Erin said, and the children's eyes were wide.

"Who knew et was so dangerous tae go for a wee walk about!" David said.

"Indeed. Takes the fun right out of it," Frank said.

The children were sent upstairs to get the appropriate clothing on while Erin and David did the same. They met outside on the grassy area in the center of the circle at the top of the driveway. "Follow me," Frank said, leading them down a well-kept, mown path. "This used to be the highway when this house was built until it was diverted.

Peter was in heaven, examining the plants, naming as many as he could, and asking the names of those he couldn't. Rosie and Charlie walked on either side of Frank, listening and absorbing everything he said, while Dan wanted to run through the high grass and brambles. "Dan! Don't go far, there used to be farm machinery buildings over there, and you might step on something rusty. I'll show you the safe places to explore, okay?" Frank said. "Do you play golf, David? There's a very nice course across the street if—"

"Ach, no, I dinnae golf. I'd rather not spend ma time gettin' angry at a wee ball that I'm meant tae chase around manicured lawns," he said.

"I couldn't agree more!" Frank said, and the two men laughed. "I thought that since you were Scottish, it was in your blood or something."

"We had a few days out during school where I reckon we were meant to be recruited, but I didn't fancy et. Ma da' wasn't a golfer either. I must say, et's rough though when I must decline an invitation from another actor or a director I admire."

"You're Scottish too, Dad," Erin said, and David raised his eyebrows.

"There's a lot more to being Scottish than being a descendant of the Scottish people, Erin. I'm proud of my heritage but not technically Scottish. I'm an American who had some good luck in the genealogy department," her dad said humbly.

"I'm not a hundred percent Scottish, anaway, ma great-grandmother's family was from Dorset, in the south of England."

"You mean the woman who married your great-grandfather, David?" Erin asked.

"Yes—Dan! You've been told tae stay close, now come back!" David said, but Frank put his hand up.

"I'll go," he said and started walking toward the head of brown hair they could see moving in the long grass. "Let's look for snakes!"

At that, Peter looked up, wide-eyed at his father and Erin. "Goh, I'll not miss that!" he said. "Wait for me, Frank!"

"Well, my dad sure knows how to get the attention of young people!" Erin said and then saw that David was looking a bit intrigued. "As well as adults... go on, you. I'll join you in a minute." Charlie wasn't far behind David, but Rosie looked frightened as she stood, watching her family walk away.

"I'm afraid of snakes," she said timidly as Erin stepped up to her.

"I used to be afraid of them too. Honestly, I'm afraid of the big ones that bite, but we don't have that kind here. We mostly have garden and grass snakes, which are harmless. My dad knows what anything bigger or more dangerous than that looks like and will make sure everyone stays away. Snakes are really neat, actually. I was about your age the first time I held one."

"You've held a snake, Mummy?" Rosie said, looking up at her with large, round eyes.

"Yes, Rosebud, I really like how they feel."

"I don't like slimy things—"

"But snakes aren't slimy at all. They're smooth and cool to the touch." Erin could tell Rosie was growing more and more curious as she began bouncing on her toes. "Would you like to come with me and see if they find one? You don't have to touch it unless you want to," she said, and the young girl smiled up at her.

"I'll touch it if you do first," she said and took her hand, pulling her up to the tall grass just as Daniel squealed.

"That was a common garter snake…" They heard Frank say just before they reached the group. "Too bad it got away, or I'd have let you touch it."

"I'll catch it!" Dan said and was just about to go after it when David caught his sleeve.

"Not so fast, son," he said, and Frank put his hand on the boy's shoulder.

"He's right, Daniel. We should allow it to live its life in peace. Now, there's a small creek down this hill. It's usually dried up this time of year, but yesterday's rain might have revived it. Let's investigate," Frank said and led them further away from the house.

After lunch, the children hung out with Frank while Erin and David were in the kitchen, helping Liz with the dishes. Erin washed and David dried. David was sent to the dining room to make sure no dishes were forgotten on the table and heard Rosie say, "That's my daddy! I'd like to play this, please, if it's not too difficult?" Then he saw the *Future Explorations*-themed Fluxx game.

"Of course! It's very easy to learn and play, Rosie," Frank said.

David groaned internally. Rosie saw him and ran over to him, holding up the game. "Daddy, Granddad told us to find a game in that big box over there," she said and pointed to a steamer trunk in the corner of the living room. I found this one! Look, it's you and Baz at the farmhouse! Will you play it with us?" she said so excitedly that he couldn't say no.

"Aye, darling," he said. He took out the last of the dinnerware and asked Liz if he could borrow her daughter for a moment.

"What's wrong?" Erin asked, reading the look on his face.

"Rosie's found the game we played last time we were here. The 'forgive the mother' night." He couldn't help but blush, remembering when Liz had walked in on him in the bath and then gotten drunk whilst playing the game that night.

"Oh, that's not awkward at all," she said with a grin. "It'll be fine. I'm pretty sure my mom's a teetotaler now… at least while you're here."

"Aye, she's not touched anathin' alcoholic since we arrived. Et's just embarrassin', yeh ken?"

"I ken. Dinnae fash, just play it cool! Have fun with it… the game, I mean."

"I just needed tae talk tae you about et. Tae calm ma nerves, yeh ken?"

"I love you. Now let's go help set it up."

Dan didn't want to play, so he and Liz played Connect Four on the coffee table, which made David's level of discomfort far less than he imagined it would be. David won three rounds, Erin one, Frank one, Rosie two, Charlie one, and Peter zero, but they all had fun and teased David about the drawing on his card. Erin and Rosie both begged him to use his John Thomas voice for three of the rounds, making everyone laugh.

That night at supper, Erin and David came downstairs after a much-needed nap to find the four children talking and laughing as they sat around the beautifully set table. "He'll never go for it," Charlie was saying to Peter.

"Who won't go for what?" Erin asked as they each found their seats.

"Peter thinks—" Charlie began, but Peter shot him a look that said, 'shut up,' so he rolled his eyes and stopped talking.

"*What* do you think Peter?" David asked.

"Nothing, Dad. Charlie doesn't know what he's—"

"I do so know what I'm talking about!" Charlie shot back. "He thinks he can talk you into moving here so he can drive sooner!" he said and scowled at his big brother. Peter didn't look happy; he stood when Charlie told on him.

"A'right boys, calm down. I'm afraid we won't be movin' here, at least not anatime soon," David said. "I've signed on for a series tae be filmed in the UK, so we're stayin' in Britain."

"I told you—" Charlie began, but Erin put her finger to her lips to shush him.

"Go ahead, Dad," Erin said, and everyone took the hand of the person next to them.

"For what we're about to eat, may we be truly grateful," Frank prayed.

Everyone said, "Amen," and as they ate their dinner, all talk of moving was forgotten.

"Have you thought about names for the baby?" Liz asked at dessert. The children started talking at the same time and didn't stop until Frank whistled so loudly it hurt their ears.

"Wow! Thanks, Dad, I think," Erin said. "Clearly, everyone has ideas on the subject."

"Maybe we could vote?" Charlie said rather diplomatically, and all the children agreed.

Erin looked at David, and he shrugged. "You're no help," she said to him. "I think we should hear them first."

Peter raised his hand, and Erin nodded to him. "Why don't we each write them down, and you can read them out for us?"

Erin looked at the group sitting around the table and shrugged. "Okay, but no promises about us choosing any of them," she said. "Mom, can you find some paper and pens while we *all* help clear the table?" The children made noises of protest but helped without a fuss.

Liz returned with a few sheets of loose-leaf paper and a mix of pens and pencils. She ripped the paper into small rectangles using the edge of the table, then wrote out her choices, seeing she'd be doing the dishes while everyone else was writing theirs down.

Once the table was cleared, the family returned to fill out their ballots as they saw them. "Dad, can I borrow your hat?" Erin asked her father and held out her hand. He raised his eyebrows and reluctantly picked up the ball cap he'd set next to his chair while they ate their meal. He handed it to her, and she put the small slips of paper inside it. "Thank you," she said and smiled at him.

"Now, has everyone had their say, who wants to?" She held up the hat for any last-minute submissions. "Dad? David?" she said, and they both nodded. "Okay then, we'll wait for mo... I mean Grandma Liz to finish." The children grumbled at having to wait. "Oh, my! If you're that impatient, you should go help your grandma!"

Rosie stood and so did Charlie. Peter wasn't about to appear lazy in the eyes of his new grandad, so he stood and joined the others. Daniel wasn't bothered by appearances and stayed put. A few minutes later, they emerged from the kitchen laughing with Liz and found their seats again.

Erin raised the hat again. "I'll read these off and make two piles. One for 'not likely' and one for 'those we'll consider.'" She pulled out the first one and read: "Patrick. Not bad, I'll consider it." The next was Ruth, then John, which got a laugh. Then Lyla, Philip, and Minnie. "Oh, I like that one!" Both Liz and Erin said together.

Next was Thomas, which got more laughs. Then there were Frank and Lily. David peered at her. "Okay, I put them in there," she admitted. Then Alexander, Eric, and William. The last ones were Annis, which David submitted, and Juniper, Liz's contribution. "Oh, my! There are so many good ones!" She looked at David, "How will we choose?"

"Hmm, I say we write down the best and ponder them for a while. We've a few months yet tae decide."

"Do you know if it's a boy or girl yet?" Frank asked. "That might narrow down your choices."

"No, not yet. It's too early for that," Erin said.

"I dinnae want tae know anaway," David said, and everyone turned, staring at him, shocked.

"Neither do I," Erin said with a really wide smile.

"Well, I'm glad we agree!"

"I like 'Ruth Annis' best," Rosie said. "Then we can call her Ruthie… Rosie and Ruthie."

"If it's twins, we could have Ruth and Juniper," Peter said, making Erin frown.

"Oh, Peter! Let's hope it's only one!" she said, and then saw the look on Dan and Charlie's faces. "Twins are amazing, but I'm not sure I could handle two tiny babies at once! I didn't mean—"

"Okay, everyone, your mother and I—" David began, and his face turned bright red. The room was utterly silent. "What I meant tae say was… Erin and I… will read these again tonight and have a long talk."

"You can call her our mother," Rosie said. "I like it!"

Erin liked it too, but she wasn't sure if David had meant her at all or if he'd meant Susannah by accident. "Alright, everyone," she said since David wasn't saying anything. "Why don't you go up and get ready for bed. We'll be up shortly to tuck you in."

The kids looked at David, clearly noticing something was bothering him. "Go on, do as Erin says," he said. The children got up from the table and made their way upstairs. "I'm sorry, Erin," David said when they were gone.

Erin looked at him and knit her brows together. "What for?" she asked. "Were you thinking of Susannah when you said it?"

"Well, no, but—"

"Then, it's fine. I liked it too. Why don't we talk—"

"Aye, we'll talk about it later," he said.

Erin wasn't satisfied with that, so she stood and took him by the hand. "Come with me please," she said, but he resisted. "Something is bothering you, and I'd rather not wait until later to talk about it. Please come with me."

He stood reluctantly and went with her. "Please excuse us," he said to Liz and Frank, who only shrugged. She led him to the steps just outside the enclosed porch. "Erin—" he began.

"What's wrong, David?" she asked and pulled him down to sit on the step next to her. "I know you well enough to tell that there's something more going on in your head. Please tell me."

"It's really not—" he said, but she gave him a 'spit it out' look, and he sighed. "A'right. Et's just that I would've liked tae talk tae the children before I started callin' you their mother… in that way, and—" he said and hesitated.

"And?" Erin repeated, knowing there was more to it. "You've had me saying they're *our* children for a while now, so I don't understand."

"And, well, et's the first time I've said that exact thing since she died, a'right? Et shocked me. I wasn't thinkin' of her fondly, et just… well, et brought back a flood of memories, especially of her… death. I haven't really thought about et since et happened, and I had a flashback, yeh ken?" he said miserably.

"I do ken, darling. Go ahead and let it out," she said and laid her head on his arm.

"Are you sure? I dinnae want tae upset yeh," he said.

"I'll be fine, David, but you need to get it out; you can't hold it in."

He looked at her hand, which he was holding, and then kissed it. "I love yeh," he said quietly.

———

Peter had just opened the window to let in the warm summer night air when he heard his father and Erin come out onto the stairs. He listened for a while and then put his hand out to quiet the others. They all gathered at the window to listen.

———

"She weighed practically nothin' when I took her out of the car; she couldn't have weighed more than Rosie! She was so frail, I was terrified I'd break her as I was doin' the compressions. I didn't want her tae die, no matter how ill she'd spoken tae yeh, and I reckon, even if I'd known then what she'd been plannin' with that Clive, I still would've tried tae bring her back.

"She—wasn't always as she was at the end. She used tae have a soft side; the money changed her so quickly. I wish the children had known her like that. I just can't believe their nanny kept them from me! Et… et makes me so verra angry! Tae think… Susannah allowed her tae do that and went along with et herself, knowin' full well how much I longed tae hold them and play with them. I wish—" he began and broke down.

143

Erin held him as he cried. She didn't say anything, she just wrapped her arms around him and gave him time to mourn.

———

Peter turned to the others, who all looked shocked. "I didn't know Nanny and Mum had done that," he said, his face red with anger. "It was their fault we didn't get to know our dad! That makes me... so angry!" Rosie had tears in her eyes, and Charlie looked as though he wanted to cry as well.

"Do you reckon he'd want a hug?" Charlie asked, and Peter nodded.

"Come with me," he said, and they followed him down the stairs and through the living room, where Liz and Frank were sitting. They seemed stunned as they watched them walk determinately past them. The foursome continued through the kitchen and then out onto the covered porch.

Peter opened the door and looked at his father, broken and hurting. He had been angry much of his life because he'd thought his 'famous' dad had had better things to do than spend time with him and his siblings. Now he knew the truth.

———

David heard the door and stood. He walked away, clearly not wanting anyone to see the state of him. "What is it, Peter?" Erin asked, worried since they'd all come down together, but he ignored her.

"Dad?" he said. "Don't walk away, please."

Rosie and Charlie didn't wait for him to stop. They ran down the stairs in their pajamas and bare feet and held onto their dad for dear life. Erin could see David shaking as he knelt to hold them.

"We... heard what you said through the window. We didn't know Mum and Nanny had kept us from you, and we didn't know you wanted to play with us or, well, wanted to be around us, really."

Peter walked down the steps and went to him. "I wish they hadn't done that to you Dad. We want to be with you and play with you as well," he said and knelt beside him, sharing the hug.

Not being much for hugging and emotions, Daniel sat on the step beside Erin and watched. After a while, he laid his head on her arm, and soon he laid his head on her lap, falling asleep. David and the three others were talking and laughing while Erin watched them, getting to know each other after all the years they were kept apart. "David," she said, having waited as long as she could while her legs slowly began falling asleep. He looked up at her, and she pointed to the sleeping boy on her lap.

David smiled and stood with the help of Peter and Charlie, then he lifted Daniel into his arms. He carried him through the house and up the stairs to the spare bedroom, laying him on the bed. He kissed his forehead, and as he straightened up, Dan opened his eyes.

"I love you, Dad," he said and then rolled over. Erin had been doing her best to tuck the others in, and they all looked at David.

"I love you, son," he said. "I love you all, and if yeh dinnae mind, I may start callin' Erin yer mum."

The three tired, happy children nodded. "Good, we're fed up with how horrible Mum was to us, and especially to you, Dad. We're happy to have Erin take her place," Peter said.

"Sweet dreams, children," Erin said as she turned out the light.

"Goodnight, Dad, and Mum," they all said.

"We... well, I, at least, love you both," Peter said.

Charlie and Rosie said, "So do I."

"I love you too," Erin said and closed the door, sighing. She turned to David, "And I love you too!" He took her hand, and they started down the stairs. Halfway down, David turned, pushed Erin up against the wall, and started kissing her. She melted into it and kissed him back.

They stayed there, snogging for quite a while, until eventually Liz came to the bottom of the stairs, planning to go to bed. She stood transfixed for a moment until Frank joined her, and they watched their daughter and David kissing. Frank decided to take a cue from David and started kissing his wife, which he hadn't done in quite a while. At first, Liz protested but then changed her mind.

Erin had heard her mother say something quietly at the bottom of the stairs, and when she didn't hear her leave, she turned her head, allowing David, who didn't seem to care who was in the stairwell, to kiss her neck. She watched her parents necking and laughed. "Copycats!" she whispered, and David then looked down and saw them.

"Let's give them some privacy," he said. "Come with me." He took her hand and led her to their room. When the door was closed, he pressed her up against it and held her face in his hands. "Ye're the best thing tae happen tae me and ma family. I thank God for yeh, Erin, and I want tae marry yeh now! I want you tae have ma name and be mine forever and ever," he said, and then kissed her, pressing himself against her.

"I... want... that... too," she said between kisses. "But it's complicated... with us... being from different countries." He was undressing her and kissing her, making it difficult to have a discussion, so she gave up for the moment.

———

He started undressing himself and took her hand, placing it on his erection, which made them both moan gently. Then he turned, led her to the bed, and lay her down. Finally, he got on top of her and entered her as he watched her reaction.

She opened her mouth, closed her eyes, and furrowed her brow. "Oh!" she said softly as he thrust himself deep inside her.

He did it again, taking his time, feeling every inch slide freely in, just to be pulled out once more. She seemed to like it as well, smiling at him as he pulled nearly all the way out, then moaning as he plunged himself back in. He could sense she was getting closer to her climax and sped up, making her cry out at the unexpectedness of it.

His eyes grew wide, and he put his hand over her mouth. "Shh!" he whispered, then moved his hand from her mouth to the back of her head, grabbing a fistful of her hair and pulling down slightly. He felt her start to pulse around him and continued thrusting hard and fast, still pulling her hair. "Ach, ma Losh, Erin, et feels like heaven tae be inside you. I've never felt anathin' like et before. I need you and desire yeh with evera breath I take," he said and then climaxed.

After a few moments of enjoying the sensations, he rolled onto his side on the bed. "Yeh make me feel... I dinnae ken, safe. Yeh ken what I need, even when I dinnae ken et maself. Earlier... yeh knew better than I did that I needed tae talk. Yeh got me tae do et without badgerin', and yeh listened without judgment. I didn't ken how much I needed that in ma life, but—" he hesitated. "Sometimes... I feel as though I'm always needin' yer shoulder tae cry on without givin' anathin' in return."

Erin shook her head and chuckled softly. "You're forgetting New Orleans... and when I left for England with you after I said goodbye to everyone. You've had to put up with my bawling and running away, my being sick, and my episode! I think we do a good job of helping each other when we need it. Plus, I love being your shoulder to lean on.I love that you feel safe enough to be yourself and cry in front of me, and I feel blessed to be the one you love and need. I need you too. I like you... your real self, the one you show only to me. I can't think of anything I want you to change or that I wish was different; you are perfect for me."

"Well then, if yeh put et *that* way," he said and sighed when she rolled toward him, laying her arm over his chest. Soon he felt her breathing become slower and knew she was asleep. *Thank you, God, for bringin' this fine woman into our lives,* he thought and then allowed sleep to overtake him as well.

Chapter Seventeen

THUMBS UP

Not counting bathroom stops, it was a two-and-a-half-hour drive from Erin's parents' home to the rental house they'd be staying at in Door County. They were all up and ready to go by mid-morning, and although it was sad, David suggested they leave after breakfast. Liz, Erin, and Rosie shed more than one tear as they said goodbye, Rosie being the worst of all. She took turns clinging to Liz and then Frank, telling them how much she'd miss them. The boys were clearly sorry to go, but they didn't become emotional about it.

Frank helped them load the car, then Liz stepped up to Erin, holding a small gift bag. "What's this?" she asked as she opened it and pulled out something soft wrapped in tissue paper.

"It was yours when you were a baby. Your grandma Marni made it," she said and wiped a tear off her cheek. "It's hairpin lace; she was known for it and made one for everyone she knew who had a baby."

Erin held out a tiny pale blue dress that had ties in the back and cream-colored ribbons woven through the waste and neckline. There was also a little diaper cover and booties with bows and little ribbon roses scattered all over them. "Oh, Mom! It's so beautiful! Thank you for this, I'll treasure it!" she said and held it up to her nose to smell it. "Mmm, smells of moth balls… yummy!" she teased then hugged her mother tightly. "Well, I hate to say it, but we really need to go now."

After final hugs and kisses, they were off, headed down the long gravel driveway. Erin drove slowly, swerving to miss the many potholes. The mood in the vehicle was somber as they headed east toward the lake and highway 43. Rosie sniffled and took short, staggered breaths all the way into Saukville, so Erin decided to take action.

She turned on the satellite radio and found a station that played Disney songs. Soon, they were laughing as they sang along and kept track of license plates from other states. They ticked off Michigan, Illinois, Minnesota, and three different Wisconsin plates right away. Then they spotted a Texas, South Dakota, and even Ontario, Canada.

When they began seeing signs for Green Bay, Dan nearly shouted, "May we see your house, Erin, please?"

She looked in the rearview mirror and saw Rosie and Charlie nodding as well. "I'll tell you what, we can drive past it on our way to the airport when we leave, okay? Everything is too raw from the party, and I'd rather not see Todd if he happens to be home. Let's give everyone some time to cool off," she said. Dan looked really disappointed, but the others seemed appeased by the compromise.

Erin headed northeast to the 'thumb' of Wisconsin, excited to be able to share it with them. It was a long drive, and after an hour or so, every field and barn began to look the same. She could tell they were getting bored when Daniel started making farting sounds and wouldn't stop when both Peter and Charlie asked him to.

"Put a cork in it, Dan," David said.

The boy stopped the noises but soon began acting like he was about to touch Rosie, making her angry. "Stop it, Dan! I don't want you to touch me!" she said.

"I'm not going to touch you," he said and pretended he was poking her up and down her arm.

"Daddy, make him stop!" she said, sounding like she was near tears.

"Daniel! That's enough!" The words left David's mouth without much energy.

"I'm gonna stop at Lautenbach's. You can stretch your legs and use the bathroom," she said, hoping that would help.

Erin pulled into the parking lot in front of a one-story, red building surrounded by cherry trees and grape vines tamed into submission along wires strung across waist-high poles. She turned off the engine with a sigh, tired of driving and trying to keep Dan in check. It was Tuesday, so it wasn't busy, and she found a spot right away.

"In spring, these trees are filled with white blossom—Wait!" she said as the doors began opening. "Please behave yourself, Daniel. Don't go running around the store—"

"Okay, I won't," he shouted, cutting her off as he nearly leapt out the door and slammed it behind him.

"Dan!" Charlie said, but his brother was already at the double doors of the touristy shop and winery and didn't hear him.

"May I throttle him, Dad?" Peter said, sounding exhausted as well.

"Aye," David said half-heartedly.

The teen's eyes grew wide, and a sassy smile played on his lips before Erin shook her head. "I know it's tempting, but please don't. Hopefully, he'll burn off some energy, and we'll have a quieter ride after this."

"Awww, but Dad said," he said, pretending to be disappointed.

"Peter! That's enough. You heard yer mum," David barked.

Peter looked upset at his father's outburst and got out of the vehicle. "Sorry, Dad," he whispered as he ambled toward the building.

Erin and David stayed in their seats for a moment, and Erin placed her hand on his leg. "He was just trying to lighten the mood," she said, and it was his turn to sigh.

"Aye, and I shouldn't have snapped at him. I'm rubbish at parenting. Daniel won't listen to me, and I'm too short with the others," he said and put his head back against the headrest with his eyes closed.

"Dan won't listen to anyone right now. He's been sitting in the car for too long and just needs a good run to wear him out. Don't be so hard on yourself, my love. I think you're a great father. You'll feel better after lunch and a rest when we get to the place we're staying. Now let's go in and make sure the boy hasn't broken anything yet," she said and leaned over to kiss his cheek.

"Ach, I'm sae grateful for you, darling. The only reason I may be worth anathin' as a father is because ye're here tae build me up. Now, I must find Peter and apologize," he said and stepped out onto the faded blacktop.

"John?" they heard someone say as they held hands and started for the building.

"They have the best pie—" Erin began but was interrupted by a man and woman rushing toward them.

"John?" the man said.

"His name's not John, Jimmy, it's David... David Elliott?" the woman said as they approached.

"Hello," David said and took a step further, but the couple moved to stand in his way.

"We are your *biggest fans!*" the woman said. "I'm Heather, and this is Jimmy. We have *Future Explorations* memorized!"

"Yeah, and we've seen everything you've ever done, too!" Jimmy said and stood smiling at him.

There was an awkward silence as they waited for the man to continue. When he didn't, David awarded him with one of his brilliant smiles. "Thank you, I'm glad you enjoy—"

"You're just the most handsome actor in Hollywood! Well, except for Hugh Jackman, of course. You're on my list, you know?" Heather said.

"Yes, Hugh Jackman is a specimen, isn't he, darling?" David said and looked at Erin with a grin.

"I guess so, but I'd still choose you over him in a heartbeat," she said. "Oh, and I don't need a list anymore. You were always on the top of mine, anyway."

"List? I don't follow," he said.

"The 'freebie list,' David," Heather said.

"The list of five celebrities you'd be allowed to sleep with if the opportunity ever arose," Erin said and squeezed his hand.

"You're number two or three on mine, and your wife is probably number one on my husband's."

David's eyes grew wide, and then he frowned.

"That was until she passed so suddenly. It was a huge shock! We're, uh, sorry for your loss. I mean, she was so beautiful and… uh, sexy. I mean… you must be so sad," Jimmy said, stumbling over his words and evidently not knowing when to stop. "That swimsuit edition was—"

"Jimmy!" Heather said, but David's eyes had narrowed, and Erin could see his face getting red.

"Well, it was nice to—" she began, but David squeezed her hand a bit too hard.

"Please… do *not* mention her to me. Now, I'll thank you to move along so I can continue my *family* time," he breathed.

Clearly worried that they'd offended him, the couple sputtered their apologies. "I didn't mean to—" Jimmy began, but David put his hand up.

"That's enough," he said quietly. "And you may cross me off your… *list*, madam, et won't be happening. I am quite devoted to ma *fiancée*, thank you."

"David—" Erin said, but he spoke over her.

"Have a lovely day," he said and stepped around Jimmy, who was fumbling with his cell phone.

"But… we wanted a selfie—" Heather said, sounding like she might start crying.

"David, darling, just give them their selfie and get it over with, okay?" Erin said softly, not wanting him to snap at her. "Um, we've had a stressful morning, sorry. Why don't you hand me your phone and I'll take a photo for you?"

"Oh, thank you *sooo* much!" Heather said and thrust both hers and Jimmy's cell phones into her hands. They then stood on either side of David, who first glared at Erin and then remained stone-faced when Erin took a photo with both phones. He was already walking away when Heather said, "Can I have a hug, too?"

"I don't think he's giving out hugs today, but thanks for… uh… stopping and saying hello. I'm gonna catch up with him now, bye," Erin said and ran ahead. He had just stepped up to the building when she got to him, and he held the door for her.

"Daniel! I'm going to tell Dad when he—" Rosie shouted at her brother just before they heard a glass jar shatter, sounding very wet as it hit the floor.

"Look what you've made me do, Rosie!" Dan said and then froze when he saw his father glaring at him with a red face. "Dad! I didn't mean to drop it! Rosie made me do it, I swear!"

"I did not!" the girl said and then ran into Erin's arms, crying hysterically.

"Outside. *Now!*" David growled and pointed to the door.

"But, Dad!" the boy protested, though David stood his ground.

"***Now!***"

"I'll pay for the jar," Erin said and ushered Rosie toward the woman who was scooping the mixture of broken glass and extra hot mango salsa into a dustpan with her hands and a large wad of paper towels. "I'm so sorry for my son—"

"Don't worry about it," she said with a slight grimace. "Happens a lot (especially when parents allow their kids to run wild unsupervised)," she said under her breath.

Erin was shocked the woman had said that out loud, but she really couldn't blame her. "You're right, and I'm sorry. My husband was detained, and I should have come in to watch them. I'll pay for what he broke, and we'll leave. I really am sorry you had to deal with him; it wasn't fair to you at all," she said humbly.

"No, I'm sorry. I shouldn't have said that; it wasn't right. You shouldn't leave because of this, okay?"

"Okay, thanks, but I'm kind of afraid my fiancé will really lose his temper, so I'd better get back out there and mediate, you know?"

"Yeah, he looked really angry," the woman said and stood with Erin's help.

"I do want a cherry pie, though," she said and then looked at the worried faces of her children, who had gathered around her. "On second thought, maybe I'll take two." She stepped up to the shelf that had several pies sitting on it and picked one up. "Oh, they're still warm! Peter, will you please carry one of these for me?"

"Sure," he said softly and took the white box that had a transparent top.

"Listen, Peter, your dad didn't mean to snap at you. He's feeling a bit… well, like he's not a very good dad right now, so please cut him some slack. He was about to come find you to apologize when a couple stopped him and were a bit rude. I understand why you're upset, and you have the right to be, but please don't stay that way for very long, okay?"

Peter cocked his head to the side and then smiled at her, making her heart melt. "I understand, but he's not a bad father. Daniel's a daft plonker, and a thrashin' is what he needs, I reckon."

"Thank you, son," David said and approached them. "Ye're right, of course. I'm sorry I lost ma temper and—"

"Aww, it's a'right, Dad. Wait, where's Dan?" Peter asked, looking anxiously around the store.

They saw the young boy standing in front of the woman who'd had to clean up his mess. His head was down, and his hands were clasped behind his back. Erin could see his little body shaking as he spoke, making her think he was or had been crying. "What happened, David?"

"Humph. Before we were in the car park, he was greetin'… I mean cryin' and goin' on about how sorry he was. He confessed that he'd been a very bad boy and deserved to be punished for everything he'd done, the whole day long. Then he fell to his knees begging me to forgive him and even said that Rosie wasn't to blame for breaking the jar."

"Wow, and what did you do?" Erin asked.

"What was I meant to do after that? I allowed *him* to hug *me*," he said, and Erin's eyebrows shot up.

"He hugged you? Dang!"

"Aye, dang! I told him that I expected better from him from now on and that he must apologize to the shopkeeper and to his siblings."

"Rosie," they heard Dan say a bit pathetically.

"What is it, Dan? You know as well as I—"

"Yeah, I know, and I'm sorry for blaming you," he said and put his head down. "I'm also sorry, Charlie, for slamming the door on you and Peter, for not doing as you said. I'll be better behaved from now on, I promise."

Rosie narrowed her eyes at him and then held out her little finger. "Do you pinky promise? It's the most powerful promise in the world! Erin told me that, and I believe her, right, Mummy?"

"The second most powerful, but close enough," Erin said, proud of her new daughter.

Dan looked up at his family, and his cheeks turned pink.

"Go on, Dan," David said.

"Goh, a'right then, I pinky promise," he said and turned away from her.

"Daniel, you have to lock pinkies and shake on it," Erin said gently.

The boy heaved a great big sigh and rolled his eyes before doing as he'd been told. Rosie's smug grin nearly made Erin laugh out loud, but she caught herself just in time. "Okay, let's pay for our things and—"

"I need a wee, so I'll meet you at the—"

"Are you David Elliott?" a woman said, and Erin stepped in.

"Wow, that's the second time he's gotten that today! I guess I can see the resemblance, but it's not him, sorry," she said and ushered the children toward the checkout counter. "Meet you at the car, Earl."

"Okay, Yvonne," David said and stole away to the bathrooms before anyone was the wiser.

Erin didn't dare look at her children as she paid for the pies and insisted on paying for the salsa as well. She knew if she looked at them, she'd lose it.

The cashier watched the lady leave the store, then she looked at the children's wide eyes. "I was going to ask the same thing," she said with a smile.

Erin caught Peter's eye and couldn't hold it in any longer. She laughed until tears rolled down her face. "Yeah, that's him, but when ya gotta go, ya gotta go, so I lied. I'm sorry, guys, I know that was a really bad example for you, but I didn't want your dad to wet his pants!"

Rosie gasped and covered her mouth. "Mummy!"

Dan and Charlie were doubled over laughing, and Peter was wiping tears from his eyes until David returned, carrying a tiny onesie that said, 'I lost my nukkie in Door County!' "What'd I miss, and did you see this, darling?" he asked, which started it all over again.

"I'll tell you in the car," Erin said through a coughing fit. "Oh, that's sweet!" She handed the onesie to the cashier and paid for it as well.

"Uh, maybe this is bad timing, but could I have your autograph… uh, Earl?" the cashier said, which made Peter snort out a snot bubble.

"Eww! Gross, Peter!" Rosie said as her eldest brother's face turned bright red.

"Yes, you may," David said to the cashier and waited for her to find something to sign.

It wasn't long before they were all back in the SUV, buckled up and ready to go, though none of them were excited to sit for another long journey. "I'm hungry, Daddy," Rosie said with a slight whine. The rest of the children piped up then, saying they were as well.

"Okay, there's a nice restaurant in Fish Creek we can go to," Erin said as they headed down a steep, curving hill lined with a rock ledge on one side and dense trees on the other. At the stop sign, she turned left and found a place to park, which seemed like a miracle with how busy it was. It was the height of the tourist season, and even though it was a weekday, there were cars and people everywhere. "Here we are. Pelletier's is just over there." She pointed to a large, white, one-story building about half a block away.

There were several interesting-looking shops nearby, including the Door County Confectionery, a candy store, that drew Daniel like a fish on a hook. Between David, Erin, and Peter, they managed to keep him with them until they entered the restaurant. The hostess greeted them, then led them to the back of the dining room. She seated themed at a table overlooking the hill they'd just come down and a large patio with what looked like a big, above-ground fire pit. The young woman, who had long, black hair and a very thick Slovic accent, handed each of them a menu and told them their waitress would be right there.

It took quite a while for everyone to decide, but eventually, they ordered drinks and then food. An older couple was soon seated at a table nearby, and a middle-aged couple was seated next to them. The middle-aged woman smiled at Erin and said, "Are you on vacation, or do you live nearby?"

"We're on vacation, how about you?" Erin said.

"Same. We're from Chicago and have never been this far north in Door County before. We've been to Sturgeon Bay but decided to have an adventure this year. Is this your first time here?"

"I've been here loads of times, but this is their first time," Erin said, gesturing to the family.

Their food arrived, so all conversation stopped as the plates were passed to the person who ordered them. Once that was settled, Erin and David discussed what they would do that day after they checked into the rental house.

"What's a fish boil, Erin?" Charlie asked as the meal was winding down and held up a card advertising the one the restaurant held once per week.

"Well, I presume it's where they boil fish," she said and laughed at his 'give me a break' look. "I've never been to one, so I'm not sure."

"It's tradition," the older man, who had wavy white hair, said from the table next to them. He reminded Erin of the main character from the Disney movie, *Up*, and she smiled at him. "The one here is alright, but we're having one at the cottage tonight. You should join us and get a feel for the real deal."

"May we go, Mummy?" Rosie said, then Charlie and Dan began to beg her, using puppy dog eyes and dimples to persuade her.

She looked at David and shrugged. "What do you think? I'm game if you are."

The children turned their attention to him, and the look of trepidation on his face faded to amusement. "I reckon we can join you as long as we won't be imposing," he said, using his received pronunciation accent to much excitement from the children.

"Wouldn't invite you if you were imposing, would I? Stop by any time after two, though we start cooking at five," he said with a friendly smile. "Emily, write down our address, honey. I'm Harry Fisher, and this is my wife Emily."

"Nice to meet you. I'm Erin, and this is my fiancé, David." His wife had a round face, short, curly, grey hair, and eyes that, behind her glasses, squinted when she smiled. She handed Erin a napkin with their address on it, then the couple looked expectantly at the children as if waiting for their names. "This is Peter, Charlie, Daniel, and Rosie."

"Pleased to meet you, Mr. and Mrs. Fisher," the four chimed in unison.

"Are you from England?" Emily asked.

"Yes," David said simply.

"I'm from Green Bay," Erin said, "though now I live in London."

David took her hand and squeezed it, adding a slight nudge with his foot under the table. "Well then, that's us, ready to go. It was nice to meet you, and we look forward to seeing you again tonight," he said and stood, pulling the chair out for Erin. "Come along, children."

"I guess we'll see you later, then. Thank you for inviting us," Erin said as David, using long strides, went to the register to pay their bill.

"What was that about?" she asked when they were outside.

"Et's best not tae give out personal information to strangers," he said.

"Well, they gave us their address, so I didn't think telling them I moved to London was a big deal. Plus, it didn't seem like they knew who you were, anyway."

"Perhaps not, but one can never be too careful in my line of work." He looked down at her frown and touched her cheek. "Never mind, darling, no harm done."

"May we go to the sweet shop now?" Dan said and made a beeline for the door before getting an answer.

"Alright, but we can't take too long; we still need to check in—" she said, but he was already walking into the building.

They ended up spending a few hours in Fish Creek, exploring the shops. At Hat Head, David bought Erin a lovely, wide-brimmed sun hat and a sweet little baby bonnet, while the children were each allowed to choose a hat for themselves.

"We should get a gift for the Fishers," Erin said.

"Aye, we passed a market on our way here. I reckon they'll have a suitable bottle of wine or perhaps champagne," he said.

"I *reckon* a twelve-pack of beer would go over better, but we can bring a bottle of wine too," she said as they stepped out of the shop.

A few minutes later, they stepped into the small market. Erin began filling a shopping basket with a few sundries, like milk and cereal for their breakfast and bread and bologna to cover any meals they didn't eat out for. It took a bit longer than she thought it would for David to find an acceptable bottle of wine.

Thirty minutes into his search, she gently tapped his shoulder and made him turn to look at his children. They were being good, but it was plain to her that their patience was wearing thin. "We should be on our way to the rental now, don't you think?"

They paid for the bottle he had in his hand and then headed back to the SUV. "Are we almost there?" Charlie asked, so Erin looked at the map on her phone.

"Only eight more minutes, according to the map, but this is a tourist area, so sometimes you get stuck behind people going way under the speed limit," she said, and the children groaned. "I know, and I'm sorry to be a Debbie Downer, but as soon as we get our things settled, we'll have to leave again for the fish boil. It's not far from there, though; maybe twenty minutes—"

"Debbie what?" David said as she got back onto the road.

"Downer… haven't you ever heard that before?" Erin said, and he shook his head. "Well, it's self-explanatory, I think. Anyway, when we get there, we should—"

"We have our own Daniel Downer," Charlie said, which made everyone laugh.

"Don't interrupt," David said, but it was useless since the kids were talking over each other, and none of them were listening to him.

"This can't be it," David said as they pulled up to an old white house with a large front porch. "I asked Tina to find us a house on the water."

"Well, this is the correct address. Did Tina leave any notes in the itinerary?" Erin asked.

David opened the original email he'd received from his personal assistant. "Ah, I missed this before. She tried tae find what I asked for, but everathin' was booked. This was the only opening available for the size we needed. Well then, I reckon we should be thankful she found this, right?"

"Agreed, now let's get unpacked and ready to go to the Fisher's. I'm sure it'll be lovely."

David helped the children with the luggage whilst Erin opened the lockbox and unlocked the back door. She stepped through the threshold into a kitchen that greeted her with a perfect blend of old and modern charm. Recessed lighting from nine-foot-high ceilings illuminated one single and one double window that retained their original woodwork. Fashionable window treatments and the perfect color palette brought them up to date.

She heard the kids talking as they got near the entrance, so she stepped outside to hold the door for them. "If your shoes are dirty, please take them off; that includes you, Dan," she said eliciting a groan from the boy.

"The kitchen is lovely," Rosie said as Peter and Charlie stepped past her, heading toward the front of the house.

"I think so, too," Erin said as she came back inside. "Now, let's find the bed—"

"This house is brilliant," Peter said, sticking his head through the swinging wooden door to her side.

Erin raised her eyebrows and followed him into the dining room. The original woodwork, including the floors and a large, built-in China cabinet filled with antique dishes and glassware, made her gasp. Two-thirds of the walls were covered by wood paneling with a wide plate rail at the top that held curiosities, like an abalone shell, vintage binoculars, and several unframed paintings.

The windows formed a bay and also had modern window treatments that didn't detract from the old-fashioned elegance of the room. The dining set was painted white, except for the tabletop, which was stained the same rich, walnut hue of the woodwork surrounding it, bringing it all together. "Well, I'm impressed," Erin said. "I can't wait to explore it more, but we need to get settled and be on our way again."

Upstairs, they found two large, spacious bedrooms and one smaller, cozy one, which Peter claimed. Once everyone and everything was sorted, they met in the kitchen. "Okay, now I know we're in a bit of a rush, but there should always be time for a slice of pie," Erin said. She delegated the tasks of finding plates, silverware, and napkins to the kids while she cut the pie into generous slices.

"We don't know exactly when the food will be served at this… event, so I think it's a good idea to put a little something into our bellies before we get there, don't you agree, David?" She handed him the first slice, cherries falling away from the flaky crust.

"I'll not argue over pie, ma love," he said and took a good-sized bite. "Ma Losh, where has this been all ma life! Ach, et's fantastic!"

Each child commented on how good it was as they began eating. Many years of memories washed over Erin then, and she felt a bit melancholy as she joined her new family at the sink to rinse off her plate. She pushed the memories behind her, and soon they were headed back out to the SUV.

Chapter Eighteen

THE FISHER'S FISH BOIL

Erin followed the map on her phone, and fifteen minutes later, they turned onto a gravel driveway, just past a white wooden shed, and parked next to the last car in line on the lawn. White smoke rose from the other side of the petite, old, white cottage with dark green trim. They got out of the vehicle, but the kids stayed close to Erin as if they were afraid of something.

"What is it? There aren't any vampires or werewolves here... at least, I doubt there are," she said as she opened the back. She grabbed the twelve-pack of Pabst Blue Ribbon cans, then handed the expensive bottle of chardonnay to David with a grin. They shrugged but didn't answer her.

As they walked up the short driveway, they heard people laughing and talking easily with each other. There were also children screaming and running around, playing in the yard. At the house, Erin didn't see their hosts, so she felt a bit awkward until Emily came out of the cottage carrying a pitcher of what appeared to be lemonade.

Her eyes nearly closed shut with the large smile she gave them. "Welcome to the cottage! I'm sorry, but I don't remember your names; was it Dan and Ellen?" she asked and continued walking toward a long picnic table that had a navy blue, oiled canvas tablecloth covering it.

"Close, I'm Erin, and this is David."

"I'm sorry, dear, I'm not so good with names. I'll remember faces for years, but Harry's the one who's good with names. Where is he?" Emily said and hurried off, presumably to find her lost husband, leaving her guests to stand awkwardly once again.

They heard a woman's laughter and turned to see a tall, slender woman in her mid-thirties coming toward them. She had long legs, and her dishwater-blonde hair was pulled back in a ponytail that swayed as she walked. "Sorry about Mom," she said. "She rarely stops moving. I'm Mary Ann Bracker, one of her *many* children."

"Hello, Mary Ann, I'm Erin, this is David, and these are our children, Peter, Charlie, Dan, and Rosie," she said and knew she'd get tired of saying that over and over.

"We should find you name tags, with how many times you're gonna have to repeat that!" Mary Ann said with a friendly smile.

"You read my mind!" Erin said. "We brought refreshments. I'd give them to your parents, but they seem to be MIA at the moment." She handed her the twelve-pack, and David held up the wine.

"Well, I think you two are gonna fit right in." She took the beer and motioned for them to follow her. "I have four daughters myself, though only three are playing right now. Pam, my youngest, is napping. Linda, Karen, and Jill are around here somewhere." Three boys came running around the side of the house and nearly ran right into them, swerving out of the way just in time. "Paul, Ed, Dave, you should look where you're going!" she yelled.

"I know, Aunt Mary Ann… Sorry!" the tallest one said and then disappeared.

"Boys!" she said and laughed.

Erin could see Dan chomping at the bit, wanting to be let loose and run around with them, but she knew he was waiting for them to say it was okay. "Yes, I'm just learning about that," she said and smiled at the children.

"Dad! Mom was looking for you," Mary Ann said to Harry as they approached him.

"Well, I guess she'll find me eventually," he said and turned to greet the newcomers. He shook David's hand and then Erin's. "Welcome! I'm glad you could make it. Make yourselves at home."

"They brought beer and wine; my kind of people!" Mary Ann said and set the Pabst on the bench seat of the picnic table. "Help yourselves to beer and pop in the coolers over there." She pointed to a row of four large blue coolers near the back door. "I'm gonna take these inside to the fridge and find a corkscrew for that wine!"

Three slender, blonde-haired girls, who appeared to be about eight, nine, and ten, ran past them, laughing and nudging each other as they gave furtive looks at Charlie and Daniel.

"Girls! Come and be friendly with this little English girl!" Harry said.

They stopped and turned to see who he was talking about. There was an awkward silence as the kids stared at each other. "This is Rosie," Erin said, trying to help.

The tallest girl took a step forward. "Hi, I'm Linda, and these are my sisters, Karen, and Jill. We were gonna head to the dock and catch some fish. Wanna come with?" she said, and her sisters nodded shyly.

Rosie looked at her dad, then at Erin, and finally at Charlie. David nodded at her, and Charlie shrugged. "Alright, I've never caught fishes before!"

"Oh, it's easy, and I'll put the worm on the hook for you if you're too squeamish, like Karen." She gave her sister a look and held out her hand for Rosie to take.

They were only a few feet away when Rosie pulled her hand away and turned back to her family. She looked at the girls who'd stopped, waiting to find out what was happening. "May my brother, Charlie come along as well?" she asked, and the boy's face lit up.

The girls looked at each other and shrugged. "I don't care," Linda said and started running away from the lake toward the road.

Rosie and Charlie ran with the girls down the driveway to a white wooden shed painted to match the house. Linda took the unlocked padlock off the latch, and the hinges groaned when she opened the door. The smell of fuel and rusted metal greeted them as she flipped a switch, and a dim lightbulb illuminated the inside. They saw a riding lawnmower, garden tools like shovels and rakes, and several long bamboo poles the girls headed toward.

Charlie followed them and was handed a small metal coffee can with a plastic lid. Rosie looked up and noticed a long chain strung from one end of the rafters to the other in a drooping zigzag pattern. It was made from what looked like hundreds of little metal things folded through each other, though she didn't know what they were. "What is that?" she asked, and Linda, who was carrying two poles, came up next to her and looked up.

"Those are old beer tabs, I think. My dad told me beer cans used to have tabs that you'd pull to open them. The adults started making that chain a *really* long time ago, like in the olden days!"

"Wow! I think it's very nice," Rosie said, and the girls giggled.

"I like your accent," Karen said quietly.

"I like yours as well. You sound like my daddy's frenchaé."

"Frenchaé? What's that?" Jill asked.

"She means fiancée," Charlie said.

"Oh! That woman wasn't your mom? I thought she was," Linda said. She lifted the poles again and turned off the light. "Let's go."

"No, not yet, but I already call her mummy," Rosie answered and held Charlie's hand as they headed toward the house again.

"Are your real parents divorced?" Karen asked.

"No, my real mummy died, but Erin is very nice, and we love her a lot, don't we, Charlie?"

"Yeah, she's wicked!" Charlie said.

"Wicked is bad, isn't it?" Karen asked.

"Blimey, it isn't bad to us. She's cracking, and we have a brilliant time with her." He looked at Rosie as if asking her to back him up.

"Yeah, she's loads of fun."

They were near their dad and Erin when the group of boys came running back around the house, yelling and laughing. "Hey! Watch it, Paul!" Linda said to one of them. The tallest boy turned to her, and Rosie thought she saw him raise his middle finger at her, but she wasn't sure.

———

"Go on, Dan, you may join them as long as you behave yourself," David said, and the boy nearly squealed with joy as he ran away.

"Oi! Wait up!" he said as naturally as if he'd known them for ages.

"Daddy! We're going to go fishing!" Rosie said excitedly.

"A'right then, have fun," he said and watched his son and daughter follow the girls to the pier that jutted into the dark blue water.

"May I have a drink, Dad?" Peter asked. "And may I walk down to the beach, please?"

"You can do whatever you want, my boy. Can you swim?" Harry said as he was passing by.

"Yes sir, I can swim." Peter looked at David, who nodded and smiled at Erin as the young man gave him a joyful smile.

"He looks just like you, David. A strapping young boy he is, too, and so polite! It's a rare thing in a child nowadays. Back when I was a kid, I'd have been horsewhipped if I'd behaved the way these youngsters do now!" Harry said, and they followed him as he began walking toward a large metal barrel placed on a sturdy stand over a blazing fire. "Stan?"

"Yeah, Dad?" a balding, thirty-something man with a cigarette, a can of beer, and a gap in his front teeth answered from his lawn chair.

"Are the potatoes ready to go?" he asked.

"Ask Mom," he said, but Harry gave him a stern look, so he huffed and walked away, apparently in search of either his mother or the potatoes.

"Gotta keep those boys on their toes!" he said and smiled at Erin. "Dick! Come meet these nice English folks from London!"

Erin smiled at David, who took the outstretched hand of a man of medium height and build, whose hair was dark brown on the top of his head but light grey on both sides. "Dick Bracker, nice to meet you."

"I'm David, and this is my fiancée Erin," he said, using his received pronunciation accent.

"Glad you could join us. Come and have a seat; do you want a beer?" he said.

"I'm not really into beer, but I'll have a soda," Erin said.

"I'll have one," David said, and they followed Dick to the back of the cottage, where a balding man with dark hair and a long beard was talking to a slender man with lighter, thinning hair and thick glasses.

"The Community Center? That's where I lost my virginity… over by the railroad tracks," the bearded man was saying.

Erin laughed, and so did the man with the glasses. "Hey, Brud, who've you got there?" the bearded man said to Dick and held out his hand.

David shook it, and Dick said, "This is David and Erin."

"Harry Fisher, but everyone calls me Junior."

"They're English," Dick said and then pointed his can of beer toward the man wearing glasses. "This is Ralph Fisher. They're Mary Ann's brothers."

"Oh, so the woman who took the wine and beer into the house was your wife?" Erin said to Dick.

"Sounds like her! You might wanna check that she hasn't downed the whole bottle of wine by herself," Junior said, and Ralph stifled a laugh.

"I was just in the house," Ralph said, and Erin noticed that he also had a gap in his front teeth. "She was sharing it with Betty, Donna, and Judy."

"So, David, what brings you to America?" Dick asked.

Peter had walked down to the pier and was sitting on the part that was over the sandy beach, watching his sister, brother, and the three blonde girls. The taller girl was yelling at a boy who was sitting on the end of it with his feet in the water. "Go home, Teddy! This isn't your pier, and you're scaring all the fish away!" she said with her hands on her hips.

"You're just jealous that my feet can touch the water from here and yours can't!" the boy said, but he got up, and Peter watched as he stomped down the wooden decking toward him. When he got to the beach, he jumped off the pier and stood in front of him with his head cocked to the side.

Peter looked up at the boy, who was probably the same age as him. He had thick glasses and the beginnings of a ginger beard, almost obscuring the acne surrounding his chin. "Hello," he said, wanting to be friendly.

"Teddy," the boy said.

"Peter."

"Girls!" Teddy said and looked down the pier at the girls who were trying to bait their hooks.

"Girls," Peter said and smiled at him.

"I have a rowboat over there," Teddy said and pointed to a short dock next door. "Wanna take it out with me?"

"Oh, well, I'd like that if we stay near the shore, I reckon."

Erin sat next to David in an aluminum folding chair, circa 1970-something, and watched the children having fun. She'd been a bit worried when she saw Peter walk out of the yard with a boy but relaxed when she saw them in a small rowboat a little while later.

"So, David, what do you do for a living?" Dick asked. David opened his mouth to answer, but a commotion near the driveway grabbed everyone's attention.

Erin heard an oddly familiar sound and searched her Rolodex of memories, trying to figure out what it was. The boys from earlier came running through the yard along with Daniel, who was clearly giddy with excitement as he ran up to her. "Come with us! You'll never believe it—" he began, but then Erin realized what it was.

"Lightsabers!" she said and stood, allowing him to pull her by the hand. David wasn't far behind them, and as they rounded the corner of the cottage, she saw two men having a choreographed lightsaber battle. "Too bad Peter, Charlie, and Rosie are missing this!"

"Here I am, Mum," Charlie said and stood beside her while Daniel sat on the grass, watching intently. "Blimey, that's brilliant!"

"I thought you were fishing?" David said.

"I was, but I needed a wee," Charlie said.

"I used to know… wait, is that John Hartley? I think I know him," Erin said. "The other guy, I'm not sure."

The show lasted a few more minutes and ended with much applause and cheering. The two men bowed, then the second one apologized and said he had to leave right away. The man Erin thought she knew shook his hand and thanked him for coming along. When he turned to the crowd, he saw her and pointed, then he seemed to notice David, and his eyes grew wide in recognition.

Erin approached him and accepted a hug. "What are *you* doing here?" she asked.

"I were invited, though I might say the same for you," he said with his thick Sheffield accent and then turned to David. "And you as well, mate! What're ya doin' wi' the likes of her, then?" He nodded his head in Erin's direction.

David flashed him an angry look, but Erin laughed. "I could say the same for your wife!" she said.

John shrugged. "Fair enough," he said. "It were me mate, Nick's nephew's birthday party this mornin'. He promised him a show, so we gave 'im a good un!"

"That was nice of you," she said and took David's arm. "This is my fiancé, David."

"Hiya, David! Didn't much like *Houlihan's Flat*, but nearly shit meself at the end of *Lost in Vengeance*!"

"Well, thanks for that," David said and looked around them. "About that, mate, I'd rather keep ma profession quiet, if you don't mind?"

"Yeah, we'd like to be treated like normal people while we're here," Erin said and then waited for his sarcastic reply.

"Normal people? Don't think I know any *normal* people, but a'right; I'll say nowt ta anyone."

"Cheers, mate," David said, looking relieved. Charlie gently nudged his arm, and he smiled at him. "This is my son, Charlie, and… Dan, don't touch!"

Daniel had just reached out his hand toward John's holstered lightsaber but drew it quickly back when he was called out. "Sorry," the boy said.

Peter and Teddy unhooked the small orange rowboat from the dock. Teddy held Peter's hand as he got in and laughed as Peter held his arms out, trying to find his 'sea legs.' "Just sit down already!" Teddy said. "I'll wait till you're settled." Finally, he managed to sit without tipping the thing over.

They rowed around for a while, watching the kids on the Fishers' pier. Peter loved the weightless feeling of the boat gliding over the water. The sound of splashing that the oars made and the slight creaking of the wood began to make him a bit sleepy. Suddenly, he felt cold water hit him on his arm and chest. "Oi!" he said as he opened his eyes.

Teddy laughed and splashed him again. "Looked like you were sleeping. I had to wake you somehow," he said and was about to reach his hand into the water again, but Peter grabbed it and managed to put his other hand over the side, coming up with a drenching deluge that soaked himself as well as Teddy. "Hey, that's not fair! I just barely got you!"

Peter was laughing so hard that he snorted, which made him laugh even harder. "Sorry, I didn't know it would be that much!" he said, still holding the other boy's wrist, afraid he would try again.

"Let go! I have to row," Teddy said, so Peter reluctantly released him. The boy acted as though he was going to splash him again but then laughed and took hold of the oar. "Where are you from?" he asked after a few moments of companionable silence.

"London, how about you?"

"Milwaukee. My grandparents own this place, and we come up for a few weeks every summer. It's pretty boring after the first week. The internet sucks ass, and there's no one to hang out with."

"Are you an only child?" Peter asked.

"Yeah… well, actually, I have two older brothers and a sister, but they're adults and have their own families. My parents had me late in life; I was an accident, they tell me. I don't think they wanted me. Actually, I *know* they didn't, but whatever," he said and shrugged.

"My mum told me and my siblings she didn't want us as well and that she'd only gotten pregnant to keep my father home… he… travels for his job," Peter said, not wanting to explain that his dad was an actor. They were comfortable together, though he knew as soon as Teddy learned his dad was famous, he'd begin to act differently. The silence resumed, and they sat, essentially rowing in a large circle. After a while, Peter could feel the sun burning him where he sat. Neither of them had put sunscreen on, so he suggested they go back. "I also don't want my parents to worry about me."

"Will they? They probably don't even know you're gone if they didn't want you," he said and glanced at the Fishers' yard.

"Oh, well, my dad wanted me, and Erin's not my birth mum; she's my dad's partner. She's brilliant, actually."

"Well then, we should get back if that's the case," he said callously and began rowing the boat toward his family's dock.

"What are you sore about? You seem upset," Peter said, sensing a change in mood.

Teddy didn't say anything; he just kept rowing until they got to the pier. He pulled the oars into the boat, wrapped the rope carelessly around one of the wooden pilings, then heaved himself out effortlessly. "Come on," he said, sounding impatient.

Peter stood, feeling uneasy, both in his mind and body, as the small craft bobbed and rocked. Teddy held out his hand and helped him crawl up onto the wooden boards and then to standing. He was about to turn away when Teddy reached up and kissed him on the lips. Peter was stunned and took a step back, quickly scanning the beaches to see if anyone was watching. "What did you do that for?" he said, resisting the urge to get angry.

"Dunno," the boy said and shrugged. "Want me to do it again?" He sounded hopeful and stepped up to him once more.

"No, I don't. I'm not gay. I'm sorry if I somehow gave you the wrong idea, but—"

"Don't worry about it." Teddy gave him a short nod and shrugged again. He tied the rope onto the piling properly then stood, not looking at Peter. "Well, bye," he said and walked away toward his cottage, leaving Peter alone.

Still reeling, he walked back to the fish boil, telling himself that he would *never* tell *anyone* what had happened *ever*. He saw Erin turn and scan the water as he approached her. "I'm back," he said quietly.

She wrapped her arm around his waist and gave him a quick squeeze as she let out a relieved breath. "I'm so glad! I was worried about you. I know it's silly, but I just want you to be safe. Did you have fun?" she said.

He smiled, knowing she really did love and want him. "Yeah," he said and returned her sideways hug.

"You missed all the excitement," she said, and he raised his eyebrows.

"Really? What'd I miss?"

"Only an epic lightsaber battle!"

That was the very last thing he'd imagined she'd say. He stood, staring at her with his mouth open, trying to process what that meant. "Huh?" he managed.

Erin laughed and took his hand. "I'd like you to meet my friend, John," she said and pulled him over to the coolers. "He was in one of the Star Wars charity costume clubs we hung out with."

"You were serious?"

They stopped in front of a tall man of about fifty with a messy mop of greying-brown hair. He was in a conversation with someone, so they stood to the side, waiting to speak to him. "Thanks, mate, I will," he said to the man and then turned to them. "Oi! I'd know you anywhere! You're the spittin' image of your father."

He reached out his hand, and Peter took it, utterly confused at his northern English accent. He looked at Erin, who laughed again and nudged him gently. "Peter, I'd like you to meet John Hartley," she said and leaned closer, saying in a loud whisper, "of Sheffield. He's Jedi, of course." She pointed to the silver and copper colored lightsaber hanging on his belt. "This is my... well, soon-to-be son, Peter."

"Pleased to meet you, Mr. Hartley," Peter said, feeling completely gobsmacked.

"Mr. Hartley were me father. I'm John," he said and smiled.

"He missed the show earlier," Erin said.

"Right," he said and took a look around him. "I'll teach you a few moves if you'd—"

"I would!" Peter said, excited and unable to hide his grin.

"Mummy, Mummy! Look what I've caught!" Rosie said as she ran up to them, holding out a good-sized fish in both hands. "Linda helped me put the worm on the hook, and then she took the fish off the hook for me. Karen let hers fall off her hook, but I wanted to keep mine! Look, Peter!"

"Well don—" Peter began.

"Where's Daddy?" she interrupted and ran off before anyone could say anything else.

"Teach a girl to fish..." Erin said as they watched her searching for her dad.

David stepped out of the screen porch door, near where they were standing. He looked in the direction they were looking and then turned to Erin. "What're yeh lookin' at?" he said, dropping his RP accent.

"Our daughter has caught her first fish and is searching for you," she said, and gently pushed him forward.

She turned to say something to John, but he was gone. "Where's—" she began, and a few moments later saw him coming toward them carrying two beat-up lightsabers. He handed one to Peter, but Erin wanted David to see, so she put her finger up. "Just wait a minute, please. I want to find your dad."

She went around the house and saw him speaking to Rosie, who was very animated, waving the fish around as she talked with her hands. "Well done, you, Rosebud," she heard him say.

"David! Come watch this, please," she said, and he turned to her. "Tell Rosie to come too."

They followed her back to where John and Peter were standing. Charlie and Dan had joined them and were sitting on the grass, watching excitedly. John said something Erin couldn't hear; he then nudged Peter, and the boy laughed. "Oi, Mum, get a move on," Peter said.

"Keep your *pants* on, you two!" she said.

"Weren't plannin' on takin' em off," John said, giving Peter the giggles.

"You know what I meant… don't get your knickers in a bunch!"

"She's obsessed wi' our knickers, mate!" John said to Peter.

"Eww!" Rosie said, making Peter laugh even harder.

"Okay, okay, you may begin," Erin said once she'd moved the lawn chairs into the shade and opened the video camera on her phone.

"Are you right-handed?" John asked Peter.

"Yes."

"A'right, right hand on the top and left hand underneath. Stand wi' yer left foot forward, bend your knees, and hold yer saber up by yer ears." John said, demonstrating everything as he went. "Then what yer gonna do; you're gonna step forward with your right foot. As you do that, yer gonna cut down, like this." John lowered the 'blade' toward Peter's left side, then waited for him to do what he'd just shown him.

"Like that?"

"Aye, now to block it, I'll step to me side… catch it in that position… when I've caught it up high, like that, with me sword straight, then I'll rotate it 'round and cut to your head, there…"

Erin watched as John led Peter in a bit of sword-play, breaking it down to make it simple for him. They went through a few moves until he became quicker and more comfortable, which didn't take long. She recorded it all and applauded with everyone who'd gathered for the lesson until they heard an ear-piercing whistle. Mary Ann then yelled, "Come and eat!"

Children and adults came from all corners of the property, laughing and talking, but they didn't find seats; instead, they all assembled around the huge barrel, standing a good distance away from it. "What're they doing?" Charlie asked.

Just then, one of the men threw something onto the fire, and the flames rose high up the sides of the makeshift pot. Everyone either took a step back or shielded their faces because of the sudden blast of heat. It only took a few moments for the water to boil up and begin pouring over the sides. "The boil-over gets rid of the oil floating on the top; makes everything taste better," Harry said from behind Erin.

"Goh! That was smashing! Do it again!" Daniel said, bouncing on his toes. "How'd ya do it, anyway?"

"Can't do it again, son. Just before it's time for the boil-over, we fill a few water balloons with kerosene and throw them onto the fire. Nifty, huh?" Harry said with a boyish grin.

"May we do that at home, Dad?" the boy asked, his smile showing off his dimples.

David laughed and put his hand on his son's shoulder. "I'm afraid not, Dan. I reckon et wouldn't be appreciated by our neighbors or the police."

Dan's face fell for all of about three seconds until he saw someone taking out the basket of grey and white fish. He ran up to the fire and followed the man to the picnic table, where the basket was set on a large platter. Back and forth, he shadowed the man as he brought a total of three baskets to the table. "Daniel!" David called out, and the boy looked over his shoulder.

"What?"

"Come here and wait," he said.

Dan looked up at the man who'd carried the baskets. The man smiled at him, and Erin heard Dan say, "I'll be back!" He then ran to where his family was standing and stood in front of his dad.

"Kids go first," Harry said. "Grab a plate and stand in line."

The children looked up at their father, and he turned to Erin. "Well, go on then, but be polite," she said and leaned on David while they watched them take a plate, fork, and napkin off the table and then stand with their new friends, laughing and talking.

When the children were done filling their plates, they found places to sit on the grass, and then it was the adults' turn to line up. Peter decided to eat with the adults since there wasn't anyone else there his age, so he waited next to Erin and David.

Harry gently pushed Erin forward as everyone began to line up. "Don't be shy, now! There's plenty to go around."

She and David joined the queue, followed by Peter. In all honesty, the fish didn't look very appetizing, but she took a chunk of it anyway. Next, she added a small pile of boiled potatoes, short chunks of corn on the cob, and coleslaw. Mary Ann was on the other side of the table, filling her plate, and startled her by plopping a hefty glob of yellow butter on top of the fish. "Uh, thank you," Erin said.

"Trust me, it tastes much better drowned in butter," she said and winked.

David and Peter were also given copious amounts of butter before they headed to a nearby table. "I've never really liked fish, David," Erin whispered, and Peter raised his eyebrows.

"I've not had boiled fish before now, though I reckon it can't be much different, right?" the boy said, looking down at the slab of white-fleshed fish covered in grey skin. He peeled back a bit of the skin, poked his fork into it, and gasped, "Oh, my days! There're bones in it still!"

"Great," Erin said sarcastically and poked a small chunk of potato with her fork, rolled it around in the butter, then sprinkled it with salt. She took a bite and sighed with relief. "The potatoes are good."

Peter took a bite of the fish, and though he didn't say anything negative, his face betrayed the fact that he didn't care much for it. "Well, what do you think, son?" Harry said from behind them.

Mouth full, the young man gave him the thumbs up and tried to smile. "Mmm," he managed to hum.

"And what about you, Erin, David?" he said, and it seemed to Erin that he was trying to hold back a laugh.

"Haven't tried it yet. I'm sure it'll be lovely," David said, though *his* face betrayed his misgivings.

Harry laughed and patted him on the shoulder. "It's an acquired taste, I suppose. When in doubt, add more butter; makes it go down easier," he said and then walked away.

"O-kay… we'll keep that in mind," Erin said, suddenly dreading the thought of eating it. Bravely, she speared a piece with her fork, checked for bones, dipped it into the semi-melted butter, and closed her eyes.

"Wait," David said, and she looked at him, hoping he'd found a reason why she wouldn't have to put it into her mouth. Instead, he was holding the saltshaker. "Here, darling, I'm sure it'll help."

"Thanks," she said and took a bite. It was very bland and a bit fishy, though the butter and salt did help make it taste better. "Eh, it's not really my thing, but I'll eat as much as I can." Her plan was to eat the fish as quickly as possible to get past it, then focus on the potatoes and corn.

"Ach, et's not so bad. I rather like it," David said.

"Humph, that's just your bland British tastebuds talking," Erin said and laughed at the look on Peter's face.

"Are you staying for the fireworks?" Erin heard over her shoulder. Turning to see who it was, she saw Dick standing there smiling.

"Fireworks!" Dan said, bouncing on his seat, much to the annoyance of Rosie and Charlie who were sitting next to him.

"Dan! Stop!" Rosie complained.

Erin looked at David, wanting to know his thoughts. "I'm—" she began.

"Oi, David," John Hartley said as he approached the table, interrupting her. "I've a question about *Future*—"

David stood suddenly. "No, I don't believe we'll be staying," he said, cutting him off.

"But, Dad!" Dan said, sounding disappointed.

"Oh, I forgot, sorry," John said. "I weren't speakin' to anyone here about it. It were me wife; she wanted to know… had a question."

"Come with me," David said and left the table, leading John several feet away.

"What was that about?" Dick asked with his eyebrows raised.

"He's just—" Erin began.

"Our dad's famous and didn't want you to know who he is, but if we're not staying, then it doesn't matter, does it?" Dan said and crossed his arms petulantly.

"Dan!" Peter barked and took him by the earlobe, making the boy cry out.

"Oww! Stop!"

"Famous, huh? What's he famous for?" Dick asked.

"I'll let him tell you," Erin said with a sigh, knowing he'd be upset.

"Meh, I don't really care that much. It doesn't seem like he wants anyone to know, so I won't let on," Dick said with a wink.

"Thanks," she said and heard a notification from David's cell phone. She watched as he finished his conversation with John, both men laughing as they parted.

"Was that my mobile?" he asked, and she nodded as she handed it to him. He unlocked the screen and groaned.

"What is it?"

"It's nothing of importance," he said and locked the screen again. He turned to his children. "If you're finished eating, you should run along and play with your mates. I reckon we can stay for the fireworks." Dan whooped, and his siblings followed him as he dashed across the lawn. David smiled at Dick and shrugged. "I reckon who I am will come out eventually; it usually does."

"Don't worry, if anyone finds out, it won't be because I told them," Dick said and walked away, having heard someone calling his name.

Now that they were alone, David turned to Erin and sighed. "That was a message from Martin. I've not read it, but I'm sure et's to do with the money I promised. I'll not be giving et to him, though I fear the retribution. Please assure me it'll be alright and that there's nothing to fear," he said and lifted her hand to kiss it.

"I wish I could, but I'm not sure of that myself. All I know is that he can't do anything now. We're thousands of miles away from him, so I guess we can deal with it later, right?"

"Aye, I reckon you're right," he said. "I need a wee, and I can't eat any more of this." He pointed to his plate and then looked cautiously around to check if anyone was watching them.

"I feel bad, but I can't either."

There was a trash can a few feet away, so he swiftly gathered their plates and tossed them into it. "That's that, sorted."

"Well done, you, now let's take a walk to the beach."

Erin could see Rosie and Charlie kneeling beside the trio of young, blonde girls. They were talking and sifting sand through their fingers. Peter was sitting on the end of the pier, leaning back on his hands, his feet dangling in the water. His shoes and socks were next to him, and he seemed content, alone with his thoughts. Dan was nowhere to be seen.

When she and David reached the short, narrow strip of beach, they slipped off their shoes and socks and stepped into the warm, cream-colored sand. "Daddy! Mummy!" Rosie exclaimed and ran toward them, smiling.

"Hello, Rosebud, are yeh havin' a good time?" David asked.

"Oh, yes, Daddy! I like it here very much," she said, and then Charlie joined them.

"How about you, Charlie," Erin said. "Are you having a good time?"

The boy smiled and nodded, then he frowned and began looking for something or someone in the yard behind them. "Yes, I am, but I think…

perhaps… you should find Dan. He was here a few minutes ago, and I heard him telling those boys that you are a famous actor, Dad. He was bragging that you were on the telly and in adverts all over London. Peter tried to grab him, but he ran away before he was caught."

"Ach, well, I reckon et's too late to do much now, but I'll try to find him," David said and slipped his socks and shoes back on.

"I'll stay here for now," Erin said, and David kissed her forehead before walking back toward the house. Rosie and Charlie went back to their new friends, so she stepped up onto the pier and sat next to Peter. "Beautiful afternoon, isn't it?"

"Mmm hmm, it is. It's so quiet here… well, except when Dan is nearby," he said and smiled at her. "It reminds me of the cottage in Scotland, though less windy."

"Yeah, I can see how it might," Erin said and took a deep breath of the clean air.

"Dad used to bring us there when we were younger. There's a hillock overlooking the loch that takes my breath away every time I see it. I've never actually told anyone about that, and I don't know what made me think of it, except I once dreamed I was sitting like this on the loch. A large fish came right up to me, looked me in the eye, and then swam away. I used to try to get to the loch without telling anyone, which I reckon wasn't smart, but I wanted to see the fish. I just knew it was there, waiting for me to come to it. It was too far away, and I never did get there."

"I know the exact spot you mean. When I was there, it made my heart hurt, it was so beautiful. I was trying to get to the loch, as well, when the cottage burned down. Your dad didn't know I'd left and thought I was still inside. I guess I wasn't very smart either." She leaned her head on the teen's shoulder and enjoyed the quietness, broken occasionally by someone laughing loudly or the kids on the beach talking.

They sat like that for a few minutes until she thought she heard him sniffle. She felt him move his free arm up to his face and sniffled again. "Bloody—" he began, and she sat up to look at him.

"What's wrong, Peter?"

He sat forward and covered his face with his hands. It took him a moment to speak, and she saw him shiver. "Oh, Mum! I wasn't going to tell anyone, but I can't keep it inside any longer." He glanced at the small pier and orange boat of the neighbors, then he shook his head and arms as if trying to get rid of a bad thought.

"What happened? Seems like it was pretty bad."

"There was another boy; his name was Teddy," he said very quietly.

"The one you went out on the lake with… in the boat?" she asked.

"Yeah, him. He was a nice enough lad, but… but when we returned to the pier… he… he kissed me! I didn't want him to, but he caught me off my guard. I didn't like it or anything, but I can't get it out of my head. I just want it to go away!" He began rocking back and forth while biting his nails. She saw another shiver run through him and touched his shoulder.

"Oh, Peter, that must've been a real shock," she began.

"Yes, and it was disgusting! I wish I'd punched him, but instead, I told him I wasn't gay and apologized for maybe giving him the wrong impression! Why'd I apologize to *him*? I feel violated every time I think about it. How do I get the memory out of my head?"

Erin looked up and saw David coming closer, so she put her hand up to say 'stop' and shook her head slightly. He nodded and went to talk to the kids on the beach. "I'm not sure I have a good answer. I've… been in a similar situation, and I also didn't know how to stop the memories from… what felt like attacking me."

Peter looked at her, frowning. "Someone violated you? When? What happened?" he said and then shook his head. "Oh, that's private. I'm sorry."

"It doesn't really matter when or what happened; the thing is, I understand how that feels. The only thing I can suggest is to talk about it with someone you trust… thank you, by the way." She smiled at him, and he nodded. "Put other things in its place. Don't sit and dwell on it. Find something to do that will add good, happy memories to your mind, and hopefully, the bad ones will get pushed out. At least they won't feel as bad once some time has passed."

"Thank you for listening to me. I'd planned to forget about it and pretend it didn't happen, but it wasn't working. It felt like no one would understand…

no one except you, Erin. You always seem to understand, and if you don't, you at least try to make me feel better."

"I'm so glad I'm able to help you, Peter. I hope you're always able to come to me. Listen, I know it might seem difficult, but I think you should talk to your dad. I believe he might know a thing or two about being violated."

"Really?"

"Do you think he wanted that woman to kiss him at the funeral? I know he didn't, and not only did it gross him out, but he knew he'd have to tell me about it. That must've been stressful. Then, to find out you'd seen the lipstick on his face... and that there were photos in every tabloid! I'm sure he was worried that people believed what they printed about him."

"Yeah, I reckon he does understand to some degree, but it was a boy, Erin!"

"Ach, an unwelcomed kiss is unwelcomed, no matter who does it," she said and patted his hand.

"I reckon so. Thanks for that."

"You're welcome, now, let's go make some of those good memories I mentioned."

The rest of the evening was spent playing and getting to know some of their hosts a bit better. They learned that the whole family took off work that week every year. It had become a tradition. At dusk, Dick and one of the other men took a wheelbarrow out to the end of the pier and set up a makeshift firework launching pad using old ceramic tiles and two metal tubes, each welded to a small base.

Everyone found a chair or sat on the grass, waiting for the show to start. Erin and David sat on a detached picnic table bench someone had set on the lawn. In the darkness, they heard a *whoosh* as a small spark was seen flying up into the sky. Then, *bang*, white sparkles burst out in all directions, making a sparkling noise. "Oooh, ahhh," Erin said, joining everyone around her. "Those are my favorites!"

The next one was three bright flashes, followed by loud *bangs*. "I like those best," Daniel said, bouncing excitedly as he sat cross-legged on a beach towel.

"I hate those!" Erin said passionately, which Dan must've thought hilarious because he began giggling.

David put his arm around her shoulders and squeezed gently. She put her head on his shoulder and sighed. "This is nice," she said.

"Aye."

The fireworks didn't last long, and then it was time to say goodbye. There was lots of hugging and handshaking before they were finally in the SUV and on the road again.

It was almost eleven when they finally got back to the rental house. Everyone except Erin and Peter, were fast asleep when she parked in the narrow driveway and turned off the engine. She touched David's arm, and he woke with a snort, which made Peter laugh. "Nice one, Dad," he whispered.

David was still a bit out of it and coughed lightly. "Are... we there... already?" he mumbled.

"Yes, darling. Please help me with the children," she said and smiled at him, then at Peter.

They were a grumpy bunch as they were pushed and prodded into the strange, unfamiliar house. Rosie was whiny, Dan was moody, and it seemed as though Charlie was sleepwalking as they stumbled through the kitchen and then up the grand staircase to their rooms. No one wanted to fight with them to get their clothes off, so they were allowed to sleep in what they had on, except for shoes, which were kicked or pulled off unceremoniously at the side of each bed.

"I'm knackered, but I had a good time today," Peter said and gave Erin a hug.

"Me too, and me too. Goodnight," she said.

"Night, Dad," the boy said to David, who was still a bit out of it.

"Night. Where's our bed?" he said to Erin, sounding a bit drunk.

"Follow me," she said and pulled him by the hand into their room.

182

Chapter Nineteen

CURRENT EXPLORATIONS

Erin was up early in the morning and began a list of places she wanted to take her new family. By the time David was up, she had a good-sized list, and as the children joined them at the breakfast table, it was already two pages long. "I think we should spend the morning here in Ephraim, exploring. We can have lunch at Wilson's, then we should hang out in Fish Creek," she said once the kids were seated with their cereal bowls full.

"You want us to wade in a creek all day? That doesn't sound like much fun," Daniel said and stuffed his face full of Lucky Charms.

"Actually, I think we *could* make a good time of it, but that's not what I meant. Fish Creek is the town where we ate lunch yesterday. There's a large park with trails. We can rent bikes and explore it."

"Sounds boring to me," Dan said.

"Hush, Dan," David said.

"There's an observation tower that's like fifty feet high. I'm sure you'd love to climb that and—"

"Fine then, we can go there," he interrupted.

"I'm glad you approve," Erin said and rolled her eyes at David. "There's also an ice cream shop, and we can find out what's playing at the drive-in; it's always a double feature."

"What's a drive-in, Mummy?" Rosie said.

"It's an outdoor movie theater," Erin said.

"Do you mean the cinema?" Dan asked.

"Yes, Dan," she said and rolled her eyes again. "Now, let's finish breakfast and get ready to go."

Once the dishes were washed, the children ran upstairs to get dressed. David was helping Erin dry and put them away when they heard a commotion, then Charlie was at the kitchen doorway, panting from his rush to get to them. "Rosie's been sick in the toilet," he said.

"Oh, no! Okay, Charlie, thanks. I'll be up there in a moment," she said, bracing herself to deal with a sick child. They could hear Rosie being sick and crying as they came up the stairs. Daniel was pacing the hall with his fingers in his ears, clearly not wanting to hear his sister.

"Go downstairs, Dan," David said, and the boy ran past them. Soon, Charlie and Peter followed, looking a bit green themselves.

"Okay, baby girl," Erin said as she entered the bathroom. "It'll be okay."

"Mummy! I'm sor—" the girl said between her sobs and retching.

"There's nothing to be sorry about, baby," Erin said and turned to David. "You and the boys should go explore the town. I'll stay here with Rosie."

"Are you sure? We can stay here," he said.

"I'm sure. Go, have fun with them. There's a big barn by the waterfront. I think it's a gallery too, but it's tradition to write your name on it, like graffiti. I think there's a place to rent kayaks and stuff nearby, too. Then, there's Wilson's, it's a diner and ice cream parlor, and the Red Putter has mini golf. Make sure to get a photo of everyone in the huge rocking chair. I'll send a message when things are back to normal here, okay?"

David looked at her and frowned. "I reckon it's better than sitting around here, but I'd rather you were with us," he said sadly.

"I know, but you should go now, it's getting late. Oh, and make sure you bring your hat and glasses… and keep that smile of yours under wraps or you'll be stuck signing autographs all morning," she said and gave him a peck on the cheek.

Soon, Rosie was in bed with a small plastic garbage can nearby, just in case. Erin found a book and read a few chapters out loud to her until she fell asleep, then she messaged David and went downstairs to work on a seaside village puzzle she found in a cupboard. A few hours later, she had just finished connecting the edge pieces when she heard David and the boys at the door.

Daniel came bounding into the house singing "Earl Had to Die" by the Dixie Chicks at the top of his voice. She went to the kitchen and put her finger to her lips. "Shh, Dan, Rosie's sleeping," she said and accepted the quick hug he offered as Charlie, David, and Peter came in behind him. "Well, it seems like you had a good time. Tell me all about—"

"I wrote my name on an old barn, and Peter won at mini golf. We ate lunch at a bangin' spot and shared a sundae the size of my head!" Dan said as he bounced around the room, Tigger style.

"Perhaps a bit too much ice cream," Erin said and received a kiss from David.

"How's Rosie?" he asked.

"She's fine now. I think she just ate her breakfast too fast. She's been asleep this whole time."

"I'll go check on her." He left the room, and Erin smiled at the boys.

"Did you have fun, too?" she asked Peter and Charlie.

Charlie gave her a hug that lasted quite a while and said, "Yes, Mum! It was smashing! I had a hot dog and so much ice cream I thought I'd burst!"

"Glad to hear it! How about you, Peter?"

"I had a brilliant morning," he said with a grin. "I won at mini golf, and we sat in the chair, as you said, and a stranger took our photo. The only things missing were you and Rosie."

"Aww, you're so sweet," she said and hugged him tightly.

"Look who I found," David said, following his daughter into the kitchen.

"Hello, Rosebud, how do you feel?" she asked and felt the girl's forehead with the back of her hand, checking for a fever.

"Much better now," she said softly. "I'm hungry."

"Okay, good. I'll make you some toast. Best to start small in case you feel sick again, okay?" Erin said.

"Okay, Mummy."

"So, what shall we do with the rest of our day?" she asked while opening the bread bag.

"We could wade in the creek, as you said earlier," Dan said as he spun in circles, making himself dizzy and then falling when he stopped.

"It's not a creek, silly boy, it's a… never mind. Please stop doing that, Dan, this room is too small. Go out to the front room, but be careful not to break—"

"A'right, Erin, but I've changed my mind," he said, his smile revealing his dimples.

"Have you, now?" David said as they waited for the punchline.

"Yes, Dad, I think it would be fun to mess about in a creek, especially if it's a wide one that's flowing fast! We'd have to hold on to each other in order not to be swept away! I'd like to do that today, please!" he said and ran out of the room.

"I'd rather not do anything like that," Rosie said, looking a bit nervous.

"Neither would I," Erin said. The toaster popped the bread up, so she placed it on a plate and put a tiny bit of butter on it.

"May I have some jam, please?" she asked.

"Take a few bites without and see how you feel first. If you can keep it down, I'll add a bit of jelly to it."

Dan was back, bouncing off the walls. "You're going to put jelly on her toast? I'd like toast with jelly on it as well!" he said, doubled over with laughter.

Erin looked at David. "What did I say?"

"I reckon he's imagining you spreading gelatin on her toast," he said, grinning at the idea.

"Yeah, and adding jelly babies and wine gums on top!" Dan said, which got a smile from his family.

Rosie kept her food down and seemed to be fully recovered. They relaxed at the house until suppertime, then found a nice restaurant in Fish Creek. After their meal, they purchased a day pass for Peninsula Park and drove through the narrow, winding, tree-lined roads up to Eagle Point, where Erin parked. She'd thought ahead and had the family put on sunscreen and bug repellant before they left the house.

Dan wasted no time climbing what Erin learned was a sixty-foot observation tower. She hadn't been there since they'd rebuilt it, along with a ramp that wound through the trees they called a canopy walk. "This is nice!" she said as she watched the kids racing to the top. "I'm going to take the ramp."

"Aye, I'll join yeh," David said.

They walked to the other side of the car park and began their much easier ascent toward the tower. The day was fine, with only the prettiest, fluffy clouds occasionally breaking up the rays of the hot sun as it began its descent toward the horizon. "So, tell me about your morning," Erin said.

"Ach, we missed you and Rosie quite a lot, but we made the most of it. Et was splendid, spending time with ma boys. We shared a lot of well-needed laughs."

"I'm glad to hear it. Tomorrow, I plan to take you to Cave Point, which is unbelievably beautiful. I was thinking about going to the outdoor theater tonight if you're up for it?"

"Aye, I go where you go, remember?" he said and squeezed her shoulders in a sideways hug.

"Mummy, Daddy, come look at the view!" Rosie said as she and Charlie ran up to them.

"A'right, love, lead on," David said and took Erin's hand as they hurried to keep up with the youngsters.

A bit out of breath, Erin stood with David on her right and Rosie on her left as they gazed out over the tall cliff onto the dark, shimmering water. Gulls and smaller birds flew below them, soaring into the slight breeze and hovering almost stationary in the air. She closed her eyes and felt Rosie take her hand. "Isn't it magnificent, Mummy?"

"Aye, baby girl, it is," she whispered and took a deep breath of the fresh air. Turning to Charlie, who was next to Rosie, she smiled at him. "And what do you think, Charlie?"

"Cor blimey, it's cracking! I've been watching for dolphins and whales," he said, and she laughed gently.

"You'll be waiting a long time for that! This is a lake, not the ocean, so they are rare indeed for these waters.

"Erin! Erin, look what I can do!" Daniel exclaimed as he ran up to her.

Before she could respond, he was standing on one of the planks that ran across the lower half of the guard rail. He spread his arms out like wings and bent forward, nearly giving her a heart attack. "Dan! Come down from there!" she said and went to him, wanting to keep him from falling.

David joined them and lifted his son off the railing, much to Erin's relief. "I'll thank you not to do that again," he said, breathing heavily.

"But Dad," Dan whined, "I'm not gonna fall!"

"Famous last words," David said and looked at Erin, shaking his head in disbelief.

They stayed another twenty minutes and after several family selfies went back to the SUV. Erin drove through the park again and then parked a block or so away in front of a colorful carved wooden sign with a rather creepy face on it that read *Not Licked Yet*. "Okay, everyone, who wants ice cream?" she asked.

The whole family erupted, even David, saying they did. After exiting the vehicle, they walked down the steep driveway and stood in front of the wooden building. "Look, Dad, it has dragons on the roof!" Charlie said and pointed to long, upright boards painted blue with a sawtooth pattern that ran along the roof peak. At each of the four gables, front and back, were fire-breathing dragon heads.

"Aye, son," David said.

"It's a Scandinavian thing, Charlie. This area was settled by a lot of people from that part of the world, so it's common to have that kind of decoration on the buildings. Now, what flavor does everyone want?" Erin asked. "There's Vanilla, Chocolate, Butter Pecan, and the flavor of the day, Ye Olde English Toffee."

"I suppose you're gonna tell us that there were quite a few settlers from 'ye olde England,' so many of the sweets and ice cream flavors are named after et, eh?" David said after rolling his eyes.

"Not that I know of, dear," she said with a laugh. They joined the line, and when it was their turn, they each told the young adult inside the building what they wanted. When they paid, there was a carafe for tips, so Erin put a few dollars into it. As soon as she did, the cashier rang a bell. The staff then began clapping and cheering as the family stepped to the side of the building to wait for their order.

Across from the building were a playground and a few photo stand-in boards with faceless gnomes painted on them. "Mummy, why don't they have faces?" Rosie asked as Dan ran to one and stuck his head all the way through the hole.

"Here, I'll show you. Stand behind that one and look through it." Rosie did as she was told, and when Erin raised her phone for a picture, she smiled at her. "Okay, come back now. She opened the photo and laughed with her new daughter at how silly she looked as a gnome.

"Brilliant! I want a go," Charlie said, then it was Dan's turn.

"Erin," David said, "come help me, please." He was being handed ice cream cones piled high with each flavor.

"Dan, Charlie, Rosie, Peter," she called out to them, and everyone came running except Peter. "Where's Peter?"

"He went inside to use the toilet," Charlie said and watched as his brother's ice cream began dripping down the cone onto Erin's hand. "I'll find him."

"Thanks, Charlie," Erin said as she tried to keep hers from doing the same thing.

A few minutes later, the two boys stepped outside, Charlie looking put out and Peter looking a bit annoyed until he saw Erin's predicament, then his red face revealed his embarrassment. "I'm sorry, Erin!" he said sincerely and took the cone from her. He then rushed to the building and grabbed a handful of napkins. "Here."

"Thanks, but what took you so long?" she asked.

"A girl!" Charlie said, rolling his eyes, and just then, a pretty blonde girl stepped out of the building and blushed when she saw Peter.

"I see, and what were you talking about, then?" Erin asked, not expecting him to give her a good answer.

"*Future Explorations*, actually. She told me that I look like John Thomas Fife and asked if I'd ever heard that before," he said and laughed as they headed for the creek that ran behind the playground.

"John, who?" Erin said, joining in his amusement. "And what did you tell her?"

"I didn't lie, really."

"Uh oh, that sounds like trouble," Erin said.

"I told her that I haven't seen the program, and before I could finish, she was explaining it to me in detail. She was gushing over it! Were you like that about it when you were young, Erin?" he asked.

"Are you saying I'm old now?" Peter gave her a wily grin and shrugged. "Why you little…" she said and elbowed his arm as he laughed brightly. "I have been known to go a bit fangirl every now and then." David stepped up to them, and she gasped. "Oh, gosh! I can't believe it's you! What's a handsome movie star like you doing in a place like this, Davidelliott—one word?"

He looked at her like she'd gone completely insane whilst Peter laughed so hard his ice cream fell off the cone and landed in the grass. "Worth it, totally worth it," he said, gasping and holding his side.

"What's all this about?" David asked. "Though I'm not sure I want to know the answer."

Erin explained what she and Peter had been talking about, and he shook his head in disbelief. "What? I haven't had a chance to fangirl in forever! You wouldn't deny me the opportunity, would you?" she said, using her secret weapon; puppy dog eyes. Peter was now doubled over, so the rest of the children gathered to see what was so funny. She began telling them what was going on and then suddenly stopped and stared at him.

"What?" Peter said, suddenly a bit more sober.

"Are you telling me that you haven't seen *Future Explorations*?"

"Oh," he said, clearly relieved it wasn't anything serious. "No, I haven't. Mum and Nanny wouldn't allow it, and then I just haven't wanted to. I'm a bit fed up with it if I'm honest."

"Humph, seems you could appreciate it a bit more, especially when it gives pretty girls an opening to talk to you, hmm?" Erin said, teasing.

"Well, I reckon it does have its advantages." He glanced toward the girl and saw her watching him, though she looked away when she saw him turn to her.

"What time does the cinema open?" David asked and checked his watch.

"Oh, shoot! We should get going now. I think it opens at seven forty-five."

"Aye, et's half seven now," he said.

Erin pulled into the Skyway Drive-In at 7:50. They were having a retro night and were showing *The Goonies* and *Dirty Dancing*. There was a line of cars already in line waiting, so she put the transmission into park and waited. The line started moving ten minutes later, and soon they were following the car in front of them behind a tall fence and row of trees. She chose a place to park in the second row which had an outdoor speaker. "What I wouldn't give for an old station wagon with a rear-facing back seat," she said as she turned off the ignition.

"What does that mean?" Rosie asked.

"Haven't you heard of a station wagon?" she asked, and everyone shook their heads. "Oh, well, it was a car with a long body made for large families I guess. Before minivans were a thing."

"We call them estate cars," David said, and the children nodded, clearly recognizing the term.

"Anyway, the one we had when I was a kid had a seat all the way in the back that folded down to make a flat cargo area. The thing was, it faced the back window, which was perfect for drive-ins. I could turn the SUV around but sitting on the edge of the tailgate isn't very comfortable. You guys can sit in front of it on the grass if you want, but first things first… snacks," she said, and Daniel whooped.

The family made their way to the snack bar, which was a one-story cinder block building that had toilets at one end and a place to buy food, drinks, and candy for the show on the other end. They loaded up on popcorn, soda, and several boxes of snacks. Erin picked up a small box that said *Pic* and set it on the counter with their things. "What's that?" Rosie asked, and Erin smiled.

"It's to keep the mosquitos away, you'll see," she said as the cashier rang them up, and David paid.

"Are you—" the middle-aged woman operating the register said, then looked around them and spoke quietly. "David Elliott? You are, aren't you? We ran Houlihan's Flat last spring. It was a hit! I distinctly remember more than one person saying how much they enjoyed it! I don't suppose you'd sign the poster if we can find it in the storeroom?"

The people behind them were growing impatient, so David leaned in close and said, "I'll make a deal with yeh; if you keep the fact that I'm here under wraps, I'll return after the films and sign et, a'right?" His smile made the woman blush.

"It's a deal, thanks," she said, and they were finally allowed to go back to their vehicle.

Erin had a bad feeling that the lady wasn't keeping her end of the bargain and was currently telling everyone she saw that a famous movie star was there. Her ears were on alert to hear if people began saying his name. She heard a few 'Johns' and one 'Thomas' on their way back, but no one was looking at them.

"What's going on in ye're head, love?" David asked her when they opened the car doors.

"Sorry, I'm just worried that people are going to figure out that we're here and that they won't leave us alone. I think we should try to keep our heads down, so to speak," she said.

"Aye, I reckon that's wise."

"What shall we sit on, Daddy?" Rosie said as she stood near the hood.

"Shoot, I didn't think about chairs or a blanket," Erin said.

"We have an extra blanket if you'd like to use it?" A young man offered from the extended cab truck parked next to them.

"Oh, well… I think we'll be—"

"It's no trouble, really. I'll get it for you," he said and hurried away.

"Uh, okay," Erin said, though he was already gone.

David turned away when he returned a moment later with two thick plaid blankets in his arms. "These should work," the man said and smiled at her. "I'm Ed, and my wife is Tasha; she's around here, somewhere," he said and looked over his shoulder briefly. A five-year-old boy came running toward him and rammed into his leg, hugging him tightly. "This is Davey." He lifted the boy and accepted the wet kiss the child gave him.

"Hello, Ed and Davey. I'm Erin. It's nice to meet you."

"Dad! Dan won't share the popcorn!" Rosie said as she came back over to them.

"This is our daughter, Rosie. This is Ed and Davey," Erin said.

"My daddy's name is David; it's a pleasure to meet you," she said.

"Same here, Rosie," he said.

"Here, Rosie, spread these on the ground and tell Dan that I said to share or he'll have to sit in the back seat for both films," she said and piled the blankets onto her outstretched arms.

"Okay, Mummy, thanks. Charlie, come help me!" she called out. Her brother came quickly and took the top blanket from her.

Davey seemed quite interested in what was happening with the children, so he squirmed out of his dad's arms and ran to the front of the SUV. Ed took a step forward and approached David, who was still facing away from them. "Hi, I'm Ed Paulson."

David was forced to turn to the man and took his outstretched hand. "Hello, et's nice to meet you," he said. "Thanks for—"

"Ed? Eddie?" they heard, and a lovely young woman stepped up to him. "Do you want any…" She looked up at David and squeaked, "Pop… corn…" Are you… Oh, my gosh! Ed, that's—"

"Please," Erin interrupted her, "Please don't say it out loud. We'd like to stay under the radar, you know?"

Ed looked confused, so Tasha whispered something in his ear. "Really? WOW!" he said, then didn't seem to know what to say.

"We won't say a word," Tasha said and stared dreamily up at David, who smiled and shook her hand.

"We appreciate it a lot, thanks," he said.

"David, would you mind checking on the kids?" Erin asked and then said hello to Tasha.

"Oh! Where's Davey?" she said, looking worried.

"Your son is with our kids; he'll be okay," Erin said and started walking toward them, followed by the young woman.

"May Davey sit with us, Mummy?" Rosie asked and patted the blanket next to her.

"That's up to his parents," Erin said and looked at them.

"Are you sure… you want him to? I mean, he can be a handful," Tasha said nervously.

"I'm sure. If we can handle Dan, we can handle him," Rosie said with a sweet smile.

"I'll be good… Mummy," Davey said, copying her accent.

Tasha placed her hand over her heart and smiled up at Ed. "Okay, but you have to promise to send him back to us if he—"

"I promise," Rosie said.

"Me too," Charlie added.

The adults looked at each other with raised eyebrows and shoulder shrugs. "Well, I reckon we should get settled, then," David said and took Erin's hand.

"Aye."

Erin and David got into the SUV, and she turned the ignition so they could put the windows down. It was a warm July night, and as it got darker, the crickets began singing. The movie screen was lit up with the decades-old ads for *Pic* and other treats to be found at the concession stand, but the volume was low on the speaker, so the nighttime sounds filled the vehicle.

David took her hand and leaned over to kiss her. "This is lovely," he said.

"Aye, though I wish this was a bench seat so we could snuggle," she said and squeezed his hand. "Oh, shoot! I forgot the *Pic*." She hopped out of the SUV and went to Peter.

"Hiya, Erin. A'right?" he asked with a friendly smile.

"I'm fine. I just need that box I handed you at the snack bar."

"Oh, right." He reached into his back pocket and handed it to her. "What is it, then?" he asked. "Oh, and are we meant to be able to hear the adverts?"

"Oh, shoot! I forgot about sound. I mean, there are speakers on the side of the car, and we can use the radio, but there's nothing up here. Um, let me think. Well, I guess you could move and sit between us and Davey's truck. We'll let you have the speaker, and we can use the radio. As for the *Pic*, I'll show you." She opened the box and placed the green coil onto the little stand the box made. "Oh, shoot! I don't have a lighter. I'll have to find one. Why don't you guys move now, and I'll ask around.

"A'right, Mum. Everyone up, we're moving," Peter said to the kids and stood.

Erin knew David wouldn't have one, so she went to Ed's truck window. "Do you have a lighter? I need to light this," she asked and lifted the coil.

"Oh, sure," he said and fished in his front pocket, pulling out a black lighter with skulls and hearts on it.

"Thanks, I owe you," she said once it was lit.

"Actually," Tasha said, leaning over her husband, "do you think he'd let us have a selfie… later, after the movies?" She discretely pointed at David and raised her eyebrows hopefully.

"Oh, well, I don't see why not. I'll ask him for you."

"Thanks a lot," she said.

Erin returned to her seat and sighed as she placed the *Pic* on the dashboard. "I have bug spray if this doesn't work."

"What's wrong? You seem, I dinnae ken, stressed," he asked and touched her cheek with his thumb.

"Not stressed, really. I don't know what it is. Ed lit the *Pic,* and out of habit, I said I owed him. Tasha then asked for a selfie with you. I can't put my finger on what's bothering me about it, I mean, I did say that I owed him, and I should be—"

"Aye, I ken the feeling well. I reckon et's that you made an opening for them tae ask me for somethin'. I've done et often, sayin' somethin' off-hand that gives whomever I'm speaking to the courage tae ask or, worse, leads me to a commitment of ma time. I dinnae mind doin' et, though, et comes with the job. Now, let's settle in… perhaps we should move to the back?"

Sitting in the back seat with him seemed like a great idea, except she knew they wouldn't be able to resist making out, and that would just lead to either frustration or doing inappropriate things with too many people around, including their children. "I'm not sure that would be wise," she said with a knowing smile.

"Why bring wisdom into et, woman?"

Halfway through *The Goonies*, Davey fell asleep, so at the intermission between films, Ed put him into his car seat. Peter, Charlie, Dan, and Rosie chose to sit in the SUV for *Dirty Dancing*. The blankets were returned to Tasha and Ed, and David took a selfie with them both, as they weren't sure they'd be staying past the credits.

It was very late when the movie was over, and people began starting their vehicles and driving away. Peter was the only one of the children to stay awake for the whole movie. He offered to stay with his siblings while Erin and David returned to the snack bar for autographs.

Erin decided to use the bathroom on their way there. When she stepped into the building, she was concerned that she didn't see David, or anyone else, for that matter. "David?" she said, but there was no reply. She heard a noise come from a back room, so she went back there to find out what was going on.

"I know it's here!" the cashier from earlier said, throwing half-unfurled posters to the back of the small storeroom. "I didn't have time to look for it—"

"David?" Erin said as she stepped into the room.

"Ach, darling, we're searching for the poster. Care to help?" he said and gave her a look that clearly said, 'please'." She knew the sooner it was found, the sooner they could leave, so she smiled and opened a rolled-up poster.

Five frantic minutes later, David found it and held it up. "Here we are, then," he said and let it snap shut.

"Oh, good! Thank you for helping," the woman said. They followed her to an old desk, and David was handed a black magic marker. Erin and the woman held the poster open while he signed it, then she found a book and glass paperweight to keep it from rolling back up while the ink dried.

"We must be off now, but we've had a lovely evening," David said, and the woman smiled warmly at them.

"Thank you again for signing this and for your patience. We'll have it framed and hang it where everyone can see it. I... hope you're successful in all your... future explorations," she said and laughed as her cheeks became pink.

"Thank you, and I wish the same for you. It was nice to meet you; goodbye," David said and held the door open for Erin as they stepped out into the warm, clear night. Every vehicle was gone except for theirs, and they walked toward it hand-in-hand.

Peter started when they opened the doors. "How'd it go?" he asked, sounding groggy.

"Humph, et took far too long, but et's over now," David said.

"We should buckle everyone—" Erin began.

"I've already sorted that out," Peter said as he pulled the strap across his chest and buckled it.

"Thank you, Peter, good thinking," Erin said. "I'm so tired I could sleep right here." She closed her eyes and jumped when there was a light tap on her window.

"I'm sorry, but we have to lock the gate now," the cashier said when Erin opened the window.

"Okay, sorry," she said and started the SUV. She drove slowly through the lot and turned right onto highway 42, headed north.

When they got back to the rental house, Erin carried Rosie, David carried Daniel, and Charlie was awake enough to walk, though he held Peter's hand. Opening the door was proving difficult, so Peter helped by taking Rosie from Erin. "I'll take her up," he said, and David repositioned Dan.

"I will as well," he said, then kissed her cheek and followed his eldest son toward the stairs.

She looked at the clock on the oven; 1:12, it read, and she sighed. After dropping her purse on the floor next to the door and taking her shoes off, she joined her family upstairs. David and Peter were taking the younger children's shoes off and getting them settled in their beds. David turned to her and smiled. "I'll help with Charlie," she said and turned to face the small bed he was lying on, fast asleep. "Okay, Charlie, time to take your shoes off," she said softly.

"I don't want to!" he said and rolled away from her.

"I'll help you."

"Leave off! I said I don't want—"

"Fine then, sweet dreams," she said, stung by his outburst, though she knew she shouldn't be.

"We're at the house now. Say goodnight to your… mum," David said to Rosie, who was asking where they were.

"Nite," she said and fell back to sleep.

Dan was out cold, so Erin bent over and kissed his forehead. "Sweet dreams, Dan." They left the room and stood in the hallway to give Peter a quick hug. "Thanks for your help," she said and accepted a kiss on her cheek.

"Goodnight, Dad, Mum, see you in the morning, though not too early, I hope?" the boy said and gave them a hopeful smile.

"Aye, I'll not be up early," David said.

"Neither will I if I can help it," Erin said and stepped into her room, longing for the comfortable bed.

——

"That was lovely, eh?" David said as they got undressed.

"Humph, I guess so," she said.

"You guess so? What happened?"

"Oh, nothing. I'm just tired and oversensitive, that's all. Charlie was grumpy when I tried to help him."

"Ach, I see. Now, come let me hold yeh," he said with bedroom eyes.

"You can hold me, but I'm too tired for anything else… just saying."

"A'right, who said anything about anything else, though I'd love tae dance with yeh," he said, thinking about the film as he watched her put her nightgown on. She got into the bed and allowed him to spoon her from behind. "That film was verra sexy. I'd like tae find a secluded place tae—" He was just about to touch her breast and tell her all the things he'd like to do with her when she began snoring lightly. "Ach, sweet dreams, darling."

Chapter Twenty

CAVE POINT

"Trust me, you're gonna love this place!" Erin said as she pulled into a shady parking spot at Cave Point County Park.

"But I'm too full to move," Charlie grumbled.

"And I'm too hot," Rosie whined.

They'd been on holiday for seven days, though it seemed a lot longer, and everyone was ready to go home. The morning hadn't gone smoothly; they'd all overslept and woke famished. Erin had been sick twice that morning and would've preferred to stay at the rental house, but she knew how much they'd love the park, so she sucked it up.

They'd had a much later start than she'd hoped and decided to have lunch on their way to the park "I know, but a good walk will make you feel better, and it'll be nice and cool by the water. You all have your swimming suits on under your clothes, right?"

"Yes, Mummy," Rosie said half-heartedly, and everyone else just nodded.

"Okay, then get out and start putting on sunscreen, then I'll spray you with—"

"But I need a wee," Daniel said, his usual boundless energy seeming to need a recharge as well.

"There's a toilet nearby; let me put sunscreen and bug spray on you first. Who else needs to go?"

Everyone, including David, raised their hand, so she sighed and got out of the SUV. "Point the way, darling, and I'll take them," David said as she took the 50+ SPF sunscreen out of her bag.

199

"Alright, it's just over there; across the road," she said and pointed to the building. "I'll join you when I'm finished." When she was done sunscreening herself, she locked the SUV and stepped into the women's room, where she heard Rosie making strange noises. "Rosie? Is that you?"

"Mummy! These toilets are disgusting!" the young girl wailed, loud enough for everyone to hear her.

"What do you mean? Do they need to be cleaned?" she asked and exchanged smiles with a woman who stepped out of one of the stalls.

The woman came close to Erin. "I think it's because it's a hole in the ground, not the kind that flush," she said and stepped up to the hand sanitizer dispenser.

"Oh, Rosie, it's not a big deal, just hurry up, and it'll be over with, okay?" Erin took the stall next to her and sighed. The toilets were rather primitive, though they had somewhat modern seats. The smell wasn't overly pleasant, and looking into the hole was not advisable, but it was better than having to hold it the whole time they were there.

"Mummy? Where are you?" she heard Rosie whine after a few moments.

"I'll be out in a minute; wash your hands."

"I can't! There aren't any taps in here!"

"Then use sanitizer."

"I've already done that." The girl sounded like she was about to cry.

"Well then, go outside and wait for your father and brothers." There was no reply. "Rosie?"

"I'll wait for you," she heard, but it lacked all joy. "It smells bad in here."

"Then wait for me outside." When she was done, she opened the stall door and saw an unhappy nine-year-old standing with her back against the wall, arms crossed. "Please try to have a good day today, Rosie. I know you're tired and grumpy, but—"

"I'm not grumpy, but it smells bad in here."

Erin used the hand sanitizer, then they stepped outside, thankful for the fresh air. She looked around for her family and saw a throng of excited people. The boys were standing off to the side with their arms crossed. "Oh dear," she said under her breath and handed Peter the bottle of sunscreen. "Please help your siblings with this while I sort this out." Then, she headed straight toward the crowd surrounding David. "Okay, everyone, please move along. Thank you for stopping by to say hello, but it's family time for us now." She pushed her way through the people and held out her hand toward him.

"But… I didn't get a selfie!" one woman said.

"Why don't you ask *him* what *he* wants to do, huh? Maybe he'd rather be with us," another one said.

"As she said, thank you for saying hello, but I must be on my way now," David said and took Erin's hand. When they were a good distance away, he added, "Ye're verra good at that; I can't believe how bold yeh are with them."

"Well, I'm not worried about image or pleasing anyone. I understand their side and know what I'd expect to happen if I did something like that. Now, let's get lost in the park," she said and pulled him across the road.

Quite a few people were hanging out in the grassy, open area that had a gazebo tucked out of the way on the side of the lawn. Many of them had dogs, and some were setting up picnics, but that's not where Erin wanted to stay. There was a bit of cloud cover, but it was getting hot and humid, and she wanted a bit of shade. "Wait, did everyone get sunscreen and bug spray?"

"Yes, Mummy," Rosie said, and her brothers nodded.

"David, did you?"

"Ach, no, I didn't have a chance," he said.

"Okay, here," she said and handed him the bottle. "Don't forget your ears and neck." When he was ready, she sprayed him with bug spray.

"What's that noise?" Charlie asked as they got closer to the trees that ran along the edge of the grass. A sound, similar to distant thunder, filled the air every few seconds, and as they approached the cliff edge, it grew much louder, like an oncoming storm.

"Below us are caves," Erin said. "That noise is the waves hitting them; isn't it delicious?"

They entered the cover of trees, following a well-used path. A group of kayakers floated silently along the shore, many feet below them, as they looked out on the horizon; water as far as they could see. "I love the ocean!" Rosie said and took a deep breath.

"This isn't the ocean, baby girl; this is Lake Michigan, which has fresh water. There is no tide, and even in August, it's very cold," Erin said.

"It must be quite deep, in that case," Peter said as he came up next to her.

"Yes, it is. When I was little, my dad and a group of his friends used to go scuba diving. They started a small museum filled with the treasures they found in old shipwrecks. I can remember being about three and walking through it. They played a recording of gulls and splashing water. I loved that place." She closed her eyes and sighed.

"May we go to Grandpa Frank's museum, please?" Rosie asked.

"I'm sorry, but it closed many years ago, and we're too far away from where it was now, anyway. Oh, I just remembered something about it! In an upstairs room, there was a mannequin dressed in a very old diving suit, complete with an enormous round helmet. I knew it wasn't a real person, but at the age of three, it made me nervous, and my imagination would worry that it might start moving," she said and suddenly grabbed Peter's arm, making him jump with a little squeal.

Daniel laughed so hard, he snorted, which made everyone chuckle as they began walking again. Totally fearless, he would run all the way to the very edge of the high cliff and look over the side, which made Erin's heart skip a beat more than once. On the path, roots and large rocks threatened to trip them up, so they had to watch where they were going, though it was difficult as their eyes examined the picturesque scenery around them.

The trail wound around, with many forks and diversions, either leading them to the edge of the water, where bleach-white or peach-colored stones were seen taking a beating from the crashing waves, or inland, into the cover of cedar, birch, and small maple and pine trees. The wind made the leaves tremble, allowing the sunlight to create ever-changing mosaics on the dirt and tree trunks around them.

Bird song, mixed with rustling leaves and the crashing, hollow noise of the water, lulled them and seemed to take them out of time, worry, and stress. Occasionally dogs were heard barking, and people passed by on their way back from wherever the trail ended. Often, they would smile and exchange hellos, but generally, everyone minded their own business.

There were several fallen trees over the path, some old and worn where thousands of people had scrambled over them and some more recent, still covered in bark. Often the fallen trunks revealed their tenacity, still sprouting foliage, though bent by the strong lake winds. Erin asked David to pose in a few selfies with her and asked Peter to snap a quick photo of them sitting on a tree trunk and then on a picturesque boulder.

A Scandinavian couple passed, speaking another language with each other, and saw Erin trying to take a family selfie. The woman offered to take some photos for them and then recognized David, saying she was a big fan. He offered to take a selfie with her, but she declined, saying that she wouldn't take up any of his family time for herself.

Ten minutes later, an excited adolescent dog with wavy golden fur came bounding up the path toward them, tongue flapping as he ran. It stopped, tail wagging with all its might, at Charlie's feet and looked up at him expectantly. "May I stroke it, Dad?" he asked.

"He seems friendly enough, so you may," David said.

Soon, the whole family was petting and playing with the pup while Erin watched for its owner. She heard someone calling out the name Charlie, then saw an older woman following a young man of about Peter's age. "Is this your dog?" she called out since it didn't appear to be responding to them.

The couple seemed relieved and approached them. "Yes, you naughty thing!" the woman said, speaking to the bundle of energy rolling around on the ground, accepting belly rubs.

"Thanks for stopping him," the young man said. "He jumped out of the car and started running before I could put his leash on him. We just adopted him a few weeks ago and haven't had a chance to start any training."

"He's a sweet boy," Erin said, "but we didn't stop him. He came up to our son and sat at his feet. Did I hear you calling out to Charlie?"

"Yeah, that's the name he was given at the shelter," the man said.

"Ach, that's ma son's name," David said and shook his head, watching the children interacting with the dog.

"Which one?" the woman said with a smile.

"Charlie," David and Erin said together, and both the boy and the dog looked up at them. "Come here, please." David finished.

"Yeah, Dad?" Charlie said as he approached, followed by his namesake, who sat at his side as if trained to do so.

"These are the dog's owners," David said.

"Hello, pleased to meet you," he said and held out his hand. The dog watched as the young man paused for a moment and then shook Charlie's hand with a smile.

"He seems to like you," he said.

"I like him as well."

"His name is Charlie... the dog, I mean," the woman said, then she put her hand to her forehead and sighed. "I suppose we should introduce ourselves. My name is Agatha, and this is my grandson, Christopher."

"Nice to meet you. I'm Erin, and this is my fiancé, David. Do you live nearby?"

"Yes, we live in Jacksonport," the woman said. "Are you local?"

"Not anymore," Erin said. "We live in London, but I'm from Green Bay."

"I live in De Pere," the young man said. I come up for a month every year to visit my grandma in summer."

Charlie had stood patiently, stroking the dog's head every now and then. When the dog lay at his feet, Erin remembered why they'd asked him to come over and crouched down to pet the dog. "I'm sorry, I forgot you were waiting. The dog's name is also Charlie, isn't that crazy?"

At hearing his name, the dog stood, wagging his tail, and panted happily. "He's a very good dog," Charlie said. He bent over to give him a hug and was rewarded with a very wet lick across his whole face. Daniel was doubled over with laughter at that until Charlie pointed at his brother and said, "Attack!" Dan's eyes grew large, and he ran away, down the trail, while the dog looked up at Charlie with his head cocked to the side as if waiting for a translation. "You *are* a good boy, aren't you?"

"Oh, dear," the woman said, and everyone looked at her expectantly. "I think those two have bonded. It's too bad you live so far away, or... well, I guess it doesn't matter."

"Yes, Agatha, I think you're right on both accounts," Erin said. "I also think we shouldn't keep you any longer, though it pains me to say it."

"Aye, et's a bit heartrending, isn't it?" David said as Christopher handed the leash to Charlie.

"Would you mind putting that on him for me? He'll sit still for you," he said.

Charlie took the royal blue nylon strap and looked at the metal clasp. His eyes betrayed the sadness he was feeling at having to say goodbye to his new friend, but he took a deep breath and bravely hooked the leash to the dog's collar. Again, the pup's tail went wild as he stood at the ready by the boy's side. "We can't keep you, boy, so behave yourself. You're a very good dog, Charlie," he said as he hugged him.

Erin fanned her eyes and turned away from the scene, wishing they could bring the dog home with all her heart. She heard a noise and turned just as Rosie ran into her father's arms, bawling. She heard Peter sniffle and even Dan, who'd come back by then, seemed a bit sad, though he was trying to hide it. "Come now, Charlie, it's time to go," David said and held out his arm, ready to hug the boy.

Charlie handed the leash to Christopher, took one more look at the dog, and then turned, burying his face in his dad's shirt. "It was nice to meet you both," Erin managed to say.

"You too," Agatha said, and as they walked away, she said to her grandson, "The poor boy."

Erin knew a pet, especially a dog, wasn't practical for them since the children were gone at school most of the year and David's schedule wasn't regular, but it broke her heart to see that instant bond rent in two. They suddenly heard a commotion and turned to see Charlie, the dog, straining at his lead, barking, and trying to return to them. "We should keep walking," she said and led them away.

The crashing waves, crunching of gravel underfoot, and twittering birds filled the silence as the family walked onward. Soon, they heard people yelling and laughing, then what sounded like splashing. As they came to a place where they could climb down onto the snow-white stones, they saw two teenage boys and a girl who appeared to be near Rosie's age.

One of the boys, whose dark hair had been buzzed off, was scrambling up the uneven rocks and dirt, using roots and tall grass to help him get up onto a dark stone ledge. The girl, her short, dark hair plastered flat against her head, had just gotten out of the water, and the other boy, who had short, sandy-blond hair, was in the lake, swimming toward the shore.

The Elliotts climbed down and watched as the boy with the buzz-cut ran to the edge of the rock and flung himself off, hitting the water with a loud *plunk*. The girl wasn't far behind and dove into the crystal-clear water that appeared to be teal and aquamarine. Peter looked at his father hopefully. "May I join them, Dad?" he asked with bright, pleading eyes.

"I dinnae ken, Peter, it doesn't seem verra safe," David said.

"I'll be careful, Dad, please?"

Rosie had taken her sandals off and squealed when the cold water washed over her feet. "I'll be staying here, thank you! Have you felt the water, Peter?"

"You're right, it doesn't look very safe, but give me a minute," Erin said. She took off her sandals and gingerly made her way to where the kids were getting out of the water. "Excuse me," she said to the boy with short hair.

"Hi," he said politely and stood dripping, his light skin a bit red from being in the water. Then the hairs on his arms began to rise from the goosebumps slowly spreading over his body.

"Sorry to bother you, but is this the first time you've done this, or—"

"No, we've been coming here all summer!" the boy said, smiling with perfect teeth, the same bright white as the stones beneath their feet.

"It doesn't look safe, though."

"No, it's fine over there," the younger girl said, having joined them.

"Your kids can join us if they want," the boy said and ran off to climb up the cliff again.

"Please, Dad, Mum? I promise to be careful," Peter said.

"May I have a go as well?" Daniel asked though he was already taking off his t-shirt.

Erin looked at David and shrugged. "I guess it's okay; I mean, those kids aren't getting hurt," she said, and Dan rushed over to the cliff. "Hold up there, Mr. Naughty Britches!"

Everyone laughed at that, even Charlie, who was still sad and quiet. "A'right, you may have a go, but I want yeh to be patient and wait until the previous person is out of the water before yeh jump in," David said. The look of glee that covered Peter's face made Erin laugh as she accepted the quick hug he offered her and his dad before rushing to get his shirt off.

They watched as Daniel ran fearlessly to the edge and dove off it with a cry of delight. When he came to the surface, his eyes were wide, and he let out another cry of shock. "Bloody... I mean, blimey, that's pure ice water!" he said and began swimming toward the shore.

The other three kids stood shivering as Peter waited for Dan, then he crept up to the edge and looked down. Just then they heard a loud *boom* as a large wave hit one of the caves. A visible shiver rippled through the boy's body, then he laughed and said something to the buzz-cut kid behind him. He looked at Erin and David and then shrugged before taking a step forward and jumping off into the lake.

He had barely resurfaced when the buzz-cut kid took a giant leap, hitting the water far too close to him. "Oi! You almost landed on me!" Peter said, and the boy rolled his eyes.

"Go faster next time!" he said and was already scrambling onto shore before Peter had even gotten his bearings. The girl was also impatient and landed within only a few feet of him.

"Oi, Peter! Get a move on!" Dan said from above.

The late morning sun made the ripples and waves shimmer as Peter finally made it to shore, dripping and shivering from head to foot. "That'll wake you—"

A loud splash followed by a dreadful scream echoed around them as Daniel emerged from the lake, shivering but smiling brightly. They all turned to see the buzz-cut boy floundering. The girl was flailing her arms and crying as she tried to stay above the water, then she dipped under the surface again. Quick as a flash, both Peter and Dan jumped back in and swam to them. Dan grabbed the girl, nearly getting hit in the face by her elbow as she panicked. Peter helped the buzz-cut boy to the flat rocks on the shore.

They lay there, trying to catch their breath and recover as the other boy came to shore and stood shivering as he gawked at the scene. The girl then began to cry loudly. "I'm telling Mom!" she wailed while the buzz-cut boy sat holding his arm, clearly in a lot of pain.

"You should've gotten out of the way, Bella!" he shouted.

"You jumped before I could!" she screamed.

"Are you alright?" Erin asked as she crouched beside the boy.

"I'm fine," he spat and glared at the girl, who ran off, crying and dripping, then the boy stood, still holding his arm. "Thanks," he said to Peter and Dan, who were still on their backs, panting from exertion as well as the adrenaline rush they'd just experienced.

Peter lifted his hand weakly, and Dan said, "Yeah, cheers."

As the teenagers walked away, Erin crouched beside her boys. "How about you; are you okay?"

"Yeah, Mum, just a bit winded," Peter said, barely above a whisper.

"Well done, boys," David said and held out his hand to Daniel, who smiled sheepishly and took it, allowing him to help him stand.

He did the same to Peter, but he held up his finger, silently asking for a moment before placing it over his heart. Erin laid her hand over it, and he smiled though his eyes were closed. "I'm a'right, truly, though my heart is racing at the moment."

"I'm not surprised! You were pure brilliant, both of you," Erin said and smiled at Dan.

"That was mental!" Charlie said, still looking a bit wide-eyed and shocked.

"Didn't consider what I was doin'… I just did it," Dan said, sounding very sober as he sat beside his twin brother.

"I was so frightened! I saw the foolish boy jump too soon, but there was nothing to be done about it. I tried to scream, but by the time it came out, that girl was already screaming," Rosie said, stuck to her daddy's side.

"Aye, I hope that'll teach them both a lesson about patience and safety," David said. "Now they're gone, do yeh wanna have another go?"

"Naw, I'm good," Peter said, and Dan shook his head in agreement. Erin handed them each a towel from the large beach bag she'd bought at Hat Head on the day they'd arrived in Door County, then she traded them for their t-shirts once they were dry.

When everyone was recovered and ready, David climbed back toward the trail and then helped the others. Little bugs, gnats, and mosquitoes began pestering Peter and Dan since their bug repellent had mostly washed off by then. "Oww! Little buggers!" Peter said after slapping his leg twice.

"Hold on," Erin said. She opened her bag again and rummaged around for a while before taking out a dark green spray bottle. "Here, you two go over there and put this on." She pointed to an open place beside a tall birch tree, its white bark glowing as the sunlight touched it.

"Thanks, Mum," Peter said with a smile and gave her back the towel.

The boys ran away, and she stood looking at the cliff face. The solid stone jutted out from the land, the colors graduating from bleached bone-white near the water to charcoal at the top, as if a great fire had swept through and scorched the stones. She marveled at it until she felt David's arms embrace her from behind, and she melted into them. "Mmm," she said, relaxing back into his chest.

They looked down at the dark green and black moss in the sage and yellow water below them. Gulls soared under fluffy white clouds, then dipped into the cold water, looking for food. He turned her to face him and smiled down at her. "I love you," he said and kissed her.

"Dan! Don't touch it!" they heard Charlie yell, but he continued kissing her. "Dad! Oh, sorry." They turned and smiled at the boy, whose face was pink.

"What is et, Charlie," David said.

"Erm, I don't—Oh yeah, Dan is about to touch a spider's web!" he said.

"Daniel! Don't touch anathin'," David yelled, hoping his youngest son would hear him, then he turned back to Erin.

"I love you too," she said and took his hand. When they approached the children, they were bent over something in the grass. "What's all the fuss—"

The children parted and Dan pointed. "It's a cracking spider's web, look!"

Before them was a large web covered with something that made the spiral design stand out. "We didn't notice it until the bug repellant began hitting it," Peter said, isn't it ledge, Dad?"

David stepped up to it and crouched down to take a closer look. "Aye, son, et's brilliant," he said. "Erin, come—"

"Oh, no! I'm not getting anywhere near that thing! There's an arachnid lurking somewhere near there, and I'm not going to be the one it... I don't know, attacks!" she said from a few paces back.

"Attacks? You are much larger than it is, yeh ken?"

"I don't care! They can jump and... they bite, and they are just... gross!" By then, she had the creepy-crawlies and couldn't help but scan the environment for what her mind had convinced her were an army of angry spiders, ready to eat her alive if she stood still. "I need to keep moving! Please, David," she said as a shiver ran through her body.

She stayed close to him as he smiled, and they continued walking. "Look at this crack, Dad, it's completely separated from the rest, and you can see down to the water. How did that happen?"

"I reckon thousands of years of the water hitting it has worn it away," he said, and then Rosie let out a shriek that made them all jump.

"What in the world?" Erin said and put her hand over her heart, which was beating hard in her chest.

The girl ran to her father and nearly climbed up into his arms. "What is it—"

"A… a snake! In the tall grass… there!" she said and pointed to a spot a few yards away.

"Oh! I see it!" Erin said and pointed to it as well. "Boys, do you see it?"

"Bloody… I mean brilliant," Dan said and took a step closer.

"Hold on," Erin said and grabbed his shoulder.

"I see it," Charlie and Peter said as Rosie buried her face in David's t-shirt.

"Don't worry, it's just a Fox snake; they aren't venomous and will leave you alone if you don't threaten them. It's a constrictor and not big enough to hurt you." She smiled up at David, and he gave her a puzzled look. "What?"

"Ye're terrified of a tiny spider and completely calm over a good-sized snake? I'm a bit baffled if I'm honest."

"I know, it's mental, but snakes are awesome! I had a friend who rescued a baby Fox snake and kept it as a pet. It was nearly that size when I used to let it lay across my shoulders and move down my arms."

The boys looked up from the snake and stared at her. "What?"

"I'd like to do that as well," Peter said, and Dan's dimples showed as he smiled at her.

"So would I," he said.

"May we go now?" Rosie said, sounding uneasy.

"Yes, baby girl, I think we're nearly at the beach anyway," Erin said.

"There's a beach?" she asked.

"Yes, and it's just up ahead." They came to an area that was more open and had the remnants of a large wooden boat, complete with an enormous anchor. The children ran around, climbing on everything while Erin took photos. When they lost interest in that, they continued walking and came to some paved paths and another toilet. "Anyone need to go, because I do," she said and led the way.

Everyone but Erin undressed down to their swimming suits; even David was wearing trunks. After adding more sunscreen, they followed the path to Whitefish Dunes State Park, where the pale tan sand was dotted with black chunks of burnt wood, remnants of beach fires from long ago. The sun shone bright as they made their way to an open spot, where Erin laid out a large towel for them to sit on.

David and Erin sat on the towel and watched as the children ran up to the water. Peter and Dan were brave enough to jump in, knowing they'd get used to it again, but the waves chased Charlie and Rosie back to the warm sand. "You'll become used to it right away if you jump in," they heard Peter say.

"I'd rather not get wet and have sand all over me," Rosie said, and Charlie looked longingly out into the water at his brothers.

"Go on, Charlie! He's right, you know. I used to go in every summer when I was a kid," Erin shouted.

"I reckon we should set an example for him, shouldn't we?" David said casually, though Erin saw the grin he was trying to hide.

"*I* reckon *you* can if you want to. I'm not letting anyone but you see my body like it is now!" she said.

"Ach, once ye're in the water, no one will see yeh."

"Ha! Nice try, but I'll stay here and watch you freeze yer arse off!"

"Are yeh sure ye'll not feel lonely if I join them?" he said, his smile brightening her day.

"I will, but I think I'll be okay. Maybe I'll dip my feet in a bit later."

He leaned over and kissed her mouth, then pressed his lips gently to her forehead. She watched as he trudged through the sand and stood next to Charlie. He said something to him, and they both posed, like at the start of a race. They ran right into the blue-green water, laced with bits of dark green seaweed. She couldn't see David's face, but she heard him yelp, and though Charlie continued bravely, he turned back. He approached Rosie and said something Erin couldn't hear, then he lifted her into his arms and ran into the waves, the young girl screaming all the way to her brothers, who were laughing hysterically.

Erin took several photos and a few short videos of her new family laughing and splashing each other. She felt brave enough to take off her sundress, revealing a swimming suit that covered everything, though she still wore a skirt of the same material to cover her thighs. She had just put the bottle of sunscreen back in her bag when a shadow loomed over her, and she looked up.

David and Peter were standing in front of her, and before she knew it, she was being 'led' toward the lake, one dripping-wet man having taken hold of each arm. "Wait! No!" she screamed, though she couldn't help but laugh as they pulled her along with them. She screamed bloody murder as the freezing water of Lake Michigan hit her legs and even harder as it inched up her body. "David! Peter! I'll get you back for this! You'll be sorry!

"Come now, Mum," Rosie said, laughing. "If I can do it, you can as well!"

"My legs are numb!" she said and began shivering.

"Go on, Peter, I've got her now," David said and held her close. While the children played and splashed each other, he continued into the deeper water, holding her in his arms as he'd done to Rosie. He began kissing her, slowly inching away from the kids. Their energy began to build up as he put his hand between her legs.

"David! I don't think that's a good idea right now," she said, then gasped when his finger eased under her suit and found her clitoris.

"I reckon ye're right, but that only makes me want to do it more. Relax, and no one will be the wiser," he said as he slipped a finger into her, allowing the cold water to penetrate her along with it. "Ye're so warm."

"I was until you forced me out here… Oh, yes," she whispered and buried her face in his neck, trying to hide the orgasm he'd brought her to. She could feel his erection on her leg as he allowed the waves to slowly moved her up and down over it. "We need to stop, David! What if one of the children comes over here? You don't want them to see you like that, do you?"

"No, but I want yeh—"

"Aye, but yeh cannae have me now; ye'll jest have tae wait," she said, using her rendition of a Scottish accent.

He pulled her up close, pressing her leg against his erection, and whispered, "Ach, I love when yeh do that! Et makes me radge, woman!"

She laughed and pushed herself away from him. "I cannae think of what tae say! Noo let me be, laddie, or I'll... I'll... I dinnae ken what I'll do to yeh, but ye'll no' like et!"

"I reckon I will," he said and managed to get her hand under the water, placing it over his swimming trunks. She couldn't help but gently stroke him as he moaned and kissed her but stopped when they heard the kids coming closer.

Erin had just enough time to fix her suit so it wasn't pinching her when Dan came swimming over to them. "There's a sand bar over there," he said and pointed at Peter, Charlie, and Rosie sitting in the shallow water.

"A'right, we'll be along in a moment," David said, and they watched him paddle back to his siblings, then he turned back to her. "I love yeh; thank you for that."

"Mmm, you'll thank me later," she said, and his eyes grew wide.

"Is that so? Well then, I look forward to et."

They spent another hour playing in the water until everyone got hungry, then they headed back to the car. Nothing extraordinary happened on the way, except that Dan found some wild thimbleberry bushes, and they each ate at least one. "Everyone should use the loo before we go," Erin said as they entered the car park.

Back at the SUV, they got in, and Erin looked in the rearview mirror as she shifted into reverse. She and Rosie made eye contact, and she noticed large alligator tears rolling down the young girl's face. "What's wrong, baby girl?" she said and put the transmission back into park.

All eyes were on Rosie then, and she blushed. "Nothing... well, I've had the best day of my life, I think, and I just... love you, that's all," she said and covered her face with her hands.

"I agree," Peter said.

"Me too!" Dan chimed in.

"Best birthday I've ever had," Charlie said, looking as though he were about to cry too.

"Birthday? It's your birthday today?" Erin said, shocked that no one had mentioned it.

He and Dan both nodded. She looked at David, mouth agape, and by the look on his face, she knew he was mortified for not knowing it either. "Oh, I see," she said, thinking quickly. "You were planning something special for supper, weren't you, David?"

He knit his brows together and began to nod but then shook his head slowly. "I'm ashamed I didn't ken et was yer birthday, boys. I'm gutted over et," he said and put his head down. "Please—"

"It's a'right, Dad! Don't be upset," Charlie said with a genuine smile.

"Yeah, Dad, we're used to it anyway," Dan said honestly, clearly not realizing how his words might hurt his dad even more.

"Dan! Honestly, Dad, it doesn't matter. As Rosie said, we've had the most smashing day of our lives, and you gave it to us, even if you didn't know it was our birthday. You gave me the gift I asked for, remember?" Charlie said.

"I did?" David asked quietly.

"Yeah, when we were at Dr. Neil's. You must remember, Mum." Erin sat for a moment, trying to recall what he was talking about, and just as it hit her, he said it. "I asked to spend the day with my family, as I've always wanted to do, remember?"

"Yes, my darling boy, I remember now. I'm so glad you got your wish, and I'll do my best not to forget it again, okay?" Erin said.

"Okay," Charlie said.

"Can we get a move on now? I'm famished?" Dan said, so Erin backed out of the parking spot and took David's hand.

They ate supper at a restaurant called *The Summer Kitchen*, where Charlie and Dan each got a piece of cherry pie with a candle in it. Their waitress and several other customers sang along with the family to "Happy Birthday to

You," then they went back to the house, tired and full, ready for a quiet, relaxing evening together.

They'd be leaving in the morning, so before they got too comfortable, they packed their suitcases and then played a few hands of Uno and Crazy Eights before heading to bed. Erin read to them the last chapter of *Anne of Green Gables*, the final line being a quote from Browning's *Pippa Passes*.

"*God's in His heaven, all's right with the world.*"

"I knew Anne and Gilbert would make up!" Peter said and then blushed as if he hadn't meant to say that out loud.

"So did I," Charlie said.

"I didn't at all!" Rosie said. "I thought she'd *never* forgive him, but I'm glad they did."

"Me too," Erin said. "We'll start the next book when we're back in London." She smiled at her family, then she and David kissed each of their heads. "Goodnight, sleep tight, don't let the bedbugs bite."

Chapter Twenty-One

PIT STOP IN GREEN BAY

They were glad to be going home; they'd had a brilliant time but were worn out. On their way to the tiny airport in Green Bay, everyone except Erin, who was driving, was nearly asleep.

"Don't forget to drive past your house!" Daniel yelled, startling everyone awake.

"But it's not my house anymore, Dan. I can't go into it now. Are you sure you still want to—" she said, and they all looked disappointed.

"I'm sure, Mummy!" he said earnestly.

"I guess we could drive past it if that would be good enough for you?" The children smiled and nodded.

Dan nudged Charlie, and Erin heard him whisper, "That works for Rosie all the time, so I thought I'd give it a go."

"Are you okay with that, David?"

"Aye," he said, though she imagined he would rather have avoided it as it held some bittersweet memories. They got off the highway and wound through the streets of Green Bay until they came to Whistlers Way, and Erin pulled over in front of a red brick ranch house with two huge maple trees in the front yard.

"Mummy, look! It's that man!" Rosie said and pointed to the front door, which was now open. Todd was standing in the doorway watching them.

"Fu—Sh—Cr—darn," Erin said. "I'd better tell him what I'm doing here so he doesn't get upset." She unbuckled her seatbelt and got out. Todd stepped onto the front porch and waited for her to approach. "I'm sorry, I didn't think you'd be home. The children wanted to see where I used to live. We were going to drive by so they could look at it. I wasn't going to go in or anything."

Todd cocked his head to the side and walked down the steps toward her. "It's okay. I had an… appointment… uh, that's why I'm home early. You… can let them come in if… you want to, I don't mind," he said gently.

"A doctor's appointment? Are you sick?" Erin knew he wasn't one to go to the doctor unless he couldn't function, so it startled her a bit. "Oh, it's none of my business, never mind," she said and turned back to the SUV.

Todd stepped up to her, putting his hand on her shoulder. "Wait—" At that, all the car doors opened, and the boys got out, ready to rescue her.

Erin held out her hand and moved it downward to tell them to relax, but David walked toward them anyway. Todd removed his hand and took a small step backward. "Now, boys, it's alright," she said, but the rest of the family had followed David and were gathering around her. "You're overreacting. He was just trying to get my attention, I'm sure." She looked at Todd, and he raised his eyebrows.

"Yeah! That's all I was doing… I… I told Erin you could come in if you wanted to," he stammered, trying to come across as friendly.

"Oh, Mummy, may we?" Rosie asked.

"Please, Mum, I'd like to see your house," Charlie said unexpectedly. Dan had already run up the steps and was looking through the screen on the front door.

Erin looked at David, and he shrugged. "Okay, you may go in and sit in the living room until I come in; I won't be long," she said, and Rosie beamed, giving her a quick hug.

"Thank you, Mummy," she said, melting the adults' hearts.

Todd put his hand out toward David, and he reluctantly shook it. "I need to apologize… well, for a lot of things. I'm sure Erin told you what I did by now. I was hurting, and I was wrong," he said. David nodded but didn't say anything. "I… I didn't have a doctor's appointment, Erin. I… signed up for the Registry, like you suggested. I just got back from meeting my match. She was nervous and wanted to meet before starting treatments. She'll be coming here later tonight. I spent all those years trying to help you, and I couldn't.

217

Well… now I can actually help someone. I can make a difference this time," he said humbly.

"Oh, Todd, you did make a difference! I'll be forever grateful for everything you've done for me," she said and wanted to hug him, but instead, she put her arm around David's waist. "I'm glad you're moving on," she said, then they heard a noise inside the house. "Oh! I'd better check on the children!"

"You finally got what you wanted, didn't you?" Todd said as she started for the door.

She turned back, not knowing how to take his comment. "What's that supposed to mean?" she asked, furrowing her brow.

"I just mean that you've always wanted English kids who called you mummy, and now you have them. I'm glad."

"You remember that?" she asked.

"Of course I do; you never shut up about it… I mean… it was important to you. I'm sorry I couldn't give it to you." They heard Daniel and Peter yelling, so Erin bolted for the door. She saw Dan halfway into the kitchen and Peter standing near the doorway.

"Alright, what's happening?" Erin said, already sounding like a mom. Daniel came back into the room and sat on the armchair with a huff.

"He was tired of waiting and said he was only going to look, not touch, so I tried to stop him," Peter said.

Erin smiled at the young man standing before her and put her hand on his shoulder. "Thank you, Peter; you've done the right thing. Now, Daniel, please apologize to your brother and to Todd since this is his house now, and you did not have permission to explore." Todd was about to protest, but Erin held out her hand to stop him.

"Sorry, Peter, sorry—" he began and then paused.

"You can call me Todd," he said, but when Daniel looked at his father for direction, Erin stepped in.

"You may call him Todd or Mr. March; either one is fine," she said and waited for him to finish his apology.

"Sorry, Mr. March." He looked at his father and bowed his head, "Sorry, Dad," he said, sounding like he meant it.

———

"A'right, son, well done," David said and smiled at Erin. *She really does have a knack for parenting.*

"Now, I will give you a tour; walk this way," Erin said. Everyone followed normally, but Dan, being sharp as a tack, started imitating her walk, making Todd laugh out loud, which caused her to turn around.

"What? You told us to walk this way; I was obeying as best I could," Dan said with a wily grin that showed his dimples. David had to stifle a laugh himself and shooed them along.

"Oh, I have something to give you before you go, don't let me forget it," Todd said to her, then he turned to David. "Your kids seem really great." The two men watched as Erin walked around the house like a mother duck, leading her little ducklings all in a row.

"Aye, Erin has been amazin' with them; she was meant tae be a mum," he said, watching them disappear into a room only to emerge a few moments later and then disappear again.

"Would you like a beer? I think I have a Guinness or two in the fridge," Todd offered.

David looked at him, trying to decide if he wanted to accept anything from him. "A'right, thanks," he said, and as Todd walked away, he saw the spot, just under the calendar, where Erin had fainted after discovering she was pregnant and that there was a slim chance it could be Todd's. It was a bittersweet moment, since that had been when Erin had said goodbye to her life there and began a journey into the unknown with him.

"There ya go," Todd said, handing him a dark brown bottle with a black label.

"Thanks." Out of habit, David raised his bottle as a lazy cheers, the way people do, and it struck him as odd that he'd done that to Erin's ex-husband.

"You wanna sit on the back deck while we wait for the tour to end?"

David was surprised at how amiable Todd was being, seeing they were invading his privacy and home. "I reckon we could do that," he said and followed him outside, where there were several red plastic Adirondack chairs and a free-standing covered swing which had seen better days. In the center was a fire dish. David could imagine Erin and Todd sitting out there on a chilly summer evening with Lily, Nick, and Ariana, talking and laughing.

Todd sat on one of the red chairs, and David sat on the bench swing. "So, tell me, what's it like to be an actor? I know I said I didn't like *Future Explorations*, but that's not really true. I liked the show well enough; I just didn't like how much Erin liked you in it." Todd said with a slight smile.

"Well, et has its ups and downs. Et can be boring work; a lot of sitting around and waiting, but other things are nice, like—"

"Like being recognized and signing autographs? Having people tell you how much they like you?" Todd interjected. "I guess the pay isn't all that bad either," he added with a grin.

"The attention was great at first, but et can be difficult tae have a real life when everaone's starin' at you and yer family. Then yeh don't know whom you can trust and who's just tryin' tae get somethin' from yeh. But ye're right, the money is nice," he said with a smile.

"What was the first thing you acted in?" Todd asked, and David had to think about it.

"An advert for—a fizzy drink," he said and laughed.

Erin and the children came out onto the deck. "What was a commercial for a fizzy drink?" she asked, and the children, each holding a small dish of ice cream, made themselves at home in the chairs. David smiled at her, and she sat next to him on the swing.

"Ma first actin' job," he said, and Erin nodded, smiling right back at him. "You've not seen et, have yeh?" he asked, and she giggled.

"Aye, I have. It's on YouTube. I saw it years and years ago." She pulled out her phone, searched for it, and let out a 'whoop' when she found it. The children and Todd leaned in to watch while David, on the other hand, put his head in his hands and groaned.

"Ach! Dinnae show that around! Et's awful!" It was too late; he could hear the announcer speaking.

"*...Lord, Chorley, I think we might use a video replay here....*"

"What? That's really creepy!" Todd said but was laughing with the rest of them. "Which one are you?"

"I'm the mate on the right.

"How long ago was this?"

"Nearly thirty years ago, I reckon."

"The bald orange dude is gross, and his genitals get way too close to the guy drinking the pop!" Todd said through his laughter.

"You look just like Peter!" Charlie said.

"Aye, he's a handsome kid," David said, trying to alleviate his embarrassment with a little humor.

"Agreed!" Erin said.

"Are you gonna follow in your dad's footsteps?" Todd asked Peter.

"No, sir, I'm going to be a botanist," he replied and smiled at his dad.

"Aye, and I couldn't be prouder!" David said.

"Me too," Erin said. "Now, finish your ice cream; we have a plane to catch. Thank you for being so kind, Todd. I really am glad you're moving on—"

"Yeah, my match is really sweet. I'm glad I took your advice. And… well, Diane and I have only just met and… well, that electricity thing helps me understand how you must've felt when you came home."

"Yeah, it was difficult. Anyway," she said, not wanting to dwell on that time. She stood, and the whole family did the same, then she went back into the house. "Bring me your bowls, kids."

"Don't worry about washing the dishes, Erin. I'll do it," Todd said.

"Are you sure?" she asked, and he nodded.

"Like you said, you have a plane to catch."

"Okay. Oh yeah, you said you had something for me?"

"Yes, just one minute, and I'll get it," Todd said and headed toward the spare room. A few moments later, he returned holding four tall, thin books. "Here, I thought you might want these."

Erin knew exactly what they were and groaned. "Oh, man! Now I'll have to show everyone!" she said and laughed at the confused look her new family was giving her. "These are my high school yearbooks. I'll show you in the car or something."

The children seemed disappointed, and David raised his eyebrows at her. "It's only fair, as I had to sit through the advert," he said.

"Fine, I'll find my freshman photo, but that's all we have time for now," she said and began flipping through the book on the top of the pile. She was having a difficult time of it because the books underneath were slippery and cumbersome, so Todd reached out to take them.

"Here, let me help," he said, so she handed them to him and continued her search.

"Oh, man! I should've shown you my senior photo instead," she said and held the book out for everyone to see.

"That's you?" Daniel said and began giggling.

"Stop it, Dan," Charlie said. "I think she's pretty."

"Thank you, Charlie," Erin said.

"I agree," Peter said, and Rosie smiled.

"Yes, you are pretty, but your hair is… different," she said and then blushed.

"Yes, well, those were different times, and the last thing on my mind was my hair. I'd just started having symptoms and, well… yeah, it wasn't a priority."

"Ye're lovely, darling," David said and placed his hand on her shoulder.

"This one's better," Todd said and handed him the next book with the page opened to her photo.

"Todd! That's not fair," she said, and he shrugged.

"Your face is full of spots!" Dan said and again began laughing hard.

"Spots?" Todd said. "Those are, uh, pimples."

Erin shot him an unamused look, and he shrugged again. "That's what they call them," she said dryly.

"Oh, sorry, but here's her junior year," he said and handed Peter the third book.

"How old were you in this one?" he asked with a bright smile.

"Junior year—Gosh, sixteen or seventeen, I think," she said.

"Goh, that's my age!" he said, looking more closely at her image. "You were choong in my book."

Erin furrowed her brows. "Translation, please?"

"Oh, uh, it means… pretty," he said and then blushed.

"Thank you, Peter, you're sweet. I didn't feel pretty! I felt out of control and ugly."

"Ugly? You were beautiful, Mummy," Rosie said and wrapped her arms around her middle.

"Thank you, baby girl," she said and looked up to see Charlie nodding his agreement. "Alright then, show them the last one already."

Todd had the book open and was gazing at the page with a slight smile. "Look at you, Erin. This young woman has so much potential—" He seemed to remember who was in the room then and shook his head. "Sorry, I just wish the disease hadn't taken your life away from you as it did for so long, that's all." He handed her the book and then turned away.

She looked at him and sighed, then she turned to David and handed him the book, pointing to her picture. He took it, and the kids gathered around him. "Stunning," David said and gave the book to Charlie to hold. He went to her and she held him for a moment.

"Thanks, but I really think we should go now. You can look at them more in the car," she said to the children. "Thanks for keeping these, Todd."

"It wasn't a big deal," he said, and she saw his face become a bit pink. "Uh, I just wanna say I'm sorry again and, uh, that I hope everything works out for you… now that you have your, uh, well, now that your dream has come true."

"Yeah, it has, and all's forgiven. I wish you the best, and take care of yourself," she said and fought the urge to hug him as the children and David said their goodbyes. They went back to the SUV, and she felt a slight twinge of the sadness she'd felt when she'd left a few months earlier. She knew he wasn't a bad person; it just hadn't worked out between them. Todd stood on the front stoop and waved as she pulled away from the curb.

"Are you a'right?" David asked after a few miles of silence.

"Yes, I'm okay. It's just bittersweet, you know?"

"Aye, et is, but now ye've made peace, and yeh both can heal. I'm glad he's found someone tae help; et truly makes a man feel as though he's not a failure, yeh ken?"

"I think I do, and I agree, he deserves to be happy too," she said as she took his hand and smiled at him.

It wasn't long before they were at the airport, and after the rental was returned, they flew through security. After about an hour's wait with people staring and speaking behind their hands about them, they were seated on a small jet headed for Chicago.

The looks and stares didn't stop until they got to the VIP lounge, and Erin noticed a message from her mother on her phone.

> Liz: *Hope you had fun in Door County. You should know that the tabloids and local news have been covering a story about David Elliott being seen all over Wisconsin with photos and short videos of your stay. There are also interviews with those you spoke to. It's a real sensation, I guess. There are quite a lot of photos of the children, too, just so you're aware. It was lovely seeing you, and I hope you have a safe trip home! Love you all.*

> Erin: *Great! I can't wait to see that! Thanks for the heads up. I love you, and it was so good to see you and Dad again! XOXO*

"You should read this," she said and handed her phone to David.

He took it and sighed right away. "Videos? For f—heaven's sake!" he said and handed her phone back to her.

Erin decided to look up some of the articles. She searched, *David Elliott,* and before she even finished typing, her search engine completed it with *...seen in Door County, Wisconsin...* She touched the suggestion and read the title of the first news story.

David Elliott Seen with Children in Wisconsin Tourist Destination. She clicked on the link and saved it. *I'll read this later,* she thought and then looked over at David. He must've had the same idea because she heard him trying to censor his language. *Or maybe I won't.*

Part Two

Chapter Twenty-Two

HOME AGAIN

David, Erin, and the children were exhausted when they finally stepped through the door of their house in London. The kids were snippy, with short fuses, and Rosie was whining. Erin's head hurt, and her ankles were swollen from the difference in air pressure on the plane. Daniel was also reminded of his grounding, which didn't improve anything.

She knew David was tired and just wanted to relax, but he had to help bring in the luggage and check in with Kitty and Francie before that would happen. A tall pile of mail was waiting for him on the hall table, and she saw him take it to the study after supper.

She did a timid search for the headlines her mother had told her about and didn't find anything overly invasive. Only one photo was unflattering, so she wasn't going to bother discussing it with him. Something she'd found and wanted to show him was the men's magazine interview he'd done on the day the house had been searched.

Knowing he was stressed and would be busy, she waited a while before knocking on the study door. "Aye?" he said, and she opened the door a crack.

"Are you busy? I found the article in *Impressive Male* and thought I'd read it to you," she said, not opening the door all the way yet.

"Ach, what are yeh doin' stadin' in the hall? Come in and show me." He was sitting on his desk chair and patted his lap.

"I didn't want to disturb you if you were concentrating on something. I know you were looking for a bit of quiet so you could relax," she said.

"Don't be daft, woman! Ye're welcome tae come in here anatime, no matter when. I'm far better at relaxing when I'm with you, yeh ken?" he said as she eased herself onto his lap.

"What are yeh doin' now?" he said and laughed. "Ye're not goin' tae squash me, love. I can take et; now, show me the interview."

She turned and kissed him, not caring about the article any longer. "I love you, Mr. Elliott," she said and hugged him around the neck, making him laugh softly.

"And I love you, as well, *almost* Mrs. Elliott; now hurry up, ma legs've gone numb," he said and laughed so hard he began coughing.

"Har har har, very funny, Mr. Elliott, or should I call you Dave?"

"Ach, dinnae do tha'! I'm not keen on bein' called that."

"Well, I reckon you should've corrected the man who interviewed you, then," she said and held up her phone.

"*The Future Seems Fab for David Elliott,* not a very inventive title, I must say, though it is positive."

"Aye, I reckon et is that, at least."

> *Isaac Marchant caught up with David Elliott recently to discuss his past, present, and future, which seems to be looking bright.*
>
> Isaac Marchant: *Hello, and thank you for agreeing to this interview, Mr Elliott.*
>
> David Elliott: *Please, call me David, and you're welcome.*
>
> IM: *Alright, Dave, I'll just get to it then. Already this year, you've completed a lovely Rom-Com, which has had brilliant reviews, had a steamy cameo on American television, and been in several adverts and the like. Do you have anything in the works for next year?*
>
> DE: *I've been offered a part, though I can't say anything more about it at this time.*

IM: *Really, how exciting? Will there be any martinis and perhaps bikinis involved?*

DE: *I'm not following—Oh, right… It's not James Bond if that's what you're referring to.*

IM: *That's a shame. Any kilts, then?*

DE: *I'm afraid not, not unless there's something I've not been told.*

IM: *Whatever it is, I'm sure you'll be brilliant, Dave.*

DE: *Well, thank you for that.*

IM: *If you don't mind, I've a few questions on the personal side. First, allow me to relate our heartfelt condolences on the passing of your wife, Susannah Sutcliffe Elliott. It must be a difficult time for you and your children.*

DE: *Thank you. It was for a time, but now we're doing quite well actually. As I'm sure you're well aware—*

IM: *Yes, in point of fact, we are, and that leads me to my next question. You have some big news, haven't you?*

DE: *I do, though could you elaborate?*

IM: *Well, now that your wife has passed, you're in love again, aren't you?*

DE: *Yes, I am, though I'd rather you—*

IM: *You met your new partner through the Fertilis Defect Registry, correct?*

DE: *Yes, I did. It's a—*

IM: *Treatments for the Fertilis Defect involve sexual intercourse, correct?*

DE: *Yes, that is the—*

IM: *Your wife, Susannah, was alive when you registered, wasn't she? Was she aware you'd done it, and how did she feel when she learned of it, and then what you'd done in New Orleans whilst filming Definite Action?*

DE: *What? Where is this going? This seems like an interrogation. I didn't come here to talk about my former marriage.*

IM: *No, of course not, but that must have been awkward; married to a supermodel and paired up with a stranger in order to have sex with her?*

DE: *I—Where are you going with this? I'm very close to walking out.*

IM: *Sorry, Dave, let me rephrase the question. It must've been quite daunting to be faced with having sex with a stranger, correct?*

DE: *Yes, it was difficult to imagine at first, but my match and I were meant to be. We both felt it from the start.*

IM: *I'm sure the woman you were paired with did. I imagine she was thrilled to have you as her match. How long did it take for her to get used to your being who you are?*

DE: *Not long. We have a chemistry that surpasses my job or whatever fame I've found myself with. We have something that I never had with—*

IM: *And what was it like for you to be matched with someone like her?*

DE: *Someone like her? What do you mean by that?*

IM: *Your new partner, Erin, isn't someone people expect a famous, attractive actor to be with, is she?*

DE: *Are you taking the piss? Are you truly gonna go there?*

IM: *It's just that she's not, well, fit, and if I'm honest, many people are surprised by your choice to continue a relationship with her, especially after—*

DE: *Is that why I'm here? Do you realise… no one ever once asked me why I was with Susannah, who was so thin you could see every bone in her body. This interview is over. Erin is a thousand times the person… and more beautiful to me than… I'll not answer LUDICROUS, body-shaming, mean-spirited questions by a hypocritical bawbag such as yourself. Perhaps you should take a long look in the mirror, as you've a nice start to your own breasts and a substantial belly as well.*

(David Elliott then stood, took off his microphone, and walked out of the room.)

"I can't believe they printed all that about his breasts and belly! Maybe the editors thought he was out of line too," she said and hugged him as he laughed.

"Aye, perhaps they did, love. Et's a good thing I did leave just then, as that's when yer call came through, and I wouldn't have heard et otherwise."

"I'm a thousand times the person… as whom?" she asked, playing innocent.

"Ach, I was wrong when I said that."

Her heart fell, and she nodded. "Okay," she said sadly.

David laughed lightly, and using his finger on her chin, he turned her head to face him. "Ye're at least a million or more times the woman Susannah was, and ye're more beautiful to me than anaone I've ever seen," he said softly.

"And you are a million times the man I imagined you'd be when I met you." She leaned over and kissed him. "I'm a bit surprised you gave him any info about your new role," she said and snuggled up against him.

"Aye, about that… not about my sayin' anathin', but about the role itself."

He seemed to become a bit upset or anxious, so she sat up and looked at him. "What's wrong?"

"Well, I'm wonderin' if I should pass on *Doctor Who*?" he said and began picking at an imaginary thread on her jeans.

"Wow, for what reason? That's a big decision" she said.

"Dinnae ken, et's a gut feelin'." He gently pushed her off his lap, then stood and began pacing in front of her. "I'm not sure… I'm afraid et might be more fame than I'm wantin' in our life. I want a quiet life with you and our bairns, and *that* role would put an end tae any peace we might enjoy now."

She'd had the same thought many times but had pushed it back. "I think you're right, David; that's the kind of thing you can't walk away from. It's an iconic part, one that could affect our lives in a way I'm not sure will ultimately be good for us."

"So… ye're agreein' with me?" he said, sounding surprised.

"Yes, and I admit that I've been a bit worried, too. I want you to do what you love; take the parts you choose, but I agree, this would be a lifetime commitment. Why do you sound so surprised that I'd agree with you?" she asked.

"I hate tae bring her up again, but Susannah never had faith in my decision-makin' skills. I'm not used to ma partner bein' so accomodatin'," he said and smiled at her, touching her cheek. "Thank you."

"The only reason I didn't bring up my concerns was that I thought you wanted to do it, and because of the fortune teller saying, '*The Doctor who would take care of me and my child…*' she said.

David shook his head and sighed. "Aye, one of the reasons I didn't say anathin' as well. Et's not been an easy decision, but I've spoken tae Becky about ma options."

"You have?" she said.

"Aye, I wanted tae know if backin' out was even an option at this point. She said I could, and they actually had someone else in mind if I did."

"They did? Who?"

"Can't tell yeh—They didn't tell me actually," he said with a laugh.

"Okay then, does that mean you're not going to do it?" she asked.

"I reckon so… I just dinnae feel right about et."

"I'm sure other amazing parts will come up," she said brightly.

He looked at her with a twinkle in his eye. "Aye, as it happens, Becky did mention that there was an interest in me for a miniseries. She said et would be a three-year commitment but as a secondary character, not the lead, meanin' I'd have more time away from the set."

"That sounds great, David! Did she say anything about it, like the theme or anything?"

"Not yet, as I was on the fence. All she said was et may be filmed in the south… Summerset or Dorset, which appeals verra much tae me."

"Oh! Me too!" she exclaimed. "Dorset is one of my favorite places."

"Mine as well, darling. I imagine she'll tell me more when I call her back. I'm chuffed tae bits ye're in agreement with me on this. I was dreadin' the thought of havin' zero privacy. The children will be better off as well, I think," he said, and she could sense relief washing over him.

"Aye, Rosie and Charlie mentioned something about being embarrassed when they saw one of your mobile phone ads on a bus stop. I don't think they'd appreciate the attention they'd have to deal with if you were the Doctor."

"When was this?" David asked.

"When the ads first came out. The day I took them shopping. It wasn't a big deal," she said, "except that inside Harrods, there was a full wall ad with you in it. You looked so handsome, but they were a bit upset."

David sighed, though it sounded a bit like a groan. "I forget they must deal with the fame as well. It can't be easy for them."

"If you weren't famous, they'd wish you were; there's no winning," she said with a smile.

"Aye, human nature, I reckon."

"Maybe, if you do take the job, I'll look at properties in Dorset."

"Aye, et seems a perfect place to raise chickens and children," he said with a smile. "That's a heavy load off ma mind. I'll call Becky now." He kissed her forehead and left the room.

Once she was alone, Erin sighed. *Thank God!* she thought. The role of the Doctor seemed ideal, except it would make their lives a glass house for… forever. She'd been getting nervous as the time got nearer and had also begun to dread it.

When David returned, he was smiling. "That's that sorted," he said and sat next to her on the sofa.

"Good. Did she tell you anything about the part?"

"Aye. I've been told et's about a veterinary surgeon," he said with a grin.

"Seriously? So… you'll still be a doctor who will take care of me and my child or children… I think it's quite clear at this time?" she said.

He laughed and pulled her close. "Seems that way. It's called *Wilde's Life*. I'll ask Tina to find a house for us to hire whilst I'm filming."

"Goodie! I'm excited now," she said. "Please ask her to find a place with a bit of charm and maybe near the sea if possible."

"Aye, that's just what I was going tae do."

Chapter Twenty-Three

DAVID'S DREAM

David was in his grandmother's kitchen. The old wooden windows were open, and the fine, white cotton curtains fluttered in the breeze. He could hear the gulls and the waves of the ocean against the billions of tiny pebbles along the shore of the Jurassic coast. His only desire was to get to the beach and scour it for shells and interesting rocks, but he had to finish his breakfast first.

"Now, Davey," his mother said. "Yeh must finish yer egg and soldiers, or yeh cannae go out tae play. The longer yeh take, the colder et'll become, love."

"Aye, Mother," he said and looked down at his egg. It looked like Humpty Dumpty in the nursery rhyme book his gran read from every night when she tucked him in. He didn't like runny yolks, especially once they'd gotten cold. Bracing himself, he started dunking his toast into the top of his egg, scarcely chewing, trying not to taste it. Then he took his spoon, dug out all the white, and stuffed it into his mouth. After swallowing hard, he sprang up. "May I please be excused from the table?" he asked.

"Did yeh chew any of et?" his mother asked him.

He nodded and then shrugged. "I've eaten et, as yeh said I should. May I please go now?" He was trying with all his heart to be patient, but he needed to get to the beach or the other kids would find all the good stuff.

"Aye, Davey, ma boy, but not until yeh give yer mummy a kiss." He smiled and gave her a kiss on the cheek, then he ran up the ladder to his loft room to get his bucket and spade. He ran back into the kitchen to put on his wellies and hat, then ran out the door. The sea breeze was fresh and energizing as it rushed over his cheeks, and he could smell the salty air. It was complete freedom, or at least as much as his eight-year-old self could imagine.

He ran across the narrow road, carefully looking both ways and not dawdling as his father had taught him. Then he ran across the grassy field to the high cliff, but never too close to the edge. Careful not to lose his step and tumble down the steep, rocky path lined with tall green and yellow grass and red dirt, he ran as fast as he could until he reached the bottom. He stepped from the hard-packed ground into the beach. It was literally 'into' because his wee feet sank into the tiny pebbles and rocks worn smooth and soft from the tide washing them over and over for thousands of years.

He loved the feel of the stones when he took off his wellies and let his toes sink into them. They were both warm and cold at the same time. The heat of the sun warmed the top layer, while the ones underneath stayed cool and wet. When they mixed, it was a feeling like no other.

His eyes scanned the beach to see what his competition was that day. There were a few older girls to his left and a big boy further past them; he would stay away from him. To his right was one of his friends. He couldn't remember her name, but she was fun to play with and good at sharing what they found together, so he walked up to her.

"Hi, Davey!" she said cheerfully and smiled at him.

"Hi," he said, wishing he could remember her name. She was pretty, with big brown eyes and long brown hair. That day it was braided into two braids that hung on either side of her head, one on each shoulder. She had tall yellow wellies and a green pail with a white handle and blue spade. "Have yeh found anathin' good this mornin'?" he asked and looked into her bucket.

"I think so," she said with a broad Dorset accent. "But you know better what's good and what isn't."

David lifted a shell from out of the bucket and turned it over in his hand. "This is nice," he said and then picked up an old key, rusty and bent. He was about to comment on it when he heard his name being called and looked up. His grandmother was calling to him from the top of the cliff. "But I've only just gotten down here!" he said and opened his eyes to find Erin standing over him, smiling.

"You were talking in your sleep," she said.

"I was havin' the most amazin' dream," he said and told her in vivid detail what he'd dreamt. "...and I couldn't remember her name. I had just picked up a rusty, old key when yeh woke me."

"There's an old key in your office, is that the same one?" she asked.

"Aye! That's right. I must've seen it and it jogged a memory, causing the dream. I do wish I could remember her name."

"I'm sure it'll come to you; now, let's get up and have breakfast so you can help me decide on a few details for the wedding."

"Emily Tuck!" David said suddenly at breakfast.

Erin looked up at him, not knowing what to think. "George Jetson!" she said in response, making David smile at her. "Well, I figured if we were going to be shouting out random names, I might as well join in."

"Emily Tuck was the girl on the beach, the one in my dream. I'd forgotten all about her... I wonder where she is now. Hmm—" he said and continued eating his Weetabix.

"Hmm," she echoed. *Just don't wonder too much,* she thought, hating the green monster already growing in her mind. When they'd talked about the move earlier, she'd been thrilled at the idea, but after his trip down memory lane, she was a bit more hesitant.

"I'm chuffed tae take yeh to the beach and show you around," he said and gave her one of his million-pound smiles.

"Me too."

Chapter Twenty-Four

A DRESS FIT FOR THE QUEEN

Although they had to wait six months after Erin's divorce was final before they could get married, now that they were home, there was a lot to do. The timing of the ceremony was set on that timeframe, and as long as the Home Office didn't investigate them, they planned to have their wedding on the day after Christmas, called Boxing Day. Erin had always liked Boxing Day and thought it would be easy for everyone to remember.

They planned to have a cozy civil ceremony at Owlgate with only their family and closest friends there to celebrate. The invitation list was very short and included David's mother, Annis and her partner Millie, their four children, Erin's parents Frank and Liz, and her best friend Lily and her husband Nick, who would be flown in first-class for the occasion. In addition, there would be Roger and Tilly, Kitty and a guest, Francie and a guest, and finally, Tim from the curiosity shop and a guest.

They were undecided on whether to have a formal reception. Erin thought a small meal and dancing afterward would be plenty on the day. They did talk about having a small party with more of their friends sometime after the baby was born, though it might end up being on their first anniversary.

David's assistant, Tina, was working on the necessary paperwork and forms to be submitted and filed for permission to marry. Erin had given her both her birth certificate and final divorce papers. She knew it would all be okay, but it still felt overwhelming, and she was thankful to have someone else to do it for her.

"Oh, Kitty, I know it's not going to be a big wedding, but I want it to be special, and I'm overwhelmed already!" Erin said during the first week in August, three weeks after they returned from their trip, as they prepared to move temporarily to Dorset. "I want a cake and at least a few decorations. I can ask David to have Tina set up the registrar, but I'll need a dress—Oh no! I'm only three months along now. I'll be much bigger at the end of December! How can I get a dress that'll fit me at short notice since I don't know how big I'll get?"

Kitty cocked her head to the side and smiled at her employer. "My gran was a seamstress to the Queen… I mean, she made some of the dresses the Queen wore, way back. She worked for a clothier what the Queen used regular like, an' she taught me mum to sew. She used ta say 'at me mum were better than 'er," Kitty said. "I reckon she'd be willin' ta make ya somfin' pretty if ya gives 'er enough time."

"For the Queen? Back in the day? And your mom sews as well? Are you sure she'd be up to it? I… wouldn't want to… overwork her," Erin said.

"Overwork me mum? Blimey! She's the 'ardest workin' person I know. I'll ask 'er and see what she says."

"Alright, Kitty, thank you. I don't want anything fancy, just a simple, flattering dress. Oh, and if it could camouflage my baby belly, that's even better," Erin said, hoping she was talking about the beautiful dresses the Queen wore, not the ugly polyester things from the 1960-70s.

That week, the family had a very long meeting concerning what the children wanted to do about their schooling and what would work best with David being on location in the south. He wanted to keep them out of boarding school, but after discussing many options, they drove down to Dorset and toured a fine school called Puncknowle.

The whole atmosphere was completely different. The grounds were large with plenty of lawn to enjoy, and the buildings were made from light-colored stones. There were many areas for sports and walking paths to explore.

Indoors, the rooms were bright and cheery, and every person they spoke to seemed genuinely pleasant and welcoming. One man and two women even had Scottish accents and were clearly not expected or encouraged to hide or change them. The student's houses were modern and comfortable, too.

It was such a drastic change from bleak, dark, unloving Carnoch, that the whole family was thrilled. The children told their dad and Erin that they loved it, and though David voiced his concerns, they decided they wanted to go there instead of a state school.

"Me mum says she'd be 'onored ta make a dress for you," Kitty said Tuesday night when she got back from her day off.

"Really? Oh, that's so sweet!" Erin said. "I'd rather that than a store-bought one any day!"

"You should pop 'round 'er house wifin the next few days, of course, for the measurements and the like. I'll give you 'er address," Kitty said.

Erin had a huge smile on her face and clapped her hands like a little girl. "Oh, Kitty! I'm so excited!" she exclaimed.

Kitty smiled at her. "I am as well if I'm 'onest, mum."

Kitty's mum, Bertha Jones, had seen the revealing photos of Erin and David Elliott and thought she was lovely! She was glad Mr. Elliott had found someone to love, regardless of appearance or social status. Susannah Elliott looked beautiful on the outside, if you liked sickly thin, fragile-looking women, but her heart was black and ugly. She'd been a horrible person who'd treated her Kitty like garbage.

Kitty would come home in tears, telling her of the evil things the woman had said, plotted, and executed. She'd told her many times that she was going to give her notice, but when it came down to it, she always changed her mind. There was something kind about Mr. Elliott that made her daughter feel sorry for him for having a wife like Susannah, so she stayed.

Now that Erin was there, Kitty came home happy and excited to go to work. She told her often how she loved and admired her. How she thought of every day as a new adventure, knowing Erin would say or do something unexpected and quite often funny or brilliant. She also told her how changed Mr. Elliott was. That it was as if a heavy weight had been lifted off him. He laughed and played, and she could tell he worshipped the ground Erin walked on.

Bertha's mother, Doris, had been a name to know in the fashion industry back when the Queen was young and beautiful. Though it wasn't her name on the label, everyone knew she was the reason her employer was as popular as he was. He knew it as well and married her several years after she'd started working for him. They had two daughters, Bertha, and Pearl, but Pearl died of Polio when she was four.

Bertha grew up in the workroom behind the storefront, watching a dozen or so women working feverishly on large, ugly, industrial sewing machines. She was taught at a young age to sew by hand and was allowed to take the smaller scraps of silk, satin, velvet, chiffon, and lace home to practice on. When she began creating gowns for her dolls that looked like the full-sized ones in the store windows, she was taught how to read patterns and create her own using only a few simple tools.

She made dresses for her friends, and before long, she was also working in the back room, using the uninspired but functional sewing machines as well. Her passion was evening gowns and using hand beading and embroidery to make something stand out. Unfortunately for her, it was now the 1960s, and fashion wasn't elegant like it had been in the 1940s.

Clothing was 'mod,' boring, and if you didn't have a figure like Twiggy, which Bertha didn't, it was difficult to look good in any of it. She made it through the '60s, hoping for a revival of elegance in the 1970s, but was disappointed. Bell bottoms, Nehru jackets, shaggy vests, and tube tops were the rage, so she began working on wedding gowns, which was something she could shine at.

She worked hard, creating the most beautiful gowns, until her father's shop closed, and she branched off, making her own and selling them at a price. She'd married for love, not that it's a bad thing, but he wasn't much for working hard, and seeing she could only sell two or three dresses per year, they often had trouble making ends meet.

Five years after Kitty was born, her husband died, as she put it, 'of being hit by a car' while stumbling home sodden one moonless night. She made as many dresses and alterations as she could, and they made do until Kitty was old enough to start working. Kitty wasn't as coordinated, being more like her father, and didn't care overly much about fabrics and clothing, but she had a strong work ethic like her mother and loved cleaning.

Bertha hadn't made a wedding gown in years, and her hands were gnarled and twisted from decades of abuse and arthritis, but she knew she could make something to rival any dress sold in bridal shops and even high-end designers, with their high price tags and ugly designs. Yes, she was looking forward to making a showstopper of a dress for the woman who brightened her daughter's day.

After a failed attempt at using London's public transit, Erin finally located Kitty's mum's house, frustrated after several wrong turns and stupid mistakes. First, she got on the correct transfer bus, only headed in the wrong direction, then she walked all the way down the 'Drive' only to figure out that it was 'Street' she was looking for. She wasn't in the best of moods when she rang the bell and waited for someone to answer the door. All that changed when the door opened and Betha Jones was standing there, smiling at her.

"Mrs. Jones?" Erin said, charmed by the sweet, round woman who greeted her. "I'm—"

Bertha stepped out of the way, allowing her to walk in. "I know who you are, love. Please come in and make yourself at 'ome. Would ya care for a cuppa?" she asked kindly.

"Yes, please," she said and smiled. She looked around her, feeling as though she'd gone back in time about eighty years. There were chintz curtains and throw pillows in the living room and pretty plates with flowers, birds, and a few commemorative ones of the Queen hung on the walls.

On the table was a lovely tablecloth in sage green and white with a design of pink roses in the center and corners. She was handed her cuppa in a pale cream china teacup with a pinstripe of gold on the rim. It had pink and white peonies on it and the beautiful saucer it was sitting on. Her home was lovely, but the thing she admired most was a framed portrait of Queen Elizabeth, young and beautiful, wearing a gown that Erin couldn't take her eyes off.

"Do you like that?" Bertha asked, standing behind her and looking over her shoulder.

"Very much!" Erin said. "Did your mum make that one?" she asked.

"Yes, dear, she did. It's my favorite," she said proudly.

"I can see why; it's stunning!" Erin said, wishing she could've seen it up close. She could sew at an intermediate level but usually got frustrated or bored with the projects she started and rarely finished them unless she just had to or it was for someone else. Sewing a wedding dress for herself would be a mission doomed to failure.

"Finish your tea, and we'll get star'ed; I've several ideas I'd like to show you."

Erin swallowed the last bit of the amazingly delicious tea, then followed Bertha into what had obviously been Kitty's room. It had been transformed into a make-do workspace by moving the bed and other odds and ends into the corner. There was just enough room for a small sewing machine table and empty floor space for cutting and piecing.

"How far along will you be at the ceremony?" she asked.

"About eight months," Erin said. "Do you think you'll be able to make something I won't look like a beached whale in?" she asked, and Bertha smiled.

"I've just the thing, dear," she said and walked to the sewing table. On it were several sheets of paper that she picked up and handed to Erin. She had sketched designs for some lovely dresses, all of them high-waisted with full skirts, each more lovely than the last.

"These are all so beautiful," Erin said, not knowing how she'd choose.

"Good. With one basic pat'ern, I can make any of these. Now, take off your kit, and I'll take your measurements," she said, pulling an old fabric measuring tape out of one of the drawers of the sewing table.

Erin undressed, except for her bra and underwear, and stood in the center of the room while the older woman measured her bust, waist, hips, arms, and along her spine. "What I'll do is work on findin' the fabrics and makin' the undergarments first. I'll sew the linin' for you ta try on and make adjustments. As the wedding date nears, I'll start makin' the actual dress. This pat'ern is easy enough to adjust if I add a drawstring, like a corset, in the back. It may then be tigh'ened at the top, loosened at the skirt, and the extra fabric can be tucked out of sight. I'd like to give you a bit of a lace sleeve and embellish the bodice and skirt with beads and silk ribbon flowers; will that suit your taste?" she asked.

"Yes, it will. I love when dainty meets elegant if that makes sense to you? I... also wonder if pure white is the best idea, seeing I'm obviously not a virgin." she said and laughed.

Bertha smiled and waved her hand, indicating it was of no importance. "It is your day, dear, so you may wear whichever color you fancy. I can make a sash of another color if you'd like? Maybe peacock blue?" she said, and Erin's eyes grew wide.

"Oh! The Elliott tartan! I just read about 'pinning the tartan,' and I want to do that at the wedding. I have a scarf I could loan you so you can find the right colors since there are several different ones. David will be wearing his kilt, so I think having a coordinating sash would be lovely."

They spent an hour or so choosing fabrics and discussing fit and design. When that was done, Erin decided not to brave the London busses and ordered an Uber to bring her home.

Now that the dress was sorted, it was time to think about a cake. Erin began scouting around to find a bakery for the small cake she had in mind. She saw one in a book that had tiny blue and white forget-me-nots with delicate vine tendrils and fell in love with it. She'd just hung up the phone after being told by the fourth bakery that they were booked solid until the next year when it dawned on her that Francie might know someone or be able to do it herself.

"Francie?" she said as she entered the kitchen.

"Aye?" their Scottish cook said, poking her head out from behind the pantry door.

"Are you busy? I have a question."

"Et's fine, dear. What do yeh need?"

"Could you… or do you know someone who could bake our wedding cake? I don't need anything too fancy or large; I just want it to be pretty, and I know you'd do a beautiful job."

Francie's face had an odd expression, and Erin didn't know if it was good or bad. The woman's hand came up suddenly and covered her mouth, then her eyes. It only lasted a moment, then she took a deep breath, straightened her back, and turned to her, her face as sober as ever. "I'd be honored tae make yer weddin' cake, mum," she said, as though the outburst had never happened, and Erin knew to do the same.

"I'm glad! We can discuss colors and styles whenever you're ready."

"Aye. I'll have ma niece help me if yeh dinnae mind et. She's verra talented, yeh ken," she said, and Erin imagined that underneath her guarded exterior, her cook was beaming.

"That's good, thank you, Francie!" she said and hugged her.

David and Erin were busy as bees the next few months planning and deciding. Erin would have liked Kitty to be in her wedding party and told her so, though she knew she wouldn't think it proper. Lily had to be there, though she couldn't decide whether to make her the Matron of Honor or a Bridesmaid. She wanted Rosie in her party as well but wasn't sure she'd be able to be the Maid of Honor. David had chosen Peter and Roger for his wedding party, and he was also finding it difficult to choose, so they decided to ask them, explaining the duties and responsibilities of each role.

They gathered the men and Rosie, then Erin called Lily on Skype to discuss it. Lily wouldn't be there for much of the planning, and Rosie didn't think she'd be able to manage things like holding both bouquets. Plus, David was leaning toward having Peter as his Best Man, and Rosie wanted to be partnered with Roger. It was decided that Lily would be the Matron of Honor, Peter the Best Man, Rosie would be the Bridesmaid, and Roger the Groomsman.

Chapter Twenty-Five

TEMPORARY START

I n late August, they moved to their new residence. Doctor Jill had recommended a temporary midwife, whose office was a mere five-minute drive away. They already had several appointments set up with her, so that was one less thing to worry about. Tina had found them a lovely, cream, stucco, thatched-roof house on top of a hill that overlooked West Bay. Cliff Cottage was old, charming, and only a few minutes from the beach. It had two bedrooms for the children upstairs at one end of the house and a nice cozy bedroom on the other end for Erin and David.

The building had once been a row of three connected cottages, but at some point, one of its owners decided to knock the partitioning walls down and make it one glorious house. There were lots of sunny rooms, and the kitchen had an old farmhouse sink and a lovely wooden table in the center.

The house was mostly furnished, but Erin, Rosie, and often Charlie spent hours on weekends scouring flea markets, boot sales, antique stores, and charity shops for pretty things to add their own special touch. They brought home old tea towels, tablecloths, dishes, trivets, and Erin's favorite, a blue and white floral transferware tea set. Rosie and Charlie really did have a flair for decorating, and between the three of them, they made the house a home.

Situated on top of a hill, Cliff Cottage was edged in from the south and east with subdivisions consisting of relatively new homes and to the north and west by farmland. It sat on an acre of garden that was long and narrow, with many trees and beautiful landscaping. Along the south side of the lot was a bridleway called Donkey Lane. Erin tried to help with the gardening as much as she could, but she didn't have a green thumb and was afraid she'd kill it all if she got too involved.

To the west of the house, a detached building that had once been used as an office now sat vacant. There was also a lovely little shepherd's hut that the owner rented out occasionally, though, for David's privacy, it sat empty as well. There were fruit trees in the garden, and when she had the energy, Erin enjoyed going out while David was filming to pick apples or pears. Sometimes she'd pluck a few figs from the tree near the kitchen when she could find a few that the birds hadn't eaten.

Every now and then, the owner of the cottage would stop by to make sure everything was alright with them. His name was Asitkumar Acharya, but everyone called him Asit. Erin was glad when he came over, enjoying his company a lot. He was kind and laid back, with a quick sense of humor. He had straight, thick, dark, though graying, hair with a cut that made her think of the early Beatles.

He usually wore the same orange, yellow, red, and black striped shirt, or at least Erin rarely saw him in anything else, not that she would ever judge him for wearing what he was most comfortable in. She was down to three items of clothing that fit comfortably and was too stubborn to go shopping, at least not until she outgrew them.

If David wasn't home, she would invite Asit inside for tea and biscuits in the small dining room. If he was home, she would invite him in, and they would sit comfortably in the living room, sharing laughs and stories over glasses of wine, cider, or juice and crisps. Erin made a point of telling Asit how much she loved his house and was glad she was able to live in it each time she saw him. In turn, he would tell her how pleased he was that someone who loved the place was enjoying it so much.

In early September, the children were installed in the new school and would come home about once a month on exeat weekends. Erin learned that an exeat was when the school closed completely for two nights and everyone boarding there must leave.

Almost as soon as they moved in, David and Erin began taking long walks down the coastal path, sometimes accompanied by the children but more often not. It was nice to take their time, looking forward to a meal at the Downhouse Farm Cafe. The small, secluded garden patio dining made it a great place for them to eat in privacy. Their primary customers consisted of backpackers who were friendly and mostly kept to themselves.

Erin usually ordered the bubble and squeak, and David had the bacon sandwich. Occasionally, the owner would come out and tell them that someone had recently stopped in asking if David Elliott would be eating there soon, having heard that he was a frequent patron. She smiled when she disclosed that she always replied that they had just missed him, as he had been in the day before. David laughed when he heard that and thanked her.

She loved the path which followed the coast, stretching up and down the red dirt cliffs with a lovely large stone beach halfway between Cliff Cottage and the cafe. She knew she'd never tire of the views or of seeing the sheep and cows as they approached the farm. At first, she took dozens of photographs of the ocean, cliffs, and rolling inland hills, but after a while, she got used to it and just enjoyed the walk with the man she loved.

Their hikes were a good bit of exercise but not nearly as taxing as going up Arthur's Seat. Plus, David would help her up the hills by pulling or pushing her, and she loved him for it. She knew that if she kept it up, she'd be in better shape, though winter was fast approaching, and she wasn't sure how many fine days they'd have then. She was used to such harsh winters that it seemed unimaginable to take long walks in December.

The hardest part for her was the walk back; the hills seemed taller, and she struggled much more. David wasn't bothered as much, being in far better shape, and helped her, making a game out of it. When they finally made it back to the cottage, she would flop down on the sofa and strip off all unnecessary clothing, making David laugh. Often, he'd try to take advantage of her nudity, though she usually pushed him away playfully, saying she was too hot.

That day, he countered with, "I'll get you hot!" and blew puffs of cool air over her bare chest while fanning her with a nearby throw pillow. "What is et about you? I feel as if I'm seventeen again, wantin' yeh at all hours. I think ma libido is at an all-time high."

"I don't understand it either. I keep getting bigger and bigger; before long, I won't be able to see my toes!"

"Well then, I'll look at them for yeh, darling. They are beautiful!"

"Uggg, not with my swollen ankles!"

"Even with your swollen ankles, my love."

During one visit, Asit told Erin about the parties he'd thrown at the cottage over the years. It didn't take much to convince him to help throw one while she and David were living there. They decided to host a Bollywood-themed birthday party for Erin, even though they only had two weeks to plan for it.

David sent a message to Tina, asking her to send out invitations to the people on the party invitation list in his address book, asking them to dress up. They assumed that very few of them would be able to come since it was a last-minute affair. Erin didn't know many people there yet, so she invited the ones she loved most in the UK, including Kitty, Tim from the curiosity shop, though she knew it was too far for him to come, and David's family, including Millie, Roger, and Tilly.

She also insisted that both Tina, David's personal secretary, and Becky, his agent, were invited, as well as everyone he was currently working with on the series he'd just started filming. She wanted to get to know them and asked Asit to invite his close friends as well.

Asit offered to help with décor since he'd hosted one a few years earlier and still had many of the decorations in storage and some that he used every day in his home. He told Erin where to find beautiful saris for her and Rosie and clothing for David and the boys. Part of the night's surprises would be the reveal, as Asit took the men to find just the right outfits and wouldn't allow Erin to see what they'd found.

Asit referred them to the caterer he'd always used. They were booked for that weekend, so they put her in touch with a family who had a small restaurant and occasionally provided catering. Thankfully, they had an opening. Asit's friend, Ananya, was hired to bake a cake, consulting with Erin to find out what she wanted it to look like. Not having ever seen an Indian cake before, she pretty much gave her creative license. They also found an artist to give Erin and Rosie henna tattoos the day before the event.

With Asit's help, they hired a man who would be their DJ and had an extensive collection of Indian music. He knew of a group of Bollywood dancers who he thought would love the opportunity to perform for her and her guests. They agreed, so the party was coming together better than Erin had ever dreamed.

She was excited as the RSVPs started coming in by email, text, and IMs, though she was only allowed to see a few of them. The majority were seen by David only, and he wouldn't tell her who they were or how many had said they'd come. She did know there'd be far more people attending than they thought would be available, so they booked several hotel rooms in town for those who might need one. She really wished that Lily, Nick, and her parents could come, but she hadn't even bothered inviting them since they lived so far away, and she'd see them at the wedding.

When the children came home on exeat a few days before the party, the whole family pitched in to prepare party favors. Erin and Rosie had found some beautiful blue glass votive candles with gold designs on them. There were also small battery-powered votives that looked the part and a good number of small elephant photo frames of different colors.

They wrapped squares of sparkly netting around them, added some brightly wrapped chocolates, and then tied them with curling ribbon, which the children took turns 'curling' with the edge of the kitchen shears. Dan managed to eat more chocolates than he added and was soon complaining of a tummy ache, so he had to go to bed early.

The day before the party was a busy day. After her midwife visit, Erin and Rosie drove into Bridport and had their henna tattoos applied. The woman, named Pragya, asked what she would be wearing and was surprised that she didn't have any jewelry. The whole idea had slipped Erin's mind, so she borrowed some costume jewelry for both her and Rosie from her. They giggled as they tried them on, posing and acting silly.

Pragya also taught them how to do their makeup, though they washed it off before returning to the cottage. They didn't want to ruin the surprise. The henna would have to dry for several hours before the green paste turned brown and could then be washed off. It was difficult not to bump them while they were still wet. Miraculously, they managed not to, except for one little smudge when Rosie misjudged the car door handle. One of the leaves got smooshed, but it was hardly noticeable.

Chapter Twenty-Six

TO ERIN ON HER 40TH BIRTHDAY

On the day of the party, Erin woke with butterflies in her stomach. She didn't know what to do with herself and needed to burn off some of the extra energy she felt raging inside of her, so she nearly attacked David before he was fully awake. She climbed on top of him and kissed his chest while grinding on him.

It took a moment for him to wake up enough to realize what was happening, but when he did, he didn't waste any time. He took hold of her hips, pushing and pulling her across his very hard cock, which was now quite wet, ready to enter her at any moment. She bent down to kiss him, and as she did, she tilted her hips, carefully allowing him to slide into her.

They both gasped as they felt their union, and Erin had her first orgasm almost immediately. She paused for a moment to allow her sensitivity to go down. "I want to change positions," she whispered. He smiled and sat up, surprising her; he'd never done that before, but it felt good, and it was nice to be face to face.

Her baby belly was starting to show now, so David laid his palm over it and kissed her. He moved his hand up to one of her breasts and then suckled it, making her arch her back and feel him deep inside her. They stayed in that position for a little while, but it was difficult to move, so she got onto her hands and knees.

—

David knelt behind her and guided himself easily back inside her body. She accepted him, sheathed him, and he knew it wouldn't take long. "Ach,

253

Erin, I'm so close now. Are yeh ready?" He'd started asking her that, fearing she wouldn't be satisfied when he couldn't last as long as he wanted to.

"Uh-huh," she whispered, and he heard her stifle a moan as he felt her release a second before he did.

He continued thrusting until she stopped pulsing, then pulled out, feeling like he'd won the lottery. "I'm the luckiest man alive!" he said gratefully as he lay on his back, one arm over his head and the other resting with his hand on his chest.

Erin rolled onto her side and snuggled up to him, using his bicep as a pillow. "Hmmm, and I'm the luckiest woman," she said as she played with his chest hair. "I can't imagine living without you. I'm so glad you're mine."

"I think you're wrong, dear. I happen to know that *you* are *mine*!" he said.

Erin smiled with her eyes closed. "Aye, ye're no' wrong. We're each other's, and that's the way I like et. I wouldnae have et ana other way," she said in a very put-on Scottish accent.

David laughed. "Go on with yeh. I wannae hear more," he said, amused. He absolutely loved when she did that. If he asked her out of the blue, she'd freeze up and not be able to think of anything, so when her tongue was loose, he liked to encourage her.

"A'right, then, I cannae wait tae hold our bairn betwixt us, jest here," she said, laying her hand where her chest and his met at a 'T.'

"Betwixt? I dinnae—"

"Haud yer wheesht, laddie, I'm no' finished. Do yeh think et'll have brown hair and eyes, our bairn? Or do yeh reckon et'll have red hair and blue eyes?"

"I dinnae ken; et may just have haz-el," he said and paused, remembering that Bran's eyes were hazel and Erin had been forced to see them far too closely. "I'm sorry, darling."

"Dinnae fash, ma love, he may jest have hazel eyes, but let's hope no'," she said softly. "I dinnae care about any of tha'. Et'll be our bairn, and as long as you're here with us, et could be green or even purple, and I'd love him just as much."

"Aye," was all he said. "Happy birthday, darling. I hope you have a bonnie day today."

"I know I will. I'm so excited! I can't wait for you to see me all dressed up, and I'm dying to see your costume! Oh! We should get a... family... photo," she began, having it hit her once more that he and his kids were now her family. "We... can send them... in our... Christmas—" The happiness of it overwhelmed her, and she cried, putting her chin to her chest. She thought of the family photos she'd seen of him and Susannah and how she'd wished *she* were the wife and mother in them.

"Ach! What's wrong, darling?" he asked, obviously not understanding her tears. "I think et's a brilliant idea."

She nodded and tried to collect herself once more. "I'm just so happy to be able to say that... you have no idea. I longed to have that with you after I saw the photos in your little album, and here I am suggesting the theme, as though... I'm... already your... wife. It just feels so good."

"I do ken et, and our weddin' day can't come quick enough," he said and pulled her to him.

She lay her head on his chest and relaxed with the smell of the detergent on the linens and one of David's delicious smells, probably the last remnants of his deodorant. Everything seemed too good to be true, and she wanted to soak it all up.

"Now, we'd better get up; we've a lot tae do today, ma love."

"Eeee! This is going to be the best birthday ever!" she said, bounding out of the bed like a young girl.

David and the boys decided to stay in their normal clothing until the guests started to arrive and then planned to excuse themselves to change. They'd had a long 'meeting' that Erin wasn't allowed in on, and they all seemed excited, except for Dan. He went along with it, but she could tell his heart wasn't in it.

After lunch, Erin and Rosie went upstairs to change. An hour later, they entered the living room looking resplendent in their matching purple and red saris and ornate jewelry. Erin even had a nose cuff with chains that connected to her earring.

Their henna tattoos had cured, and the beautiful designs were now a deep burgundy brown. Their shoes were silk slippers with sequins and glass beads sewn on the top and sides. Rosie had lots of bangles, and her hair was braided with gold chains plaited into it. She told them she felt like a princess and saw Erin as a queen.

Neither of them expected the reaction of David and the boys. David stood with his mouth wide open, then smiled his best smile at them, asking playfully if they knew where his wife and daughter had gone off to. The girls laughed, and Rosie played along. "It's me, Daddy!" she said and gave him a hug.

Peter also had his mouth open but then he closed it and looked proud. Charlie was clearly thrilled and walked around Rosie, looking her up and down, admiring his sister's costume. Daniel stood looking impatient. "What do you think?" Erin asked him, knowing he might say anything.

He shrugged and crossed his arms. "Looks like you're wearing a fancy bed sheet, but I like the nose ring. I hope you don't... no, I hope you *do* sneeze and I get to see it fly off and hit someone in the face!" he said, suddenly animated and showing off his dimples as he smiled wickedly.

"Dan!" David said, but then everyone seemed to have the image go through their heads and laughed with him. "A'right, let's organize and prepare the best we can, then we'll get dressed."

"I can't wait!" Erin said, "Now, what can I do to help?"

"I think we've got it sorted, darling. When the caterers arrive, please lead them to the kitchen; otherwise, just be your drop-dead-gorgeous self. Yeh really do look amazin'," he said once the children had scattered.

Chapter Twenty-Seven

INTRODUCTIONS

Guests had begun to arrive in earnest, and Erin realized she'd forgotten to put out the bright red tablecloth covered with gorgeous mandalas on the punch table. She was just coming out of the house when she heard at least two of the children say, "Judi!"

She turned to see who they were speaking to, but one of the catering staff needed her attention, so she didn't see who it was. Soon, she heard Rosie coming up behind her, calling out, "Mummy," but she had to give her attention to the staff just then and couldn't turn around. "Mummy! I want you to—" Rosie said, sounding excited.

"One minute, Rosie, please don't interrupt," she said and finished her instructions. "Now, my Rosebud, what do you—" she said, and when she turned, she nearly fell over. It wasn't unlike what happened when she'd first laid eyes on David in New Orleans. "Good night nurse!"

"Mummy, this is Judi Dench, and I want you to meet her. She's very nice and really funny. I think you'll like her a lot."

Erin did her best not to stare or go all fangirl, but it was difficult. Judi was wearing an indigo-blue sari with a silver border that had a wide band of silver embroidery dotted with emerald and silver beads and gemstones along the edge.

"Dame Judi! I... don't... I mean... it's so nice to meet you... ma'am," she said, not knowing how to address her. The grand lady was so gracious; she laughed and took Erin's hand in hers.

"My name is Judi, dear; now, let's get to know each other," she said and led her to a bench in the shade of a large, rose-colored hydrangea bush. "I realize you'll be needed shortly, but Rosie and Charlie have done nothing but praise you for the last ten minutes straight. I find that I simply must get to know the woman who has given this family so much joy."

Erin blushed scarlet. She'd loved Judi Dench for so long, and to be sitting there with her was something she'd never imagined. Rosie and Charlie sat near them, Rosie on the bench between them and Charlie on the grass. She was trying to think of anything to say when they all heard David call out, "Boys!"

Erin looked up and saw Peter walk past them, smiling like his father. He gave a little wave to Judi, and she blew him a kiss. He pretended to catch it, placed it on his cheek, and then laughed like a child.

"Come on, Charlie," he called out, "time to get dressed." Charlie smiled and kissed both women on the cheek, making them both laugh. Rosie followed him, so the two women were alone.

"I've a soft spot in my heart for those children, and I shouldn't speak ill of the dead, but their mother was, well, not a good one. They were forced to walk around like little robots without joy or fun. I can see that you're what they need."

"Thank you... Judi," Erin said, humbled by her kind words. "I love them so much."

"And they simply adore you, dear! Oh, Johnny!" she said, gazing at someone standing behind Erin. "Hello, you handsome boy! Come here to me; I'm an old woman and don't wish to get up." Erin saw the twinkle in her eye as she spoke to the person she couldn't see. Judi held out her hand for a kiss as the man walked around the bench to greet her.

"Judi, my love, you're as beautiful as ever," the man said, and Erin instantly recognized the voice as that of Johnny Depp. She was suddenly face to face with him and knew she was on the edge of losing her cool. He was wearing a jet-black tunic with tiny seed pearls embroidered around the neck, matching black trousers, and an ivory sash across his chest.

"This is David's partner, Erin—" Judi said in introduction, looking at her to finish.

"March. Erin... March," she said, trembling.

"Nice to meet you, Ms. March," he said and held out his hand.

Erin was red in the face as she held out her hand, and he lifted it to his lips. "The... pleasure is all mine, believe me," she said, managing to find her sense of humor just in time.

"Johnny!" Rosie said when she returned and went to him, holding out her arms for a hug.

"Hello, Rosie, dear; it's good to see you again," he said and crouched down to accept her embrace.

"Charlie will be so happy to see you! You always make parties fun," Rosie said.

"I'll be sure to find him," he said, then looked at Erin. "Do you know where David is? I've been told he wants to speak to me." His gaze was mesmerizing, and it was all she could do to stop staring and answer him.

"He and... the boys are inside changing. They should be out soon."

"Alright, well, if you'll please excuse me, ladies... I see some punch with my name on it." Erin nodded, and so did Judi.

"Okay, I'll talk to *you* later," Judi said with that familiar twinkle in her eyes and a mischievous smile, then they watched him as he walked away. "That was lovely, wasn't it?"

"Yes, though I'm not sure it was real! I have a lot to learn about meeting celebrities, I know that much for sure," Erin said, still reeling.

"You're with David Elliott, dear—" she began, but Erin knew the gist of what she was getting at.

"Yes, and it was just as surreal when I first met him. I actually fell on my rear end before I could say anything."

"Oh my! Now, that sounds like a story I'd like to hear," Judi said as Johnny returned with a fold-out chair. He sat on it and lifted his glass toward them. "I'm glad you've returned so soon, Johnny. Erin was about to tell me an embarrassing story, weren't you?"

"Uh, well, I was, but..."

"Come now, Ms. March, the whole world knows *all* my embarrassing stories; it's only fair," Johnny said.

Erin blew out a long breath of air. "I've heard David say it dozens of times, so it feels odd to say it too, but please call me Erin."

Johnny smiled and nodded. "Noted. Please go on," he said.

"Well, uh, I'm not sure where to start. Long story short, I have the Fertilis Defect, and the only treatment for it is…" she looked at Rosie and beckoned to her by waggling her finger. She placed her hands over the young girl's ears and whispered, "…uh, coitus." She dropped her hands, and Rosie turned, surprising her with a hug.

"Please excuse me, Mummy, but I'd like to speak with someone who has just arrived," she said with such maturity that Erin put her hand on her heart.

"You don't need to ask permission to leave, but I'm glad you were so polite; thank you," she said. Rosie gave her another quick hug. She waved at Judi and Johnny, then ran off while the adults watched her. "She's just amazing, isn't she? Her brothers are just as… as unbelievable. I don't understand how Susannah…well, that's not what I want to talk about right now. Where was I? Right, coitus… with the proper man, of course. There's a lot of science involved, but I won't bore you with that. Anyway, my doctor didn't tell me *whom* I was meeting, so when it turned out to be David, well…" Erin fanned her face, which was burning.

"Your doctor didn't tell you who it was? I might find a new one if I were you," Johnny said wide-eyed.

"Yes, well, I gave him a talking-to when I saw him again. He was sufficiently contrite, plus I will be… well, I presume I'll be living here full-time soon, so I don't need to worry about that anymore. Where was I? Oh, yeah; I was standing in the doorway of a room, having just opened the door, and saw him standing before me in all his glory," she said and laughed at her dramatics. "I was shocked, to say the least, so I took a step back and tripped over the edge of the area rug behind me. I fell flat on my arse, right in front of the man of my dreams," she said.

Johnny laughed, and Judi covered her mouth, trying to hide her amusement. "Wasn't one of my finer moments, but he was sweet and helped me up. As soon as he touched my hand, I knew there was something special between us. There's this… energy between people who are matched… a chemistry of pheromones and something I can't explain, but it's heavenly."

"And how long ago did you meet?" Judi asked.

"Just over five months ago now, but it seems like years!" Erin said, happy to be telling their story.

"Five months? That's remarkable!" Judi said.

"Yeah, it is, isn't it," Erin said and smiled at her, then at Johnny.

Erin began hearing whispers around them. She saw Rosie running toward her, looking excited, and pointing to the cottage door. "Mummy, look!" she said.

Johnny and the two women stood to see what she was pointing at. Dan and Charlie were stationed on either side of the front door, wearing brightly colored, simple tunics and puffy black trousers. They were surveying the crowds of guests until they saw Erin walking toward them, then they made a show of bowing low.

That must've been Peter's cue, as he stepped out of the small, covered entryway looking like a young prince. He was wearing an ornate, dark golden-yellow, embroidered coat with a sash of deep crimson, which was also embroidered with beads and shining golden thread. His trousers and turban were crimson as well, and his slippers made Erin think of elf shoes.

"Good night nurse!" she said as she approached him and admired the young man standing before her. He looked like an adult instead of the child she always saw him as. "You look absolutely stunning, Peter!" The crowd was oohing and ahhing, and he blushed, beaming at her, then he also bowed and moved aside, joining his brothers.

Erin and her guests held their breath as they waited. Finally, she couldn't take the suspense any longer and stepped forward. Peter straightened up and smiled at her, then he waved his hand out in front of him like an usher pointing out the way to go. "He knew you'd do that; please enter," he whispered. He bowed again, and as she passed them, the boys resumed their post, standing as if guarding the door.

"You must've rehearsed that, David!" she said as she stepped into the house, but then he stepped out of the shadows, and she gasped. She was utterly speechless, in awe of the regal figure standing before her.

His coat was cream-colored embroidered silk with crimson accents at the wrists and collar. His trousers were crimson, and his slippers matched beautifully. His sash was also crimson with elaborate embroidered decorations in golden thread, and his turban was cream with a twist of red. He hadn't shaved for a few days and had shaped his beard into a goatee that was perfect with the costume.

"Do yeh… fancy it?" he asked, as if unsure of her reaction.

"You—" she whispered, and he took a step forward to be able to hear her. She stepped back and nearly tripped on the hem of her sari, but David caught her outstretched arm just in time.

"Ye're lookin' at me as yeh did when yeh first saw me… why?"

"You… look like a… king. I… feel… I don't know, humbled or… something." David placed her hand on his chest and came closer, smiling. "I don't even care that I was just speaking to Johnny Depp in the garden; you… are—" she realized she was fangirling and blushed. "It's just that I guess I get used to you… and me, but sometimes, when I see you, it all comes back. Then, I'm just one of your fans again, and I can't believe I'm in the same room as you."

"Ach, Erin, yeh really do ken how tae make me feel like a king," he said as he bent down to kiss her. He held her, kissing her for a long time until she finally managed to break away for a few seconds.

"Everyone is going to wonder what we're doing in here," she whispered, not actually caring; she didn't want to leave his arms, ever.

"Let them wonder," he replied and continued kissing her.

When David and Erin emerged from the cottage, she was surprised that the boys were still standing guard. As they stepped out into the covered entryway, the twins parted and bowed. Peter raised his voice to the crowd, who had started to turn away and resume their previous conversations.

"Ladies and Gentlemen: May I present your hosts, David and Erin—" He was clearly going to say something more but caught himself and finished, then he stepped aside and bowed to them as they walked past. They were both impressed with his commanding presence and beamed with pride. Erin wanted to hug him and praise his performance, but she knew it would have to wait.

The crowd, who had grown substantially since Erin had entered the cottage, cheered, and applauded them as they walked out, arm in arm, looking so regal. People were taking photos and they heard comments like, '*Oh, how beautiful!*' and, '*Stunning,*' repeated several times.

David took the opportunity to address them. "Thank you for attendin' this last-minute birthday do for Erin. I never imagined so many of you would show up with so little notice, and et warms ma heart to see you all. Please enjoy yourselves and save room for cake. Namaste," he said, using a much gentler version of his accent. He placed his hands in a prayer-like pose and bowed slightly. Erin joined him, and the crowd cheered, some returning the greeting.

Erin didn't think she could ever feel as amazing, beautiful, loved, and happy ever again for the rest of her life. She shook hands with some of the most amazing people that day, including Sir Ian McKellen. She was introduced to Thomas Boyd McMillan, who had been in several films that she had either enjoyed or really wanted to see.

She met Paul Gossamer and Laurel Hammond, who were a very popular couple. He was a highly sought-after freelance photographer, and she was an award-winning director. Erin was introduced to Barney Peterson, who played the lead character, Michael Wilde, and David's son, on *Wilde's Life*, and Valentine Gregov, who played his assistant.

She met Akshara Anand, who was famous for her role as a high-powered solicitor in a recent UK television program and had just been one of the celebrity guests on *Strictly Come Dancing*. "Oh, I can't believe you're here!" Erin said when she saw her coming toward her. "I watched your whole season and fell in love with you! You were so graceful and should've won! I can't believe you didn't! I voted for you every week!"

Akshara smiled and laughed. "Thank you, Erin, that means a lot to me. I was terrified each week until the end. Do you dance?" she asked. Erin told her that she did, and they talked for a very long time about form and following and having everyone in the crowd watching you. They laughed and promised to keep in touch after the party was over.

Excited to tell David about her encounter, she went searching for him. She turned the corner at the side of the house and saw David speaking to a man whose face she couldn't see. She didn't want to intrude, but then she saw David smile at her and wave her over. Just then, the man turned, and she saw that it was Barry Thompson, the man who'd played Joe Whitehall on *Future Explorations*.

"*Le Potage!*" she said before she could stop herself. The two men laughed, and Erin blushed. "Will I ever stop saying that in front of you?" she said, exasperated at herself.

"I hope you never do," David said. "Erin, you remember Baz?"

"How could I forget? It's so good to see you again! Is Vincent here?"

"Alas, he is home with... drumroll, please... our new *baby*," he said dramatically.

"Baby! That's wonderful! You look amazing for having just been pregnant," she said and laughed.

"It was Vincent who did all the work, my dear. I was there to hold his hand through the whole painful ordeal," he said and hugged her.

"Oh! Is—Tilly here?" she asked suddenly.

David furrowed his brow, obviously not understanding why she'd asked. "I received their RSVP, so if not, she should—Well, there's Roger," he said and pointed. "Why—"

Erin turned and saw him behind her. "Please stay here! I'll be right back!" she said before David could finish his question. "Roger!" she called out, and he turned, seeing her for the first time that day.

"Ma Losh! Erin? Yeh... look sae... bonnie!" he said and blushed. She laughed and went to him, giving him a hug, then she looked him over and nodded. He was wearing jeans and a tunic-like shirt. "I made an effort, dinnae take the Mickey."

"I can see that you did. I wasn't going to tease you," she said and couldn't help but laugh at the look on his face. "Honestly, I wasn't! Where is Tilly? I need to introduce her to—"

"Erin? WOW! You look amazing!" Tilly said as she walked up to them. "I can't believe who's here! I just saw Joe and Billy Joplin talking with Moses Tuttle, and did I actually see Johnny Depp?" she said, her eyes wide.

"Aye, Tilly, you did! I can't believe it either! But I came over here to find you! You've gotta meet someone! Come with me!" she said excitedly. She pulled her friend, and Roger's FD match, by the hand to where David had been standing a few moments before. "David?" she said, looking around. He and Barry were gone. She put her hands on her hips and sighed. "I asked them to—"

'*Happy Birthday to You...*' she heard the crowd begin to sing, and when she turned, David was there holding out his hand. She took it, feeling a bit like she had on Bourbon Street, with everyone staring at her. She blushed and was suddenly too warm in the heavy silk sari she was wrapped up in.

He led her to a table with the most beautiful cake she'd ever seen. The main cake was shaped like the body of a peacock, painted with some sort of iridescent paint that was blue, purple, and green all at the same time. The tail was made of cupcakes, each decorated with the teardrop pattern at the end of a peacock feather. There were forty lit candles, each in a little rose of icing around the base of the whole thing.

"Make a wish, ma love," David said, smiling at her.

She scanned the crowd and smiled, feeling so blessed. "I can't think of a single thing to wish for. I have everything I've ever wanted and some things I didn't know I did. I know that sounds corny, but it's true. I guess... all I want is to be your wife and for our bairn to be born healthy," she said, hardly able to keep it together. "Please help me blow these out." She started blowing out the candles, walking clockwise around the table, while David did the same, going anti-clockwise. When they met on the other side, he put his hand on her cheek and kissed her, making their guests cheer.

"The cake won't be served just yet," David said to the anticipating crowd. "I wanted Erin to see et before sundown and before et was destroyed by you, yeh greedy buggers." Everyone laughed and then went back to their previous conversations. David turned to her and smiled.

"Thank you for thinking ahead like that. It's a stunning cake! I would've been sad if I hadn't gotten to see it in its full glory."

"I'm glad yeh like et, but et wasn't my idea, I admit," he said.

Tilly walked up to them, and Erin remembered what she was doing before the cake. "One second, Tilly," she said and put her mouth up to the side of

David's face. "Can you find Joe... I mean Baz? I want to introduce him to Tilly," she whispered in his ear.

"Aye, I can do that," he said and walked away from them.

"This is an amazing party, Erin!" Tilly said. "I'm so glad we were able to come."

"And you're going to be even more glad in a few minutes." Erin saw David and Baz walking toward them and waited until just the right moment to turn her friend around. "Tilly, I want you to meet someone," Erin said as they watched the men approach them.

The sun was positioned so that the women had to squint. All Tilly saw at first was David smiling warmly at her, then Barry stepped out from behind him, and she gasped. She looked at Erin with tears in her eyes, which was not what she'd expected. "I'd like yeh tae meet ma friend, Baz Thompson," David said, and Baz held out his hand to her. "This is Tilly Maxwell."

"Hello, Tilly, it's a pleasure to meet you," he said and seemed to be toning down his flamboyance a bit for her.

She stared at his hand until Erin nudged her, then she finally took it, and they shook hands awkwardly. "He's just a man, like David, Till," Erin whispered to her, but she shook her head.

"I'm... sorry you died," Tilly said as her cheeks bloomed pink. "What I mean is..."

"So am I," Baz said, smiling, "though David did a fine job of things, I reckon."

"I agree," Erin said.

"I'm sorry. I know I'm being ridiculous and making a horrible first impression, but you don't know what this means to me. I'm sure you probably hear that all the time," Tilly said, still holding his hand.

"Not so much anymore," he said and looked at David, who smiled. "Thank—" he began, but Tilly wasn't finished.

"You are the reason I moved here! I know everyone loves John Thomas, but not me... no offense, David."

"None taken," he said, obviously enjoying the scene.

"You were the one I connected with. I was so glad they brought you back in other seasons!"

"So was I, actually. I really did love being part of the program. It's especially nice when lovely people like yourself say such kind things," Baz said, sounding genuinely grateful for her remarks.

Tilly was red in the face, and David looked at Erin. He moved closer to her and put his arm around her waist. "I love yeh," he whispered as Tilly tried to collect herself.

"Tilly, did you see who's here?" Roger said as he came up behind Barry, unaware of who he was.

Tilly's eyes widened, and her blush grew even deeper, spreading to her neck and the tips of her ears. "Roger! Uh, hi," she sputtered.

Baz turned to face him, and Roger froze. "Oh... right, I see... well, then," he stammered and narrowed his eyes at him.

"This is Baz Thompson," David said.

Roger nodded curtly. "Aye, I ken who yeh are. Roger Blackwood," he said, shaking the man's outstretched hand. "I'm her... partner." Things suddenly felt quite awkward.

"Nice to meet you as well," Baz said.

Erin watched Tilly staring at her idol; she knew her friend had wanted to meet him for a long time, and she wasn't going to let anything ruin it for her. "Could I get your advice on something, Roger?" she asked, knowing he was not happy at the moment. She led him away, determined to keep him from making an ass of himself.

"Huh? Oh, aye," he said, clearly reluctant to leave Tilly's side. "What do yeh need, Erin?" he asked distractedly, looking over his shoulder at the scene they were walking away from.

She took him to a place where he could no longer see Tilly and then saw Judi sitting alone with a glass of wine, so she approached her. "Good evening, Judi. Would you mind some company for a few minutes?" she said, amazed at being able to say that to her.

"I was thinking of that very thing but was too comfortable to make an effort to find someone. How fortuitous. Please do introduce me to this fine-looking young man you've brought with you," she said with one of her devilish grins.

"This is Roger Blackwood; he works for David's mother in Edinburgh. "Roger, I'd like you to meet—" Erin began, then noticed he was blushing. She hadn't seen him look that shy since the day he met Tilly.

Judi held out her hand, and he took it, giving it a light kiss. "Et's nice tae meet yeh, Ms.—I mean, Dame… Dench," he said adorably.

"Dame Dench… honestly. Please call me Judi and come sit with me. Tell me something interesting about yourself, young man."

"Ach, well, tha' will make for a short conversation, I'm afraid," he said. Judi laughed, and Erin shook her head.

"That's not true, Roger!" Erin said but then couldn't think of anything to suggest.

"I can tell you of someone who *is* quite interesting," he said and looked at Erin wickedly.

"Oh, ho ho! If you're going to talk about me, I'll leave you to do it behind my back!" she said and could feel her cheeks getting warm. "Anyway, I need to find the loo. Oh, and one more thing before I go." She leaned in close to his ear and whispered, "Baz is gay, very gay, so don't stress, okay?"

Chapter Twenty-Eight

OVERHEARD

Erin stepped into the cottage, making a beeline for the toilet. She wasn't sure how she'd be able to manage the sari by herself, but the need was greater than the dilemma. She made it to one of the upstairs bathrooms, wanting to keep the others open for their guests. The ordeal wasn't as difficult as she thought it would be, and soon she was washing her hands. After a quick hair and make-up check, she was about to open the door when she heard two women talking on the stairs nearby.

"The size of her!" one of them said.

"I know! I wasn't aware one could *find* a sari that large. It must be terrible for poor David now that he's gotten someone like *her* in trouble. She should've had an abortion like Susannah did so many times. She told me she only kept the ones that made him stay home," the second one said.

"She said as much to me as well."

"I guarantee she'll *hate* her gift from us. I bought it for Susannah, and it will *never* fit her."

"Well, maybe it will give her incentive to lose a few… well, *more* than a few pounds."

"I doubt her *skeleton* would fit in it. It's a sexy little teddy I thought David would *love* on Susannah. I'd be tempted to put it on and see what he thinks of it myself if I wasn't with Jules. I imagine he'd *enjoy* a little eye candy right about now. Maybe I'll wait until she's too big to waddle over and stop me. Then she can *watch* him devour me," the second woman said, and the two women laughed.

Erin heard the stairs creaking and waited to open the bathroom door until she thought they were gone. From the balcony that overlooked the living room, she watched as the women left the house. All her imagined beauty left her, and she felt disgusting again. She wondered how many more people at the party were thinking the same thing as those two ladies.

The temptation to go to her room and hide was overwhelming just then. She very nearly did, except David and around a dozen men and women, most of whom she recognized as actors or musicians, exited his office and flooded the living room. Wanting to get out of sight, she turned, and David saw her. "Hello, ma love. What're yeh doin' up there?" he asked, smiling so beautifully at her.

Several of the men, including Johnny and Baz, looked up at her and waved, saying, 'hello,' or 'happy birthday,' before heading outside again. David must have seen that something was troubling her because he excused himself and rushed up the stairs. She nearly swooned over how handsome he looked in his costume, and she felt even worse about herself in comparison. "What's wrong, hen?"

"It's... nothing," she said, knowing he wouldn't believe her. He gave her a 'come on... spit it out' look, and the dam broke. "I overheard two women saying nasty things about me," she said, trying not to get too worked up. She didn't want to ruin her make-up and have red, swollen eyes when she went back outside.

"Who were they?" David asked, looking angry.

"I don't know them."

"What did they say?" he asked, pulling her into Rosie's bedroom for privacy.

"David—"

"What did they say?" he repeated.

"They were commenting on my... size." She told him some of what she'd overheard and tried to act like it was no big deal. "Then she said some other rude things—"

"What other rude things?" David demanded.

"I don't want to say it," she said, but the look on his face implored her to do it anyway. "Fine." She told him what the gift was and how the second woman said she was tempted to put it on, "...to see what you'd think of it on her if she wasn't with... what was the name... Jules, I think? She said that it must be terrible for you... getting someone like *me* in trouble, and that I should've gotten an abortion like Susannah did so many times, and that she only kept the ones that made you stay home. Oh, and she thinks you'd like some eye candy, and—"

"And?"

"And she might wait until I'm too big to waddle over and stop her and that I could watch you devour her!" Erin said and hung her head. "Everyone thinks I'm fat, David. I mean, I am, but... I did feel pretty... now I... don't."

David's face was dark red, and the blue vein on his forehead jutted out like an angry river. He took her by the hand and nearly dragged her, caveman style, through the house. She protested the whole time with, 'What are you doing?' 'David!' 'What are you going to do?' 'Please, David, don't embarrass me!' and the like.

When they got outside, it was quite dark, but he stood in the glow of the porch light and tiki torches. "May I have your attention, please?" he said, still holding Erin's hand tightly.

"Good night nurse, David! Please... please don't! Please!" she begged quietly at first, but as she saw that he wasn't going to listen to her, her pleading grew louder. "Stop it, David! You're embarrassing me. Let me go!" Soon, the whole party was gathered around them as Erin struggled, and David ignored her, waiting patiently.

"David! What is this? Can yeh no' see she's upset by et? Let her be!" Roger said, coming to the front to try to help Erin, who was wide-eyed and crying.

"Roger! Please tell him not to—"

"I'd like tae thank all of you for attendin' our party. Ye've been pure brilliant. There are two of you, in particular, whom I'd like to give special mention to."

"No! David! Stop, or I'll never—"

"Jules, please come here, and Roxanne, as well. Penny, please join them," he said, and Erin saw the two women she'd heard say the rude things about her step forward.

271

"David… please," she said and started tugging on his arm earnestly, trying to get away from the whole situation.

"I hear ye've an extra special gift for ma love. Would yeh bring et to me so she can open et now?"

Roxanne blanched white, then her face burned scarlet. "I hardly think that's—" she began, but Jules was already fetching it for her. He returned a few moments later and proudly handed Erin a very small black gift bag. He seemed like a nice man, unaware of the serpent he had for a partner. "Jules! Don't—" Roxanne spat at him.

"Thank you, Jules. Now, Erin, please read the tag," he said. She refused, so he took it from her and looked for something, anything to indicate whom the gift was from. "Well, et seems as though you've forgotten tae include your name. How will we send our appreciation if we've no idea where it came from? Never mind, now we know." He handed it to Erin, but she wouldn't take it, hanging her head in shame at the spectacle she felt he was making of her.

"David, what's this about?" Roger asked again, but he was ignored.

"Well then, I reckon I'll have tae open et maself," he said and let go of Erin's hand. She flew to Roger, allowing him to hold her while David carefully took the small bundle, wrapped in glittering tissue paper, out of the bag and slowly peeled back the layers. He saw a small note card tucked inside and put it into his pocket. Once the paper was removed, he held up a microscopic piece of black silk and lace lingerie. It was painfully obvious that Erin would never fit into it. "What's this? Interesting. Let's read the card, shall we?" Roxanne was wide-eyed, and it seemed as though she was looking to find a place to run, revealing that she'd forgotten about the note she'd included.

"*Susannah*—" he read, and the whole crowd gasped collectively, with small comments being heard traveling around. Even Jules was looking at Roxanne with disgust. "*I hope this will help get you in the mood for David. If not, give me a shot. R.*"

David frowned at her. "What's the meanin' of this? Ye're invited intae our home and insult us with yer— I dinnae even ken what tae call this! Et's disgustin' and I want you and yer friend here—" he said, pointing to Penny, "tae leave. Ye're not welcome any longer."

Roxanne and Penny looked around at the crowd of angry faces and walked toward the field where the guests had been allowed to park for the evening. Jules stepped up to Erin, looking mortified. "I'm so sorry, Erin. You don't deserve to be treated like that," he said and leaned in closer. "I think you're lovely and never cared for Susannah at all. I don't much like Roxanne either, come to think of it." He smiled at her, then turned to David. "I'm sorry, mate. I reckon that's the proverbial straw that broke the camel's back. I've had enough of her as well."

David shook the man's hand. "Ye're always welcome, mate, just dinnae bring *her* again, a'right?" Jules nodded and followed the women. "Now, I believed we'd only invited respectful people, but as you can see, that's not the case," David said, turning back to their guests. "So, if any of you feel the need tae shame ma true love, as those vultures did, and if there are other gifts of this nature... intended tae humiliate her, I'll ask that yeh take them and leave."

He was still holding the gift, and after stuffing it back into the bag, he found Erin still holding onto Roger. Taking her hand gently this time, he walked out to the bonfire that was happily burning in the side garden. Erin was still upset and looked at the ground as he handed her the insulting gift. "Erin, look at me," he said, but she shook her head.

"You have utterly embarrassed me, David. Just end the show now, okay?"

"The only way tae stop someone like her is tae rub how horrible they've been in their face. The joke loses et's humor when they're exposed for the wallopers they are. None of the people here are ever goin' tae trust those two women again. I hope you can see how much that's worth?"

"That may be so, but you've disrespected me. I asked you, begged you not to say or do anything, but you steamrolled over what I wanted and made me into a spectacle in front of all these people who... I admire and idolize a little bit. I know what you were trying to do, and you might have succeeded, but it cost me feeling utterly exposed. It's like you just stood up at the Oscars or Baftas and yelled, 'Hey... look at Erin, we all know she's fat, but you don't have to be a dick about it.' You've helped everyone but me. I don't want these people to feel sorry for me! I want them not to see me at all now. I feel foolish wearing this stupid costume! I look like a sausage roll, and I want to hide." The last thing she wanted was condescending pats on the back from his friends and acquaintances that meant they also didn't care that she was fat. She didn't want it to be a thing; she wanted to be normal, to be like everyone else and blend in.

"But, darling—"

"I want to… never mind. What do you want me to do with this?" she said, holding up the bag. "Throw it into the fire? Will that make anything any better? Fine, here." She threw the bag into the flames, and it lit up, making sparks fly. She wanted to run to her room, take everything off, and pout, feeling sorry for herself, but that would only make things worse.

"Erin—"

"I'd like to be alone now… please," she said quietly, wanting to end the scene they were making. "I need to take a walk and clear my mind."

"Aye. I'm sorry," he said, kissed her temple, and watched her walk away.

Chapter Twenty-Nine

SAGE ADVICE

Erin needed air, a quiet place where she could think. Trying to look natural, she slowly made her way to the garden's side gate, which was mostly hidden by branches and leaves. She slipped through it and found herself completely removed from the star-studded affair, standing on an ordinary, empty subdivision road. The streetlights, high above her, tried to illuminate her path through the evening mist, making it look like a film set.

As she walked, the smell of the sea and the sound of gulls and crashing waves lured her forward. She noticed several people watching her through their family room windows and sighed. *I must look insane!* she thought, *A fat, white woman walking down the street through the fog, dressed like an Indian bride.*

At the bottom of the road was a bench that looked out over the pebble beach and ocean. She sat, enjoying the strong winds while she took turns admiring the water and then the tall, golden cliffs with their green grass tops still glowing in the last rays of the setting sun.

"May I?" A man's voice said from behind her. She knew who it was immediately and sat up taller. "It's a lovely night, isn't it?" Ian McKellen stood at the end of the bench, waiting for permission to sit beside her.

"Sir Ian, of course you may," she said and then didn't know what else to say. She sat, staring at the waves, finding peace in their steady rhythm. Neither of them spoke for a long time. "When I'm upset... I need to get away... to walk away and sort out my thoughts and feelings."

"If I may be so bold as to give my opinion? I believe you are missing a piece of the puzzle as far as how David behaved tonight, my dear," Ian's gentle, classically trained voice offered.

"The last thing I want to do, Mr.—"

"Ian, please."

"Ian, is to be disrespectful or contradict you, but you don't understand," she said.

"Don't I?" he said and turned to face her.

She looked up into his gentle, caring, compassionate eyes. She'd seen interviews with him about how he had dealt with being a gay man in the twentieth century and realized that he probably did understand, at least to some degree. "Perhaps you do, after all. Please go on."

He took her plump hand in one of his soft, aged, yet manicured hands, and used his scarf to wipe the mascara off her cheeks with the other, then he smiled at her. "David poked the elephant in the room, yes. He was, perhaps, a bit insensitive and hasty, but you must consider his past. We have all witnessed how he was crushed and bullied by people like Susannah, Roxanne, and Penny. What he said and did tonight was as much for him, cathartically speaking, as it was to avenge you."

She lowered her gaze and gently shook her head. "I can see that, but he took the elephant and made it into an enormous, psychedelic, tie-dyed lava lamp that everyone can't help but look at. I don't want that to be how people see me, and I don't want their pity."

"I assure you, my dear, none of the people remaining see you any differently. Look at you; you're a true Bollywood vision. I have learned that the things we dislike most about ourselves stick out to us, but rarely do the people around us even notice them," he said.

Erin moved closer to him and lay her head on his arm, still holding his hand. They sat silent for a few minutes, then she sighed. "Thank you, Ian, you've helped a lot. May I take you home with me?" she said and laughed. "Don't know why I said that except you have a way... a gentle, convincing way about you that I love."

"Thank you, Erin. Now, do me a favor?"

"Anything."

"Take a selfie with me?"

Erin looked at him and laughed really hard. "I'm supposed to ask you for that! I'd be honored, but you have to promise to send me a copy, deal?"

"Deal, and I'll even pinky promise," he said and held out his little finger for her to shake.

"The second most binding promise, next to the…"

"Unbreakable vow," they said in unison and giggled.

"If I weren't engaged, and if you fancied women, I'd ask you to marry me right now!" Erin said and kissed him on the cheek. *Snap,* she heard his camera as it caught the act, then she looked up at it, and he took several more, including a silly face. "Okay, if you won't marry me, at least adopt me?"

"I believe you have a deal. You may now refer to me as your honorary grandad," he said. "Now, there's a man who loves you dearly waiting, and most likely worrying, about you at the top of this road. Do allow me the privilege of escorting you back to him. I enjoy playing the hero."

"I'd like that, Gramps," she said. They walked slowly up the hill, Erin holding his arm. "For the record, I believe you did the world a great disservice by turning down Dumbledore when Richard Harris passed."

"Is that so?"

"Yes. I'm sure Michael Gambon is a lovely person, but I don't think he was meant for that role. Albus Dumbledore was whimsical and gentle; he had a tenderness that Mr. Gambon just doesn't have. I think you would've been the perfect replacement, even if Mr. Harris didn't agree." They continued in silence for a while; the hill was steep and not easy going. "I know you didn't want the part; another ancient wizard might have typecast you. I just think, in my humble opinion, that you'd have been perfect. Especially if you'd been able to show this side of you."

"Thank you, my dear," he said simply. "Allow me." They were at the gate, and Erin waited for him to open it for her.

"I'm so glad you came to speak to me. I'll never forget it," she said and kissed his soft cheek, feeling his end-of-the-day stubble on her face just before stepping through.

"Erin!" David said, seeing her reenter the garden. "I was beginnin' tae worry."

"Ian has been keeping me safe," she said and took David's offered hand. "He's excellent company, and I have good news! He's adopted me, right, Grandpa?"

"I'm delighted to say I have." Ian took her hand and brought it to his lips, bowing as he kissed it. "I haven't forgotten my pinky promise either. Here you are," he said and handed her his mobile phone, open to his contacts. "Please add your name and etcetera for me, dear."

"Ye'd be wise tae keep yer eyes on her whilst she's in possession of that," David said. "Yeh may end up with a few surprises the next time yeh open et." He smiled at her, and she remembered what she'd done with his mobile after their special meal in New Orleans.

"A man my age might look forward to a few surprises now and then," Ian said, taking his mobile back since she was finished. "Now, if you'll please excuse me, I need a word with *Dame* Judi." He walked away and David turned to her.

"I'm sorry, my darling, I can see how what I've done has—" he began to say.

"It's okay, David. Ian helped me to see it differently. We have a lot to learn about each other. Thank you for trying to avenge me; I know you meant well. I love you," she said and held him.

They turned and saw Ian and Judi holding out champagne flutes to them while many of their guests watched. "To Erin," Ian began, raising his glass in a toast.

"And David," Judi continued.

"Cheers!" they both said together.

"Cheers!" the crowd roared, took a drink, then began clapping and talking amongst themselves.

"Thank you," Erin mouthed to them. David raised his glass to Judi and mouthed the same thing. She had an inkling that the two wise thespians were in cahoots. "Did Judi speak to you while I was gone?" she asked him quietly.

"Aye, she passed on a bit of wisdom to me. I reckon our two elders were playin' the role of guardian angels."

"I'm glad. They are lovely people! Now, let's get some food and cake; I'm starving! Oh, and drink this for me, please. I can't, it's alcoholic," she said, handing him her glass.

They stepped up to the colorfully decorated table, laden with delicious-looking food, and filled their plates. There was a sofa, bedecked with a myriad of pillows and brightly colored fabrics set aside especially for them, in front of the spot where the dancers had been performing throughout the event. As they took their seat, festive Indian music began to play, and several Bollywood dancers assembled and got into position.

The moves and hand gestures were mesmerizing, and they sat, delighted by the show. After one very long dance, the cake was cut, and they were served generous slices. "Mmmm, this is so good, isn't it?" Erin said.

"Aye, et's fabulous."

Daniel was seen running past them, the knees of his trousers filthy with grass stains and dirt, then Charlie and Rosie came along and joined them. "This is the best party ever, Daddy!" Rosie said. "It's much better than our Christmas parties."

"Yeah, Dad, it's a right stonker!" Charlie said. "Johnny was just telling us stories about when he filmed *Pirates of the Caribbean*! He taught me how to hold a sword and said you'd make a jolly good pirate, Dad. I agree with him!"

"Is that so? Well then, I'll be on the lookout for that sort of film," David said.

"I'm glad you're having a good time. It's the best birthday party I've ever had, but I'm getting really tired. I might have to turn in soon," Erin said and yawned so hard her eyes watered, which set the rest of them off.

"Aye, I reckon I'll be done in before long as well," David said.

Soon their guests began to stop by to say goodnight. Erin was amazed by all the people she'd seen on TV and in movies, people she'd never imagined being in the same room with, let alone speaking to them and accepting their genuine birthday wishes. She hugged Judi Dench and kissed her cheek as she said goodbye. "I do hope you like my contribution to the gift table. You seem the kind of person who will appreciate it thoroughly," she said and giggled, her impish smile lighting up her face.

"Oh, Judi! I'm sure I will! Thank you so much for coming; it's one of the highlights of my life... having met you, truly!" Erin said and hugged her again. "Please... don't be a stranger—Oh, that's kinda forward of me, isn't it, but—"

"No, not forward at all. I was going to say the same, but you beat me to it."

"It's been an unforgettable night," Johnny said and kissed Erin's hand. "I might just have to find a way to top it soon. I'll expect you to join me when I do."

Erin giggled and hugged him. "Wouldn't miss it!"

That night, when their costumes were off and Erin's makeup was washed away, she and David lay in bed, exhausted. "Thank you for one of the best nights of my whole life."

"Aye, darling, you're welcome," he said, then he kissed her temple and rolled over.

She got comfortable and was just about to fall asleep when she felt the bed shaking slightly. "David?" she said and rolled toward him. There was no answer, but she thought she heard him sniff. "What's wrong?" She saw him slowly shake his head in the faint moonlight that filled the room through the light window coverings. "Are you… crying?" She pulled on his shoulder, and he rolled toward her.

He held her, sobbing. "Did she… really say that, Erin?" he gasped.

"Did who say what? I'm confused," she said.

"Roxy… did she say Susannah had… multiple abortions?"

Erin's heart dropped and hurt for him. She'd said it so flippantly earlier that the full meaning of it hadn't hit her before then. "Oh, David! I'm sorry, but she did."

He nodded and then rolled away again. "Ma whole life, for the last eighteen years anaway, has been a lie, Erin. I've no idea what might come next in this nightmare of discovery. I've scarcely come to grips with what I've already learned, and I don't know that I have the constitution for more. How many of ma bairns did she… rid herself of?"

He was still for a few moments, and she wrapped her arm over him, kissing his shoulder. "The very worst bit is that I can do nothing about et; any of et. She's dead and cannot be brought tae justice or even confronted about et any longer. '*Cursed is the woman who dies, but the evil done by her survives.*' And cursed am I, the one who bears the weight of it." There was nothing she could say, so Erin held him, allowing him to mourn the loss of untold lives.

In the middle of the night, she woke with a start and saw David kneeling on the floor next to her. "What—"

He took her hand and kissed it. "I didn't mean tae wake yeh, love. I was watchin' yeh sleep and… thankin' God for the gift of you. I'd be a broken man if you weren't here tae help mend me and keep me away from the darkest of places… the abyss I'd have fallen into otherwise."

"Honestly, I feel unqualified and at a loss for what to say or do to help you. I want to encourage you and build you up, but all I can do is sit here mute. I know that what you've gone through… what *she's* done to you and the children is so much more than I can fully comprehend. I can't give you anything but my love and my ear—"

"Ach, Erin, don't yeh understand? That's the verra thing I need from you. That's the best thing… the only thing I reckon yeh could do for me or the children. The last thing I wanna hear when I am as low as I've been over the last months are platitudes or trite, threadbare adages. I need tae give vent to et; tae rant a bit, sometimes rage, occasionally cry… and know ye'll still be here when I'm finished and spent."

"Aye, but I feel so guilty for what I said to you when you were in the spare room, drunk. I *never* would've hurt our baby! I was just—"

"I ken it, love. You were desperate; I told yeh there was another bottle… what else could yeh do? I was wrong tae be so self-destructive. I'm not upset about that anamore."

"Good, I love you," she said and pulled his hand toward her. "Come make love to me, okay?"

"Aye, as you wish, darling."

Chapter Thirty

GIFT OPENING

The next day, Erin woke hearing voices at the bedroom door. *"Shhh! You'll wake them up!"*

"You 'shhh'! You're the one talking."

"Shut up, both of you. They're obviously not awake yet, and it's rude to listen at the door. Come—"

She put on her robe, opened the door, and raised her eyebrows at the startled trio of boys. "You're full of beans this morning! What's all this?" she asked and crossed her arms.

"I told you to be quiet!" Charlie said to Dan. "The study is chockablock with presents, Erin, and we want to watch you open them."

"Sorry, Erin, I tried to get them to come away from the door, but they wouldn't listen," Peter said. Charlie glared, and Dan stuck out his tongue at him.

"Where's Rosie?" Erin asked, surprised she wasn't with them.

"She's in the study admiring the fancy wrappings. I told her not to touch anything," Peter said.

"Okay, we'll be down shortly. Are there really that many?"

The children smiled and nodded. "Yes, and they're beautiful," Charlie said. "We'll go down and wait for you." Peter and Charlie turned and headed down the striped, multi-colored carpeting toward the stairs.

"Yeah, and you should hurry," Dan said, "Looks like they cost a bomb!"

"Dan!" Peter said from the end of the hall, so Dan turned and ran after them.

"*What? I'm not exaggerating!*" Erin heard him say just before she closed the door.

"Cost a bomb, huh?" she said to David, who was already getting dressed. "Are you gonna keep that goatee? I kinda like it!"

"I'm sure many of them did 'cost a bomb,' though that doesn't mean ye'll like them," he said and rubbed his chin, looking at his facial hair in the mirror. "Yeh like et, eh? Perhaps I will keep et for a few days."

When they finally made it downstairs, Roger and Tilly, who had been invited to stay the night in the shepherd's hut, were sitting at the dining room table, helping themselves to cereal, milk, coffee, and tea.

"Good morning," they all said together.

David pulled out Erin's chair, which had a lumbar support pillow on it, and once she was settled, he sat next to her. "That was a night tae remember, was et not?" he said, and then they heard a knock on the cottage door. "I'll go." He stood and left the room.

"Did you two have a good time?" Erin asked Roger and Tilly.

"Did we ever!" Tilly said, and Roger tried to hide a frown.

"Aye—" Roger began, but then David returned with Jules, the man who had been with Roxie.

Erin was about to stand, but David shook his head and put his hand out. "Dinnae stand, darling. I don't believe any of you have been formally introduced," he said. "Julian Gordon, allow me to introduce you to Roger Blackwood, who works for ma Mother in Edinburgh, and his partner Tilly…"

"Maxwell," she supplied.

"Yes, of course, Maxwell, and you met my fiancée, Erin. Please sit and have a cup of coffee," David offered.

"It's a pleasure to meet you all," he said with a genuine though anxious smile. "Are you… sure, David, Erin? I don't imagine you're overly thrilled at having me show up on your doorstep after what Roxanne and Penny did last night.

"Nonsense, Mr. Gordon. It was obvious you had nothing to do with that. I'm only sorry you were called out along with them," Erin said. "Please join us for breakfast. Would you like tea or coffee?" she offered graciously, pointing to the empty spot next to David.

"You are very kind, and please call me Jules," he said and sat in the wooden, straight-backed chair, looking relieved. "Roxy left for London earlier, and good riddance to her, I say. I wanted to stop by and… well, I'm not entirely sure what I wanted to do, exactly. Make amends, I suppose? I've also brought you a small birthday gift to replace—"

"Oh, Jules, that's so sweet, but you didn't have to do that," Erin said, blushing. The short, bald man, who reminded her of Stanley Tucci, set a small green box with a cream-colored bow on the table near her mug of tea.

"Please accept it, Erin. It's the least I could do," he said, and Erin understood that he needed to do it to make peace with himself just as much as with her.

"Thank you; shall I open it now?" she said, her eyes shining.

"Yes!" Tilly said and blushed, obviously thinking others would join in on her vote.

Erin looked at Jules and smiled. She picked up the box and slowly pulled the bow off, then lifted the top. Inside was a dark green, velvet-covered jewelry box, the kind antique bracelets and necklaces come in. The box was just a bit bigger than a business card and rather heavy for its size. She couldn't imagine what it could be as she opened the hinged lid and gasped.

"Good night nurse! But this is too much! It's… beautiful!" she said and lifted a silver, gold, and enamel compact with a jewel-encrusted peacock on the front in shades of blue, teal, green, and purple. She opened it to reveal a mirror that could be set up on a table if you opened the case all the way over onto itself. She looked back up at Jules and shook her head, not knowing what to say.

"So, you… like it?" he asked, looking a bit worried.

"It's exactly my taste… it's better than my gaudy taste," she said and laughed.

"Good. Last night, when I drove Roxy back to the hotel in Bridport, I took a walk. I passed an antique and consignment shop and saw it in the window. I... don't know why, but it seemed to speak to me," he said and laughed, plainly embarrassed at his flowery sentiment. "They were closed, only just, but I got the owner's attention, and she allowed me to purchase it. "I have to say that I am normally one of the worst gift-givers. I'm known for it, actually. That's why I allowed Roxy to choose the gift. I've never experienced a draw toward a particular item as I did for this, and I'm glad I listened to... well, it." His cheeks were pink as he poured a cup of coffee from the French press on the table next to him.

"I am, too," Erin said softly.

"Roger, I think we need to take a diversion into Bridport on our way out of town," Tilly said.

"As you wish, darling," he said.

Erin had just finished a bowl of cereal and downed her one allotted cuppa of the day when they heard an ominous noise come from the room David used as an office. "I was just about to mention that the children were being far too quiet," she said and stood. "Please stay, Jules, if you'd like. I'm going to open the rest of the... undamaged gifts now."

"Thank you, I will then," he said.

Each of them held their breath as they headed to the opposite end of the long house, wondering what the noise might have been. They heard arguing until the door was opened by their angry-looking father. "Dan—" Peter began, but David put his hand up.

"What did you do, Daniel?" he asked sternly.

"It was Charlie's fault! He made me—"

"I did not! You were—"

"Lads, we'll talk about this later. Is anything broken?"

Dan put his head down. "Yes, sir," he said quietly, pointing to one of Asit's lamps, which didn't look overly expensive.

"I'll clean it up," Tilly said and began picking up the largest shards of the lightbulb, then put the lamp upright again.

As they found comfortable seats, Erin looked at the piles of gifts hastily stashed on every surface or stacked neatly on the brightly colored area rug. "I don't know where to begin! Will someone with good handwriting please record what each thing is and who it's from?"

It was crickets until Tilly spoke up. "I'll do it," she said and smiled at Erin.

"Thanks, now, someone hand me something, please," she said as David found a pad of notepaper and a pen for Tilly.

Erin was handed an elaborately wrapped package. It had golden paper and a beautiful ribbon and bow. The tag read, *'Happy Birthday —Judi x.'* She didn't want to open it, it was so pretty, but she did, and nearly peed her pants when she saw a beautifully embroidered throw pillow that on one side read, *'Welcome,'* and on the other, *'Fuck Off, You Twat.'*

"Holy Moses! That's perfect! Absolutely perfect!" she said and put it on her lap. "Throw pillow from Judi Dench," she said to Tilly.

The next gift was a green, wicker, heart-shaped purse with a gold chain and a red, heart-shaped clasp. "Wow, this is… interesting," Erin said and looked at the tag. "It's from Penny."

The room was silent for a moment, then Tilly said, "At least it's pretty and not insulting, right?"

"Yeah, you're right, Tilly," Erin said.

"I think it's beautiful," Rosie said, and Erin smiled at her.

"Well then, that's perfect because I'm giving it to you," Erin said and watched as the nine-year-old's eyes lit up.

"Really?"

"Really."

"Oh, thank you, Mummy!" she said and reached over to hug her. "Open this one next; it's from Baz."

Rosie handed her a soft package wrapped in what looked like silk fabric. She untied the wide ribbon and realized that he'd cleverly wrapped the gift in itself. She held up a beautiful silk dressing gown with exotic birds and flowers printed on it. "Oh, my! This is extraordinary!" she said and put it on. She reached into the pocket and pulled out a small card that she read out loud. *'I do hope you love this as much as I do. I've the very same one at home and wear it nearly every day. Happy birthday, much love, Baz, Vincent, and Caroline X.'* "A silk dressing gown from Baz and Vincent Thompson," she said to Tilly."

"Well, I never thought I'd be writing that out anywhere in my lifetime," she said and blew out a short breath.

The next gift was an impossibly soft throw blanket from Ian McKellen. "Ooh, this is fantastic! I'm gonna wear it all winter!"

She got a Cocktail Keurig from Akshara Anand with a note that she read out loud. "'*I know you'll not be able to use this for a few months, but I do hope you'll enjoy it after the baby arrives, Akshara x.*' I had no idea anything like this existed! What a cool gift!" Erin said.

"Open this one next, Mummy! It's from Johnny," Rosie said and handed her a large, turquoise-blue, fabric tote bag.

"Oh, that's so pretty!" She looked inside, gasped, and pulled out an eye mask, house slippers, a feather-light blanket, a small pillow, and another robe, all made with the most exquisite robins-egg-blue silk and embroidered with cream and red peonies. All she could do was stare at it and shake her head, trying not to cry. "I've never seen anything like it. I don't know what to say," she said and stroked the pillow with her thumb.

"Best gift ever from Johnny Depp," Tilly said as she wrote it down.

Erin would've been thrilled if there were no more gifts to open, but there were quite a few more, so she pressed on. She got fancy wine glasses; a silver candelabra with leaves and flowers that was very pretty; an odd feather scarf stole that she gave to Tilly, who laughed as she put it on.

Next was a box of chocolate body paint and a rose gold necklace that looked sort of like a long nail. It didn't have a name on the tag, only a winking smiley face. "What should I write down for that one?" Tilly asked.

"What is it, anyway?" Roger asked and lifted the box up to read it. After a few moments, his face grew red, and he began to cough. "Well then, that's somethin' yeh dinnae see everaday," he said and handed it to David, who had a very similar reaction.

"What is it?" she asked, noticing the men's red faces and David's odd smile. She took it out of the box and held it. It was a bit heavier than it looked and had a small button on the side. She pushed on the button and nearly dropped it when it began vibrating. "Wow, I think I might like this one the best! I guess you don't have to write it down since there isn't a name on it," Erin said and laughed at Jules, who'd just read the box David had handed him and began coughing.

She opened a bag with a big, comfy, cashmere sweater, a box of heart-shaped candles, and chocolate truffles from Haley Cunningham, the woman who played David's daughter-in-law on Wilde's Life. Next was a photo collage wall frame from Valentine Gregov, then a Coach handbag from Una Gupta, one of the Bollywood dancers and a very popular Indian film choreographer.

The last few gifts were a Burberry logo hair scarf in black, tan, and brown; a ceramic vase that looked like an eardrum; wall sconces that looked like amoebas; and finally, oversized cat eye sunglasses which she loved, from Barney Peterson, the lead actor on Wilde's Life, and his wife Heather.

David's mobile dinged, meaning either Becky or Tina had sent him a message. Out of politeness, he left the room to read it and returned to show Erin. Becky had sent him an email with a link to an article about the party. They opened it, and Erin read:

Bollywood Birthday for David Elliott's Baby Mama

Apparently, the star-studded Bollywood birthday party for David Elliott's pregnant partner, Erin March, was a success. Several celebrities posted tweets and shared images of the do on Instagram and other social media platforms.

Erin smiled at the image of David in his costume, bowing to their guests.

"Namaste!" said Una Gupta in her post.

The event was certainly worth talking about with a turnout such as that.

There were two photos of the beautiful cake, one before the candles were lit, and one after.

"Look at this cake!" said Akshara Anand.

She flinched as she gazed upon an image of her and Paul Gossamer, smiling for the camera.

"Happy birthday to Erin March!" said Paul Gossamer.

Next was a picture of the decorations and one of the boys, guarding the cottage door.

"Stunning! This is the place to be tonight!" said Thomas Boyd Macmillan.

Erin gasped at an image of her bending over to pick up a dropped fork. Her rear end looked enormous, and she closed her eyes in disgust.

"Well, look at that!" said Roxy Foxx, though we don't believe she meant it as a compliment.

David looked over her shoulder. "Who's the hot babe in the sari?" he said and bent down to kiss her cheek.

"Some chick you were seen with this weekend."

"That reminds me, I was invited to an event page for the party by Tina. She said she was sorry she couldn't come but set the page up for you and added everyone we invited to share photos and stories."

"Yes, I was also invited, but I've been too nervous to look at it. Can we look together later?"

"Aye, we can use ma laptop."

The rest of Sunday morning was spent relaxing and laughing with her friends. Jules excused himself just before lunch, then David and Erin helped the children pack up their things since they would be returning to school later that afternoon. Tilly had to go back to work the next morning, so she and Roger volunteered to deliver them on their way home.

Finally, at about four o'clock, the house was empty and quiet. "There's one more gift, darling," David said after a supper of leftover Tikka Masala and birthday cake.

"Who from?"

He began swiping his phone and then handed her his mobile, opened to a message from Becky.

> Becky: *I will send this to the papers today: David Elliott and Erin March officially announced their engagement today. The wedding will be small, with only family and close friends in attendance.*
>
> David: *Thanks, Becks.*
>
> B: *It should run next week.*

She looked at him, not knowing what to say. "Really? So... it's official?" she said.

"Aye. I hope ye're pleased?"

"Aye, it's just a shock, that's all. It's also surreal seeing it written out like that, you know? It's just so hard to believe." The shock had her reeling; they hadn't discussed it, and it had come out of left field.

"Yeh dinnae seem verra—" he said, sounding trepidatious.

Erin shook her head and smiled at him. "Aye, I'm chuffed to bits! It was just such a surprise that... Well, thank you, honey!"

The last word hung in the air for a moment. "Ach, I want everaone tae know about et. I'm thrilled tae be makin' you ma wife." The atmosphere was a bit strained, and they were silent until she handed him his phone. "Would you like tae look at the event page now?"

"Not really, but I'll do it," she said and followed him to his office.

The first photo to show up wasn't too bad; she was standing next to David while everyone was singing *Happy Birthday* to her. The spectacular cake was glowing, as were their faces from the many candles on it. "I like that one," she said.

"Ach, ma darling, yeh look bonnie," he said and then scrolled down.

There was one with Judi and Ian and one with her and Johnny Depp, which was surreal, but she looked bloated and ugly next to how attractive he was. Many of the photos on the site were taken by the guests and weren't flattering in the least. "Good night nurse! I look like a big red sausage! Is that how I really looked? Why didn't anyone tell me? I... can't look at anymore—"

"What are yeh on about? Yeh look lovely!" he said, but she stood and walked away from him and the awful reminder of how mismatched they were. "Erin?"

"I'm sorry," she whispered and went to their bedroom to cry.

Chapter Thirty-One

A PERILOUS EXPEDITION

On Monday, Erin walked to West Bay to find thank you cards and then filled them out when she got back home. Finding the many celebrities' addresses on David's phone when he got home that afternoon was exciting. She just couldn't believe he had all that information at his fingertips.

On Wednesday, she went out for a few odds and ends at the supermarket and was putting her things in the trunk. A vehicle pulled into the spot next to her with its radio playing, and she couldn't help but overhear a DJ talking. *"Have you heard the latest about our favorite kilted time traveler?"* Her ears perked up at that.

"I believe I have," said the second DJ. *"He's made a statement to a reporter revealing that he intends to marry the woman he's been seen with so often, even before his wife Susannah Sutcliffe Elliott died so tragically."*

"Yeah, it was really tragic," she whispered.

"One wonders what he could be thinking? Does she honestly believe he'll ever actually tie the knot with her after being Susannah Sutcliffe's husband?"

Erin's heart was pounding as she shut the trunk lid. Her face was hot, and she could feel tears prick her eyes. *Ignore them! It's just one opinion,* she thought and then got in her car. She touched the start button and heard Elton John singing, *Goodbye Yellow Brick Road.* The song ended, and it was time for the radio personalities to banter. *"This just in… David Elliott plans to marry his new partner."*

"Has he said it, or is it only a rumor?"

"Says here that he's made an official statement."

"He's gonna marry her? But why? Is she pregnant?"

"Some might say she certainly looks as if she is. Didn't you see the photos from her birthday gala? Pregnant or not, she certainly has enough belly to go around!"

"David must be feeling guilty or perhaps trapped; I mean, she is sick, and he's apparently the only one who can cure her. If he buggers off, she'll most likely die and—"

"Oi, and before she does, she'll almost certainly give a vindictive interview. The poor man, caught between a rock and a fat woman!"

The two men laughed, and Erin turned off the radio. *I can't do it! It's not fair to him! He'll be a laughingstock if he marries me! What were you thinking? You're deluded!* she thought miserably.

When she got home, she stepped into the thatched cottage and set down her bag of groceries. Her heart hurt, and she felt numb. She'd have to tell him as soon as he got home that afternoon, but she didn't know how.

The last thing she could think about was cooking, and wasn't hungry anyway, so she decided to go for a walk. She and David had walked the Jurassic coast path together many times, so she didn't think anything of heading out on her own.

The wind was high, but it pushed her along, up several steep hills and down again. She began to feel a bit tired, so she turned to head home; however, now the wind was against her. She pushed and trudged up one hill, having to stop three times to catch her breath. Even the way back downhill wasn't easy; the wind fought her every step. At the bottom of the next hill, she looked up and knew she wouldn't be able to do it.

Good night nurse! How are you gonna get home now?

"I'll call him!" she said out loud and put her hand in her jacket pocket. No phone. She tried her jeans. Nothing. She patted every pocket she had and even a few imaginary ones, just to be sure. "FUCK!" she said into the wind, which ate it up, making it lose its meaning. *It's in the car! Dammit!*

It took her nearly an hour of stops and starts, but she managed to climb the next hill. She was so far from home that she couldn't even see it from where she stood, panting. Had she kept going the other way, she would have come to a small town where she might have been able to get an Uber or call David, but she couldn't go back at that point. She sat on the path, looking out to sea, hoping someone would walk past and let her use their phone.

A good hour later, the sun was setting, and there was no sign of anyone on the trail. It was also getting colder, and her jacket wasn't keeping the biting wind out any longer. *David, please help me! Please come looking for me!* she thought desperately. She had no idea what to do and was beginning to panic. The day had been warm for the first week in October, but she guessed the nights could dip to around freezing at that time of year, and she wasn't dressed for it. "Help!" she yelled, but again, the wind took it and ran away.

It was now dusk, and she huddled in the tall grass, hoping it would give her at least a tiny bit of shelter. It didn't. *Where are you, David?* Out of nowhere, it was as if someone turned off the fans, and the wind died down. She heard dogs barking and voices in the distance, but she was so cold that it hurt to move. "Help!" she called out again, but there wasn't much power in it that time. She managed to sit up and saw little dots of light below her and on the tops of the hills headed home. *It's too late in the year for fireflies,* she thought.

"Erin?" she heard from a great distance away. "Erin March? Can you hear me?" She recognized Asit's voice and wanted to call out, but it was so difficult.

"Help!" she whispered, "Help me, please."

She felt a blanket cover her and a strong person lift her. Next, she was moving across the path very quickly and wondered why she wasn't falling out of whatever was transporting her. When she looked up, she thought she could make out David's co-actor, Val Gregov. She was sitting on his lap, and he looked worried. "Where's David?" she whispered.

"He's out searchin' for you. He's on the other side of West Bay, past the East Cliff. Are you warm enough, then?"

"I think so. I just want to see David."

"Yes, I imagine you do. He's been out of his mind with worry. I reckon he'll—" A cell phone started ringing, and the man answered. "Yes, I've got her with me now. Barney's drivin' the cart, and I'm holdin' her. Yes, hold on, a'right." He held the phone up to her ear, and she heard David's voice.

"Erin? Are yeh a'right? Are yeh hurt?"

"I'm better now," she said and then realized that her teeth were chattering. "I'm cold, David. I'm really cold."

"Oh, darling, I'm on my way home now, and I'll warm yeh up, ma love," he said.

"Okay. Wait, there was something important I needed to tell you, but I can't remember it now. I'm so tired and hungry, too. I just wanna be home now," she said.

"Almost there," Barney said.

"I heard that," David said. "I love you, Erin, and I'll see you in a little while."

"I love you too."

Valentine took the phone away from her ear. "Right, well—" he listened for a moment and then replied, "Don't thank me till we're there. See ya in a tick, cheers."

"Thank you for rescuing me, Val. I guess you're the hero of the day," she said and hoped he hadn't lost all feeling in his legs because of her. "Thank you, Barney. You guys are the best." She was exhausted and didn't feel like talking anymore so she tried to concentrate on Val's warmth.

She woke in the morning, only recalling snippets of what had happened after Val and Barney helped her into the cottage, where Asit had been waiting with a cup of hot drinking chocolate for her. She'd been bundled up in as many blankets as they could find while they waited for David to arrive. The men tried to make small talk but soon gave up when she stopped answering them.

She remembered David charging through the door and heading straight for her. He held her and kissed her, then he thanked everyone who had helped. Next thing she knew, they were in their bed, naked; David was spooning behind her, rubbing her cold skin with his warm hands and feet. She remembered waking up and going to the bathroom but then shivering when she returned, feeling the cold again.

She had to pee again as she lay in their bed, listening to David breathe. Finally, she flung off the covers and groaned as she stood. Every muscle in her body ached horribly. Muscles she didn't know she had as she hobbled to the bathroom. The towel warmer was on, so the room was heated and comfortable. She didn't want to return to their chilly bedroom and stayed there a long time.

"Are yeh a'right, love?" David said and then knocked gently on the door.

"Yeah, it's just nice and warm in here. I'll be out in a minute. Can you please bring me my sweats and my big robe?"

"Aye," he said and returned a few moments later.

"You can come in. I'm not using the toilet," she said when he knocked again.

He entered the room looking anxious. "Erin, why did you do that?"

"Do what? I told you, it's warm—"

"Why did you go off on yer own like that? You left the groceries on the counter, and… et seems yeh just walked out. I don't understand."

"Oh, yeah, I was upset."

"Upset? What about, love?"

"Doesn't matter—"

"Et matters tae me," he said and took her hand. "Please tell me."

"Well, the thing is… you can't marry me, David. It just won't work."

"What are yeh on about? Why can't I marry you?"

"It'll be a mistake. You'll be a laughingstock, and well, you already are, so—"

"If I already am, what difference does et make? You're talking nonsense, Erin. How many times must I tell yeh that I dinnae care—"

"But *I* care. You should've heard the DJs on the radio yesterday, they were cruel! They speculated that I had some kind of dirt on you or that I was pregnant; those being the only reasons you'd say you were going to marry me and that you really wouldn't, not after being *Susannah Sutcliffe's husband*." She was now pacing and wringing her hands.

"Ma Losh, why do yeh torture yerself by listening tae that bullocks?"

"You should find someone who fits you better; someone beautiful and slender and—"

"Fine, is that what you want? You want me to find someone else?" he said, raising his voice. "Yeh won't listen tae anathin' I say! Could yeh, for once, give me the benefit of the doubt and believe me? Yeh go off into the cold without a care for yerself, our bairn, or me, all because you were too foolish tae turn off the talking heads? I dinnae understand yeh!"

"That's not *why* I did it. I needed to think and clear my head. I just went too far and—and what do you mean by *fine*? You were mighty quick to say that! Have someone in mind, do you?" she spat.

"Don't be ridiculous, Erin, now ye're being paranoid. You seem determined tae sabotage our relationship, and I don't understand et. Don't yeh want to be with me anamore?"

"More than anything, but I don't want people to look down on you because of me."

"They won't… don't you understand? The people saying those things only do it for ratings and to cause a stir. Everaone who matters is on our side. And to be frank, yeh seem to believe that yer enormous, and yer not, not by a long shot. I'm not sure who or what made yeh think that way, but et's a lie."

"Everyone and everything have made me think that way. I look like Aunt… what's her name, on Harry Potter, when he blew her up like a balloon! Look at my hands, David!" She held them out to him. "They're like ugly little sausages, and my feet are so swollen, all I can wear are your bedroom slippers! I know you don't like skinny women, but this is just disgusting! I… I feel ugly and unlovable, and completely undesirable. Those talking heads are only telling the truth," she said and began crying so hard that she couldn't breathe.

David held her and didn't say anything until she'd calmed down a bit. "Erin, ye're pregnant. I understand it must be difficult to see yourself in photographs right now, but darling, do you truly believe that I only love you for how you look? We both know that this weight gain is temporary and soon you'll be free of et. I love you for everything you are, inside and out, but especially inside. I reckon yeh can't understand that, but et's true. Please stop telling me that I can't marry you because I'll not listen to et any longer. Ye've given me yer word that you'll be ma wife, and now ye're stuck with me, a'right?"

"But… if I'm stuck with you, that means you're *stuck* with me! How do I know if you're regretting that promise? Don't you understand that words are… nothing? Words mean nothing. All I've heard are words… I love you, Erin… I'll get rid of the porn, Erin… No, I didn't buy any more of it, Erin… I'll never do it again, Erin. All words. If you did wake up thinking that I was too ugly and fat, you wouldn't tell me! You'd *deal* with it until you found someone else."

"I'm so sorry you've been through that with so many other men, but I am not one of them. You might never believe me, but I'll not do that to yeh, ever. Actions speak louder than words, right? So, when you can't believe my words, believe my actions, a'right?" She nodded and allowed him to lead her to their bed. "I'm going to make love to you now," he said and kissed her passionately.

She gazed into his soft brown eyes and melted at his touch. "Okay, I'd like that. Thank you for loving me," she said when he stopped, and he kissed her again.

Chapter Thirty-Two

TUCK EVERLASTING

David was gone for the day filming, as he had been for the last week. It was windy and cold that day, so Erin wanted to build a small fire in the fireplace. She'd been over-emotional lately, feeling lonely and sometimes crying when he came home, but her doctor told her it was normal to feel that way during pregnancy. It was also suggested that with the Fertilis Defect, her mood swings and emotions might be even more unpredictable.

She pulled an old newspaper out of the recycling bin and started crumpling it up. Just as she was about to ball up the piece in her other hand, she saw a photo that made her look twice. It was David and another woman sitting at a cozy-looking restaurant. He was leaning in close to her face, and it was hard to tell if he was kissing her or saying something in her ear. She froze and instantly felt the bile come to the surface of her stomach, just waiting to come up and out.

She flattened the paper and read the caption at the side of the photo.

David Elliott Seen with Partner in
Dorset Pub... Story on page 4c.

Erin knew it wasn't her and was already starting to panic. She turned to page 4c and saw another photo of David and the woman; they were both laughing, and she wanted to smash her face in. She had a few extra pounds on her like she did before she'd gotten pregnant and blew up to the size of a whale, with big eyes, a pretty smile, and perfect teeth. She read the story.

David Elliott, *45, best known for his role in Future Explorations, was seen at the Anchor Inn on Wednesday afternoon with his partner, Erin March. They had a few drinks, a meal, and several hearty laughs. Will they last? Who knows, but the two lovebirds sure know how to have a good time together.*

Erin was beside herself. *Why didn't he tell me about it? That was... a week and a half ago! Just after my birthday party.* Everything inside her wanted to drive herself to the film set and demand an answer, but she knew that would be the worst thing to do, so she tried to explain it away. *Maybe it's a co-worker or... a fan he couldn't get away from? No, he looks completely comfortable; too comfortable!*

'The two lovebirds.'

Most other women would be able to stay calm and wait for an explanation. She wanted to be like them, but she was nothing like that. Jealousy and fear gripped her heart, and by the time David returned from the set, she'd convinced herself he was cheating on her or was probably thinking about it. At the very least, he was seeing other people on the side.

———

"Erin? I'm home, darling," David said as he stepped into the house. "That's so nice to say!" He hung his jacket on the hook by the door and went to find her. She wasn't in the sitting room or the conservatory. Not in the kitchen or bathroom, either. "Erin? Where are you, love?"

He went upstairs to their bedroom to change into something more comfortable and found her lying in bed with a newspaper crumpled up in her hand. There was also what appeared to be a whole box of used tissues scattered around her, so he hurried to her side and put his hand on hers. "What's the matter, darling?"

Her eyes were closed, and all she did was shake her head and sob. He managed to get the newspaper page out of her hand and opened it. When he turned it over and saw the photo, terror swept over his whole body. He knew what Erin was thinking, and she was NOT going to believe him, at least not right away.

"Ma Losh, this isn't what et looks like, darling," he said and knelt in front of her again. She held out her other hand, which had the continuation of the story in it. He read, "*David Elliott... was seen... with partner, Erin March...*"

"You were obviously familiar enough with her for people to think you were together... lovebirds... and to think she was me," Erin said, gasping for air.

"Erin, calm down, please. That's Emily Tuck, the girl from my dream. She learned I was shooting down here and came to see me. We had lunch, that's all. Please believe me."

"She looks like me; she's bigger, like me... before I got *this* big... and she's... pretty and has perfect... teeth," she said between sobs. "Apparently you have a connection with her... look at you! That's your best smile! You obviously like her."

He looked at her, utterly confused. "Yes, I like her, she's nice and funny. We talked about our childhood and—"

"You're going to fall in love with her and leave me, just like everyone else. So... you might as well go now. Why draw it out... why not rip the band-aid off right now?" she said, sobbing.

"Why would I do that? I'm not gonna—"

"We aren't married yet, David. Maybe you're having cold feet, or maybe you want to make sure... or... maybe you really want to change your mind but don't know how to say it?"

"Erin, that's the farthest thing from—I had lunch with a childhood friend. I wasn't thinking romantically about her at all, honestly. I have all the romance a man could ever desire with you; I'm not looking for more or other—"

"No? Then why didn't you tell me about it? Why were you hiding it from me?" How do you think it feels to find out about it in a gossip column... where they think it's me you're with?"

David sat on the floor, not knowing what to say. Susannah wouldn't have had a problem with him having lunch with another woman, but he had to remember that she wasn't Susannah. "I... I forget to mention it; it slipped my mind," he said, and she shot daggers out of her eyes.

"You forgot? It slipped your mind to tell me that you had lunch with a woman who looks an awful lot like me, and you're quite attracted to me... unless... you aren't now!" she said and curled up into a fetal position.

"It wasn't a big deal to me, honestly," he said, trying to convince her and defend himself.

"Are you really telling me that seeing this girl you haven't seen in nearly forty years, who you've been dreaming about and spent all kinds of time trying to remember the name of wasn't important to you? Do you think I'm stupid! I'm sure it was extremely important to you! Don't you dare lie to me!"

"I reckon et was, but I didn't think of it that way, and I'm not attracted tae her at all. I'm not going tae fall in love with her. It's not like that. And what about Roger?" he said.

"Roger? Are you still thinking something was going on with us?" she said, and David shook his head.

"Aye, I mean, no, but ye're friends with him. If he were in town and stopped by, ye'd have lunch with him, wouldn't yeh?"

"But that's different; you know Roger, and you know he's not a threat; plus, he has Tilly now. I don't know this woman. What if she tried to seduce you? And what if you let her?" She was crying again, hugging herself tightly.

He knew that every relationship she'd ever been in had ended with the guy cheating or leaving her for someone who had something she didn't, whether it was bigger boobs, a thinner body, or boredom. She'd explained it to him many times before; it was all she knew, so he was doing his best to be patient with her tirade. "Aye, I reckon I can see how et might make yeh feel, but I honestly didn't think of et as anythin' more than if ye'd gone tae lunch with our Roger. As for her seducing me, et wouldn't happen, and if she tried, I'd not let her! That's just insultin' if I'm honest."

"No, that's reality... the only reality I've known, apart from Todd, though instead of another physical woman, he allowed porn to seduce him. What's insulting is not telling me and then trying to say it meant nothing to you! Why, on earth didn't you text me or tell me about it?"

David's patience was wearing thin, and she was starting to make him angry. "I dinnae ken. I didn't think of et."

Erin shook her head. "See, that proves it! You didn't think of me when you were with her! All you were thinking about was her and you. That was it, right?"

"Mebbe I didn't tell yeh because of this! Mebbe... I wanted tae have an innocent meal with an old friend without the third degree! Did yeh think of that in yer overblown fantasy about what I was thinkin' and feelin'?" he said and instantly regretted it. That wasn't what he'd been thinking at all, but now he couldn't take it back.

———

Erin wilted; she melted and felt like something died inside her. She hated herself and Emily Tuck. "I see," she said calmly and stood.

He took her hand, still on his knees, and held it tight. "I didn't mean that. I wasn't thinkin' that at all. I only said et because I was angry. As soon as I come home, the events of ma day fade away, and all I want is tae be here, comfortable, and myself with yeh. I'm sorry I didn't tell yeh about Emily. I swear tae you et wasn't because I wanted tae hide et from yeh.

"Just tell me what yeh want me tae do in the future if somethin' like that happens again. If yeh want me tae tell her tae fuck off, I will. If yeh want me tae text yeh and invite yeh tae join us, I will. Please, please, dinnae go away; stay here and be with me."

It was unhealthy and wrong for her to forbid him from associating with other women, she knew that, but she didn't know how to trust. If it had been someone they both knew, someone she was comfortable with, she would've been fine with it, but this was a stranger and therefore a threat. He'd told her that actions speak louder than words and to watch his actions. His actions were screaming at her in her aching mind, and she knew what would come next... she knew the routine down pat.

It might start as an innocent encounter, but it never stayed that way. She'd heard, *'It didn't mean anything,'* or *'It was just lunch, Erin,'* or *'I'm not attracted to her at all—I'm not going to fall in love with her—It's not like that,'* and *'That's just insulting,'* too many times before. It was the beginning of the end, and she could do nothing about it. The more she fussed, the sooner it would happen; it was inevitable. All she could do at that point was shut down and wait for the end. She was just going to have to turn off her feelings so that when it happened again it wouldn't matter.

"You do what you want to do, David. You're a grown man and don't need a mommy at home telling you what you should do in a crisis situation, such as finding yourself in the presence of a female who isn't her. I'm… sorry I overreacted. Let's have supper." He stared at her, and she figured he was confused. She'd just been furious and was now apologizing, but she couldn't explain it to him.

"A'right ma love, I'm… sorry," he said, watching her as she stood, looking down at the floor and wanting it to swallow her up.

She didn't care about supper, but when he let go of her hand, she walked down to the kitchen and methodically set the dishes on the table. Then she put the food she had warming in the oven on her dainty trivets. Her dishes were pretty and so was the vintage cotton tablecloth. The cutlery had mermaid tails for handles, and she used a conch shell to weigh down the napkins so they didn't blow off the table in the wind coming through the open windows.

Gulls cried as they flew over the nearby water, and she could smell someone having a barbeque nearby. She cut up the roasted chicken and tried to smile as she put a drumstick and thigh on his plate. After dishing out the corn and mashed potatoes, she set it in front of him and started to fill hers. She could feel his eyes on her as she put the smallest bite of chicken breast on her plate and only a spoonful of corn and mashed potatoes. She wasn't hungry and couldn't help it.

"Erin, I don't understand," he said and tried to take her hand, but she got up before he could, heading to the fridge to get some juice.

"Neither do I," she said.

Later that night when they went to bed, David touched her, tenderly. She knew he wanted to make love to her but she pretended to be asleep. The image of him with his face so near to the other woman wouldn't stop tormenting her, and she was quickly convincing herself that it *was* a kiss, not a whispered comment. *'The two lovebirds,'* the article had read. *Of course.*

A few days later, on Wednesday, Erin got a text from David.

> David: *Darling, Emily is here again and*
> *would like to have lunch. Why don't*
> *you join us?*

Erin wanted to beg him not to go to lunch with her but knew she couldn't do that.

> Erin: *No, thank you.*

> D: *Are you sure? I'd like for you to come.*
> *I want her to meet you.*

Erin didn't reply. She went to their room, held onto the compass pendant he'd given her in New Orleans, and cried. When David got home, she set out the dishes and put the food on the trivets, but they didn't look as pretty to her. The dishes sat on the vintage tablecloth, both looking dull and worn. She loaded David's plate with meatloaf, green beans, and mashed potatoes, then gave herself a tenth of what she'd given him.

"I missed yeh today," David said, and she nodded.

Not enough to stay away from the other woman, she thought.

"Let's go for a walk on the beach after supper tonight."

Erin tried to smile, but she couldn't. "I'm tired. I'm gonna go to bed early." *Maybe you can ask Emily to walk with you,* she thought, then worried that he might just do it. They finished their meal, and David helped her clean off the table, then he dried and put the dishes away after she washed them. When that chore was finished, he took her by the hand.

"I love yeh, and… I want tae make love tae yeh so badly, Erin," he said.

She imagined she heard a slight hesitation when he said her name and thought he was making sure to use the right one. He started kissing her neck and touching her breasts through her shirt. All she could think about was him imagining that she was Emily as he did it. "No, David. I said I was too tired," she said and backed away from him, wanting to vomit. Then she went to their room and shut the door.

"Why don't you ask Emily," she whispered and began sobbing. She heard him knock, but she didn't answer. Just then, the baby kicked her, a real solid kick. She should have been happy and run out to tell David so he could put his hand on her belly, hoping it would do it again, but she didn't care.

"Erin? What's the matter? Is et because I had lunch with Emily? But I asked yeh tae come, and yeh said yeh didn't want to."

Silence.

"Erin? But yeh said yeh didn't want tae come," he repeated.

Chapter Thirty-Three

EPISODE TWO

Three weeks went by for Erin without sex and without feeling. David had stopped asking her for it, so she knew he was getting it from *her*. The children had been home on their half-term break for two of those weeks and had just been taken back to school on Sunday. She was now around six and a half months pregnant and had been tired the entire time they were home. It had taken everything she had to get up and dressed every day.

Monday, she felt a tightness in her chest and thought it was indigestion. On Tuesday, she had a hard time catching her breath, but she hid it from David, figuring it didn't matter anymore. On Wednesday, he sent her a text from the set.

> David: *I'm going to come for you today at lunchtime. I want you to meet Emily. And don't bother saying no, as I'm coming whether you like it or not.*

> Erin: *I don't want to go anywhere. I don't feel good.*

He didn't reply. She was feeling extraordinarily tired and had already experienced several alarmingly serious struggles to catch her breath that day. At one o'clock, a car she didn't recognize pulled into the driveway. She didn't want to see anyone; she hadn't done her hair and was wearing sweats, so she hid in the study, hoping they'd go away.

"Erin? Where are yeh?" David's voice came closer, and then he was standing in the doorway, smiling at her. "I've come tae—" he began, but when he saw her, he stopped. "Oh, ma God, Erin! Yer lips are blue!

She stood so she could leave the room. *He had* her *drive him here? How could h—"* Her head was whooshing, and she saw tiny dots before her eyes, then everything went black.

Erin woke with her head on David's lap in the backseat of a car, being driven very fast by a woman. "What's happening? Where are we going? Who the fuck are you?" she asked the driver.

David happened to have his hand on her belly, and the baby kicked, making him jump and gasp. "Was that our bairn? Erin, yeh didn't tell me et was kickin'!" he said, sounding so excited.

"I want to go home," she said, ignoring him. When there were no signs of the driver slowing down, she got angry and tried to sit up, but she didn't have the energy. "I said to turn around you... homewrecker!" she exclaimed and started sobbing, absolutely wailing. "Let me out of this fucking car!"

David held her tight and seemed shocked at her outburst. "What in the hell are yeh on about, Erin? She's not a homewrecker! She hasn't done anathin'—"

"We haven't had sex in over three weeks, and you're going to tell me you're not getting it from her?" she said bitterly.

David let go of her, lifting his hands as if she were diseased, and he didn't want to touch her. "Is... that what yeh think I've been doin'? Do yeh really believe that? We haven't had sex because ye've turned me away evera time I suggested et!"

"Tell her, David," Emily spoke up from the driver's seat.

Erin thought she was going to have a heart attack.

"Tell her!" she said once more.

"Why don't you tell me yourself?" Erin spat. "For how long? Since the first time you showed up and he didn't tell me? When I had to find out from the gossip section? Couldn't find someone of your own, so you had to—"

"I'm a lesbian, Erin, and I'd say for about forty-two years," Emily said softly.

She wanted to say something, to yell at David for not telling her and letting her waste away, torturing herself, but she couldn't catch her breath. She opened her mouth and tried to sit up, fear filling her mind with nothing but *Please, let me breathe! Please!* "Wha—" was all she could say before the coughing started, and David panicked.

"Oh, God, NO! Erin, okay, I've got you, darling. I'm sorry, my love, just relax, et'll be over soon, just feel my arms around you. Emily, please hurry," Erin heard him say before she passed out again.

Erin opened her eyes and didn't know where she was. It was pitch black, and the last thing she remembered was being driven somewhere by... *her.* "*Who is David?*" she heard, and every hair on her body rose in terror and confusion.

"Todd? What's going on? Where am I, and where's David?" she asked in complete darkness. She heard something move, and then the room was suddenly thrown into light. She shielded her eyes with her hand and groaned.

"Who *is* David?" Todd's voice asked again. Erin moved her hand and saw her ex-husband standing near the light switch in her old bedroom on Whistlers Way. She began to panic, not understanding what was happening. "Answer me! *Who* is David? You've been saying his name in your sleep. Are you having an affair, Erin?" Todd said, glaring at her with anger in his eyes.

"Is this some kind of joke? How did I get here? You know perfectly well who David is. Why are you doing this?" She felt like she'd been run over by a lorry and wasn't in the mood for games. "I need to use the toilet. Please ask David or Kitty to come help me," she said and sat up on the side of the bed.

"Who's Kitty?"

"OH, MY GOD! WHAT HAPPENED? WHERE'S MY BABY? WHERE IS IT?" Erin screamed, realizing that she was no longer pregnant. Todd was looking at her as though she'd lost her mind and started backing away.

"This isn't funny, Todd! I was over six months pregnant! It's not just going to disappear! Please tell me what happened! Did it… die? Oh, God! Does David know?" she wailed.

"What in the fuck are you talking about? You can't have children. It's impossible that you were pregnant! Stop this! Now, who the fuck is *David*?" he said again.

Erin sat shaking with fear and dread. "He's… my fiancé… David Elliott. We've been together since May. I'm… pregnant with his baby. You and I are divorced."

"David Elliott?" Todd laughed. Nice one, Erin. You got me! I've heard of elaborate April Fool's Day pranks, but this one is over the top!"

Erin stood, angry that he was mocking her, and felt the whooshing in her ears again. "I'm not joking," she said before everything went black.

Erin woke again, hearing a heart rate monitor and something else that sounded like '*whah-whah-whah-whah*' non-stop. She felt heavy, and it was difficult to open her eyes, as though she'd been drugged. "Where am I?" she whispered and tried to sit up. It was very difficult, and an alarm began to go off.

"*Erin?*" she heard her true love, David Elliott, say, and her eyes grew enormous.

"DAVID! OH GOD, DAVID! Is it really you? Touch me! Please!"

"Aye, et's me," he said but didn't touch her; he also didn't sound all that pleased with her.

"I was just in my old home! Todd was there and—" She could feel her eyes growing heavy as she saw a nurse change an empty IV bag. "He… said you… weren't… real. Are you—" Her eyes were so heavy she had to close them for a second.

Erin was startled awake by the slamming of the kitchen door. Her chest was tight, and it was hard to breathe. She was sitting with her legs up on the couch like she'd done more times than she could count, trying to rest. *Wait! This is wrong! Where's David?* "David?" she called out.

"God, Erin! You're not engaged to David Elliott!" Todd said from the kitchen.

"NO! I am! I just saw him! Stop lying to me! I don't love you anymore, Todd! You're going to have to get over me!" she cried.

"You… don't love me anymore? Nice! You're insane! How on earth could you have even met David Elliott? He lives in England!"

"Come on! We met through the treatments! May sixteenth of this year… in New Orleans!"

Todd came into the living room and stared at her. "Alexa, what's today's date?" he said.

"Today is Tuesday, the second of April, " their Echo Dot replied.

"But… that's impossible! I was just with him! I want to go back! I want to go home!" she cried.

"Well, you are home, so you'd better get used to it… again." He looked at her, obviously disgusted with her, and turned away. *"Now she's fucking hallucinating; what's next?"* she heard him say under his breath as he went back to the kitchen.

Erin woke in a hospital room; she was exhausted, and something was hitting her. "What's hitting me?" she said out loud, but there didn't seem to be anyone around to hear her. She was hooked up to an IV, and tubes and wires were coming from everywhere. She didn't want to be there and sat up, which made one of the machines start screaming, telling on her that she wasn't lying still.

A nurse rushed into the room, and David came in after her. Her vision was blurry, but as he got closer, she could see him a bit more clearly. It looked like he hadn't slept in days and had dark circles under his eyes. He had the beginnings of a beard, and she could see much more grey in the hair at his temples than he'd had before. "David! Is it really you? I was... with Todd, and he was angry because he didn't believe me... that I was... with you... and the baby was... gone, David!" she said.

The anger on his face reminded her how she'd gotten there, and she looked down. "And... something was hitting me—" she said slowly, feeling quite out of it. Her eyelids felt heavy and swollen, and so did her hands. She felt cold and really, really heavy. "I'm cold, I have to pee, and I don't want to be here! I want to be home in Dorset," she said, but it was hard to think clearly.

"You have a catheter, dear; we'll remove it in a bit, but until then, if you need a wee, just do it. Now you must lie flat. There's a belt around your belly monitoring your baby's heart rate," the nurse said and tried to get Erin to lie down, but she felt like she'd been lying down for a very long time and wanted to get up. "Please, ma'am, you must lie flat, or you'll risk going into premature labor."

Erin looked at her and then at David and did as she was told. "What... happened?" she said meekly.

"I'll tell yeh what happened!" David said with his voice raised. "You nearly killed yerself with all yer frettin' and worryin' and must now stay put or yeh may lose our bairn!" Erin's heavy eyes filled with tears, blurring her vision even more. "Yeh had an episode in the car after yeh fainted in the house, *three days ago*!

"Why did yeh not talk tae me about how you were feelin'? Why did you let et go this far, and why did yeh not tell me our bairn was movin'?" He turned away from her and added quietly, "Yer... yer startin' tae behave like... like... Susannah. Starvin' yerself, turnin' me away, and not lettin' me experience ma bairn's growth. I dinnae understand yeh." He sat perfectly still in the chair next to her bed and put his face in his hands.

The nurse left, telling Erin to be sure to lie still and that someone would come back soon to remove the catheter. She didn't know what to say or do; she could see David was a mess and started to think she'd been wrong. "David?" She could see his shoulders shaking now and wanted to hold him. He didn't look up. "David, I don't understand either—" she said slowly, measuring each word. "You didn't tell me. You were hiding it from me!" she said, which is what she'd convinced herself was the truth. She knew she sounded like a broken record, but her mind wouldn't let it go, and she needed truthful answers.

He stood and stared out the window. "So that's what this is about, then? You were killin' yerself because yeh dinnae trust me. I've shown yeh naught but love and have told yeh every day how much I love you and that nothin' could ever change et, but you just won't trust me. What do I have to do tae make yeh understand?" he said.

Erin could hear the hurt in his voice. "You... lied to me. You met another woman behind my back—" she said, feeling crushed by the weight of it. "I told you about Todd hiding things from me... and how it hurt me so badly. You... you know how I reacted to the bikini woman, and you promised! You don't understand." Her heart hurt, and she really felt like she was having a heart attack; however, she was so angry she kept speaking. "How could you think I wouldn't be upset at this? Why couldn't you just tell me?"

"I already told yeh, et slipped ma mind!" he yelled.

"Something as important as that, and it slipped your mind? No way! You wanted me to suffer! Why didn't you tell me she was gay? Why didn't you try to set my mind at ease?" she yelled back.

He looked at her and shrugged. "I dinnae ken," he said. "Mebbe, I wanted yeh tae trust me?"

"So, you had the power to... to make me feel less insecure, but you were too proud and... and stubborn to do it? That makes you just as guilty as I am for how bad things got!" she shot back at him. They weren't getting anywhere, so she took a deep breath. "There's something I swore to Lily I'd never tell, but I'm going to break my promise," she said, trying to calm herself down. It was taking a lot of energy to speak clearly. She wanted to slur her speech, but this was important, so she shook her head and did her best to enunciate.

"What does Lily have tae do with us?" he said, shaking with rage.

"Lily was married before she met Nick. I'd just started my job as a bus driver and had only talked to her a few times. She started showing up to work with red eyes and her head down, so I asked her what was wrong. She didn't want to share it with me, but it began our friendship. Eventually, she told me her husband, Simon, was seeing another woman. She told me how one day, he was running late for work and didn't have time to make his lunch, so he went to a diner to eat.

"Soon, she noticed he was running late at least once or twice a week, so one day, she decided to surprise him by joining him. That's when she saw them together. He told her that on the first day he'd gone to the diner, he'd seen the woman, who worked at the office where he did, sitting alone, so they sat together. He said that it didn't mean anything, and he wasn't attracted to her, so she decided to trust him and didn't make a big deal of it.

"After four months, his attitude started to change, and she'd call me, crying, afraid that it was more than just lunch. He started acting cool toward her and would snap at her for the slightest thing. At seven months, he would come home an hour, sometimes two hours late, without explanation. Eventually, he left her for the other woman, breaking her heart. He swore up and down he wasn't attracted to her, that it didn't mean anything to him, and he didn't tell her, just like you didn't tell me," she said, tears falling from her already puffy eyes.

David sighed and shook his head. "I… told yeh tae tell me what tae do… and yeh said something about me not needing a mother telling me—"

"How could I tell you not to see someone? I… I wanted you to *choose* not to see her because you knew it made me upset. I wanted you to… to choose me over her, but…you didn't."

"But if et made yeh that upset, why didn't yeh just tell me you preferred that I didn't? I can't read yer mind, Erin."

"You didn't *need* to read my mind! When we were in New Orleans, you said you never wanted me to be upset like I was about the bikini woman ever again. Why then, when you knew I was upset about Emily, did you allow it to keep going?"

"I… thought you were… okay with—That et was a'right with yeh… yeh said I could do what I wanted—"

"I told you that I was afraid, but you ignored it, and… apparently, you could've set my mind at ease by telling me that she was gay, but you didn't. I heard her say to tell me; it obviously wasn't the first time she'd said it to you; why didn't you?" Erin said.

"I dinnae ken. I reckon ye're right, et was pride or stubbornness. I wanted you tae just trust me. Et was foolish and stupid, I ken it well enough now. But… why didn't yeh talk with me? Yeh just shut down, and I couldn't say anathin' to yeh without it upsettin' yeh."

"I'd convinced myself that it was too late. I didn't have anything to offer you that was better than whatever she had. I wasn't going to use the baby, 'cause … maybe that wasn't good enough, or… that was why you'd gone to her. Maybe I was too fat or whiny or a miserable companion."

"But you knew how much our baby meant to me. I don't understand."

"Why did any of the other men leave me, David? They said the things I wanted to hear, but it was all lies, or they changed their minds when they saw a different make or model. Something shinier or faster or sexier. Why wouldn't you do the same? Todd told me once that it wasn't that the girls in the porn were prettier or thinner than me; they were just different. How can I compete with just being different? Then I remembered how you said that actions speak louder than words… and that I'd know your feelings by your actions. How can you blame me for being scared out of my mind?"

"Aye," was all he said and sighed. He slipped off his shoes and motioned for her to move over on the bed. She slid over, making the alarms sound for several seconds, but once she was laying still again, they stopped. He got into bed with her, lying on his side, and placed his hand on her stomach. "I didn't think of that, but yeh should've told me about the bairn, and yeh should've been honest with me about how yeh felt when I texted you," he said quietly, rubbing his hand over her belly button.

"I figured my initial reaction was proof enough of how I felt about you being with another woman," she said, feeling even more exhausted than before. "Listen, I can't begin to understand how it was you didn't know how I felt. I thought I'd made it plain, but I guess I didn't. I know I should've told you, but I was just so stunned by the photo in the paper and the idea they thought it was me!" She was getting worked up again, so she took a deep breath, although tears ran down her eyes, anyway. "By the time you got home after I'd found the article, I was already convinced that you were hiding things and you would end up with her in the end.

"I overreacted, and it's my fault. It all revolves around my insecurities and past experiences. I should—I need to learn how to give you the benefit of the doubt. I wish I knew how to cope, but I don't know how yet. I don't know why I go to such extremes; it's like I can't stop it, even when I can see what I'm doing. Please forgive me, and tell Emily I'm sorry as well."

David suddenly remembered that Erin's doctor in America had warned him that she might be affected by the twenty-plus years of oxygen deprivation she'd sustained because of her disease. "Ach, no, yer Doctor Nan warned me about this, but I forgot all about et. Et's my fault that et went so far, and I'm sorry, ma darling."

He explained what the doctor had told him over the phone in New Orleans, then placed his ear on her belly and spoke to it. "Ma darling bairn; et's yer da'. Yer mummy and I have a lot tae work out between us, but we both love yeh with everathin' we've got." He laid his hand on her stomach, then kissed it, and the baby kicked his hand.

He looked up at her and smiled his beautiful smile, then he kissed the place it had kicked. He kissed every place he felt it kick and then worked his way up her body, kissing her over the hospital gown, all the way up until he put his lips on hers and kissed her for a long time.

"Three days?" she said.

He nodded and kissed her some more. "I've missed yeh," he said between kisses. He placed his hand on her neck and looked her in the eyes. "Please dinnae leave me like that again. I can't live without yeh!"

Erin looked down, emotionally worn out. "I've missed you too, and I've missed myself. I thought I'd lost you to her, and obviously, I can't live without you either." They lay together for a few minutes, listening to the monitors make their various noises. "David?" she said, which took more effort than it should've.

"Aye?" he replied.

"I had the worst dreams! They were so real! I don't want to go back to sleep, ever!"

"Yeh woke yesterday, sayin' somethin' about a dream with Todd, but then you fell back asleep."

"I don't think I've ever felt so frightened," she said.

316

"You were, I could tell."

"David?"

"Aye."

"I need a treatment," she said, knowing it sounded like she was being funny, but she was completely serious. "And I... really, REALLY need to make love to you."

"Aye, so do I," he said, not laughing.

"Do the doors lock?" she asked. They looked at the door and saw what appeared to be a latch for a deadbolt.

"I think so, but yer monitors will go mental if we try that! Plus, I dinnae think et's safe! I reckon we should wait until they say yeh can leave, don't you?"

"But,, I'm so very tired and I feel lonely from the inside out. I need you! Maybe we should ask them to talk to Dr. Jill? She'll know how important the treatments are, even if she does scold me for not telling her about the exhaustion or lead-up symptoms," she said.

———

David nodded; he wanted to bury his face in her neck and his fingers someplace else. "Aye. I think yeh should," he said, breathlessly. He had managed to subdue his sexual desires as Erin distanced herself. He'd done it in the past and knew how, but they were at the surface again, and he couldn't put them down for much longer. Erin pushed the call button, and he sat up, swinging his feet off the edge of the bed. After a few moments, a nurse came in.

"Ya a'right, love?" she asked pleasantly.

"I need someone to contact my doctor about whether or not I can have a long overdue treatment whilst... well, today, and whilst I'm here," she said breathlessly. "Her name is Jill Westin, and she's doing a residency in London."

The nurse wrote down the information. "A'right, dear, and what sort of treatment do you receive?"

"It's... for the Fertilis Defect. If you use the word treatment, she'll know what it means. Please tell her it's been nearly four weeks since my last one; that's important," she said emphatically.

"I'll see what I can do," the nurse said and left the room, obviously annoyed she wasn't told what the treatments involved.

"Well, done," David said. "Et's not a good idea tae let the whole hospital know."

"Aye. Now come back here!" she said, patting the empty place next to her. He got back into the bed and snuggled up to her.

Chapter Thirty-Four

LONG OVERDUE

David and Erin slept for over an hour until a nurse came in to check Erin's monitors, and she woke. "How long will I need to be here?" she asked the young woman.

"Things seem to be settling down, and you're no longer having contractions, so the medication is working."

"Medication?" Erin said.

"Yes, you are on progesterone, which is used to stop uterine contractions," she said.

"Is that why I feel like an overstuffed rag doll?" she asked, and the nurse chuckled.

"I reckon it is, though I've never heard it described as such. I should think they'll be takin' ya off it before long, so you'll be feein' better soon. I'll speak to the doctor and see what he says. Meanwhile, try to stay calm and lie still," she said and left the room.

They were just getting comfortable again when David cleared his throat. "Erin, I… want yeh tae meet Emily," he said, and Erin's stomach dropped. "She's verra nice, and I know you'll like her."

"Humph," Erin said. "You said you wanted me to tell you my honest thoughts, right?"

"Aye, I do."

"Well then, can't it just be the two of us right now? Do you *have* to bring *her* up now? Why are you thinking about *her* all the time? I don't want to think about her, not now, not… yet. Give me some time—Can you just think about

319

me for now and not her?" she said. She didn't care that she was a lesbian; it was still too raw.

She could feel herself getting worked up, and tears stung the corners of her eyes. "I'm sorry," she continued. "It's just that she's been my every waking thought for the last three-plus weeks, and I don't want to think about her or… or hear her name anymore! Can we just close the 'Emily box' in your head for a while? I am starting to hate the name!"

"I see," he said. "I… didn't know she was yer every waking thought. I didn't realize." He wiped away one of the tears gliding slowly down her face. "I had no idea et hurt yeh so badly, and what yeh were so worked up about this whole time… I mean, after the day you found the article. I thought et was that yeh didn't like tae be alone, or because I was gone all day. I dinnae think about her all the time; I think about you… every waking moment of ma day and night… I even dream of you—"

"And her!" Erin said sharply and then felt bad. "I'm sorry."

He took her hand in his and kissed it. "Is that how far this goes back? From ma dream?" he asked, sounding baffled.

"No! No, your dream was innocent, but it got you to start thinking about her and what happened to her, and then… well, then she just magically shows up without you contacting her? I know that if *I* knew someone when I was, what… six, who grew up to be famous and suddenly a widower, I wouldn't just assume he'd remember me. And I most definitely would not presume to show up at the place he was filming… unannounced… unless… either I was hoping he'd be interested in me, or… or… did you contact her?" They were interrupted by another nurse coming in with a clipboard.

"I'm… sorry. I can come back later," she said, obviously realizing she'd interrupted an argument.

"No, it's okay," Erin said, not feeling as much like having a treatment as she had a few hours earlier.

"I've a message from Dr. Westin. She says you may perform one very gentle treatment and see how it goes. She also said," she cleared her throat, "that only David may climax. Erin is not to under any circumstances, as it can bring on labor. She said if you don't think that will be possible, then treatments are forbidden until things are normal again with the pregnancy. At that time, you may continue treatments as usual, only they must be gentle, without roughness of any kind." She cleared her throat again. "Also… nothing may be inserted into her vagina except for… David's penis, nothing else." She finished reading the message and swallowed hard. All three people in the room were bright red when she was done.

"Well… a'right, then. Ah, if that's the case, could we please have some privacy, and may we lock the door? Oh, and could the belt be taken off for a while, please?" David asked. Erin was shocked at his bluntness; she put her head down and closed her eyes while the nurse raised her eyebrows.

"Ah, I reckon so," the woman said and approached the bed to remove the belt around Erin's stomach. The alarms sounded, making a horrible noise until the nurse turned off the machine. Her face was crimson, and she wouldn't look either of them in the eye. "You may lock the door, but once the… uh, treatment is completed, please unlock it as soon as you are… able," she said and quickly left the room. David followed behind her and locked the door.

Erin could feel the electricity in the air even before he turned around. She wanted answers, and she would get them, but right then, she wanted her treatment. It didn't seem possible to stop herself from having an orgasm; she could feel it in her already.

David closed the drapes on the windows and then began taking off his clothes. She watched him, suddenly aware of everything around her; the smell of the bedding, the feel of the tape keeping her IV in place, and as David got closer, the smell of him.

"Et's not gonna take me verra long, but yeh might wanna—"

She didn't need to hear more and took hold of him. He was already hard and ready for her. All she wanted to do was bring him to the point where he would only need one or two strokes, but she thought even that would be too much. She could feel her body readying itself for him, just waiting for its chance to release, but she needed him.

The energy increased as she put her mouth around his cock. He gasped and said, "Dinnae move!" He held her shoulders and pushed them back slowly. After a few seconds of hardly breathing, she was able to pull her head away. He got up onto the bed, threw the blankets off, and laid on top of her.

"Baseball," she said and closed her eyes. "No, football! Yes, football! The ball is snapped... Rogers throws it to... to Driver, who catches it at the forty-yard line."

David stopped and stared at her as though she'd gone completely bonkers. "What are yeh doin'?" he said.

"Go on... please. I'm not allowed to—Just go," she pleaded.

As soon as his cock touched her, she nearly climaxed, and as he entered her, she had to tell him to stop. "Oh, God! Stop! Just don't move, please. Driver runs, he's in the pocket... he—Okay, David, but you have to be quick!" He moved, one stroke... two.... "The crowd is cheering—" One more stroke, and he climaxed; she could feel it filling her up. "Touchdown," she whispered breathlessly. "Please, you have to pull out!"

He rolled off her and held her tightly. "You're shaking!" he said, sounding worried. She was breathing very hard and still had her eyes closed, wanting to climax, to feel the release. Her body felt like there was a wild animal caged up inside her, and it was almost torture. "Are you a'right, darling?"

She shook her head, not wanting to move. "Yes, my body... it wants to keep going... it's begging me for an orgasm," she said, smiling but still feeling like she wouldn't be able to stop it.

"Oh, darling, I'm sorry. Can I do anathin' tae help yeh?"

She didn't think so, but then she remembered what they'd been talking about before the nurse had come in. "David, please tell me the truth; did you contact Emily? Is that why she came to find you?" She still had her eyes closed, but she could feel the shift from needing to release to trying not to be angry or upset.

"No, Erin, I didn't," he said and swung his legs off the edge of the bed.

Erin opened her eyes and saw that his head was down and his shoulders were slumped. He stood and bent over to pick up his clothes. "Wait! No! Please, don't get dressed yet! Wait!" she practically begged him, but he shook his head, looking sad.

"The treatment is complete. I must unlock the door as the nurse said," he told her without emotion, and Erin felt slightly heartbroken. He put everything on but his shoes, then he walked back to the door, unlocked it, and opened it a crack. He returned to the bed and was about to get back in and hold her when there was a soft knock on the door, and a nurse poked his head in.

Chapter Thirty-Five

AN UNWELCOME GUEST

"You've a visitor," the male nurse said cheerfully. Before either of them could say it wasn't a good time, the door was opened, and Erin saw Emily step hesitantly into the room.

"I… don't mean to disturb you," she said with a strong Dorset accent.

Erin wanted to tell her to go away. She'd already succeeded in bringing on an episode, and now she threatened to ruin their time together after their first treatment in forever. However, after the way she'd spoken to her in the car, she knew she had to bite her tongue. David was looking at her, so she nodded, feeling like she had no choice.

"Come in," David said cautiously.

"Hello, Erin, I'm—"

"I know who you are," she said coldly, then glanced at David and looked down.

"I wanted to come by to—"

To see David, I'm sure, Erin thought.

"…see that you were alright. I was scared to death when you stopped breathin' as you did," she said.

"I'm fine now. I'm sorry for what I said in the car," Erin said, trying to sound sincere, but Emily shrugged.

"It's alright; I understand. David's told me all about you, Erin; you're all he ever talks about. No matter what I say about… anythin', actually… he's got a story or an anecdote about you. He's told me how you get on brilliantly with his children and family and basically thinks you've hung the moon. I've never actually met anyone so head-over-heels in love with someone before," Emily said, smiling.

Erin looked at David, and he shrugged.

"He's said over and over how much he wanted me to meet you and how he knew I'd love you as well."

Erin was ashamed of herself; her face was bright red, and tears sprang to her eyes.

"I understand why you'd feel threatened by me, especially not knowing that I'm gay," she said and shot David a look that plainly said 'I told you so.' "I'm sorry I wasn't paying attention. I wouldn't have come back if I'd known how upset you were, but… well… David didn't tell me, and with the way he carried on about you, I—"

"I… guess that was my fault," Erin said. "I didn't exactly tell him. I mean, I thought I had, but I didn't spell it out clearly enough, I guess. I'm sorry… to both of you. I was blinded by fear and jealousy when I saw the pictures in the paper, and then they thought you were me, and it just stung that he didn't tell me… but… I guess it doesn't matter anymore."

"Oh! I get that, truly! I'm just the same with my girlfriend. It can be difficult to know what to think, especially in a new relationship. I thought you were one of those 'superwomen' who had no flaws. At least David is fully convinced you don't," Emily said with a tentative smile, and Erin frowned.

"Did you really say all those things about me?" she said with tears running down her face, looking at David who was standing next to the bed.

He smiled sheepishly at her and took hold of her hand. "Aye. I've told yeh, Erin, I'm yours. I dinnae want anaone else for the rest of ma life," he said with so much feeling, it made Erin's heart hurt again.

She put her head down as the tears continued. "I've been so stupid, and I'm sorry," she said. "I've just had so many bad—"

David sat next to her on the bed and kissed her hand. "Shh, I ken, ma love. Dinnae fret. It's a'right now," he said, soothing her.

"I… should go," Emily said, but Erin shook her head.

"No, don't go. I want to hear more about how much David loves me," she said with a grin. "Please stay a while."

Emily looked at the two of them and nodded. "A'right, but please let me know if I wear out my welcome."

"Oh, trust me, I will," Erin said. The nurse came in again and attached the belt around Erin's belly. He waited for everything to start reading normally and allowed Erin to raise the bed so she was sitting up a bit.

"Everything looks good. Hopefully, you'll be discharged in the morning," he said and smiled at the two of them. David was now sitting next to Erin, all the way up on the bed, holding her hand and kissing it every once in a while.

Erin saw the young man watching them and looked up. "Is there something else?" she asked, back to her normal, polite self, and he blushed.

"Oh, uh, no. I'm sorry, I was just thinking how nice you are together, and… it's daft, but I was hoping I'd find someone… well, a soulmate, I reckon, like you are," he said, blushing deeper and deeper every second he stood there.

"Sign up for the Fertilis Defect Registry. You've nothing to lose and a true love to gain." David said, which made Erin laugh.

"Sounds like a slogan, but he's right, it'll change your life for the better, and it will change some woman's life as well. Another slogan! We're on a roll!" she said.

The nurse laughed, "I'll look into it. Thanks," he said and left the room.

"I'm glad I don't have that… the Fertilis Defect. I can't imagine having to… be with a… man," Emily said, looking like she'd just tasted something bitter.

"I never thought of that. I wonder what happens if a gay woman has it?" Erin said, thinking about how horrible it would be for her. "Although, being with a man isn't so bad." She looked at David, and he kissed her, then put his head on her shoulder.

They told Emily how Roger and Tilly had met and how it was meant to be right from the start. They talked about the baby, and David touched her belly, which apparently woke it up, as it started kicking. He laughed and beamed with pride.

"Do you want to feel it?" Erin asked Emily, and she raised her eyebrows.

"I would, actually," she said and stepped up to the bed, placing her hand on Erin's belly.

"Just be patient; he's working up to it, ready to kick the field goal," she said, remembering how she'd used football to keep herself from climaxing. She put David's hand on her belly, and like magic, it kicked Emily.

"Oh! That's amazing! It must be so strange to feel that from the inside!" she said to Erin.

"It can be, especially when he kicks my bladder." David was looking at her with an odd expression. "What?" she asked after a few seconds.

"Yeh just said 'he' instead of 'it' more than once. Is there somethin' I dinnae know that yeh do?"

"No, I don't know why I said 'he,' it just came out that way," she said.

Twenty minutes later, Emily stood and looked at her watch. "I'd better go now. I'm so happy we've made peace, Erin. David was right, I really do like you, and you truly were made for each other," she said sweetly.

"I'm glad you came here today. It can't have been easy for you; I've been a real bitch." David and Emily laughed but didn't contradict her. "I hope we can get to know each other better while we're here. I'd love to meet your partner, too," Erin said.

"Deborah will fancy you; I know she will. You're just her type."

"Well, if that's the case, I'll be flattered, but I'm not into chicks, so no need to worry." Erin smiled at the woman who did look a fair amount like her, though Emily had deep dimples, green eyes, and perfect teeth. "Oh, and I won't be upset if you have lunch together. Maybe I'll join you next time without the theatrics."

"Thank you," Emily and David said at the same time.

"Snap!" they both said, then Emily said it again, faster than David.

The two laughed comfortably. "I'd forgotten about that!" David said. "We used to do that all the time when we were kids. It was the thing at the time."

"When we were babies," Emily said. "Well, see ya soon, then." She walked out the door, shutting it behind her.

"You were right," Erin said as they prepared to go to sleep that night, "I do like Emily."

David nodded and smiled. "I kent yeh would," he said. "I reckon I thought you could use a friend tae talk to whilst I was on set day in and day out. I never once thought of bein' with her, or… well, anathin' like that. I actually felt like a right eejit, talkin' nonstop about yeh, but I couldn't help maself."

"Holy Moses, David, you don't even know how foolish I felt when she told me that. I don't know what's wrong with me! I can imagine other men being faithful to their partners, but for some reason, it's like my mind thinks that as soon as a man falls for me, he becomes infected and will go behind my back as soon as I turn around. I have been so stupid, and I can't tell you how sorry I am."

"We've both been stupid, and all we can do is grow from it. Now, I'm knackered, so be quiet and let me sleep, a'right?"

"A'right, David, I love you."

"Love you too."

Chapter Thirty-Six

PROMISE ME

David woke needing to stretch; the bed was small, and it was hard to stay in the same position all night. He rolled onto his back, his shoulder completely off the bed, and tried to stretch out. Erin rolled onto her side, and he knew the alarms at the nurse's station would be going off, although it stayed quiet in the room, as the machine was in sleep mode.

Sure enough, the nurse they had spoken to earlier came in to make sure everything was okay. He saw Erin lying on her side and David trying to get comfortable next to her. "Tight quarters, eh?" he said, and David shrugged.

"Aye," he said. "Is she a'right tae lay like that?"

"I reckon so, as I've been told she can leave in the morning," he said and turned off the machine.

"Really? Does that mean she's officially off bed rest now?" David asked quietly, and the nurse nodded.

"Yes, sir," he said.

"When yeh leave, I'm goin' tae lock the door for a while, but I'll unlock et within, oh... half an hour or so," David said. The nurse nodded, not looking at him, and acted like he was still doing something with the machine.

"I... did some research on the Fertilis Defect Registry and... well, do you mind if I ask you about it?" the man asked sheepishly, so David sat up.

"I dinnae mind, what do yeh want tae know?"

The nurse faced him. "Does it... really work? I mean, it seems so—" he began nervously.

"Aye, et works, as long as yeh keep et up," David said. "Yer wonderin' why Erin's in here if et works, right?"

The nurse shrugged. "Well, yes, I suppose I am," he admitted.

"Aye, Erin and I had a verra profound misunderstandin', and we... well, she didn't have a treatment for three weeks. I'm ashamed I didn't take care tae... I dinnae ken—I failed her, I reckon. I should have pressed her instead of allowin' her tae push me away. Anaway, et's my fault she's here, but if yeh pay bloody attention, et works beautifully," he said and looked down at his love, sleeping so peacefully.

"But wasn't it... awkward, meeting a stranger to have sex with them? It seems like it would be awful!" he continued, and David laughed under his breath.

"Aye, et's torture leading up tae the day yeh meet, but when yeh do, there's... electricity. When yeh meet her, ye'll just know et's right. Et's butterflies in yer stomach and the thrill of accidentally touchin'. Et's pure, unadulterated attraction, like a drug yeh know you'll become addicted to, but yeh want tae be an addict until yeh die," he said passionately, still feeling that way about Erin.

"Wow, I think you *should* do public service announcements," he said. "You're selling me on it!" The young nurse walked to the door, then turned back. "Thank you, Mr.—"

"Call me David."

"Thank you, David. I... I'm going to do it... soon," he said, and left the room, closing the door behind him.

David got up and locked the door, then he took his clothes off and got back into bed with Erin, spooning behind her. He untied her hospital gown and slid one side over her shoulder, then he kissed it and worked his way to her neck. He pressed himself against her, pulling her hip back toward him.

She inhaled sharply, waking from a deep sleep. "David?" she said, and he knew it was to make sure it was him after what happened with Bran.

"Aye. Et's me, love," he said, moving his hand from her hip to her breast. "Ye're officially off bedrest, and I've locked the door; will yeh make love tae me?" he asked, his voice shaking with anticipation. She rolled onto her back, then he got on top of her and kissed her breasts. He wanted her badly, but he also wanted to savor it instead of rushing, like last time.

"David, please, I need you! I don't want foreplay; I want you now!" she said, but he ignored her.

"Aye, and ye'll have me, but yeh must be patient. I'm goin' tae have ma way with yeh first," he said and started moving downward, kissing her as he went.

"NO! Don't do that!" she said, sounding horrorstruck. He looked up, startled, not understanding. "I haven't bathed in three days, or is it four now? You don't want to go there! Do that the next time, okay?" she said and tried to pull him back up by his arm, but he hesitated, so she grabbed his hair and pulled gently. "I'm serious, David; please don't."

"Ach, a'right," he said and slid his chest up hers, stopping with a kiss that made him melt. "You want me, don't yeh? Yer achin' for me tae enter yeh, eh?" he said, teasing her.

"Aye! I do… put me out of my misery!" she begged.

"Promise me something first. Promise ye'll never doubt ma love again, no matter what," he said and began pressing himself against her vagina, guiding himself with his hand. "Say it, and I'm all yours."

She looked at him in shock. "I don't know if I can honestly do that."

He pulled away, flabbergasted. "What? Really? After all this, you still can't trust me?"

"I could lie to you and say I promise, but I can't seem to control my mind when it goes off like it did this time. We have to work together because I can't talk myself out of it. I tried with the woman in the bikini and with Emily. Okay, maybe not so much with her, but it's like a disease that consumes me, and I can't, I just can't. I told you that when Officer George brought me back," she said, clearly getting upset. "I'm sorry."

"Aye, I remember. But I dinnae ken how tae tell what will make yeh upset. Tae me, there is no woman tae compare with yeh, and no matter what any other woman does or says, or tries tae do, that's never gonna change, so you MUST communicate with me. Think of me as though I'm five and dinnae understand."

"And you must pay attention to me; you know how I am with you, my personality. If it changes, there's something wrong, and you need to do your damndest to figure it out. You can't give up, even if it means a big fight, because I might not be able to bring myself to say it, or I'm too afraid it's true, or… that you'll leave me if I say whatever it is—"

"Leave yeh? Erin! I dinnae understand you sometimes! I just told yeh I'll never leave yeh. Ach, I'll do ma best tae pay attention, but yeh can't get angry if I ask yeh too often when yer upset about somethin', a'right?" he said, feeling exasperated. "Can we promise each other that? Tae work together and talk instead of thinkin' one of us will get the hint?"

"Aye, I promise. It's not that I don't love you or… I don't know—I just get so afraid of losing you that I push you away, which I know is mental!" she said and laughed softly.

"Aye, I promise. Yeh can't get rid of me; I'm here forever, remember?" he said and lay back over her. The baby kicked, and he kissed her again. After a minute or two, he was ready once again and slid into her.

He moved slowly at first, building feeling upon feeling, enjoying the sensation of being sheathed and surrounded by her. "I love you," he said. "You turn me on. Just the sight of yeh turns ma legs tae jelly, and when yeh smile at me… goh, I can't tell yeh what et does tae me, Erin."

"I feel exactly the same way about you," she said.

"Tell me, when yeh saw Johnny Depp at yer party, did et make yeh wanna cheat on me or leave me?"

"No, not at all."

"If he'd come on tae yeh? If he'd kissed yeh, even, would that have changed yer mind?"

"No, I highly doubt it, anyway," she said, smiling wickedly. "It might've been fun, and I'd have a great story to tell in my dotage about the time Johnny Depp kissed me, but I'm all yours." He doubled his efforts, and it became more difficult to talk. "Though… had it been Ian McKellen," she gasped, "it wouldn't have been… such an easy… decision."

David felt her climax and then shuddered as he also reached a powerful orgasm, so much so that he thought he might not be able to stand for a few minutes. "Ach, Erin, please… don't deny me again. I need tae be with yeh."

"Good night nurse, I've missed that! I've missed you! I'm so sorry, darling!" she said, and the tears started falling. "I've wasted so much time being angry and scared. Soon the baby will be here, and I won't be able to do as many things as I can now with you. I'm not going to waste any more time!" She nearly smothered him by rolling halfway on top of him and holding him tightly.

"Good, because I was hopin' ye'd come down to the beach with me tonight?" he said when she finally let him go.

"Tonight? You mean they're gonna let me go today?" she said, and then they heard a knock on the door.

"Ms. March? The doctor is here to see you," a disembodied voice said through the door. Erin put her hospital gown back on, and David got himself dressed quickly, then went to the door and unlocked it.

"Sorry," he said as a doctor and nurse came in. The nurse looked at David and smothered a laugh. He went back to the bed and turned to stand next to Erin, but she laughed as well.

"Oh, David, go look in the bathroom mirror, and come back, please," she said.

He did what she asked and realized that not only was his shirt on inside out but backward as well, and he had a tag flapping under his chin. "Fuck!" he said under his breath as he took it off and put it back on right way around. He returned to the bed smiling, a bit red in the face, and listened, holding Erin's hand.

The doctor was telling her how it was vital she had regular treatments, every day, twice a day, if possible. "Eat plenty of good food, lots of protein and vegetables, don't go overboard on carbs, and above all, avoid major stress," he said.

She sighed. "I'd love to, but that has been my existence for the last six months… no, longer than that, nearly a year! Constant, never-ending stress! This baby is either gonna come out looking like Einstein or have the most *hakuna matata* attitude after having been through so much! But I will do my best to avoid it."

"Good, if you can do that, I don't see why you can't have a perfectly healthy, full-term baby. Now, if you'll excuse me, I must be going, but it was nice to meet you and… I hope all goes well for you in the future," the doctor said with a grin at David.

"Thank you, doctor. Wait, can I leave now?" she asked.

He turned to her and smiled. "Yes, you may leave," he said, then he and his nurse left the room.

Chapter Thirty-Seven

AN IMPORTANT VOW

David called for a car, and they were home within an hour. He opened the cottage door for Erin, and as they entered the kitchen, she saw her cabbage rose teapot sitting on her flower sack tablecloth and smiled. Everything looked pretty again. "Would you like a cuppa?" she asked him.

"Aye; let me help you," he said and filled the electric kettle while she got out the cups and filled the beautiful china teapot with hot water from the tap to warm it up. She took down the box of tea, and David put his hand on her shoulder.

"I try tae be a man of ma word, tae set a standard, yeh ken? I even joined the Registry because I'd made a promise tae host a charity telethon, after all! I dinnae always live up tae those standards, but I try. How can I show you just how much yeh mean tae me?" He looked around and took her left hand in his, then he kissed it and ran his thumb over the diamond on his great-grandmother's ring.

"This ring... there are few things I own that I value above it. Et means so much tae me, and I'm not goin' tae throw et away. By giving et to yeh and asking you tae be ma wife, et's—I'm confirmin' that I value you and yer love just as much and more than I do the ring. Et's not just a metal thing I purchased at the mall. This counts, et matters, *you* matter tae me. I'm no' goin' tae cast yeh aside tae have sex with someone else."

It hit him then, why it would be so difficult for Erin to trust him. "Oh, darling, I'm a fool. I see et now. I cheated on and left Susannah for you, why wouldn't I do et again with someone else? I can't tell yeh how different et is tae me. "Swearin' tae God or on one's life has become meaningless tae some, but no' tae me, and I swear tae *God*, I'll never cheat on yeh. I dinnae want tae be with anaone else. Just... please, look at the ring when yeh feel worried. Et's a promise; the most valuable promise I have tae give yeh, next tae ma life and ma children."

"But... we're not married yet, and I was afraid you'd changed your mind," Erin said softly, looking at the floorboards.

"Erin, I ken that what Martin said to yeh at the Savoy cut to the quick, but... I... I've only ever been with two women in ma life, yeh ken? Susannah and you, and that's all. I have never been one tae sleep around, not ever."

"Just us? Really?"

"Really, and yeh need tae know what this ring means tae me. Et means forever, Erin. Et means I'll love yeh till the day I die, and that's final. I want a marriage that lasts as long as my great-grandparents' did. I was wrong when I married Susannah; I can see it plain enough now, but I'll no' be wrong when I marry you.

"If yeh ever start tae doubt me or ma love, look at et and remember, then tell me how yer feelin'. Even if yeh think I'll get angry or yeh think yeh can't believe what I'm sayin', come tae me, and I'll remind yeh," he said, and she hugged him.

"Thank you for being patient with me. I'm learning, and it's gonna take a while to get to know who you are and how you operate," she said and held him as they leaned against the countertop. The kettle was boiling, so she poured out the hot tap water from the teapot and put the tea bags in it, then she added the boiling water.

"I've been thinking about it, and maybe the root of the problem is that I don't trust myself anymore. I used to; I'd have sworn up and down that I'd never leave Todd. I was convinced I'd love him forever, but it didn't end up being that way. I think I'm afraid that if I could do something so inconceivable as cheating on the man I loved, then anyone could, even you. Does that make sense?" she asked.

"Aye, I reckon so, only yeh ken what we have together; neither of us has had anything like et before. Are you afraid ye'd cheat on me?" he asked, feeling a bit shocked and alarmed.

"Well, no, I don't think I could, and I don't want to, not in the slightest. I'm just afraid I'm not the person I thought I was, and it scares me. If I could do it to Todd, and you could do it to Susannah, even though your marriage wasn't healthy, then perhaps… someday… we could do it to each other as well," she said, feeling miserable again.

"I… dinnae want tae think about that. I give yeh ma word, Erin, that I'll not run off or cheat on yeh with anaone, ever," he said.

Erin's eyes suddenly grew large. "David!" she said suddenly. "The show! Your job? You've been away for four days!"

"Aye, I've spoken with the Assistant Director. They've been working around it, but I'll be expected on set come Monday," he said, and Erin bit her lower lip.

"I'm sorry to put you through all this. I feel like such an idiot," she said.

"Dinnae fash," he said, then filled the cream pitcher and sugar bowl. "Ach, I remember now why et slipped ma mind! The first day I had lunch with Emily was the same one that I came home to find you missing. I'd come home chuffed tae tell yeh all about et, but when yeh weren't there, the only thing on ma mind was findin' you."

"Oh," she said and put her head down. "Yes, I can see how that might happen. God, Erin, you're so stupid!"

"Dinnae say that, darling."

"But I am! If I'd just put two and two together instead of freaking out, none of this would've happened. Well, I'm sure I still would've been jealous and upset, but we might've been able to talk about it like adults instead of me shutting down and—"

"Ach, et's all over now, so dinnae fash. Let's sit together on the sofa so I can hold yeh, a'right?"

"I'd like that," she said, and David carried the tea out to the living room, where they snuggled, watching *Doctor Who* reruns.

After supper, David and Erin stepped out the cottage door. They walked through the gate at the back of the fence, then down the steep road that led to the small seaside village. They reached the beach, where stones of all shapes and colors substituted for sand, and Erin had a hard time looking up, wanting to see them all.

She picked up a handful and sorted through them. There were black, red, white, tan, and even blue. One stone was two completely different colors on either side, and a rectangular one looked like a ribeye steak with a fatty layer and thin veins of marbling spaced randomly throughout it. "I could spend all day here looking at these," she said, showing him a black stone the size and shape of a small egg that had tiny dimples all over it, like a golf ball.

The gulls were crying as they soared overhead, and she heard a child playing nearby. When she looked up, she saw a young boy trying to outrun the waves, but they were too clever for him. David moved into her line of sight, and she smiled up at the most beautiful man she'd ever seen. He placed his hands on either side of her face and kissed her. "I want tae live here; close enough to walk tae the beach and have this with you and ma bairns everaday. Would yeh like that as well?" he asked and looked out at the immense ocean before them.

"Aye, David, I would love it, though I don't care where we live, as long as we're together, you, me, and our bairns. I'll go where you go, and I'll stay where you stay," she said.

———

David smiled at another one of her random Bible passages; this one from the story of Ruth and Boaz, where Boaz, the wealthy, important man, rescues the widow, Ruth, although in his case, he knew it was Erin rescuing him, not the other way around.

Chapter Thirty-Eight

HELP NEEDED

It was the third week in November, and Erin was seven months pregnant. Though they were keeping up with her treatments, she was often tired, and managing the housework was difficult. "Do you think we could ask Kitty to come and help me out for a while?" she asked David after a particularly trying day.

"Ach, of course, darling, I should've thought of et," he said.

Erin looked up at him seriously. "Yes, David, you really should have. I don't understand why you never think of the things I need," she said and saw his face fall. She couldn't hold it in any longer and started laughing, smiling up into his rich brown eyes. "You can't think of everything, my love," she said, "that's why I'm asking."

David rolled his eyes at her and picked up his mobile. "I'll send her a message now," he said.

Erin watched as he found Kitty's name in his contacts list, then started typing. She loved watching the expressions he made while doing everyday things. She'd never seen him look anything but beautiful, except for the few times she'd seen him very angry, and even then, she thought him attractive.

"What is et now, love?" he asked.

She had started to zone out and lost track of how long she'd been observing him. "Sorry," she said, blushing. "I was just admiring you again."

He shook his head and leaned in close to her on the sofa. "I believe et's ma turn tae admire you for a while, then, but first, I need tae speak tae our bairn." He lifted her top and ran his hand gently over the bump that was

338

getting quite large, the skin becoming taught around it. He traced the dark brown vertical line starting to appear at her belly button and put his face up to it. "Hello ma lovely; et's yer da'. I can't wait tae meet yeh! Keep growin' strong, darling," he said, then kissed her belly and stood, taking her hand to help her up.

His phone made a noise, and he looked at it. "Kitty says she'd love tae come help yeh," he said and put his mobile on the coffee table. "Come with me," he said and led her to their bedroom.

Erin was tired; she felt like she wouldn't have the stamina to make love, but when he smiled at her, she somehow found the energy. They were supposed to do it at least once or even twice a day, and sometimes she felt like it wasn't fun anymore, but then he'd look at her and she'd melt.

"Close yer eyes," he said, and she sighed, but she did as she was told. He led her to the bed and had her sit on the edge. "Keep them closed, no peeking." She heard him take something out of the closet and come back. "A'right, you may open them now," he said and smiled at her, holding up a long dress. "I got yeh somethin'."

Erin stood and took it from him, admiring it. "Oh, David, it's lovely! And… it's a maternity dress too!" It was a soft knit in royal blue, with a knot just over the belly; the skirt was full, and it seemed like it would be both comfortable and flow beautifully. "I love it, darling," she said, meaning it.

"Kitty helped me," he said. "She knew you'd like it."

Erin laid it on the bed and kissed him, running her fingers through his hair. "Kitty was right, I do. It's perfect. Thank you." She continued to kiss him as they moved to the side of the bed, and she sat on the edge of the mattress. Just then, David's phone notified him that he had a message. "Go on and look; it might be important," she said, and he picked it up.

He frowned and said, "Ye're not gonna tae believe this!" She looked up at him, waiting for an explanation. "Et's Martin!"

She raised her eyebrows. "No way! Really? What does he want now?" she said, not wanting to have anything more to do with the man. He handed the phone to her, and she read it out loud.

Martin: *How're you doing, Mate? It's been too long. We should have lunch soon.*

"Lunch means he needs something," he said. "I'm not sure what tae do. Should I ignore his message or tell him to fuck off?" he said.

Erin blew out a puff of air. "I don't know; maybe just ignore him for now and see what happens?" David was a nice guy, and he'd known Martin for a very long time. She could tell he was more conflicted about what to do than he was letting on.

"Aye, et's a bit premature tae tell him where tae go. I'll—"

She lay her head on his lap and sighed. "You don't have to do what I say, my love; it was just a suggestion. I know you're dying to find out what he wants, so—"

"You do know me well," he said. "I'm no one for burnin' bridges, but his behavior at the funeral is hard to ignore."

"And he tried to gaslight me at the Savoy, he sold photos of us to the tabloids, and… most likely orchestrated the woman kissing you at the same event," she reminded him, having to swallow hard at the memory of the last one.

"Aye." He nodded as he ran his index finger along her bare arm, making the skin break out in gooseflesh.

It wasn't overly warm, but she was prone to hot flashes and was wearing a short-sleeved shirt. She lay her arm out with her palm up, hoping he'd continue. "I love when you do that!" she said and sighed. He ran his fingers lightly down the inside of her arm to her palm and back up, making her almost purr. Then he lay his hand on her baby bump again. "We should think of names; pin a few down, you know?"

"Aye, what were the names yeh told me ye'd thought of, Henry and Olive?"

"Yeah, but they aren't set in stone. There are also the ones everyone came up with at my parent's house. Whatever we choose, I want us to decide together. Olive Elliott is nice, but so is Cecilia or Celie. What about Sam? Oh, wait, there's an actor named Sam Elliott, not that it matters. There's also Lucy or Charlotte—" she said.

"I like Henry," he said, "and Lucy Elliott is nice as well. Celia is lovely too. There are too many good names!" he said.

"Henry Oliver Elliott," Erin said, testing out the sound of it. "I like that."

"Aye, that's nice; I had an uncle by the name of Oliver," he said. "I think that should be the name we choose for a boy."

Erin smiled. "Okay, agreed. Now for a girl's name," she said.

"Ach, but ye're always referring to et as a 'he,' so do we really need a girl's name?" The baby decided to move just then; it wasn't a kick, just a stretch or a change in position. "Ooh! I felt that!" he said.

"Aye, so did I!" she said with a groan. "He's sitting on my bladder, now help me up!" David pulled her hands to help her stand. "I feel like a beached whale!" she said, and he held her.

"Ach, though ye're *my* beached whale!" he said, and she swatted his arm playfully.

———

While she was in the bathroom, David sent a message to Martin.

> David: *What do you want? Do you honestly think I'm going to meet with you after what you've done? I think you should find someone else to manipulate and leave us alone now.*

He had a family to look out for; he needed to sever the old ties that bound him up and who had leeched off him for far too long. He received a reply right away.

> M: *I see. I reckon that means you're not interested to learn that I've spent the past month in jail because you didn't loan me the money you promised.*

"Jail?" David said out loud.

"What about jail?" she asked, having just returned from the bathroom and waddled back to the bed.

"Mmm, Martin says he's been in jail because I failed tae give him the money I promised."

"And you believe him?" she asked. "What did you say to him?" David read his message and Martin's reply. "Hmm, sounds like a guilt trip to me, darling. He knows you're a big softie, and he's pulling your heartstrings like a marionette."

"Aye, yer right, of course. I need tae stand ma ground."

Erin took his phone, and started typing, then she gave it to him before hitting send, and he read it with a heavy heart.

> D: *I'm sorry to hear that. Didn't you make enough selling the photos to the tabloids? I won't be at your disposal any longer. I wish you well, but I'm done.*

"You don't have to send that," she said. "You can change or delete it; it was just a suggestion."

He sighed. "No, et's brilliant; I just worry about retaliation. That's what I've always feared, I reckon." He put the phone down without sending it.

"I'm gonna take a nap now. Care to join me?" she said and began undressing.

He smiled and cupped his hand around her bare breast. "Aye," he said.

Martin waited for a reply for quite some time, and when it didn't come, he got angry. "*You're better than that boy! He's a weak pushover, and if you play your cards right, son, you'll never want for a thing. But… you must play hardball sometimes, Martin. If he won't budge, you must make him move. Call his bluff and play dirty when necessary. That's how you get what you want from a person like*

him, too perfect for his own good!" His mother's voice seemed to rise from the grave, reminding him of what she'd told him so many times.

He picked up his mobile and searched his contacts, remembering a name that had come up several times at the Elliott home during parties and events, Clive Dawson. *If he has anything on David Elliott, I'll get it out of him,* he thought. He tapped the call button and waited.

"Dawson," a man's gruff voice said.

"Hello, my name is Martin Green. I believe we have an acquaintance in common, and I thought we could have a chat?"

"I'm acquainted with a lot of people, Mr. Green, so don't waste my time," he said.

"David Elliott," he said, knowing he'd have his full attention.

The man grunted and paused. "Meet me outside the yard tomorrow night at half ten."

"I'll be there," Martin said, feeling the adrenaline rush once again.

Martin stood in front of the sign that read *New Scotland Yard,* each letter backlit in white. The smoke from his cigarette drifted away, swallowed by the dark mist that hung ominously over his head. He'd just noticed how film-like the atmosphere was, the irony of his clandestine meeting not being lost on him when the dim shadow of a large, forbidding figure stretched before him.

"Green?" a gruff voice said, sending a shiver up Martin's spine.

"Yes," he said, not turning to look at the man behind him.

"Now, what's all this about?"

Martin suddenly felt as though he were under interrogation and wiped the sweat off his forehead with his jacket sleeve. "Right, well, I believe we—"

"Don't waste my time repeating yourself. Cut to it."

"David Elliott has been a… nuisance and… and hindrance to me for… well, since I've known him."

"And?"

A bead of sweat rolled down the back of his neck. He knew he must be concise, but his thoughts had become muddled. "He has always gotten what he wants… he has everything… things I would like—"

"And what is it you'd like me to do about it, then?"

His mind raced, trying to convey what he was asking of the man. Earlier that day, it had been clear to him what could be—what must be—done, but as he stood in the darkness, it left him. "I… I want him to suffer, if I'm honest. He's never suffered a day in his precious, privileged life, and I'd like to see to it that he… does… for once." It hadn't come out as elegantly as he'd hoped, but it was the truth, and it would have to do.

"Suffer, eh? And how do you envision this suffering, Mr. Green?" Dawson said, sounding intrigued.

"I've an idea or two," he said and turned his head. Speaking just above a whisper, he laid out a scenario that had the man laughing when he was finished speaking.

"I must admit, I appreciate how you think, Green. If you were speaking to any other officer, they'd have laughed and sent you on your way. However, I am not one of them, and I believe we might be able to suss out a plan that'll leave us both appeased with the outcome. I will begin setting up the operation, and you may rest assured you'll have what you've asked."

Martin was pleasantly surprised by the man's amenability and held out his hand to shake. Clive took a step back and tisked. "Not so fast, mate. What are you willing to do for me, then?"

"Uh, well, I, um—" Martin sputtered. "I've nothing to give. I've no income to speak of, and all I own has been repossessed."

"You know people, mate. When the time comes, I'll want the press and media ready and waiting in the wings. If all goes to plan, they'll not be disappointed," Dawson said, then held his hand out.

The two men shook on the deal and turned, each going their separate ways. *This ought to be good! I'll finally be awarded the payback I deserve,* Martin thought as he lit another cigarette and quickened his pace.

Chapter Thirty-Nine

LAST MINUTE SHOPPING & PRINCES STREET GARDENS

As the wedding grew near, the girls were fitted for dresses. Rosie and Erin found the perfect dress online through Harrods and bought Lily the same one in several sizes to make sure at least one of them fit her. The men were also measured for their kilts. Roger would wear his family tartan and already had one, while Peter needed a new one, as he'd outgrown his. Frank had been measured by Liz, and a Wallace tartan kilt was being custom-made for him, as well.

One week before the wedding, they spent the night in London. David spent over an hour in the study while Erin slept. She looked a bit leery as he led her into the room and sat her on the sofa. "I've a surprise for yeh," he said excitedly.

"Do I like surprises?"

"I hope ye'll like this one." He opened the panel that hid the safe and pointed to it. "It's right there," he said.

"You're giving me the safe? I'm confused."

"I've changed the numerical code. Can yeh guess what et is?"

"Not a clue, please tell me."

"Et's 2612."

"Um, okay. Is that supposed to mean something to me?" she asked, frowning.

"Yeh mean et doesn't?"

"Not... yet."

"The twenty-sixth day of December?"

"OH! Oh, I get it now! I'm not used to the date being written backward. That's so sweet, David! Thank you!"

He drew a long breath and took her into his arms, holding and kissing her. "I can't wait until you're ma wife, Erin. I ken et's only a week away, but et seems like et'll never come."

"It still doesn't feel real... except now, with your little surprise, it feels a bit more tangible. That was so thoughtful."

"Ye're welcome. Et was work, though. Took me an hour tae sus out how tae change et, all the time fearin' ye'd come in and catch me," he said with a laugh. "Now come upstairs with me so we can celebrate my achievement.

"Okay," she said with a knowing smile.

There was so much going on with the wedding plans that Erin nearly forgot about Christmas. They headed to Owlgate a few days after picking the children up from school and still had quite a lot of shopping to do. Edinburgh was abuzz with Christmas activities in The Princes Street Gardens, including the large Ferris Wheel.

Roger offered to watch the children in the gardens and was given money for rides, food, and gifts, while David and Erin did the last of their shopping at Jenner's department store and the shops nearby. Erin wasn't used to having lots of money for Christmas gifts and had a difficult time spending as much as David was used to.

At the end of the day, Roger was asked to take the packages back to Owlgate, and the family rode the Ferris Wheel together. Then they wandered around the booths filled with gifts and food. A few last-minute gifts were bought in secret while the recipient wasn't looking. Finally, they had hot drinks from a hut in the gardens while waiting for Roger to pick them up. "The weather is so nice here!" Erin said, glad she didn't have to wear three layers and still end up freezing, though she proudly wore her cashmere Elliott tartan scarf, which she loved.

Logistics at Christmas was a nightmare, and poor Roger was the one who bore the brunt of it. Erin's parents' plane arrived on time on the twenty-third of December, but Lily and Nick's plane was delayed, so instead of making Liz and Frank wait with him at the airport, he drove them to Owlgate. They would be staying in Millie's room, while Nick and Lily would stay in Peter's. Neither Kitty nor Francie had a guest coming with them, so they would use Roger's flat.

Erin had tried to get Kitty's mom to come, but she'd declined. Francie flat out refused to take a plane, saying that she'd never flown in an *aeroplane* and had no plans of doing so, so she and Kitty took the train. Roger managed to deliver everyone safely to Owlgate, and Erin asked the children to go out and help him with the gate when he arrived each time. Needless to say, the house was packed with people.

Having new people at the house was not something Millie cared for much but seeing that they were friends and family of Erin, she made a real effort to be civil and was actually kind and likable. Even Francie and Millie managed to get along since Francie was wise enough to know not to interfere with another woman's kitchen. She actually complimented Millie's meat pie and cranachan, which Millie was secretly proud about, even though she hated compliments, as Erin had learned at her first stay in Owlgate.

Liz and Annis got along quite well and told stories to everyone after lunch on the first day about Erin and David when they were young. One or two of the photo albums were taken out of the small tropical bird cabinet, and those who hadn't already seen them laughed at how adorable David was. Liz had brought quite a few photos of Erin and showed them around as well.

"Ma Losh, yeh were sweet in your pigtails and missing front teeth," Millie said and handed the picture to David, who smiled and kissed Erin's cheek.

"Aye, adorable," he said. He nuzzled her ear and whispered, "I think you should put your hair in pigtails tonight for me."

"You think so? Will you pull them as you enter me, doggy style?" she whispered back and saw him turn a bit pink.

"Aye, if yeh want me to, I will. I'd like tae take yeh upstairs with me right now," he whispered and kissed her a bit too passionately because the children all groaned and turned away.

Erin thought she heard Peter whisper 'get a room,' but she wasn't sure. "I'm going to be Mrs. David Elliott in only a few days; I can't believe it!" she said quietly to him and traced the outline of his ear with her finger. She wanted to curl up next to him on the sofa, but her baby belly was just too big for that. David smiled at her and placed his hand on her stomach. As soon as he touched it, the baby started moving and kicking. "Ow! Hey, you in there, this isn't gym class!" she said.

Liz jumped up and went to her. "Ooh! I want to feel it moving!" she said.

Before Erin knew it, nearly everyone had surrounded her and was touching her belly, which made her laugh since the baby had decided to stop moving. "David, please wake it up?" she said and took his hand, laying it on her swollen belly. With all the hands already on it, she felt like she was in a seance and her stomach was the crystal ball. The baby didn't disappoint, kicking everyone's hand at least once.

Liz had tears in her eyes as she looked at her baby girl and smiled. "I'm so proud of you, Erin. You are going to be a really good mother," she said, and David smiled.

"That's what I keep tellin' her, although she already *is* a good mum, right, children?" he said and looked at the young faces, each trying to get a look at the baby moving.

"Yes, sir," Peter said.

"*I* think so," Charlie said.

"I think she's the best mum in the world!" Rosie said.

Dan said nothing until the baby kicked so hard that Lily screeched, then he laughed so hard he landed on the floor. "She's a lot of fun," he said, as though she were a sideshow at the traveling fair.

"Thanks, everyone. Wait, tomorrow is Christmas Eve, isn't it? Ooh, Millie, I have a recipe for you if you'd be willing to take a request for breakfast tomorrow morning? I have the strongest craving for *Risgrynsgröt!*"

"Rice pudding?" Tilly said, and everyone looked at her, not believing she'd understood the alien word. "What? I'm Swedish, and my mormor used to make *Risgrynsgröt* every Christmas Eve morning since I can remember. Then she'd make the most amazing dessert for Christmas supper with the leftovers, something with eggs and vanilla, but I don't remember what it was. Oh, please,

Millie, would you please make it for us?" she said like a young girl, begging sweetly.

"Ach, how can I refuse the two of yeh? What's in et then?" she asked.

"It's really simple! Just make up a lot of rice and cook it until it's almost done. Then add a ton of whole milk, bring to a boil, and cook it, covered, on low for forty-five minutes. When it's done, it'll be really mushy, kinda like porridge, right?" she said and looked to Tilly for confirmation.

"Yeah, that's right. Then you dish it out and add butter, cinnamon sugar, and a bit more cream to cool it down," Tilly said. "Oh, and don't forget the almond!"

"Oh, yeah, the almond! I know you're supposed to add one, and I always do, but I don't know why."

"It should be a blanched almond, Millie. Put it in the pot when it's ready to serve; the person who gets it in their dish will get married in the next twelve months," Tilly explained.

Erin's eyes grew wide, and she started laughing. "Oh, man! Last Christmas Eve… I got the almond! No, I really did! I thought it meant you'd be lucky or something. I mean, I *have* been about as lucky as anyone could be. That's so funny!"

"Aye, but the weddin' will be two days past twelve months, so ye'd better find the almond this year as well," David said.

"That can be arranged, I reckon," Millie said with a wink.

"I'll try to find you a recipe for ratios," Erin said and blew her a kiss.

Supper that night was amazing, as usual, and Erin felt so blessed. They'd added three leaves to the table so everyone would fit, and she couldn't help herself, asking to take a group selfie and a panoramic shot as well. She also got a few small videos during the night, which she shared with everyone.

"I wish your dad could've been here," Erin said out of the blue in David's ear. "I wish I could've met him. Do you think he'd have liked me?"

"He'd've loved yeh dearly, Erin. What made yeh think of that?" he asked.

"I was just thinking how nice it is that my mom and dad are here, and I'm so glad I know your mum and Millie. The only thing missing is your father, that's all."

"Aye," he said and stood. "As our meal comes to an end, I'd like tae raise ma glass in a toast tae those who couldn't be with us tonight, especially ma da'. He'd have loved this and all of you, as well. He would also have loved Erin, don't yeh agree, Mother?"

Annis nodded, smiling fondly at him and Erin. "Aye, son. He'd have loved her dearly," she said, not knowing that she'd quoted exactly what David had said moments before.

"Agreed," Millie said. "He was a good judge of character, our Charles was. Jest look how he found the right man in our Roger. He was a wise one, and I admit I miss his wit and sunny disposition, not to mention his good looks." Millie laughed with everyone at that and then smiled fondly at Erin.

"To ma da', Erin, and to family," David said, raising his glass.

"To family," everyone repeated.

Chapter Forty

CHRISTMAS EVE

"This is surreal, isn't it?" Liz said to Erin after a delicious breakfast of *Risgrynsgröt* in the morning as they watched the men put the lights on the tree. "I mean, to be in David Elliott's mother's house on Christmas Eve is not something I thought I'd be doing... ever."

"I know! I can't believe it either," Erin said.

Tilly walked in and stood next to Erin. "Isn't this crazy?" she said.

"We were just saying the same thing. Aren't they handsome? Lily, come here," Erin said, and the four women stood together, watching the four men until Frank happened to look over at them.

"I think we have an audience," he said and jerked his head toward the women.

Liz and Lily blushed and looked away, but Erin and Tilly smiled and continued watching. "As you were, boys, we're enjoying the show," Erin said, and Lily nudged her.

Nick went to his wife and kissed her, making the girls say, "Aww." Not to be outdone, the rest of the men joined their partners for a kiss as well.

Annis walked into the sitting room and joined the group of women. The men looked at each other and nodded, then each of them gave her a kiss on the cheek, making her laugh and shoo them away playfully. "Ach, yeh ken how tae make an old woman blush!" she said.

Erin figured her mother was probably jealous, but she knew David was not about to kiss her. The memory of that summer was still too fresh in his mind for that.

Once the lights were on the tree, they hung the garland, then the boxes with the ornaments were opened. The children were allowed to hang quite a lot of them, although they were directed by Annis as to where she wanted them. Everyone in the family had their own glass orb, each one unique.

The children hung theirs first, then Roger, Millie, Annis, and finally David. Susannah's ornament was the only one left in the box. Peter suggested they throw it into the fire, remembering all the letters from them she'd hidden from his dad. Charlie proposed they crush it, and Daniel seconded the motion. Before anyone could protest, the children were outside on the front stoop, arguing over who should be allowed to step on it.

"Children, are you sure you really want to do that? I mean, she was your mum," Erin said, concerned at their eagerness to be rid of anything that reminded them of her.

"Erin should do it!" Charlie said and held the burgundy glass ball out for her to take.

"No, Dad should do it; she hurt him the most," Peter said, and everyone looked at him.

"I'm afraid I agree with Erin. Are you sure—" he began, and then with tears in her eyes, Rosie took the ball and threw it down the nine stone steps. She watched, along with everyone else, as it bounced down the first two and smashed apart as it hit the next three, stopping midway down. Rosie turned and ran into her father's arms, crying, while Daniel kicked it the rest of the way down. He was about to pick up the largest remaining piece, but Roger stopped him.

"A'right then, I'll clean et up," he said. "Go back inside now."

There was an odd atmosphere in the house after that, a mixture of pain, release, and discomfort. Erin could tell that Lily, Nick, and her parents were more shocked and worried about what they'd witnessed than they wanted to admit. Erin was both brokenhearted and touched and sat quietly in thought for most of the morning.

Just before lunch, Rosie climbed onto her lap, only barely able to fit around her pregnant belly, and stayed there without saying anything for a long time. Erin thought she was asleep, but then the girl pulled the compass pendant out from under Erin's shirt and watched the pointer spin until it found North.

"I'm sorry we've upset you, Mummy," she said quietly, and Erin had to smother the sob that wanted to escape after hearing her innocent apology.

"Oh, baby, I'm not upset, not in the way you're thinking I am, anyway. It's hard to explain what I'm feeling right now. I've been trying to put my finger on it, but it's too complicated," she said and noticed that the rest of the children and the nearby adults were listening too, evidently wanting to know her thoughts as well.

"It made me very sad to see you throw your mum's ornament down the steps, not because it broke, but because of the anger and hurt I knew you must have been feeling in order to do that. I… wish I could somehow wave a magic wand and take all the pain away from you and your brothers. I'm also, I guess, a little bit afraid—"

"Afraid? What are you afraid of, Mummy?" Rosie asked, pressing the cool metal compass to her cheek.

"So very many things, darling, but the thing I'm most afraid of right now is that I might somehow hurt you and add to your pain."

"Erin," Peter said from beside her. "I don't think that's possible, at least not in the same way or to the degree our mother did. What Rosie did surprised me as well, but it also seemed to help a bit. I didn't know just how angry I was at her until I saw that glass ball smash into a thousand pieces. It reminded me that I won't ever have to be afraid of making her angry or disappointed in me again, and it was a relief."

"I wanted to smash it into a *million* pieces! I wanted to pick it up and throw it down again on the pavement and stomp on it!" Daniel said, sitting near the fireplace with his knees drawn up under his chin and his arms wrapped around his legs.

"I don't know what I wanted to do to it," Charlie said, but I'm glad it's destroyed! I don't ever want to see it again! I want to see one with your name on it, Erin. I want your ornament and mine to be on the same tree."

"I want that too! Come here and hug me, okay?" Erin said, knowing Rosie would get smooshed but thinking she probably wouldn't mind. Peter and Charlie were quick to join Rosie in a group hug. Daniel didn't move, which didn't surprise anyone, as he wasn't much of a hugger. The three children got up, feeling much better, but Dan stayed in his place. His face was now covered by his legs, and Erin thought she heard him sniffle.

"Dan? Are you—" she began, and the eleven-year-old boy looked up, saw that her lap was empty, and rushed to her, nearly slamming into her belly. He climbed onto her lap the best he could, bawling and gasping for air.

"I hate her! I hate her, Erin! I'm glad she's dead, and I'm glad you're here! I don't want to think about her ever again!" he said, shaking violently with anger and frustration at what his mother had done to them.

Erin held him and smoothed his hair, making gentle shushing noises as she tried to comfort him. All the grief and mourning he might've felt at his mother's funeral or soon afterward was revealing itself through waves of pain and hurt washing over the young boy's body.

The adults watched the inconsolable boy pour his heart out until he fell asleep, hiccoughs still wracking his body as he held the woman who would be his official new mother in only two days. Erin felt exhausted by his grief and lay her head on his, kissing his temple every now and then.

"Shall I lift him off yeh?" David asked after a few minutes, but Erin shook her head.

"No, let the poor baby rest. I'm comfortable now." His grief had reminded her of how she'd felt after telling David that Bran had raped her. She'd cried harder than she thought possible and was thankful beyond measure that Annis had held her until she felt a bit better. Several tears fell down her face at the memory. The truth was her arm was falling asleep, and she really had to pee, but she was determined to stay put until her arm fell off and she'd wet the loveseat she was sitting on.

Eventually, though, the baby started kicking, and Millie, who hadn't witnessed Daniel's outburst, came in and loudly announced that lunch would be ready in less than ten minutes. Dan woke and found himself curled up in Erin's arms. It seemed the events of the last hour returned to him, and he nearly jumped off her, allowing the blood to flow back into her arm, making it tingle with a thousand pinpricks. She shook it, and her eyes watered as she half-laughed and half-groaned with the feeling. Dan looked embarrassed and ran off to play with Gurty, his favorite of his gran's dogs, until he was forced to wash up for lunch.

"David, help me up. I've gotta pee so badly you might have to wash the floor behind me as I head to the bathroom!" she said, which lightened the mood in the room. David came to her and held out his hand. She took it, and between the two of them, she was heaved off the couch. He began to hug her, but she pushed him away. "I wasn't kidding," she said, starting to panic a bit, thinking she'd not be able to hold it after all, and made a mad dash to the bathroom. She didn't even close the door before she sat on the toilet.

Having followed her, David laughed and closed the door for her.

After lunch, the children begged their soon-to-be new grandma and grandpa Wallace to go for a walk to Dr. Neil's. It was a fair, sunny day and they couldn't refuse them. Nick and Lily were also invited, but they decided to stay at the house instead.

"How's Ariana?" Erin asked Lily as they sat near the fire and listened to Christmas music.

"She's okay now," she said, and both David and Erin frowned.

"What do yeh mean by *now*?" David asked.

"Last month, she was in the hospital for over a week with pneumonia. It was a bit touch and go for a few hours, but she's a trooper and pulled through again," Nick said.

"That must be terrifyin'!" Annis said. "I take et she's been in hospital for that before then?"

"Yes, she's in the hospital a lot, Mrs. Elliott," Lily said.

"Call me Ann, dear," the regal older woman said to her guest. "And why is that then?"

Lily explained that their ten-year-old daughter had been born with birth defects that no one could diagnose. "She also has a rare blood disorder, and bacterial or viral infections make things worse for her."

"She's verra sweet, Mother. We sang a duet together when I was at their house earlier this year. Et was unforgettable!" David said.

"Yes, and we've had to watch *Future Explorations* every day since then, and I swear she said 'John Thomas' the other day. She's smitten!" Nick said and laughed.

"Every day? Yeh poor things!" David said sympathetically.

"Well, it's better than the same three movies she'd only wanted to watch for three months straight before that," Lily said. "At least it's three seasons worth of shows now. That breaks it up a bit, you know? I just hope they don't remove it from Netflix any time soon!"

"Yeah, that would be dramatic! We'll have to break down and buy it if that happens!" Nick said.

"You could always ask Father Christmas," David said.

"Now, don't go getting any ideas! That's not why I brought it up!" Lily said, looking between Erin and David.

"He didn't say to ask *us*, silly. How would we get a copy this late, anyway?" Erin said. "Relax! Plus, David's already finished signing Santa's 'nice list' requests, haven't you, dear? How's your hand? I know it was cramping up a few weeks ago."

"Right as rain once more, ma love. Thanks for askin'," David said, playing along.

"Ye're all children!" Annis said, chuckling lightly.

"Aye, Mother, and what's wrong with that?" David asked just as "Have Yourself a Merry Little Christmas" by Barbara Streisand, began to play.

"Ach, this is ma favorite Christmas song," she said.

He stood and held out his hand to her. "May I have this dance?"

"Ye've a screw loose, but aye, yeh may." She stood, and David danced with her. Roger had just come back from the flat, where Tilly was taking a nap, so he stood and held out his hand to Erin. She laughed as she took it and with his help, they hoisted her up off the couch.

"Well, I'm not going to be the only one not joining in," Nick said and asked Lily to dance as well. The song ended, and they were about to return to their seats, laughing at their spontaneity, but the next song was "The Christmas Song" (Chestnuts Roasting on An Open Fire) by the King Cole Trio, so they switched partners. David took Erin's hand, Nick took Annis's, and Roger took Lily's. They danced and talked and laughed, not wanting to stop as that song came to an end. The next one was too fast, so David asked the Echo device to play "Silver Bells" by Dean Martin. They switched partners once more; Erin danced with Nick, David with Lily, and Roger with Annis.

About halfway through the song, Daniel came running into the house and stopped, staring at them with his mouth open. He ran back to the door, and they heard him shout to the others, "*They're dancing! All of them! You've got to see it!*" The children ran inside and stood, watching the adults.

Erin smiled and laughed at their befuddled faces. "What, haven't you ever seen people dancing before?" she asked.

"Not our parents," Dan said, and Peter nudged his arm.

"What?" he said defensively.

"Ach, Daniel," Annis said when the song ended, and "White Christmas" by Bing Crosby began. "Would yeh honor me with this dance?"

The boy's eyes grew large, and he looked at his siblings as if for permission. Peter gently pushed him forward and then went to Erin. "I'd love to dance with you… that is if you're not too tired or—"

Erin smiled at the young man and held out her hand to him. "I wouldn't deny you, Peter, even if I were an inch from collapsing," she said, then her parents stepped into the room.

"Look what we're missing, honey!" Frank said to Liz and took her hand.

Rosie danced with Roger, and Charlie with Lily, though everyone switched partners at least once. They continued dancing and changing partners through "It's Beginning to Look a Lot Like Christmas" by Johnny Mathis. After that, Erin was too tired to keep going, but the kids danced and laughed during "Jingle Bell Rock" by Bobby Helms, then "Rockin' Around the Christmas Tree" by Brenda Lee.

Supper that night was filled with laughter and joy. It was the best Christmas Eve Erin could remember having since she was a child. Christmas had lost some of its magic for her over the years because of her illness, which had become all-encompassing. That night, all the wonder and anticipation returned, and she felt the childlike happiness she could see on Peter, Charlie,

Dan, and Rosie's faces. There was nowhere she'd rather be than at Owlgate with her friends and family.

At bedtime, Erin and David tucked the excited children into their beds. She then read her favorite Christmas story from the *Little House* books by Laura Ingalls Wilder.

"When Ma opened the door, Laura and Mary heard the creek roaring. They had not thought about the creek. Now they knew there would be no Christmas, because Santa Claus could not cross that roaring creek…" Erin read.

"Did they really not have a Christmas?" Rosie asked, sounding shocked.

"You'll have to wait and see, Rosebud," she said and continued reading.

"Now go to sleep," Ma said, kissing them good night. "Morning will come quicker if you're asleep." She sat down again by the fire and Laura almost went to sleep. She woke up a little when she heard Pa say, "You've only made it worse, Caroline." And she thought she heard Ma say: "No, Charles. There's the white sugar." But perhaps she was dreaming.

Then she heard Jack growl savagely. The door-latch rattled and someone said, "Ingalls! Ingalls!!" Pa was stirring up the fire, and when he opened the door Laura saw that it was morning. The outdoors was gray. "Great fishhooks, Edwards! Come in, man! What happened?" Pa exclaimed.

Laura saw the stockings limply dangling, and she scrooged her eyes into the pillow. She heard Pa piling wood on the fire, and she heard Mr. Edwards say he had carried his clothes on his head when he swam the creek. His teeth rattled and his voice shivered. He would be all right, he said, as soon as he got warm. "It was too big a risk, Edwards," Pa said, "We're glad you're here, but that was too big a risk for a Christmas dinner."

"Your little ones had to have a Christmas," Mr. Edwards replied. No creek could stop me, after I fetched them their gifts from Independence."

Laura sat straight up in bed. "Did you see Santa Claus?" she shouted.

"I sure did," Mr. Edwards said…"

"Where? When? What did he look like? What did he say? Did he really give you something for us?" Mary and Laura cried.

"Wait, wait a minute!" Mr. Edwards laughed. And Ma said she would put the presents in the stockings, as Santa Claus intended. She said they mustn't look.

Mr. Edwards came and sat on the floor by their bed, and he answered every question they asked him. They honestly tried not to look at Ma, and they didn't quite see what she was doing."

Erin read how Mr. Edwards told the two young girls all about the nice long conversation he'd had with Santa Claus, who was riding a pack mule, seeing there wasn't any snow.

"But everyone knows Santa's sleigh can fly!" Rosie said.

"He can fly now, but way back then, he had to glide across the snow, like a sled does," Erin said, thinking fast, and continued.

"Something was shining bright in the top of Laura's stocking. She squealed and jumped out of bed. So did Mary, but Laura beat her to the fireplace. And the shining thing was a glittering new tin cup. Mary had one exactly like it.

These new tin cups were their very own. Now they each had a cup to drink out of. Laura jumped up and down and shouted and laughed, but Mary stood still and looked with shining eyes at her own tin cup.

Then they plunged their hands into the stockings again. And they pulled out two long sticks of candy. It was peppermint candy, striped red and white. They looked and looked at the beautiful candy, and Laura licked her stick, just one lick. But Mary was not so greedy. She didn't even take one lick of her stick.

Those stockings weren't empty yet. Mary and Laura pulled out two small packages. They unwrapped them, and each found a little heart-shaped cake. Over their delicate brown tops was sprinkled white sugar. The sparkling grains lay like tiny drifts of snow.

The cakes were too pretty to eat. Mary and Laura just looked at them. But at last Laura turned hers over, and she nibbled a tiny nibble from underneath, where it wouldn't show. And the inside of the cake was white! It had been made of pure white flour, and sweetened with white sugar.

Laura and Mary never would have looked in their stockings again. The cups and the cakes and the candy were almost too much. They were too happy to speak. But Ma asked if they were sure their stockings were empty. Then they put their hands down inside them, to make sure. And in the very toe of each stocking was a shining bright, new penny!

They had never even thought of such a thing as having a penny. Think of having a whole penny for your very own. Think of having a cup and a cake and a stick of candy and a penny.

There never had been such a Christmas..."

"What would you say to someone who had risked his life crossing a flooded creek to bring you a tin cup, one piece of peppermint candy, a little tiny cake, and a penny?" Erin asked them.

"I think we would all thank him, but I'm not so sure Daniel would," Peter said, and Daniel shot him a stony look.

"Well, let's see what happens," she said and read on.

"Now of course, right away, Laura and Mary should have thanked Mr. Edwards for bringing those lovely presents all the way from Independence. But they had forgotten all about Mr. Edwards. They had even forgotten about Santa Claus. In a minute they would have remembered, but before they did, Ma said, gently, "Aren't you going to thank Mr. Edwards?"

"Oh, thank you, Mr. Edwards! Thank you!" they said, and they meant it with all their hearts. Pa shook Mr. Edward's hand, too, and shook it again. Pa and Ma and Mr. Edwards acted as if they were almost crying, Laura didn't know why. So she gazed at her beautiful presents.... That was a happy Christmas."

Erin smiled at her young brood, and they smiled back at her. She knew they'd have many more gifts under their tree in the morning than Laura and Mary had gotten such a long time ago, in a land far, far away from them, and she hoped it helped them realize just how blessed they were.

"Now it's time to go to sleep or Santa... I mean, Father Christmas won't come!" she said, and kissed each of their foreheads. Peter had joined them, and they followed him to his room, where Erin tucked him in and gave him another kiss for good measure. "Sweet dreams, Peter."

"Sweet dreams, Mum, Dad," he said.

David and Erin went back downstairs, and while Erin sat laughing with her friends, David and Frank watched them, enjoying a wee dram of sherry. "It's going to be hard to say goodbye when we leave here," Frank said.

"Aye, but you're welcome tae visit us anatime."

"Funny you should say that. We had a lengthy conversation last night about possibly moving abroad."

"Is that so?"

"We haven't made any plans, but we agreed that being near our daughter and grandchildren would be something to think about, anyway."

"Well, if talking becomes planning, please let me know. I'd be happy to help you find a place nearby, though… not *too* near, if you ken my meanin'," David said with a light laugh.

"Understood, thanks," Frank said with a smile.

David saw that Erin was looking a bit droopy-eyed and went to her. "Perhaps we should go up now?" he said.

"Hmm, aye, that's a good idea. I'm beat!"

She excused herself, and David followed her up the winding staircase to his bedroom. "I dinnae think I've ever been so happy at Christmastime," he said as he was getting into bed, but there was no reply. In the dark room, he heard Erin begin to snore softly and smiled. "I love yeh, Erin March, nee Wallace, and verra nearly Elliott."

Chapter Forty-One

FIRST CHRISTMAS

On Christmas morning, David and Erin woke to someone knocking on the door of their room. "Come—" Erin began, but the door was already flung open, and three children came rushing into the room, smiling and full of joy.

"Good morning, Mummy!" Rosie said. "Oh, and you as well, Daddy."

"Good morning, Mum and Dad," Peter said, and Charlie parroted him.

"Good morning, my lovelies! Merry Christmas!" Erin said, and they laughed.

"Happy Christmas," David said.

"Oh, right, I forgot," Erin said. "Happy Christmas, then. Where's Dan?"

"He's gone downstairs to wait by the tree and see if Father Christmas remembered us," Peter said.

"Has he forgotten you before?" Erin asked.

"No, Mummy, he's impatient, that's all," Rosie said.

"My first Christmas with you! I'm so excited." Erin looked at the children smiling at her, then turned to David. "I love you all," she said and gave him a peck on the lips.

"Let's go down and have breakfast," David said, and the children groaned.

"But, Dad! Shouldn't we open our gifts first?" Charlie said.

"Mmm, I think I need some food in my stomach first. I'm feeling a bit queasy," Erin said.

"Why don't you lot go help anaone who needs… helping," David said. "We'll be down shortly."

When the children were gone, David turned to Erin. "Happy Christmas, love."

"Merry Christmas," she said and laughed until he leaned in to kiss her. "Guess what?"

"What?"

"We're getting married tomorrow; can you believe it?" she said and squeed.

"I can't wait!" He leaned over and gently pushed her backward, then he lifted her nightgown and kissed her large belly. "Happy Christmas, ma love," he said, then put his ear over it. "Aye, I will… You are? I believe you, darling."

He lifted his head, and she laughed. "And what did you hear, then?"

"First, I'm to wish you a happy Christmas. Then, the bairn is hungry, so ye'd best hurry to the breakfast table, and finally, the wee thing can't wait for tomorrow either—Oh, and to be born, as well."

"Oh, David, I love you," she said.

Erin and David came downstairs, and Erin headed straight to the kitchen. David went to the dining room, where he found Liz, beside herself with giddiness. "Did you mean it?" she asked him.

He honestly didn't know what she meant. "Mean what, exactly?" he asked.

Liz looked at Frank and motioned with her head for him to explain. "I believe she means moving to England," he said.

"Oh, right," David said.

"It's so generous!" Liz said, tearing up.

David looked at Frank, wondering what he'd told her. "Liz, honey, I don't know what you're thinking, but I said he'd *help* us *find* a place, not he'd *buy* us a house," Frank said.

She looked at her husband, then at David. "Oh, I see. I'm sorry, I misunderstood, I guess," she said, her red cheeks revealing how embarrassed she was.

"Ach, dinnae worry about et, Liz. Of course I'll help yeh if ye'll allow me to," David said.

"Thank you, David," Liz said quietly.

———

Erin entered the room and noticed her mother's discomfort. "Okay, what'd I miss?" she asked.

"Yer parents are considerin' becomin' ex-pats," David said.

"Oh really?" she said, sounding excited. "What brought that up?"

"I'm going to miss you when we go back home," Liz said to her, looking emotional. "Your father and I had a discussion the other night, that's all. Foolish dreaming, I suppose."

"Not foolish at all, Liz," David said with a genuine smile.

"Thank you, now let's take our seats, and we can talk about it another time," she said.

"Mom?" Erin said and took her to the side. "What happened?"

"Oh, Erin, I should just learn to keep my mouth shut, that's all," Liz said and began wringing her hands.

"What did you say?"

"Your father came to me last night and said that he and David had spoken about finding us a house... here. I don't remember exactly what he said, but I took it to mean he was willing to *buy* us a house. I came down here all excited and thanking him, and now I feel like an idiot. David was gracious about it and said he'd help us if we'd allow him to, but now I feel like I somehow coerced him or put it into his mind. That's not what I meant to do at all."

"Oh, Mom, please don't let it ruin your day. You must know that we'll help you buy a house if you really want to move here. My guess is that Dad worded it poorly or was just vague enough that it's no wonder that's what you thought. Trust me, David isn't going to be upset about it. He understands things like that can happen."

"Yes, but I still feel ridiculous."

"You'll feel better after brekkie," Erin said and hugged her mother.

"Oh, I'm hungry," Erin said as she sat at the dining room table. "What's on the menu?" She peered at the many china dishes filled with mounds of delicious-looking food.

"Cold gruel and water, and you'll like it!" Frank said.

"But, Father, that's what you feed us *every* morning! Can't we have hot gruel… just for the holiday?" she said pleadingly.

Her dad gave her a stern look and then put his hand on his chin, rubbing an imaginary goatee. "Well, I suppose, since it is Christmas… you may have lukewarm gruel and water, but don't expect it every day, young lady!"

Erin bounced on her chair and clapped her hands excitedly. "Thank you, father! This will be a Christmas like no other!" she said and then noticed the faces of those sitting around them. "Holy Moses, you should see your faces!"

"You're so much fun, Grandpa and Mummy," Rosie said.

"Aye, ye're off yer heid, I reckon," Annis said and then began to laugh.

"Glaikit, the lot of yeh!" Millie said with a warm smile.

"Where do yeh come up wi' et, out of the blue, like tha'?" Roger asked.

"Must be genetics, I guess," Erin said. "And lots of practice."

Daniel wasn't paying much attention to the conversation, and as soon as the prayer was finished, he piled bits of this and that onto his plate, then hoovered it up faster than Father Christmas headed back up the chimney. "Daniel, you'd better slow down, or you'll get a belly ache," Frank said, but the boy just shrugged and took a drink of his milk.

"Aye, son, you'll not be any closer to opening gifts by—"

"But, Dad! Why can't you eat faster? I just can't wait!" he said.

"Ah, to be a kid again when Christmas morning was all about finding out if Santa brought you the thing you wanted most," Frank said with a bit of melancholy.

"May I be excused?" Daniel said.

"He's already given me everything I've wanted most and more," Erin said and took David's hand.

"Aye, he has for me as well," David said.

Apparently, their ardor was taking too long, and Dan cleared his throat loudly. "Come on, Dad!"

"Ach, Daniel, have a wee bit of patience, boy," David said.

"But, Dad!" he said impatiently. Peter shot him a look that clearly told him to cool it, but the boy only rolled his eyes.

"Aye, son, yeh may be excused, though—" David began, but Daniel was off his chair in a blink, and he had to raise his voice to finish, "you're not to touch anathin'!"

"I'll watch him, Dad," Peter said and wiped his mouth with his napkin. "May I be excused?"

"Aye, Peter, we'll be along shortly," David said and saw the eager looks on Rosie and Charlie's faces. "Ach, ye're all excused, but heed what I said."

"Thank you, Daddy!" Rosie said and then waited for Charlie to push his chair back in before hurrying to the sitting room.

"Yeah, Dad, thanks," he said before following his sister.

"I'm tempted tae make them wait, if I'm honest," David said with a smile.

"Oh, show mercy, David!" Erin said and took his hand. "There may just be a few things *you'll* be waiting for soon, and you'll be happy if I don't decide to dilly-dally, right? Anyway, I'm finished, so if *I* may be excused, I'll join them."

"Ach, yeh drive a hard bargain, but I can see yer point," he said and put his napkin on his plate. Then he stood and pulled Erin's chair out for her.

"I'd say that's a wise decision," Frank said and stood, doing the same for his wife.

Soon, everyone was gathered in the sitting room, finding seats. The children's eyes were bright and their faces eager to get started, though Erin knew it was taking all their discipline to remain seated quietly. Finally, she saw Daniel close his eyes and scrunch up his face. "Dan! What's wrong?" she asked since it looked like he was in pain.

The young boy shook his head and closed his eyes even tighter. The adults looked at each other and then at the children, hoping for an answer. "I told him that if he wasn't perfectly well-behaved and if he didn't wait until someone was asked to begin handing out the presents, I'd convince Dad to send him to his room until we were finished," Peter said, and then blushed.

"I see," David said and tried to hide a smile. "Charlie, please begin handing out the gifts, then."

Dan opened his eyes and smiled, revealing his deep-set dimples. "Whew," he whispered and then turned to face the tree.

Charlie picked up a box and read the tag, "To Erin, from Annis," he said out loud and then handed it to Erin, smiling.

"Ooh! Thank you, Charlie," she said and resisted the temptation to shake it. It was wrapped in duck-egg-blue paper covered with trees filled with little birds. "This paper is just so beautiful, isn't it, Lily?" she said, making the children and half of the men groan.

"Yes, it's stunning!" her friend replied and laughed as everyone watched Erin try to find the least intrusive way to unwrap it.

"Open et, already," David said, exaggerating his impatience, "or I'll do et for yeh." He smiled and acted as though he'd grab it from her.

"No!" she squeaked and held the gift close to her chest, laughing. "I would be thrilled if the present was just this paper," she said as she tried peeling the tape off without ripping it. David shot her a look, raising his eyebrows. "Humor the pregnant lady, a'right?"

She finally got the paper off and used Roger's pen knife to carefully break the tape on the ordinary brown cardboard box. Upon opening the flaps, she discovered something wrapped in duck-egg-blue tissue paper. She lifted the flat object that, thankfully, wasn't taped and unwrapped it, revealing a small watercolor painting of a yellow rowboat tied to a small wooden pier surrounded by tall grass, rushes, and long, brown cattails. "Oh, Annis, this is lovely! Did you paint it?" she asked and looked up, though she could've stared at it all day.

"Aye, ma dear, there are more in the box; et's a set, you see," she said and pointed at it.

Erin hugged the framed artwork and then set it down next to her on the tissue paper. She opened two more paintings; one with a red boat and the last one was blue. "Will they come back?" she said to herself as she admired them.

"What did yeh say, dear?" Annis asked.

"Oh, sorry, it was nothing. I was just thinking about the story behind each boat, you know? I was wondering if the owners would come back, that's all." Erin's cheeks turned pink, and she shrugged, feeling silly.

"Ach, that's a verra good question. What do yeh think, then? Will they come back or leave them tae rot, along with the pier they're tied to?" Annis asked.

"May I open something now, please?" Rosie asked sweetly.

"Of course you may, darling," Erin said, then turned to David's mother. "I think they'll come back."

"As do I, dear."

"I love them, truly! Thank you," Erin said quietly as the rest of the gifts were being handed out. The children opened quite a few presents each, and as the area beneath the tree cleared out, Erin nudged David and pointed to the small cube toward the back of it. He crawled over and pulled it out, groaning as he did so. "I'm too old for this," he said, then handed the gift to Lily. "Happy Christmas."

Lily figured out what it was as soon as she took it from him and blushed dark red. "But I said you shouldn't—" she began to protest.

Erin put her finger up to her lips to shush her. "Read the tag, Lil," she said.

Lily sighed and read it out loud. "To Ariana, from John Thomas Fife." She nodded but didn't say anything right away. Erin put her hand on her best friend's shoulder, and when she looked up, saw tears falling down her face.

"Oh, Lil," she said and hugged her.

It took Lily a few minutes to compose herself, and then she laughed. "Sorry, but it's just so sweet!"

"Yeah, guys, thanks," Nick said and put his arm around his wife.

"And it's signed!" Lily said as she pulled out the first of the three-disk Blu-ray set of *Future Explorations*.

"Of course! I reckon Ariana would be disappointed if it weren't," David said.

Suddenly, Erin yawned so big that her eyes watered. "Dang, I think I'll take a nap before lunch."

"Aye, and after that, we should have a rehearsal for tomorrow," David said and helped her up from the loveseat. "Children, please help tidy up the room."

"Yes, sir," Peter and Charlie said, and Rosie just got to work picking up torn wrapping paper. Daniel grumbled but held out a bin liner bag as the others filled it.

"Now, please behave until we return—" Erin said, and everyone looked up at her, especially the children. "Dad." She looked at her father and laughed as he rolled his eyes.

"You're no fun at all!" he said. "Sweet dreams."

Chapter Forty-Two

I WANT TO MARRY DAVID

Finally, the day had come. Erin stood at the far end of the sitting room at Owlgate, nervous as she began to advance down the aisle. All her friends were seated in chairs to either side of her; they smiled and stood as she passed them. The wedding party was standing at the other end of the room, David looking so handsome in his kilt. She couldn't wait to get to him and finally become his wife.

She made it down the aisle, stood in front of him, and the next thing she knew, she was saying, "I do," thinking how quickly everything was going. She wanted it to slow down so she could enjoy it. The Registrar asked the guests if anyone had any objections, and the room was silent for a moment. Then, in true *Four Weddings and A Funeral* fashion, the doors flew open, and both Todd and Martin rushed into the room.

"I object!" Todd said. "She was my wife first, and I want what is mine!"

"No, *I* object! David isn't allowed to do anything without my approval, or I'll make his life miserable!" Martin said.

Todd had come up the aisle and was dragging her away while Martin stood behind David, holding him and keeping him from rescuing her. Erin screamed, then shouted, "But I don't want to go with you! I want to marry David!" She sat up in bed, realizing she'd just said that out loud.

David sat up as well, startled awake. "What's the matter, love?" he said drowsily. "Did yeh just say you want tae marry me?"

Erin had finally caught her breath and nearly tackled him, needing him to hold her. "I had the most awful dream! Todd and Martin were both

370

objecting at the wedding," she said and told him everything that happened. "I felt so helpless and really angry. I yelled at Todd, saying something like, 'I don't want to go with you! I want to marry David.' That's when I woke up. Are you sure Martin doesn't know and won't know about the wedding or where it is? I'm not worried about Todd, not after we spoke with him on holiday, but Martin, or what Martin is capable of, scares the shit out of me."

"Aye, I'm as sure as I can be, and I dinnae think any of the people we've invited would tell him, or even know who he is, for that matter. Dinnae worry, my darling."

"But he seems to know things he shouldn't and manages to find out things there should be no way of finding out about. I wish he'd just find another hobby instead of making it his life's ambition to ruin yours," Erin said, holding him tightly, not yet able to erase the memory of her dream.

"We should—" David began, but Millie interrupted him with a knock on the door, saying that lunch would be ready in half an hour.

When Erin got to the table, Liz mentioned that she looked a bit peaked. "Are you alright, honey?" she asked and placed the back of her hand on her daughter's forehead. "You don't have a fever."

"I'm fine, Mom; I just had a nightmare," Erin said, and after Annis's prayer, she told them all about it.

"Oh my gosh!" Lilly said. That's awful!"

"Tell me about it! I just want it to be perfect... I mean, I know it might not be *perfect* exactly, but I just don't want anything like that to happen!"

"You're just nervous, Erin. It'll all be okay; I'm sure of it," Frank said and blew her a kiss across the table.

Erin laughed and caught the kiss mid-air. She pretended to fumble it, then pressed it to her cheek. "Thanks, Daddy. I know you'd beat up anyone who tried to ruin my wedding day, right?"

Frank put up both hands, clenched into fists, and said, "Just let 'em try!"

After lunch, they set up just the main aisle with a few chairs on either side and the place where the couple would repeat their vows. Since he didn't have a role in the wedding, Nick stood in for the Registrar. Everyone who did have to do something during the service was instructed on what to do and how to do it, then they went through the whole ceremony twice.

When everyone felt confident that they knew what to do and when to do it, they all pitched in and set up the rest of the chairs. The pretty floral hall rug was rolled up and moved to the aisle, and the Christmas tree was carefully pushed into a corner, out of the way. David, Roger, and Peter went upstairs to pack for their overnight stay in a hotel so that, per tradition, the groom wouldn't see his bride until their wedding day.

"I'll miss you," Erin said as she walked into his childhood bedroom and sat on the edge of his bed.

"And I'll miss you as well, darling. Sod tradition! I'd much rather stay in here with you tonight! Do yeh reckon anaone will notice if I sneak in after midnight?" he said.

Erin stood and wrapped her arms around him. "Probably, but I won't kick you out of bed if you do. Just make sure I'm a-wake—" she trailed off, not wanting to think about Bran.

"Aye, love. I reckon we can be apart for one night, right?"

"Aye," she said and held him tighter. "What are you boys gonna do tonight?"

"Well, that's up tae Roger, though I dinnae plan tae drink, and there'll not be any strip clubs or the like, no worries there. I reckon we'll order room service and play poker until the wee hours of nine-thirty and then be off to our slumber."

"That sounds like fun. I hope you win!"

"Ach, I've already won, yeh ken?"

"Aww, David, you say the sweetest things," she said and allowed him to kiss her, then she followed him down the grand staircase toward the front door.

"I'll miss you, darling, and I'll see you tomorrow. Sleep well, ma' love," he said and kissed her cheek.

"See you tomorrow. I love you!" she said and then hugged Peter, who had just joined his father. "Have fun, but not *too* much fun without me!"

"Okay, Mum," Peter said.

"Wouldn't dream of it," David said and opened the door, allowing Peter to step out ahead of him, then he smiled at Erin and closed the door behind him.

"I wonder what David and the boys are doing right now," Erin said to everyone as they ate Millie's shepherd's pie, which she had requested.

"From what I know of David," Lily said, "I bet he's pining away, missing you so badly that all he can do is pace the room and wring his hands."

"Wouldn't surprise me," Liz said, and Frank nodded enthusiastically.

"That's exactly what I imagine him doing, though I bet Roger and Peter will get him to have fun doing something," Erin said.

After an amazing dessert of cranachan, she invited Kitty, whom Erin insisted was there for the wedding, to join her mother and bridesmaids for the festivities. Sadly, she wouldn't allow herself to do it, saying it wasn't proper. Instead, she scurried into the kitchen to help with whatever preparations Millie needed for the next day.

They watched Houlihan's Flat and then searched YouTube for old commercials and things that David had done when he'd first started acting. He was so young and handsome, reminding her of Peter. She was determined to go through her viewing history when her new family was gathered and watch them again. She knew David would protest, but she and the children would talk him into it.

Later in her bedroom, the women laughed as Erin told them about falling on her ass when she'd seen David through the doorway on their first treatment weekend. There was a knock on the door, and Annis stuck her head into the room. "I hope I'm not disturbin' yeh?" she said with a lovely smile.

She was in the house coat she'd worn the night Erin had decided to return to Wisconsin. That terrible night, after she'd told David about what had happened with Bran, and he'd not taken the news well. She was glad she'd left but more glad she'd come back. "Come in, Ann! I was just telling them about when David and I first met," she said.

The older woman stepped into the room, carrying something in her hand. "I won't take up much of yer time—" she began, but Erin stood and put her arm around her soon-to-be mother-in-law.

"Nonsense! Come join us," she said, but Annis shook her head.

"Ach, thank yeh, dear, but I've quite a lot tae do tae make maself presentable," the older woman said, and Erin saw her cheeks bloom in a soft, rosy blush. "I've come tae loan yeh somethin' if I'm not too late." She held out a light blue, velvet, drawstring bag.

Erin couldn't imagine what could be in it and took it from her. "You may recognize et from ma weddin' album. I wore et for ma Charles, and I'd be honored if ye'd wear et for ma son," she said as Erin opened the bag and took out a thin, delicate, silver tiara. "Et was a gift from ma mother."

Everyone in the room gasped and gathered around her to see it better. "Oh, Ann! It's beautiful. Thank you for thinking of this; it'll be perfect!" Erin said and hugged her tightly.

"Aye, I think so as well. I'll leave yeh now tae get on with things. If yeh need anathin', find Millie or me, and we'll help yeh." She turned and walked out the door, and the girls squeed over the lovely hairpiece.

Chapter Forty-Three

THE MORNING OF—HER SIDE & HIS

In the morning, Erin woke feeling sick, which wasn't anything new. She'd had several months without morning sickness, but now that she was in her third trimester, it was back, though her doctor said it was normal for that to happen. She'd missed David in the bed with her overnight and couldn't wait to see him again in only a few hours.

She brushed her teeth, took a shower, and heard women talking in her room when she got out and toweled off. She put on David's robe, inhaled his scent, and then stepped out into his bedroom, seeing her wedding party and mother standing near the end of the bed. They had a tray with breakfast waiting for her on the desk near the window, and each greeted her warmly with 'good morning.'

"Good morning! Have you already eaten, then?" she asked, and Lily laughed while Liz smiled.

"Why, yes, *dahhling*, we have, quite," Lily said, making fun of the way she'd asked with an overdone British accent.

"Why you mocks me?" Erin said, pretending to be hurt. "Would you rather I said, 'Did ya'll rustle up some grub and eat your vittles before I had a chance to join ya?' Or, how about, 'Did ya eat, eh? I'm hungry, don't ya know!'?"

"No, I think the first was best, but it does sound mighty posh to us," Lily said.

"Well, thank you for bringing me food, anyway. I'm really hungry! I… can't believe this is going to happen today! You don't think… he'll… change his mind, do you?" she said, suddenly terrified.

"Not a chance!" Liz said.

"Never! Can't happen!" Lily added.

"My daddy loves you, Mummy! He won't do that," Rosie said.

"Don't worry, honey. Eat your breakfast and let's get you ready to become Mrs. Elliott," Liz said.

"That sounds good, doesn't it? I need stationery that says, 'Mrs. Erin Elliott' at the top!" she said. "And a fancy ink pen with our names and wedding date engraved on the side. Oooh, and a pretty little porcelain box filled with stamps, each with the queen's..." She gasped softly, still saddened by the Monarch's passing. "Or, I guess, the King's profile on them, though I don't know who I'd send anything to. I don't know many people in the UK, but it would be nice to have them, just in case letter writing becomes the new fad, like vinyl LPs," she said and laughed too hard. "Good night nurse, I'm nervous! Somebody slap me!"

Rosie's eyes grew wide, and she shook her head. "No! Don't slap my Mummy! What if we all kiss you instead?" she said and gave her a kiss on the cheek.

"Yes, Rosebud, that's a much better idea," Erin said, and the baby decided to wake up and kicked her. "Oww!"

"Did I hurt you?" Rosie said, looking shocked and alarmed.

"No darling girl, your baby brother or sister did!"

Rosie smiled. "May I touch your tummy?" she asked sweetly. Erin leaned back on the chair and allowed her and the rest of the women to feel the baby assault her from inside.

Two hours later, Erin asked Rosie to go downstairs and see if David was there yet. She ran out of the room and came back, shaking her head. "Not yet, Mummy."

David woke in the morning at the hotel feeling nervous and excited. The night before, Roger and Peter had a little stag do for him without the strip club and alcohol. They ordered room service, drank Irn-Bru and coke, and watched movies, laughing a lot.

He was the first one up and took a shower, trying to imagine what Erin's morning would be like. He hoped nothing would go wrong; that's all he wanted for the day. As he stepped out of the shower, he heard Roger and Peter laughing and smiled. He knew Roger was a good example for his sons. He was a fine, upstanding man with more integrity in his little finger than most men had in their whole body, so he was glad they got on as well as they did.

"Hurry up! Ye're no' the only one needin' a wash!" came Roger's voice from the other room.

"Ach, I must look ma best for ma bride! Gie a man some time!" he replied.

"You look yer best everaday! Yer worst is near ma best!" They continued their banter until David came out wrapped in the robe provided by the hotel.

"Are you nervous, Dad?" Peter asked as Roger went into the bathroom.

"Aye, does et show?" he asked and watched as his eldest son reflected his own smile back at him.

"No, I just wondered if you would be since you've been married before. Did you feel nervous when you married Mum?"

"Aye, I did, but I dinnae remember much of that mornin'. Martin had taken me out the night before, and I was verra hungover. I'm much happier to be sober."

"I'm... glad you're marrying Erin; she fits with us, if you know what I mean?"

"Aye! I'm verra glad you feel that way about her now, seein' yeh felt quite differently when yeh first met." Peter blushed and shrugged, clearly remembering how he'd behaved. "Dinnae worry, Peter, a lot was happenin'. We understand," David said.

"Yes, but I'm gutted about it sometimes," Peter said sadly.

"I assure yeh, son, she's forgiven' yeh and doesn't think on et," he said and pulled him close for a sideways hug.

———

Peter watched his dad getting dressed and admired him. He wanted to be like him, honest and friendly, even to strangers who were always stopping him and asking for selfies and autographs. He thought of his dad as a good man and was proud of him. He really was happy for him and Erin, knowing she was one of the best things to happen to their family.

———

David started watching his son, who seemed to be daydreaming. "Penny for your thoughts?" he said, ignoring the fact that he'd been staring at him steadily for at least five minutes.

Peter blushed and smiled sheepishly. "Sorry for staring. I... well, I'm chuffed for you, that's all," he said and walked to the bathroom door. "Roger's taking too long!" He knocked on the door and then tilted his head. "Wait. We've adjacent rooms. I'll use the other bathroom for my shower." He grabbed his underclothing and left the room through the connecting door.

It was finally time to leave for Owlgate. Their bags were packed, and they looked each other over to make sure nothing was amiss. "Ach, we make a fine-lookin' trio if I do say so maself," Roger said, catching a glimpse of them walking down a corridor with a mirror on it.

"Wait! We need a picture!" Peter said as they entered the lobby. He saw the concierge and asked him to take it for them. The man took several and made sure they were what they wanted before he accepted their thanks. David tipped him, and they walked out into the overcast day and into a limousine idling outside the hotel doors.

"Et's odd bein' in this half of the vehicle," Roger said since he was usually the one driving.

David didn't say anything the whole way there. His mind had begun tormenting him with thoughts that something would go wrong or that Erin would remember the horrid things he'd said to her in the past and change her mind.

"Dad? What's the matter?" Peter said as they turned onto the old street in Duddingston and pulled into the drive, past the wrought iron gates, which someone had already opened for them.

The limo stopped at the bottom of the nine stone steps that led to the grand entrance of his mother's home. "What? Ach, nothin', son, I've a lot on ma mind, is all," he said as they got out of the vehicle. It rolled slowly away, out of sight. It would return after the wedding to take them to the Royal Mile for the surprise honeymoon he'd planned for them. For the time being, however, they didn't want too much attention on the house.

He noticed one of his mother's neighbors appear, close the gates for them, then discretely exit through the side door. *I must remember tae thank him for that,* he thought as he and his groomsmen ascended the stairs and were ushered into the formal reception room. The Christmas decorations were still up, but they added to the beauty of the ceremony.

Chapter Forty-Four

THE PERFECT MATCH

All eyes were on David as he took his position to the right of the registrar, who would be officiating that day. David thanked her for being there on Boxing Day, and she smiled, saying she was pleased to have been given the honor of marrying him and his bride.

"She is… here, right?" he asked the woman, feeling weak in the knees. His heart fluttered, and his stomach felt as though it had already tied the proverbial knot inside him.

"Aye, I believe so, sir. A wee lass has been sent tae check if ye've arrived several times already," she assured him.

There was a sudden hush as everyone took their seats, and the stringed quartet began to play softly. David got goosebumps up and down both arms and legs as he saw Rosie pop her head around the door frame and give a tiny squee of joy at seeing the three men standing at the ready.

"Hi, Daddy," she said and gave him a little wave.

"Hello, Rosebud," he responded and waved back. He was beginning to sweat and worried it would show on his starched shirt, but then a signal must have been given because the quartet began playing the music they'd chosen to start the ceremony.

Another hour, and several more trips down the stairs later, Rosie came into the room beaming. The music of the string quartet followed her, drifting up the stairs like the loveliest alarm notification telling them that it was nearly time to get started. "Daddy's here, Mummy! He looks really handsome! Peter and Roger do as well."

"Thank you, sweetheart! Are we ready? Are we forgetting anything? The tiara is on—My makeup is on—My… dress is on," she said, and Rosie giggled. "That's pretty important, Rosie, isn't it? I wouldn't want to get married without my dress on!"

There was a knock on the door, and Lily opened it. "I've been sent to ask if you're ready," Frank said.

"Oh, Mr. Wallace! You look really nice!" Lily said.

"Yes, Daddy, I'm ready," Erin said, and Lily opened the door all the way. "You look scrummy, Daddy!"

"You look breathtaking, sweetheart," Frank said, smiling.

"Does everyone have everything? Umm, Mom, you should go down and let them know we'll be down soon. I love you… thanks for helping me today."

"You're welcome, baby girl. See you in a few minutes. Frank, you *do* look scrummy!" she said and left the room.

Rosie picked up her small bouquet, smiled at Erin, and then walked out of the room. Lily took up her bouquet, handed Erin hers, then followed Rosie after making sure Erin looked perfect. Erin heard the musicians begin playing the song they'd chosen for when they were supposed to get ready to walk down the aisle. She took a deep breath and smiled at her father in his red Wallace kilt.

"Ready?" she asked, and he beamed.

"When you are," he replied.

"No time like the present, right?"

"Don't want to keep the man waiting too long! He looks as if he'll swoon at any moment already."

"Swoon? Like… that he doesn't want to—" she said, suddenly worried.

"No, like he's nervous and excited and can't believe his luck," Frank said, much to her relief.

They left the bedroom and walked down the hall, stopping at the final landing. Their photographer took a few photos of the moment, then they proceeded into the large entryway, where a small fire was happily crackling in the fireplace. The sun came out from behind the clouds just long enough to shine through the stained-glass windows, providing some lovely shots of the dappled light falling on Erin's face.

Erin stood just out of everyone's, especially David's, sight in the entrance hall. Rosie and Lily did their final checking on Erin and waited at the door. The mothers were wiping tears off their faces, waiting for their cue to start down the aisle. Liz took Erin's hand and whispered, "I'm so proud of you." She then stepped aside, and Annis took her place beside the bride.

"I'm so verra glad yer marryin' ma son, Erin. You were meant tae be together," she said.

"Thank you; I'm so nervous!" she said as the mother's music started.

"Ye'll do just fine, dear," she said and left the room after Liz.

Everyone stopped talking, and in the window, Erin saw a reflection of their guests turn to watch the mothers. It was then Lily and Rosie's turn. She watched them as they walked slowly toward the place where the ceremony would be conducted and stood to the left of the registrar since that was the traditional Scottish wedding setup, opposite of what is done in America.

Frank patted his daughter's hand and smiled at her. "Your mother and I are so proud and happy for you, sweetheart," he said as they stepped into the doorway to the sitting room, where a cheery fire was lit in the fireplace and the string quartet played. The guests stood and turned to look at her.

She saw Peter, whose kilt matched David's, and Roger, his kilt a striking green against the blue of the Elliott plaid. Everyone they loved was there, and as she walked in time with the music, she saw snippets of them but couldn't keep her eyes off David. He was immaculate, and her heart skipped a beat as he smiled at her.

He was breathtaking to behold in full Highland dress, his kilt made with the blue Elliott tartan. Everything faded away, and she couldn't believe she was there at all, let alone the bride for *that* bridegroom. She didn't want to cry, but the tears came forth and rolled down her cheek nonetheless.

When she finally arrived at the platform, she turned to face her father. He kissed her, told her he loved her, then handed her over to David, who took her hand and brought her close, their mutual energy flowing between them. She gave her small bouquet to Lily, then took David's outstretched hands, which were trembling.

He pulled one hand away and gently wiped the tears off her cheeks with his thumb, then he touched his forehead to hers. "I love yeh," he whispered, then they turned to face the registrar, who smiled at them and told the guests they may be seated. She began by speaking about marriage and how important it is, but neither Erin nor David heard much of what she said.

Next were the vows; the registrar stepped forward again and had them repeat after her.

"Do you, David Peter Elliott, take Erin Grace March to be your wife, to be her constant friend, her partner in life, and her true love? To love her without reservation, honor and respect her, protect her from harm, comfort her in times of distress, and grow with her in mind and spirit?"

David smiled at Erin and then held out his pinky. She laughed and wrapped her pinky around his. "I pinky promise that I do," he said. They continued to hold each other's pinkies while Erin made her promise.

> "Do you, Erin Grace March, take David Peter Elliott to be your husband, to be his constant friend, his partner in life, and his true love? To love him without reservation, honor and respect him, protect him from harm, comfort him in times of distress, and grow with him in mind and spirit?"

"I pinky promise that I do," she said.

"Now, who has the rings?" the registrar asked.

"I do," Peter said and reached into his left breast pocket, pulling out a small, silk-covered box. He handed it, opened, to the woman, and she held it out. David lifted his great-grandmother's ring and held it on the tip of Erin's left-hand ring finger.

"David, please repeat after me," the registrar said, and he repeated it.

> "Erin, I give you this ring as a symbol
> of my love. I ask you to wear it as a
> sign to the world that you are my
> wife. With this ring, I thee wed."

He slipped the ring all the way onto her finger. The woman turned to Erin as she took David's father's ring out of the box and asked her to repeat after her. Erin had secretly taken it and had it engraved with '*An ever-fixed mark—D&E Elliott*. She'd show him later; right then, she repeated the words the woman said.

> *"David, I give you this ring as a symbol*
> *of my love. I ask you to wear it as a sign*
> *to the world that you are my husband.*
> *With this ring, I thee wed."*

She then slipped it down his finger. Her face hurt from smiling so much, but she couldn't help it. It was the best day of her life, and there was no way to hide it.

The official had them hold hands and asked the guests if there were any objections. Erin held her breath, and the room was silent. "Good," she said, "I now pronounce you man and wife." The room exploded in applause. "You may kiss your bride." David pulled Erin close and kissed her as their small group of friends and family cheered. "I'm pleased to present to you, Mr. and Mrs. David Elliott."

Erin turned, and from a small table next to the registrar, she carefully lifted a small, silver, two-handled bowl, called a quaich, filled with whisky. She turned to face their guests, careful not to look any of them in the eyes since she didn't want to cry anymore. Raising it up, she held it out to her new husband.

He took a drink from one side, then she took a tiny sip from the other that made her cough and make a face. It was very strong, and she didn't like whiskey anyway. Some of the guests laughed, and she blew out a breath of air, feeling as though her mouth was on fire.

The bridesmaids set their bouquets on a designated table behind them. Erin managed not to spill as she handed the quaich to Lily, who took a tiny drink. Next was Rosie, who'd been given the choice to take a sip or not. She said she'd like to try it, and since it was just a wee nip, they said it was okay.

Lily passed the quaich to her, and she lifted it to her lips. Though she only took a dribble, she started coughing, so Lily took it back. Millie went to the kitchen to fetch her a tall glass of punch. She drank down half of the rose-colored liquid, which seemed to help a lot.

The quaich was then passed to Peter, who, wanting to be a man, took a larger drink than he should've. Everyone watched as he tried to keep his face neutral, but first his cheeks, then his neck, and soon his whole face turned bright red. Millie held out the crystal glass of punch she'd taken from Rosie. He was about to refuse it when Roger leaned over.

"There's no shame in chasin' a strong draft of whiskey with somethin' a bit more palatable, son," he said, so Peter smiled and gratefully accepted it. He downed it all in one swig, making several people chuckle again. Roger then took the quaich and drank the bowl dry.

"You may now pin your tartans," the officiant said.

Peter took out another box from his sporran and opened it. "Frank... Grandpa, I mean," he said and smiled at him. "Please take this Wallace crest of arms and pin it to my father's tartan." Frank did as he was asked, kneeling to pin it to the front opening of David's kilt, which was a bit awkward, but then he stood and shook David's hand. "Grandma Annis, please take this Elliott crest of arms and pin it to Erin's tartan." Annis stood and pinned the crest to Erin's sash, then kissed her cheek and returned to her seat.

The newlyweds then held hands and began their journey back down the aisle to start their life as husband and wife. The wedding party followed them, then the guests and family. All they did was go in a big circle through the house and gather in the sitting room for photographs while the guests had drinks and hors d'oeuvres.

While the photos were taken, the dining room was being transformed into a dining hall. They'd hired waiters and a bartender and had rented tables, chairs, and linens for the dinner. The smell of roasted meat filled the house, and Erin couldn't wait for the photo session to be over so she could eat.

Chapter Forty-Five

DINNER AND DANCING

Forty-five minutes later, the wedding party stepped into the dining room. The long dinner table was pushed to the wall for them, and the smaller tables were set up for guests. Each table, draped in white linen, had a small bouquet of rosebuds and greenery in the center. "Oh, that's so pretty!" Lily said as they made their way to the head table.

"It's even prettier than I imagined it would be," Erin said, then felt the baby kick her bladder. "Shoot! I need the toilet. Be right back."

When she returned, the tables were full of people, and David stood to pull out her chair for her. "I missed you, Mrs. Elliott," he said with a sweet smile.

"What did you just call me?" she said, which surprised him so much he began to frown."

"I... said I miss..."

"No, the last part."

"Mrs. Elliott?"

"Yes, that's it. Ooooooh, I like the sound of that! Say it again!"

"As you wish, Mrs. Elliott," he said and shook his head, smiling again.

The meal was delicious; Erin heard several people mention it as they ate, and she felt so proud and pleased that Millie had cooked for them. She and David were made to kiss many times during the meal when their guests began clinking their glasses. Each time they kissed, everyone cheered.

When the meal was nearly finished, Roger stood. He straightened his jacket, smoothed his kilt, then turned, smiling at his friends, and cleared his throat. "I'd like tae say a word or two about the lovely couple before yeh. I met

David when he was in his twenties, and I was verra much down on ma luck. His father, Charles, God rest his soul, gave me a position and a second chance at livin'.

"Charles was a carin', thoughtful man who listened before he made decisions. He was a wealthy man but never acted as though he were. Charles Elliott was generous and unselfish; I feel blessed to have known him.

"David has never once acted superior around me either, even though I was just the family's handyman and driver. He has always been respectful and kind toward me, and I've wanted tae thank him for that for a verra long time." Roger raised his glass toward him in salute, and David returned the gesture.

"Et may no' be appropriate tae bring this up at yer weddin', mate, but please hear me out. Erin, I must ask for your forbearance as well. I remember when David sat on the sitting room sofa, convinced he was in love with a supermodel and wanted tae get married. He was nearly bouncing off the walls, but his father knew better. Charles took David aside and warned him that it would be a huge mistake, but being young, and... excuse me for sayin et, foolish, he married her anaway.

"Whilst it's true, she gave him four of the most delightful children I've ever met, she was no' the woman David Elliott was meant tae be with. I reckon it was pure stubbornness and a desire to prove his father wrong that kept them together, but ach, I digress. I won't go on about her.

"What I mean tae say is that between the two of yeh, David and Erin, yeh equal one Charles Elliott. I know beyond a shadow of a doubt that he, yer father, would've loved Erin dearly and would've blessed this marriage wholeheartedly. You were made for each other, and I'm blessed tae know yeh as ma friends, and I think of yeh as kin." The guests clapped, and some said, 'here-here,' but Roger wasn't quite done yet.

"One final thing before I sit and wipe ma brow. Erin, yeh are the light in our lives. We didn't ken how dark and dreich our lives had become, livin' every day, one after the other. Then you showed up and made us remember sunny days and warm weather. We've all been in love with yeh at one time or another, maself included," he said and blushed dark red.

"Also, because of you, I found ma woman, Tilly, the joy of ma life. If you and David hadn't encouraged me, I'd never have thought tae register, or I'd have chickened out and canceled my appointment. I... we have so many reasons tae thank God for bringing yeh intae our lives, Erin. Congratulations on yer blessed union! Tae the Bride and Bridegroom!" he said and raised his glass in a toast.

Everyone followed his lead, repeating his words. David whispered, "Thank yeh."

Erin blew him a kiss and said a quiet, "Thank you, Roger," as he sat in his chair again.

David stood, and the room was silent once more. He lifted his glass and looked at Erin, who was smiling at him. "On behalf of maself and ma wife, we'd like tae thank you, Frank, for traveling so far with yer lovely wife Liz. Thank you, Nick and Lily, for comin' so far and tae Lily, for attendin' tae ma wife's needs today. Thank you all for comin' tae celebrate our union with us today. To the rest of yeh, thank you for yer gifts and well wishes; we're blessed tae have yeh in our lives.

"Above all, I must thank ma new parents-in-law for their blessin' tae marry their daughter. I ken et's a bit old fashioned and seein' that neither of us lived with our parents before we wed, et may have been unnecessary, but havin' their permission was important tae me. I'd also like tae thank ma Mum and her partner Millie for makin' this day so verra special.

"Thank yeh for the use of yer home and for the food. I reckon ye'll be worn out come tomorrow, Millie, but you have our heartfelt thanks! Also, thank you both for acceptin' ma darlin' Erin as yeh have. Ye've made her part of the family, and I ken how much yeh love her. What's not tae love, right?" he said, and Roger raised his glass.

"Hear, hear!" he said, and several others repeated the same thing after him.

"Next, we'd like tae thank Erin's Matron of Honor Lily and our lovely bridesmaid Rosie for everathin' ye've done tae help her. A toast tae the bride's wedding party! *Slàinte mhath!*" he said, holding up his glass. Everyone repeated after him and took a drink from their crystal stemware. "One more thing before I'm finished blatherin'. Erin, please stand."

Erin stood and took his hand, looking into his eyes. "Erin, ma love, thank you for takin' me as yer husband and for acceptin' ma children as yer own.

Ye're one of a kind, and I became the luckiest man on earth today when yeh said I do."

Erin shook her head, trying not to cry again, but it wasn't working, and several tears fell down her cheeks. He placed his hands on either side of her face, bent over, and kissed her passionately, to much applause. "Oh, David, I can't believe I'm here. I can't believe you want me as your wife and the mother of your children, but I'm so glad you do. Thank you for loving me, trusting me, and to all of you for accepting me... us... as a couple, and thank you, children, for wanting me as your mom. You fill my life with joy, and I don't ever want to live without you. I think we make a good couple, since when you said, 'I do,' you made *me* the luckiest *woman* in the world," she said and hugged her new husband.

Everyone stood and applauded, then the newlyweds sat, and Peter stood, holding several index cards and looking quite nervous. He took a deep breath and let it out slowly, then he smiled at his dad and new mum. "Being Best Man, I'm meant to respond on behalf of the attendants. I'll get to that, but first, I'd like to say a few words to my father and his bride, my new mum.

"Dad, I've spent much of my life not knowing who you were and being resentful about it. I've recently learned that there were reasons behind that, which you didn't know about and... well, I'd like to tell you that now that I'm learning who you are and have spent more time with you, I... well, I really like who you are.

"I believe Erin has helped us all become closer. I see how you are with her and how much you love her, and it makes me want what you have as well. You've become a good example of how to treat the people you love.

"Erin, as you know, we didn't have a good example in our mother; however, now we do, and I couldn't be more chuffed about it. You've a way of helping me to calm down and seem to know what I need even when I don't. I know I can come to you about anything, and you'll listen and care about whatever it is. I'm proud to call you Mum, and I know my siblings feel the same as I do." The other three children nodded and smiled at her, confirming their brother's statement.

"So, now I'll say that your attendants all feel blessed to have been part of your wedding party. We also wish to thank Erin's parents Frank and Liz

Wallace, my new grandparents. Also, my gran, Annis Elliott, for being here and for hosting and helping. Millie, I haven't forgotten you. You are the glue that holds this house together; we all know it well enough. You helped raise my dad, and so, in my book, you are just as much his parent as our gran is, so please raise your glasses 'to the health of all four parents.'"

"The health of all four parents!" everyone repeated. Erin saw that both Annis and Millie were in tears, which made her eyes well up again. Peter turned and shook his father's hand, then went around him to hug Erin.

"Peter, my darling son, that was the most beautiful toast I've ever heard! Thank you so much," she whispered in his ear.

"I meant every word, Mum," he said and kissed her cheek.

Frank Wallace wasn't one to be left out when it came to toasts, so he stood and got everyone's attention. "I have a confession to make," he said, and everyone stared wide-eyed at him, giving him their full attention. "I confess when I first met David Elliott, I thought that nothing good would come of the relationship between him and my daughter. I thought it was infatuation and that being a famous actor, she'd just get hurt in the end when things cooled off and they came to their senses, but I was completely wrong.

"These two people were made for each other, or I'm not an old Scottish/American fool, which my wife and daughter can both attest to. David Elliott has made my little girl the happiest and healthiest I've ever known her to be. He's also made us the most blessed grandparents ever, with the gift of his delightful children and the blessing of the child on the way, which we all thought was impossible.

"When Erin's mother and I learned what we'd done by taking Fertilis, we mourned her loss of health and wished, at times, that we'd not made the choice, as it subjected her to so much pain and misery. David Elliott is the silver lining in our grief, and I need to personally thank him for everything he's done for our baby girl." He walked up to David and shook his hand, then gave him a hug, complete with heavy pats on the back and the shaking of shoulders. Then he stood in front of his daughter, kissed her, and held her tightly as they both cried.

"Oh, Daddy, thank you for that. I love you!" she said in his ear.

"May I say something, please?" Lily said and stood.

"Of course!" Erin said, not believing she'd worked up the courage to do it.

"Umm, I'd like to... ask for—No, propose a toast to my best friend Erin Elliott and her husband David. I never imagined I'd be sitting here with... him... and his family, watching my best friend become the luckiest woman—" she said, and Nick cleared his throat, making everyone laugh. "Umm, the second luckiest woman ever.

"You're all so normal and welcoming. I... just want to say thank you for making Erin's... and David's, of course, but mostly Erin's day so beautiful. And... thank you, David, for... falling in love with her, and... for forgiving me for what I said at Margarita's, though it turned out to be true anyway, right?"

She'd lost most of the people there by that point and lost track of what she was doing. She sat and looked around as if wondering why everyone was so quiet and still looking at her. "Oh! Sorry. Public speaking was never my thing. Umm, where was I? Well, anyway, cheers!" she said. Her face was red, but everyone applauded.

"Well done, Lily. I love you," Erin leaned over and said.

"Aye, thank you, and yer quite welcome for all of it," David said.

"Shoot! Now I don't remember what I said," Lily said.

Finally, Annis stood, and everyone was silent. Erin was in awe of her ability to command a crowd without saying anything. She smiled, and Erin noticed that she also had dimples, like Daniel, though they weren't as prominent and blended in with her wrinkles.

"I'd like tae say a few words to and about this lovely couple. From the moment I met Erin, I knew there was somethin' special about her. When I saw how she and our David were with each other, I knew they were meant tae be. Then, when I observed her with the children, I knew she'd been sent by God Himself tae heal and restore that family.

"She's been through more than any woman should have tae endure and has risen from et stronger and with more grace than I believe any other woman I know would have done. I admire and love her dearly, as I ken all of us here do as well. Tae David and Erin Elliott! Long may they live as one," she said, and the room was silent, except for many sniffles and a few noses being blown.

When the guests were completely sure she was finished speaking, they all rose and held up their glasses.

"To David and Erin Elliott! Long may they live as one," they said in unison.

The dishes were being cleared away, and Erin had yet to see a cake, so she was a bit worried. However, it wasn't long before Francie wheeled out a table with the most beautiful cake she'd ever seen. It wasn't large since they didn't have many guests, but the detail of each forget-me-not was exquisite. The vines and delicate ribbons made of frosting looked real. "Francie! Ye've outdone yerself!" David said, and all Erin could do was cover her mouth and stare at it.

"It's more than I could have ever dreamed," she finally whispered and hugged her cook for a long time.

"Ach, noo, yer makin' too much of et, though I'm glad yeh like et, dear," she said with a genuine smile. "Go on and cut et."

"Where's the photographer?" Erin said.

"Ah'm here," he said, "and ma wife's right over there." He pointed with his lenses at his wife, who nodded, ready to take the photos while he took the video of the cake cutting.

"Wonderful; are you ready, David?"

"Aye, darling," he said with a mischievous smile.

"If you do, you'll regret it later tonight," she said.

"I wouldn't dream of mashing the cake onto yer face; why would yeh think that?" he said and laughed.

"Humph, I'm glad to hear it," she said.

The photographer posed them holding the knife whilst showing off their rings, and his wife took a few shots. Then Erin and David cut the cake together and pulled out the first slice. That layer was a white cake with pink filling. David laughed at Erin when she gave him a 'don't you dare' look and was a perfect gentleman when he placed a small bite into her mouth. The filling was whipped cream with fresh strawberries in it, and Erin rolled her eyes as she let the flavors burst in her mouth.

"Holy Moses, Francie! That's fabulous! What's the other layer?" Erin asked.

"Ye've the knife, give et a go," she said, smiling.

She and David acted like it was their first slice again and fed each other. This time it was chocolate with raspberry whipped cream, and Erin nearly started dancing, bouncing up and down on the balls of her feet. "Good night… Francie! That one is even better!" Erin said and then turned, getting everyone's attention. "Excuse me, friends, family, and esteemed guests. Due to extraordinary deliciousness, and the bride's selfishness, there will not be any cake for you. I apologize for any broken hearts and sweet teeth denied."

David's laughter rang out pure and sweet through the house. "Losh, I love yeh! You surprise me all the time. You make me look forward tae every day in anticipation of what ye'll do or say. I need yeh like I need the air I breathe and the sun that occasionally shines on this island," he said and fed her another bite of chocolate cake.

After the meal, everyone waited while the sitting room was cleared for the small reception dance. The rug had already been rolled up and taken away, and the band resumed their positions. The wedding may have been small, intimate, and private, but they would have a good time, no matter how few people were there to witness it. They had many of the same traditions as larger weddings, for instance, a lovely father-daughter dance, followed by the first dance of the married couple.

"I'm sorry it's not grander than this, darling," David said as they danced together slowly.

"I don't need grand, David, I need this. You and me and our family; I couldn't be more blessed and happy."

"Yer so different from… well, everaone I've known, outside ma family. I dinnae need grand either; all I need is you," he said and kissed her.

Everyone danced with everyone; even Liz got to dance with David more than once. Erin noticed near the end of the day that David was acting a bit peculiarly and then saw him nod to the small band. He took her hand and led her to the dance floor, then smiled down at her, looking nervous. "I've a surprise for yeh," he said and nodded to the musicians, who all nodded back.

They started playing something that Erin recognized but couldn't place right away. David handed her a note card with words on it, and she laughed as the band continued the opening bars of the song "I See the Light" from Disney's *Tangled* in a loop. She wasn't sure she'd be able to keep her composure and sing well, but when the song got to the beginning again, she began the first verse. When she sang, *'blinking in the starlight,'* tears sprang to her eyes. He *was* a *star*, and it just didn't seem real.

After the second verse and chorus, there was a break in the song that transitioned it into a different key. David smiled at her as he began to sing the third verse. She couldn't believe how appropriate the words were, and as he sang about living in a blur and not seeing things the way they were until she arrived, tears ran down both their cheeks.

At the next chorus, they sang together in harmony, and when the song was done, they stood looking at each other. Somehow, they kept it together until the band hit the final note, then all hell broke loose. Everyone was on their feet, applauding and crying.

Erin could feel the tears flowing down her face, running down her neck, and into the valley her cleavage made, but she didn't lose control. She stood staring at the man who'd been made for her and whose tears were falling onto the front of his stiffly starched dress shirt. She knew if she looked away from him at her friends and family, she wouldn't be able to take it and would start bawling, so she kept eye contact with him and waited for the commotion to die down. "I hope someone recorded that," she whispered.

"Aye," the photographer said with a smile.

That evening, before the limo came back for them, David sat Erin on a chair in the middle of the dance floor and made her giggle when he reached his hand under her skirt. Often, the act of removing the garter is all play, without true feelings of excitement. This time, she could feel his energy coursing through her, and it took quite a lot of effort to not start breathing heavily. She did turn red and was thankful for Millie's folding fan to create a breeze.

He inched his fingers up her calf, then her thigh, staring at her the whole time. No one saw what he did next under the privacy of her layered skirt, but when he kissed her, she longed for more. He smiled at the whoops and hollers he was getting before slowly pulling the elastic band, decorated with lace and silk, off her leg.

Privately, she was embarrassed at how large it was, especially since it had stretched out by the time he took it off, but she didn't say anything. David made a hilarious show of spinning it on his first finger as though he'd won a prize. He threw it to the single men, including his three sons. Roger caught it and blushed painfully red, first because everyone, especially Tilly, was watching him intently and second because of where the garter had just been.

Next, Erin threw her bouquet to the unmarried women, just for fun, including Annis and Millie, who had to be dragged onto the dance floor. Annis caught it, and both she and Millie blushed. After that, Annis and Roger danced together until halfway through the song, then Tilly and Millie came out to cut in and finish the dance. The children seemed to have a marvelous time as well. They danced with each other, with David and Erin, and with anyone else who was willing.

Chapter Forty-Six

OLD TOWN HONEYMOON

At the end of the day, Mr. and Mrs. Elliott hugged everyone as they left Owlgate and headed for the waiting limousine. Erin didn't know where they were going, but that didn't matter to her. She got into the back with her husband and snogged him for a good two minutes before noticing two travel cases on the opposite seats, one for each of them. "Ooh, where are we going? Will you make love to me when we get there? Will you make love to me now?" she whispered, touching his bare leg and inching her hand under his kilt, closer to his private bits.

"We dinnae have time now, love," he said laughing. "That tickles!"

"Good, maybe you deserve it after what you did under my dress earlier. I know you need this—" She lifted his kilt and knelt before him, taking his limp cock into her mouth.

It soon woke up, and he moaned. Then he tried to get her to stop. "Ach, Erin! Dinnae—Oh, God… there's not enough time for—Et won't go down in time if yeh dinnae stop… now! Erin!" He pushed her away by her shoulders, though she resisted.

"You're no fun! Where are we going?" she said and straddled him on the seat, feeling his bared cock against her lacy panties.

"Ach, Losh, Erin! Yer makin' me radge, woman."

"How? I don't understand," she said and rocked herself against him, wanting to move her underwear to the side and slide him into her, but she wouldn't do that in the limo.

"Erin, stop!" he whispered in her ear and held her hips stationary. He was breathing heavily and closed his eyes.

"Where are we going?" she asked, but he didn't respond, so she tried to rock her hips, but his eyes grew large, and he shook his head. She saw sweat beading up on his forehead, and his eyes fluttered slightly as he closed them.

"Dinnae... move!" He sat beneath her, panting and frowning. The car stopped, as it had done several times for traffic lights and pedestrians, but when they heard the driver's door open, she saw genuine panic in David's eyes. "Oh, God! Get off me now," he said and tried to cover himself with his kilt, but he couldn't hide his erection. He gently lay his sporran over it and moved very slowly to the door just as the driver opened it.

Erin felt awful; she knew he was worried and self-conscious, and if a fan saw his condition, or worse, a tabloid photographer, things could get bad. He held out his hand to help her, then thanked the driver, who took the two suitcases out of the trunk and brought them into the hotel.

She gasped when she turned and saw Edinburgh Castle behind them, then followed David into a very old building. She saw their bags, which the driver had set on the floor in front of the check-in desk. "I'm sorry, David, really, I am!" she whispered as they walked slowly up to the counter.

"Welcome, Mr. Elliott!" The man behind the counter said warmly. "And is this your new bride?" he said with the faintest French accent.

"Yes, this is Mrs. Erin Elliott," he said and managed a semi-convincing smile. She could tell he was, if not in pain, at least in extreme discomfort, both physically and socially at the moment, and she made a mental note to never do anything like that again.

"We are pleased to host you for your honeymoon and hope you will enjoy your stay with us," The middle-aged man said and held out an old key with a large tassel. David nodded at Erin, so the man, whose name tag read 'Pierre,' handed it to her.

"Thank you, Pierre," she said.

"You are quite welcome, madame."

"What is this place?" she asked David as they were led back outside by the concierge, down Jollies Close, to another building where they had to climb a narrow spiral staircase that led to their rooms.

"Et's the Witchery by the Castle, and yer gonna love et."

"I already do," she said, looking around her at the luxurious yet dark decor. *It's like the Hogwarts dormitories*, she thought. They stepped into an entry with walls covered in a rich wallpaper and a staircase with a velvet rope banister. They led to a water closet and the bedroom door, which looked like a bookcase.

They opened the door to their room, and Erin gasped. "Holy Moses! This can't be for real!" The room was dark yet cozy. The main lights were wall sconces and two narrow windows that looked out on the Royal Mile. She entered the room and stepped onto the dark wooden floors covered with beautiful area rugs, then she looked up. The ceiling was overlaid with a holly leaf patterned wallpaper.

As they were given a tour of the rooms, she noticed a small, round dining table with a white tablecloth under a small, round, metal chandelier. Then she saw an oddly shaped sofa that appeared to be quite comfortable, but the crème de la crème was the bed.

The wooden headboard was one of the most ornate and beautiful things she'd ever seen. It looked like it had been taken out of a castle or even a cathedral, with fabric valances and lights on a delicate, carved arm that swung out for reading. The bedding was luxurious, with copious amounts of pillows on top. "David!" she said but couldn't finish.

"The television is here," Pierre said while Erin flipped through a guestbook on an old wooden desk. He pressed a button on an upholstered box at the foot of the bed, and the lid slowly rose, revealing a shiny, glass screen. "There are old guestbooks on the windowsill, madame if you are interested. There have been many unique guests who have stayed with us. Here is a hidden door leading to the closet and another one that leads to the kitchen."

"Kitchen? Are you planning to cook for me?" Erin said to David and laughed.

"Stranger things have been known to happen."

As she followed Pierre and David, Erin noticed a fireplace with old books on the mantle and carved wooden accents on the walls. She nearly ran into David as he and Pierre stood before a bookcase. "This is your ensuite bathroom," Pierre said and pushed on the wall. A panel swung open, revealing a room that looked like a library.

The walls were covered with faux book spines, and there was a deep, standalone bathtub with a red and white striped wraparound curtain. She stepped up to another fireplace and shook her head. "This is unbelievable! I wish our whole house was like this!" she said, and David laughed.

"Thank you for the tour, Pierre. I'm sure our stay will be lovely," David said and handed him a tip.

"You are quite welcome, monsieur. If you need anything, please do not hesitate to ring the desk, and we will do our best to accommodate you and your lovely bride," the man said and stepped out the door.

Before Erin could take another breath, David was pulling her by the hand to the bed. "Now ye'll pay for what yeh did tae me in the limo, Erin," he said and pressed her against the edge of the high mattress.

"Is that so?"

"Aye, and I reckon yer punishment should start now." He took his jacket off and let it fall to the floor, then he began unbuttoning his shirt.

"What are yeh doin'? I'm a married woman now! I cannae be intimate with yeh, no matter how sexy you are in yer kilt," she said in a poor Scotch accent.

"Ach, woman, and what kind of husband leaves his virile, young bride alone in a city such as this tae fend fer herself?"

"Ach, laddie, I'm no' young anamore, but I'll allow yeh tae have a wee feel of what you'll be missing out on," she said and saw the mischief in his eyes.

"Well, now, yeh may jest change yer mind when *you* feel this," he said and took off his belt and sporran. He lifted her hand and pressed it against his tartan-covered erection.

"Ach, I admit," she said breathlessly, "ye're wearin' down ma resolve."

"Good," he said and put his hand up her skirt. He ran his finger under the edge of her undies and moved them to the side, then he spread her lips and caressed her clitoris, making her moan. "How about now?"

"Ach, aye! Aye, take me!" she gasped, feeling herself on the edge of a delicious orgasm. "Oh, yes, David!"

"Get up on the bed," he said and smiled at her attempts to heave herself up.

"I… need… help," she said, laughing. She ultimately had to crawl up onto it and lay on her back. He pulled down her underwear and then began kissing her thighs. She felt his fingers rub her and then enter her. Next, she felt his hot breath and then his wet, rough tongue on her. "Yes! Don't stop!" The now familiar sensation of climax rolled over her as his fingers thrust. "Make love to me, husband."

"It will be my pleasure, wife," he said and pulled her to the edge of the mattress. He ran the head of his hard cock over her until he was wet enough to enter and then moaned as he did. "Do you realize I nearly made a mess in the limo? All I could think of was that ye'd move yer panties, I'd slide into you, and that would be it. I reckon I've never needed more self-control."

"Yeah, about that, I'm sorry, David! I was wrong—" she began, but he covered her mouth with his hand and doubled his efforts.

"I'll never forget et, Erin. That was the sexiest thing, and—" He closed his eyes and moaned. Erin could feel his balls clenching and his cock pulsing inside her. "You are so verra sexy, and I forget how traditional conventions don't seem to apply to you. You often do the verra thing I've not considered and catch me off ma guard. Et's intoxicating, and I never want you tae stop, ever, okay?"

"Oh, okay. I thought you were mad at me," she said as he rolled off her, and she turned over to snuggle up to him.

"Ach, aye, I was, but only because I wasn't prepared, though that's the best part of who yeh are. I want to live the rest of ma life unprepared for the outrageous things you come up with, and when I die, I'll be a happy, well-fulfilled man."

"Well, if you put it that way, it's a deal. This has been, I'd say, the second-best day of my whole life," she said and sighed.

"Second-best?"

"Aye, the first best was the day I met you, of course." She could feel his chest move with his light laughter.

"Aye, darling, and I feel exactly the same."

Erin closed her eyes and woke to David getting out of bed. Now that her heat source was removed, she shivered in the chilly room. *There must be a thermostat in here somewhere,* she thought. "David?"

"Aye," she heard from the bathroom.

"Can you turn up the heat?"

"Aye, one moment."

She heard him wandering around the suite, so she got up to use the bathroom. As she washed her hands, she saw that her hair was a mess, and her makeup had been mostly rubbed or cried off by then. "Ugg," she said and stepped out into the amazing bedroom where her husband, wearing only a kilt turned to look at her.

"Ugg?" he said and went to her.

"Yeah, I just looked in the mirror."

"Ach, so the looking glass was so jealous of yer beauty et spoke?"

She rolled her eyes and then smiled. "Yeah, something like that. I'm hungry, but I really don't wanna leave our room," she said.

"Is that so? Well then, what say you to room service, and then I'll draw you a bath?"

"Room service and a bath would be nice, says I. Or how about, I say! Room service and a bath would be jolly good fun!" she said and laughed at herself.

That night, after supper, David filled the bathtub and helped Erin climb into it. He watched as she carefully descended into the warm water. Having only filled it about half-full, the very top of her belly was above the waterline. "Ye're sae bonnie, love," he said and wet the fluffy washcloth he'd taken off the heating rack near the tub.

"Aren't you going to join me?" she asked.

"Not just yet. First, I'd like tae bathe yeh."

"Bathe me? Ooh, that sounds nice."

"Aye," he said and lathered the cloth with soap. He began with her neck and shoulders. She laughed when he lifted each arm and washed her armpits, then he worked his way down her pale, plump arms. He kissed each of her fingers and then washed them individually. "Slide down a bit."

Her large breasts weren't quite floating, as the water wasn't deep enough. She slid herself down until all he could see, besides her head, were her erect nipples on the surface. "How's that?"

"Hmmm," he said and gently touched each one with his soapy pointer finger, leaving a few small bubbles behind. Next, he blew little puffs of air onto them, which made them rise even higher.

She shivered and dunked them into the warm water. "That's cold!" she said, then let them rise to the surface again.

He leaned over the tub and kissed the breast closest to him, then he gently sucked it into his mouth while using the washcloth to wash the other one. Then he stood, went to the other side of the tub, and did the same thing again. He asked her to sit forward and washed her back, then she sat back, and he washed her belly. The baby kicked him once but then seemed to relax as he rubbed what he assumed was its back. "It likes that, eh?"

"Aye, and so do I, but there's another place I would enjoy much more," she said and smiled at him.

"I reckon so, but yeh must be patient, hen." He decided to change tactics and build the anticipation by moving to the far end of the tub. He reached in and took out one of her feet.

She squirmed and wiggled as he washed between each toe. "Stop! That... tickles!"

He ignored her pleas and continued with the other foot, then he washed each leg up to her knees. Her skin was smooth and soft, freshly shaven. "How'd yeh manage that?" he asked. She'd told him she wasn't going to shave anymore, not until after the baby was born since she wasn't bendy enough to do it.

She laughed and blushed. "I... asked Lily to help me. She was as timid as... I don't know what, worried she'd cut me, but she managed to do it without any blood spilled. Do you like it?"

"Aye, and I also like the thought of her doin' et to yeh if I'm honest."

She splashed him and then laughed as he stood, water running down his bare chest and dripping off his dark wavy chest hair. Her gaze landed on his erection, and her eyebrows shot up. "Well then, I guess you weren't kidding," she said and reached out to touch it.

He narrowed his eyes and then smiled as he stepped into the tub with her. The water rose as he sat at her feet, having to wrangle his legs around hers. "Now, where was I? Ah, yes, the best bits." After soaping up the flannel again, he ran it down her vulnerable inner thigh and then up the other side.

"Oh, David, please!" she said, breathing heavier.

"Ach, a'right, have it your way." He grinned, took a deep breath, then plunged his whole head into the tub, splashing water onto the floor when he did. He pulled her up a bit by the ass, as he couldn't bend that far in half, but then he began kissing her and flicking her clit with his tongue. Air bubbles ascended as he blew some of his reserve over her sensitive skin. When his breath was gone, he emerged with a smile and watched her with her mouth open, panting.

"Good night nurse, David! Do it again!" she said and closed her eyes.

"A'right, once more, but then I'm going to make love to you."

"Okay, but let's go to the bed; it'll be more comfortable."

"A'right," he said and after fulfilling her request, managed to get out of the tub. He then helped her out and dried her off.

That night, as David made love to her, Erin cried. Her life would be forever changed, and it just didn't seem possible for any of it to be real. "David?"

"Aye?" he said and slowly thrust into her.

"Please… tell me… am I dreaming, or is this real?"

"Which part? Be more specific," he said a bit breathlessly. They gazed into each other's eyes, and he smiled at her.

"Well, all of it, I guess. You, me, all of it."

"Aye, ma love, et's all real. Ye're ma wife and—Ach, there it is," he said and began moving faster.

"Oh, oh, yes!" she whispered, and they both reached climax together. "I don't ever want to be without you, okay?"

"Aye, and I never want tae be without you, forever. I ken we already vowed our lives to each other, but I'll not ever forsake yeh, Erin. You can count on me tae be here for you and our family. Even if I am away filming, I'll bring yeh with me, or I'll not be gone for long—Ach, I'm blatherin', but yeh ken what I'm saying, right?" he said and finally rolled off her.

"Aye, I ken what you're saying." She rolled onto her side and snuggled up close to him. He smelled so good, she just wanted to sniff him. "I admit," she began as she ran her fingers through his chest hair and then twirled it in her fingers, "I don't look forward to you being away for work, though I know it's going to happen. I guess that makes me too needy, but I guess I am."

"As I said, I'll bring yeh with me. We'll have adventures on set together," he said, sounding like he was only half awake.

"Aye, every day is the best adventure with you," she whispered, then inhaled his scent as deeply as she could.

Chapter Forty-Seven

HARSH REALITY

What is—hey— "Hey! Oww! That... hurts!" Erin said, feeling a hand between her legs. It wasn't like David to be so rough. "Stop! That—"

"Shut it!" he said and continued roughly groping at her. He was breathing heavily, making an unusual wheezing noise she'd never heard from him before, so she was confused. Next, he grabbed his cock and was trying to enter her, not being gentle with it, either.

"David, that hurts! Why are you—"

"What did yeh jest say?" He grabbed a large fist full of hair and pulled it toward him.

She gasped, and tears sprang to her eyes. "I said it hurts!"

"No, what did yeh call me?" he whispered in a way that made her shiver.

"What? I... called you David—That's—" she began, but he pulled harder on her hair so that she could see his face.

"Yeh fuckin' cunt! Jest for that I'm goin' next door," he said and violently pushed her away.

She tried to stay as still as she could, hoping he'd go away and leave her alone. The bedding reeked of sweat, body odor, and piss. She wanted to flee, but he was still in the room, so she didn't move.

"Yer no' gonnae beg me tae stay?" he said as he put on his tracksuit. "Get up, cunt; ye're meant tae feed the bairns."

She could hear him light a cigarette, and then he was on top of her again, pulling her hair, the ashes of his fag falling onto her forehead. "Okay! Just… get off me," she said.

He pushed her head forward and got off the bed, then he opened the bedroom door. "Ye'd best be ready for me later, yeh ken what I'm sayin'? And if yeh *ever* call me David again, *I'll kill yeh.*"

She nodded and sat up, wanting to vomit. Suddenly, three children, aged six and under, came into the room. Realizing she was naked, she covered herself with the duvet, which was stained with who knows what; some of it looked like vomit.

"Mummy," the oldest-looking boy said. "We're hungry, and Annie's crying. Owen's hiding in the cupboard, and John's bleeding."

"What? Okay, let me get dressed, and I'll be right out," she said, and the children left, closing the door behind them. She stood and saw that she was pregnant, very pregnant, and cried when she looked around her at the filthy room she'd woken up in.

All she could find to wear were dirty, stretched-out yoga pants that she had to wear under her belly and a smelly, stained, cut-off t-shirt that said TENNENT'S across her breasts with a bright-red, block letter T above it. She looked in the small mirror that hung on the wall by the door and didn't even recognize herself. Her hair was bleached badly, and one of her teeth was chipped in the front. She had an ugly, cheap ring on her left hand, and the only shoes she could find were Pound Saver flip-flops with dirt-encrusted pineapples on them.

"John's bleeding," returned to her memory, and she rushed to help whomever John was. As she stepped into the hallway, she almost turned back. There were filthy toys, dirty clothes, soiled diapers, and dishes with petrified fish fingers and mushy peas everywhere she looked.

She was close to hyperventilating, but John was bleeding, so she went to the kitchen and saw a puddle of red liquid spreading over the floor, starting from behind the island, and she screamed. A boy, no more than a year and a half old, crawled through the puddle and began splashing in it.

"John?" she said, and he looked up at her. She walked around the island and saw a packet of diet drink powder open on the floor and a half empty-bottle of water dripping off the edge of the countertop. A baby started screaming in another room, so she went in search of it. She found it in a crib, surrounded by what looked like rags, then she smelled the poop.

The wall, bedding, and baby were covered in shit, and she didn't know what to do. Children were crying and saying they were hungry, John was drenched with red juice, and this baby, who she couldn't remember the name of, was encrusted in poo. She didn't have a choice and stepped into the room, nearly puking from the smell.

She stripped the sodden diaper off the child, rushed to the bathroom, and set the baby in the filthy bathtub. Then, finding a washcloth that didn't look quite as nasty as the rest of them, she ran warm water from the tap to wet it. There was a dried-up, dirt-encrusted sliver of a bar of soap she had to pry off the olive-green bottom of the tub. She wet it and began washing the baby as the other children screamed.

The older children came in and began fighting. "Stop!" she yelled. "Where's your dad?"

"Next door with Lydia," the boy, who looked a lot like David, or a very young Peter, said.

"What's his name?" she asked.

"Who's name?"

"Your dad's name," she said, feeling stupid.

"Daddy," said a girl of about four, who had eyes like hers and wavy brown hair, though it was matted and stuck to the side of her head. She also looked a lot like David, and maybe Annis as well.

"His real name."

"Oh, his name's Bran. You know that, Mummy! You're being silly!"

"Do we have any cereal?" she asked, wanting to cry and scream and run away.

"No. We have Clover spread and oil in the fridge," the boy said. Then there was a noise that terrified the children. It was the door to the flat opening and closing.

"*What the fuck is going on! Where's your mum, that fucking cunt?*" she heard Bran say, and she was also frightened. The children scattered, and then Bran was standing over her. She had just finished washing the baby and looked over her shoulder. He glared at her with bloodshot eyes. "What the fuck is this?" he said and then hauled off and hit the back of her head, making her forehead bump into the baby's teeth.

The baby wailed, and she cried, feeling blood run down the bridge of her nose. "She was covered in shit, Bran! Did you want me to leave her like that? Is she bleeding, or am I?" she said, and stood too quickly. She thrust the baby into his arms, heard the whooshing, saw the stars, and then everything went peacefully black.

"*Erin? Are you a'right?*" She heard and covered her head protectively as she waited for the pain of her forehead to flare up or another blow to it. "Woah! What's wrong? Yer actin' as though yer expectin' a thrashin'. You were talkin' in yer sleep; somethin' about… Bran and a baby covered in poo."

She lifted her head and held him tightly. "Oh, David! Oh, God! I had the worst, most realistic dream!"

"Obviously."

"I was married to Bran, and we lived in a council flat." She told him what Bran had been trying to do to her and that he'd gotten angry when she'd called him David. "It was filthy, David, everything was—I was pregnant and looked like white trash. There were so many children!"

"Wow! That does sound awful."

"That's not even half of it!" She explained how the flat was full of garbage, and one of the babies was supposed to be bleeding, but it was a drink mix. Then she told him about the baby in the crib, covered in shit. "They were all crying, wanting food, but I had to clean the poo baby, and the older ones said there wasn't any food in the house. Bran had gone to some other woman's flat, and I was alone. I'd just finished washing the baby when he came back and knocked me and the baby's heads together."

"That's dreadful!"

"I wanted to escape, but the children needed care. I stood and handed the baby to Bran before I fainted and ended up here again. I don't ever want to fall asleep again! Not till I have our baby! How long will that be?"

"Too long, darling," he said compassionately.

"What if—What if this is the dream and I don't wake up from what I *think* is a dream? If—David—I'd... kill myself if that happened!" she said passionately and cried even harder.

"Now, now, this is your reality, darling. Don't worry, love, I'm sure that as soon as you give birth, everathin' will return tae normal.

"I don't want to go back to being married to Bran again! Good thing he gave up trying to—You weren't... touching me, were you?"

"Not this time, darling," he said and stroked her hair.

"Okay, good. Just don't... okay... not while I'm sleeping, anyway," she said and kissed his chest.

"A'right," he said and held her until they both fell back asleep.

That beeping is getting on my nerves! Erin thought and tried to roll over.

"Don't move, honey, it'll be over soon," she heard Todd's voice say.

She tried to open her eyes, but they were so heavy. "What do you mean? What will be over soon? Where's David?"

"Ignore her; she has this delusion that she's married to David Elliott," he said, and she heard someone in the room laugh.

"I'm not delusional, Todd! I am married to David Elliott, and I'm pregnant with his baby! I know you're wrong, so laugh all you want!" Suddenly she felt a horrible pain, a terrible pinching inside her. "Oww! What's that? That hurts!"

"Just relax, Mrs. March," an unfamiliar voice said. "We are extracting the fetus now. It will only hurt for—"

"What? Extracting the fetus? What are you talking about? I don't want you to extract anything! David! David, help me!" she called out, but all she could do was whisper.

"Put her under again," a voice said, and then she felt an oxygen mask being placed over her face.

"But... I don't... wan—"

Erin woke, gasping for air in a place she didn't recognize. She couldn't place any familiar sounds or smells, and it was very dark in the room. Somewhere nearby, she heard a toilet flush and then heard footsteps on a creaky floor coming closer.

She fought off the urge to panic and sat up on the side of the bed. Her feet felt the cool, smooth, wooden floorboards, and she couldn't figure out where she might be. Everywhere she'd lived in the last few years had been carpeted, or there was an area rug on the floor next to the bed.

"Are yeh a'right, love?" she heard. It was David, and her heart leapt.

She felt him get into the bed, so she turned toward his voice, but she was hindered by her large belly. "Oh, David! Oh, my love! Oh, please hold me! Are you really here, or am I dreaming again?" she said and flung herself on the bed toward him the best she could at eight months pregnant. She straddled him, attacking him with kisses and felt his face, then she reached around above his head, trying to find a lamp to turn on.

"What... Erin, what are yeh doin'? Yer smotherin' me!" he said, sounding shocked by her sudden outburst.

"I need to see you; where's the lamp? Where are we? I don't recognize anything!" she said, and he grabbed her jutting hand.

"The lamp is... wait... there's a switch—What is all this about?" he said as she scrambled off him and felt for a lamp on the other side of the bed.

She finally found it and pulled the small chain to turn it on, but nothing happened except it fell on the floor. Next thing she knew, the light on David's side of the bed was on, and she clambered back to him and stared at her husband. "Oh, David, please tell me you love me and that it's really you! Wait... where in the hell are we?" she asked, finally able to look around her.

"I love yeh, though ye're mad, and aye, et's me; I'm not goin' anawhere, remember? We're in a hotel on our honeymoon, darling. What's goin' on with yeh? Are yeh feelin' a'right? Yeh look a bit peely-wally, now that I can see yeh," he said and touched her face. "Did you have another dream? Who were yeh married to this time, Roger or Martin?" he asked, teasing.

"It's not funny," she said and buried her face in his neck. "Oh, David, just stay awake with me now, please?"

"A'right, ma love, I'm sorry. I reckon et's not funny at all. I have an idea of what we can do to stay awake," he said and smiled at her.

She couldn't help but smile back at him. "Yes, I'd like that! Please make love to me."

"As you wish, Mrs. Elliott," he said and pulled her toward him.

The way he said her new name made her feel warm and fuzzy all over. "I already like being your wife."

Chapter Forty-Eight

EXPLORING EDINBURGH

They stayed at the Witchery for five nights, and because of his disguise, they were able to explore the city together, though they usually ventured out at night. Princes Street was abuzz with Christmas and New Year activities, including shopping, food, and amusement rides. On the second night, after bundling up, though it wasn't nearly as cold there as it usually was in Wisconsin, they walked through the streets and closes of the Old Town and crossed Waverly Bridge to the New Town.

They found a lovely old cemetery and spent over an hour there reading old headstones. As they were headed back toward the Princes Street Gardens, in front of the Balmoral Hotel, Erin was a few steps in front of David. She reached her hand back, expecting him to take it, but nothing happened. Turning around, she saw that David wasn't there. Instead, there was an older man with a kind face, looking smart in his tweedy suit.

He looked at her hand and then up at her with a humorous smile. "Ach, I'll hold yer hand for you," he said with a rich, Scottish accent and reached out to her.

She laughed, took the stranger's hand, and said, "I'll hold yours instead." They continued, hand in hand, for several paces, then she let go and thanked him. He walked away into the crowd, and then she saw David. He had somehow managed to get ahead of her without her noticing; he was facing her and laughing.

"Well, that doesn't happen evera day, does et?" he said.

"Aye… that was amazing! I'll never forget it!"

"Only you, ma love, only you would do somethin' like that. I reckon he'll never forget et either."

At the Princes Street Gardens, they rode the Big Wheel, a large Ferris wheel, and the Star Flyer, which had spinning, swinging chairs, similar to Erin's favorite ride at Bay Beach. They drank delicious hot drinking chocolate and ate loads of junk food.

On the third night, they ventured deeper into the Old Town, losing themselves in the winding roads. They ate haggis, neeps, and tatties at the Haggis Box then stopped at Mimi's for a bit of pastry.

On the fourth day, they wandered around, finding galleries and shops to waste time in. After a much-needed nap at the hotel, they headed back out, looking for more urban adventures. When they found themselves on Victoria Street, Erin suggested they visit Tim at John Kay's, or what she called 'the curiosity shop.'

"Aye, it would be nice tae catch up," David said and followed her up the winding street with its colorful storefronts. They opened the door, but a woman was sitting at the register, reading a book.

Erin approached her, and she looked up. "Hello, Sara," she said, reading her name tag. "Do you know if Tim is working this weekend?"

"No, he won't be here, sorry," she said.

"Okay, thanks," Erin said and turned to leave.

"He'll be at the Tron location."

"The what?" Erin asked.

"Tron Kirk; et's not far from here," David said, and the woman gasped.

She looked at the poster he'd signed earlier that year and stood. "You're… him, aren't you?" she said and pointed to the tall, cardboard cutout of him wearing a kilt next to a display of *Future Explorations* merchandise.

"Aye," he said and agreed to give her his autograph and allowed her to take a selfie.

"Were you planning to visit Tim today?" she asked.

"We were hoping to," Erin said.

"We close in…" She looked at her watch and said, "half an hour." Erin's face must've shown her disappointment because the woman cocked her head to the side and smiled. "Here is what I'll do; I will call him and tell him to leave the doors unlocked for a little while. Should I tell him who you are or that you're looking for something we don't have here?"

"Oh, Sara, that's great! Please don't tell him it's us. I'd like to surprise him," Erin said. "Thanks so much!"

They left the shop, and she followed David to a beautiful old church. It wasn't far, but Erin was out of breath with excitement as they climbed the old stone steps to the doors. The sign had been flipped to say, "CLOSED," but when David tried it, the door opened.

The shop only took up a portion of the enormous room, and the vaulted and beamed ceiling rose high above them. A gigantic stained-glass window towered, dark against the night sky over their heads. The portioned-off room was filled with similar curiosities as the other store; however, in that location, a large zeppelin and many hot-air balloons hung at far greater heights, making it seem all the more amazing and surreal. "Hello?" Erin called out, not seeing or hearing anyone.

"*Hallo, ah'm over here,*" they heard Tim say from the far end of the shop, though he was still out of sight.

"Tim… or should I say, Marco?"

They heard a jolly laugh and then, "Polo!"

"Marco," she said and headed toward the sound of his voice. David was shaking his head but laughing along with them.

"Polo!" Tim said and stepped out from behind a tall bookshelf.

"Tim!" Erin said and went to him. She wrapped her arms around his neck and gave him the best hug she could with her belly sticking out as far as it was.

"Ach, Erin!" he said and looked down at it, his eyes wide with surprise.

"Aye, I know! Isn't it crazy!"

"Aye, and beautiful! Et's sae good tae see yous! Hallo…" He hesitated and his cheeks turned pink as he finished with, "David."

David laughed and held out his hand for a handshake. "Hello, Tim; I hope we're not keeping you from anything," he said.

Tim laughed as he shook *David Elliott's* hand. "Not likely! Anaway, ah'd rather be surprised by a visit from the two of yous than nearly anathin' else ah can think of. What brings you out so late? Well, ah reckon et's no' tha' late, and ah reckon et's none of ma business—" he floundered, then his eyes grew wide. "Ach, ah'm sae sorry ah couldnae come tae yer weddin'! Ah was chuffed tae bits when I received your invite but—"

"Oh, Tim, no worries. We missed you, but we haven't come to scold you," Erin said and laughed. "We're on our honeymoon and decided that seeing our dear friend would warm our hearts." Tim's face turned bright red, then it seemed to shrivel up a bit. He put his finger up and then turned away from them. "Tim? What's wrong?" She looked at David, but he shrugged.

After a moment, Tim turned to face them and sniffed. Erin could see that his eyes were a bit bloodshot and moist. "Sorry, but... yeh caught me off ma guard. Ah'm touched ye'd think of me." He smiled at her and rolled his eyes. "Ah'm a grown baby, I ken et."

"Good thing I like babies," Erin said and patted her belly. "Why don't you come along with us as we explore? Do you mind, David?"

"Dinnae mind at all. Actually, I was about tae ask the verra same thing."

Tim's eyes grew large, then he looked around him at the store. "Ach, I'd love tae, but I'm meant tae close up—"

"Don't be silly, baby Tim; we'll wait for you and even help if we can. And before you make another excuse—"

"Erin," David said.

"Just hear me out. Before you try to get out of it, I'm officially kidnapping you. Well, after you close and all that stuff, of course. I'm not an unreasonable kidnapper, after all. I'll start facing everything, so chop, chop."

"Facing everything?" David said, giving her a confused look.

"It's retail jargon for making sure everything on the shelves is facing out and pulled forward. It also involves putting things back on the shelf it's meant to go on or whatever. Just do what I do," she said and tidied up a display of hand lotions and soap.

The two of them spent the next fifteen minutes making sure everything was just so while Tim counted the till and put the money in the office safe located behind the counter area. It was dark outside, and with all the lights low, everything inside the church was a bit eerie.

Erin screamed when a stranded bird fluttered across the vaulted ceiling. Tim laughed and put his hand on her shoulder. "That happens to me all the time! I sound like a bloomin' bird maself, though you beat me to et tonight."

"The poor thing!" she said.

"Dinnae fret, they come in durin' the summer when the doors are held open. Tryin' tae get them out is nearly impossible, though most likely, they'll find their way out come May when the doors stay open all day again. Ma boss is a kind woman, though, and feeds 'em. I reckon she's a name for each one and thinks of them as her pets."

"Well, good, I'm glad," Erin said as they stepped outside and stood on the sidewalk while Tim locked up. Then, they began walking down the Royal Mile, away from the castle. "Are you hungry? I'm starving," Erin said.

"Aye, let's try the World's End," David said.

Three minutes later, they entered the old pub. It was crowded, so David kept his head down. After waiting for quite a while, the host appeared, shaking his head. "We've nothin' for over an hour," he said and turned away from them.

"Oh, my God, it's David Elliott!" an American man of about thirty said far too loudly. "Can I have your autograph?"

The host perked up and turned to face them again when he heard David's name. Then, when David was finished signing the man's ball cap, he waved them over. "How many, Mr. Elliott?" the young man said.

"Ach, we can't wait an hour," David said quietly.

"We have an immediate opening for you and your guests, sir," he said and waited for a response.

"Oh, well then, three," Erin said and looked up at her husband, then at Tim.

The host grabbed three menus and led them to a small, nicely decorated room, apart from the rest of the dining areas. Within moments of being seated, a waiter arrived asking for their drink order. He was very polite and said, "Yes, sir," and "Yes, ma'am," almost exclusively.

As soon as the man left the room, Tim shook his head and laughed. "Bloody hell, ah've never heard him speak tae anaone sae hospitably b'fore. Ah frequent thes *fine* establishment often enough, and ah've only ever heard contempt from the man," he said.

"Aye," David said, and Erin saw his cheeks bloom pink.

417

"Don't be upset, darling. You don't get special treatment every day. It's okay to enjoy it now and then," she said and took his hand.

"Aye," he said and gave her a half-hearted smile. "I ken, ye're right."

"A reluctant celebrity," she said and smiled at Tim. "But that's one of the many things I love about you."

"Ah reckon I'd no' enjoy the extra attention and preferential treatment, either. Never thought about et, but ah'm well suited tae verra few people knowin' who ah am," Tim said.

"Well, I can tell you it's really weird getting recognized!" Erin said. "I guess I'll just have to get used to it. Except… I've mainly just been recognized as the naked woman in those photos, so I'd better find something more interesting for my CV, eh?"

David laughed, and Tim blushed. "Aye, though yeh already have, I reckon. You're now the wife of a famous movie star!" Tim said.

"Well now, there is that, though I don't think the media fancies me very much. I reckon… actually, I *know* they think he's settled and that I'm not good enough for him."

"That's rubbish! I reckon he's found just the right bird, and ah'll be the first tae tell anaone who disagrees with et as much!" Tim said.

"A-hem," David said. "I am sitting here with you, yeh ken?"

"I don't think he likes being talked about behind his back… in front of his face." Erin laughed.

Their drinks were brought out to them quickly, and they chose their meals. The room was a bit too excluded for Erin's taste; she enjoyed hearing people talking around her, especially in Scotland. Before they knew it, their food was brought out. Erin didn't care much for her dish, so David traded her for his, which was much better. "You're a good husband, David," she said and leaned over to kiss him.

When their bellies were full and the check was paid, they headed out to the High Street again, managing to avoid any fan encounters. Erin took a deep breath of the night air and sighed. "Where shall we go next?" she said and held David's arm.

"How're yeh feelin', darling?" David asked, and she frowned.

"What do you mean? I feel great," she said and saw him glance at her belly. "Oh, right; honestly, I feel fantastic!"

"Wouldn't want yeh tae overdo, now," Tim said, apparently sensing David's concern.

"Good night nurse! I'd rather savor this feeling and have to be picked up by a taxi once I drop from exhaustion than go back to the hotel right now. Oi, fancy a mug of hot drinking chocolate?" she said and pulled David's hand as she headed toward the New Town. "There's a booth we went to with the children last week that had phenomenal hot chocolate!"

They rambled through the closes and narrow stairways of the Old Town, laughing and not paying much attention to the people around them until Erin heard a man's voice nearby as they waited for a crossing signal. "Fer fuck's sake, Angus! Et's ruddy John Thomas Fife, standing 'ere, incarnate!"

"Ooch, beltah! Ye're pure dead brilliant, mate!" the man who'd been called Angus replied.

"Thank you," David said.

"No, yeh truly are, mate!" the first man said.

The light had changed, so Erin turned to her husband. "David," she began.

"Oi, wait yer turn, yeh mingin' gurk! I were 'ere first," the man said, and out of the corner of her eye, she saw Tim moving quickly toward him.

She took a step closer to David and watched her friend, who wasn't a large man, punch the first guy square in the jaw. "Ye'll not insult ma friend without blows, mate!" he said and clocked Angus a good one on his cheekbone.

David gently pushed her to stand behind him and stepped a bit closer with his fists raised. "David!" she cried just before he hit the first man in the jaw, the same place Tim had hit him.

"Oi, and ye'll not insult ma wife again, either!" David said.

A crowd was quickly gathering, and Erin saw phones being held up, obviously taking photos and videos of them. She heard comments using David's name, so she tried to intervene. "David! Stop! You're being filmed! Please—"

"Take Erin away from here, David! I'll catch up with yeh," Tim said and dodged a blow from Angus.

"I'll not leave yeh, Tim," David said.

The first man threw up his hands and backed away. "She's yer wife?" he said. "Angus, tha's enough!"

Angus also put his hands up and took a step back, then he wiped his bloodied nose with the back of his hand. He said something to the first man with such a thick accent she couldn't understand it, and the first man replied with the same accent. Finally, he turned to David. "Ach, mate," he said. "I apologize fer what I said tae yer bird. Et were rude, and I should learn tae shut et, I reckon." He put his head down and looked sincere enough as he held out his right hand.

David hesitated and looked at Tim as if to gauge his thoughts on the apology. "Good night nurse, David; just shake the man's hand, and let's go, alright?" Erin said.

"Humph," David said and shook his hand, though he didn't smile or act in any way amiable. "Aye, shutting et would be wise."

"Aye, now get on with yeh," Tim said, and the men turned to leave. "Wait! I reckon an apology tae Mrs. Elliott would be appropriate!"

Erin just wanted to leave and forget the whole thing, but she stood and watched the first guy turn to her. "Ach, I'm sorry, Mrs. Elliott, ma'am, I didn't ken who yeh was… Fuck me, ye're not gurk, ye're with child! I *am* a right git."

"I accept… your apology. Now, let's just go, okay?" she said, feeling a bit less energetic.

"A'right, darling," David said and put his arm protectively around her.

They walked in silence for a long time until the gawkers finally got tired of following them. Erin noticed Tim rubbing his right hand, then she looked at his face and saw a cut on his chin. "Oh, Tim, you're bleeding!" she said, then pulled a tissue out of her purse. "Come here."

"Et's no' a big deal, Erin," he said, but she'd stopped walking, so he grudgingly went to her. "I'm fine, truly."

"I reckon he called me fat, then?" she said and gently wiped the mostly dried blood off his small wound.

"Aye, he did; what dae yeh expect me tae do, leave the bloody bawbag get away weth et?" he said a bit defensively.

She looked at him and sighed, then she turned to her husband. "Hot-heided Scots! Those guys were twice as big as you! What were you gonna do when they started really beating you up, hmm? I'm proud that you stood up for me and my honor, but a bit of wisdom might do you good in the future, okay?"

"Aye," David said, but she narrowed her eyes at him.

"And you… what happened the last time you got into a fistfight? Five hours in the emergency room and then having to wear a plaster on your nose for a week! People were recording you, you know!"

"Aye, but—"

"That's gonna be all over the internet now, and guess who'll be in those photos and videos? Me, your fat… grunt wife, who you just had to—I don't want to be in some jerk's vlog, where more people can judge me."

"Gurk, not grunt, and I ken well enough et was foolish, but that eejit should be held accountable for what he said," David said, and Tim nodded his agreement.

"And do you think anyone caught what he said in their recording? Highly unlikely! 'Raging David Elliott Seen Punching Ned Near Princes Street Gardens.' I can see the headlines now! Clickbait, where no one cares *why* you did it, just that you *did*." She sighed again and continued walking, leaving the men to exchange glances then catch up to her.

"I'm sorry, Erin. You're right, but once Tim threw the first punch… I was all in. I can have Becky do a bit of clean-up, maybe somethin' tae explain what happened," David said.

"Aye, I've a mate who's a vlogger; he'll set the record straight," Tim said. "Please dinnae be sore, Erin."

"I'm not angry; I'm just a bit exasperated with the way men think and behave sometimes. I still love you both, don't worry," she said and smiled at them, then she took David's hand and squeezed it just as they approached the hot chocolate booth.

They spent the rest of the evening wandering around the park and riding the amusement rides until, it seemed, the whole of Edinburgh was aware that David Elliott had been spotted. After that, they were either being watched, filmed, or asked for autographs and selfies, and it wasn't as much fun. It turned out that Tim lived in the New Town, so after a tearful goodbye on Erin's part, they parted ways, and David hired a taxi to take them back to the hotel.

Chapter Forty-Nine

A HAPPY HOGMANAY

The children were on holiday until January seventh, so the next morning, which was New Year's Eve, David and Erin returned to Owlgate to spend Hogmanay with them. They took the children to the center of town, where they rode the amusement rides and ate food from many parts of the world. There were small wooden huts selling almost anything you could think of. At one of them, David bought a bottle of whisky, a pretty jar of sea salt, and something small and black that Erin didn't recognize when he put everything into a bag. When she asked him about it, he told her he'd explain it later.

They were allowed to go into the VIP area, where there was a band and dancing and the best view of the fireworks. At midnight, the fireworks over Edinburgh Castle began. They were incredible, and as soon as the last one faded into the night sky, the whole city began singing.

Should auld acquaintance be forgot and
never brought to mind... Should auld
acquaintance be forgot and days of auld
lang syne...

Everyone took hands around them as they sang, the whole city in unison. Erin didn't know the words to every verse, but she listened and sang along with the chorus. On the last verse, everyone crossed their arms and held hands again.

They tried to move forward in a large circle, but the crowd was far too big for it to work well.

After much laughter and wishes for a happy new year, it was time to go. She'd had such a lovely night and was sad that it was over. "Now for the first footing," David said as they filed out to Princes Street along with everyone else in the city. It was slow going, but eventually, they made it to a quieter side street and hailed a cab. She was asleep when the taxi pulled up to Owlgate. "Darling, we've arrived," David said and gently nudged her.

"Hmm? Oh, right. Okay," she said, feeling groggy and very heavy. David paid the driver, then between him and Peter, they pulled her out of the cab. "I'm sorry, I'm just so tired."

"No worries, Mum," Peter said as they took the shopping bags out of the back seat.

All the lights were on in the house, and Erin was confused when David began ascending the formal front entrance instead of the side door. "Why... I don't want to climb all these steps!" she said, knowing she was whining, but all she could think about was getting into their nice, comfy bed.

"Ach, ye'll see, ma love," David said, then rang the doorbell, which shocked her even more.

"What... Millie is going to be angry," she began, but when she opened the door, she was smiling and laughing as she held out a cut crystal glass filled with amber liquid.

"Happy New Year, Davey, Erin, Children," she said.

David took the glass and drank it down, then he gave it back to her and said, "Happy New Year, Millie!" He held out the bottle of whisky he'd bought at the market, and she took it, then he held out the jar of salt and the black nugget. "Coal for warmth and salt for health."

"Oh, it's coal! I was trying to figure that out all night," Erin said as David stepped over the threshold. "Happy New Year, Millie," she said and hugged her friend.

"Ach, Happy New Year, dear, yeh look a bit knackered," she said.

"I am! I'm not used to staying up this late."

"Happy New Year!" Annis said as they reached the entry hall, where a small fire was crackling in the seldom-used fireplace.

"Happy New Year," everyone said in unison.

"Come, have a glass of punch," she said and ushered them into the sitting room.

Erin sat on the sofa and accepted a crystal glass filled with a pink frothy drink that tasted heavenly. Rosie came and took her cup when it was empty; she placed it on a side table and then sat next to her. "This is the best Hogmanay ever," she said softly and hugged Erin's arm.

"Yes, it is, isn't it?" she replied, having a difficult time keeping her eyes open. The next thing she knew, she was being shaken awake.

"Et's time for bed, darling," David said and helped her up.

"Oh, I'm sorry! What did I miss?" she said, feeling horrible for falling asleep.

"Ach, nothin' much. Let's get you tae bed."

Chapter Fifty

RETURN TO DORSET

On January second, the Elliott family returned to Dorset, and David continued filming *Wilde's Life*. The children attended to Erin's every need, fetching and carrying things in addition to tidying up here and there. They spent many joyful hours playing on the beach and managed a few brief walks on the Jurassic Coastal path together. It genuinely did seem like the *Sound of Music* when the wind carried their laughter and occasional sing-a-longs inland or out to sea.

On January seventh, the children returned to school, not without a few tears, mostly on Rosie's part. Afterward, the house was far too quiet. David and Erin missed them terribly but were very happy together and began counting the days until their baby was born.

Lunch with Emily became a regular event for them both. They even invited her and her partner Deborah to the house for lunch one Sunday. There was a knock on the cottage door, and as she got closer, Erin overheard voices on the other side of it.

"This is ludicrous, Em! They're on a level so much higher than me! I won't know what to say to people like them!"

"Don't be ridiculous, darling; they're no different than us, trust me."

Sympathetic to how Emily's partner might be feeling, she opened the door with a smile. The women stopped talking, and Emily held out her arms for a hug. "Hello, and welcome!" Erin said as she embraced her friend. Then she turned and took Deborah's hand. "It's so nice to meet you; please come in!"

Deborah was almost the exact opposite of Emily. Her tall, slender frame revealed her inner turmoil as she lifted her trembling hand to smooth her short, white-blonde hair. "Thank you for inviting us, Mrs. Elliott," she said formally.

"Now, none of that. I'm Erin, and my husband is David. We don't put on airs or pretend we're superior to anyone else, though I do think David is exceptional compared to most men I've met, but I'm biased," she said, then David entered the room.

"Sorry I'm late, but… well, never mind, not important." Erin noticed him blushing and would ask him about it later. "What are you biased about, love?" he asked before embracing Emily and shaking Deborah's hand.

"Just you, that's all," she said and looked at Emily for introductions.

"David, this is my partner Deborah Collins. Deborah, this is David Elliott, my childhood friend," she said with pride.

"It's such an… honor to meet you, Mr… I mean—" Deborah began and then floundered.

Erin saw her give the slightest curtsy and then noticed Emily roll her eyes. "Debbie, darling, he's not a prince, for goodness' sake," she said, and both David and Erin laughed out loud, which made Deborah blush deep red.

"Oh, I'm so sorry, Deborah! We had a memory just then, didn't we, David?" Erin said and held his hand.

"Aye, a verra pleasant one, actually."

"Come in and get comfortable. We'll tell you all about it, alright? Would you like something to drink?" Erin asked as David led them to the sitting room.

"Whisky sour on the rocks with a twist of lime, please," Deborah said, and Emily's eyebrows shot up.

"Isn't it a bit early for that?" she said, making David and Erin laugh again.

"Ach, another memory; please excuse our rudeness," David said.

"Aye, it's five o'clock somewhere, right?" Erin said. "I don't think we have any limes, but I'll see what I can do. Actually, I'm not a bartender, but I'll show you where everything is. You may fix yourself anything you'd like, any way you'd like, if that's alright?"

"Oh, well, Emily is probably right—"

"Nonsense. I'm not in any way judging you, my dear. Honestly, the first time I met David Elliott in the flesh, I longed for something strong to calm my nerves. If I weren't about to burst with this baby, I'd ask you to make me one as well."

"My Debbie has tended bar in some of the trendiest clubs in the world," Emily boasted.

"Really? I can't imagine remembering all the different cocktails off the top of my head like that! I bet you have some amazing stories!" Erin said.

"A few," she said humbly.

"Okay, change of plans," Erin said. "We don't have a bar, but our store of booze is in the room David uses as an office. I say we sit in there and talk. I'm sure you'll feel more comfortable doing something you are familiar with, right?"

"I... might, but that's your personal space. I wouldn't want to—" Deborah said, looking quite uneasy.

Erin stood quiet for a moment, with everyone watching her. She rubbed her chin and then grinned. "Alright, new change of plans," she said and took Emily's hand. "Come with me." She tugged her friend along with her as she advanced toward the staircase. "David, I think you're gonna have to push me."

He chuckled and took his increasingly routine place behind her. He pushed while Emily pulled her, laughing as Erin grunted and groaned the whole way up. Deborah followed slowly, smiling, though she still seemed unsure. "This is our upstairs hallway. The cottage was once a row of three small houses, but at some point, someone took down the divider walls and made it into one lovely home. We're only renting it, though. I love how this hall is open so you can see down to the room below. Follow me," she said and turned left. "This is our daughter Rosie's room. She and her three brothers are at school now." She opened the door, and Emily pulled Deborah to the door to look inside.

Erin opened another door at the end of the hall. "This is our three boys' room; they share when they're here." Emily and Deborah peered into that room, too. "Did we make the bed, David?" she asked as she turned back and headed to the other side of the house.

"Aye, we did," he said and laughed.

"This is our bedroom," Erin said and opened the door. Deborah gasped, but Emily tugged her to the door. "I hope there aren't any dirty underwear on the floor!"

Emily laughed. "None that I can see," she said.

"Whew! Well, you'd know if they were mine! A small elephant could wear them!" Erin said and laughed as she patted her large belly. "There now; you've seen the most personal parts of the house. I imagine the office isn't out of bounds anymore. Oh! Ouch! Hey, you in there... this isn't kickboxing class!"

"Is the baby moving?" Emily asked.

"Aye. Come feel it if you want to," Erin said, and Emily beckoned Deborah to join her.

The two women placed their hands on Erin's belly. They were astonished when Deborah began to giggle. "Bloody hell, that's amazing!" she said, then covered her mouth with her hands, clearly shocked and dismayed that she'd said it out loud. David, Erin, and Emily were nearly doubled over with laughter, so she shrugged and laughed with them.

Suddenly, Erin's eyes grew wide. "Oh, shoot! Go back downstairs. I'll catch up to you," she said and rushed into the bathroom.

When she entered the dining room, the women looked at her as if worried. "Sorry, but it's dangerous to laugh at nine months pregnant! What did I miss?"

"Nothing, actually. I was just leading Deborah to our bar supplies. Now, I believe we've some explaining to do," he said and smiled at her.

"Explain... oh, right! We were rude, weren't we," Erin said and told the ladies about the first time she met Rosie and Charlie. "I was really nervous and tried to find things to talk about that might interest them. I mentioned princesses, which of course led to princes. I told Rosie that I'd always dreamed of meeting prince Eric. Quick as a wink, she said, '*You did meet your prince Eric, but his name is David.*' Then she caught us kissing and whispered, '*Prince David.*' When you said that David isn't a prince, it made us think of that. We weren't laughing at you."

"Aww, that is a very nice story, Erin," Emily said, and Deborah nodded, smiling at her.

"And the other was when I was in Wisconsin... no, wait, et started in New Orleans, didn't et?" David said and looked at Erin.

"Aye. Go on and tell it."

"We'd just met and were wandering about the city... ach that was a lovely day," he said and took her hand. He kissed it and then leaned over to kiss her gently on the lips. "Where was I? Ach, aye, New Orleans. We ate at a lovely restaurant, and I ordered a Guinness—"

"I said something like, *'Isn't it a bit early for a Guinness?'*"

"To which I said, *'Et's never too early or too late for a Guinness.'* Then, when I was in Green Bay, Erin, or was it Lily... I can't remember; anyway, one of you suggested margaritas for lunch. If memory serves, et was eleven o'clock when et happened. Thinking I was a clever lad, I quipped, *'Isn't et a bit early for margaritas?'*"

"But Margarita's is a local Mexican restaurant, so I had him, though being eleven o'clock a.m. in Green Bay meant it was five o'clock p.m. here. See, we didn't mean to be rude; we're just sentimental, I guess," Erin said and pulled David's hand up for a kiss.

"Aww, I love stories like that! That's all I got out of him the first few times we had lunch," Emily said. "As I told you later, I'd never met a more besotted man in my life."

Having already asked David what he'd like, Deborah set a tumbler in front of him, then she began preparing another one. She set Emily's down and cocked her head to the side. "I reckon you're right, Em, they are like us," she said and smiled at Erin. "I can make you an alcohol-free cocktail that'll knock your socks off if you'd like?"

"Yes, please! I haven't had my socks knocked off in such a long time! I'm about due, I reckon! Wait, am I even wearing socks? I can't see my feet," she replied.

They sat in the study with their drinks, talking and laughing for nearly an hour. When the oven timer went off, Emily helped Erin bring out the large lasagna, salad, and garlic bread. "Did you make this yourself?" Deborah asked after several bites, followed by moans of pleasure.

Erin laughed and then shrugged. "Yeah, though David helped me, of course. It's my mom's recipe. I know it's not how you guys make it, but this is the one I grew up eating. Personally, I prefer ricotta and cottage cheese to béchamel sauce in a lasagna."

"It's superb! There's so much flavor and texture! I'd go out of my way for this at a restaurant!" Deborah said.

"Oh, well, thank you," Erin said. "I'll be sure to tell my mom how much you like it. I can give you the recipe, though I'm not overly precise in my measurements."

Deborah laughed and looked at Emily. "I'm not much of a cook, but I'm sure Em would be clever enough to do it justice."

"I'll copy it out for you, or if you don't mind, I'll just send you a photo of the one my mom wrote for me. Her handwriting is much better than mine."

"It's a deal, then," Emily said.

After a few cocktails, Deborah relaxed quite a bit and told them stories from her younger days as a highly sought-after bartender. She told them how she and Emily met, then asked how Erin and David had. When Erin mentioned that she wasn't told who her match was, Deborah gasped and said, "No way! That's so unfair!"

"I agree, and I gave my doctor an earful when I got back… though, in a way, I'm kinda glad it happened that way. Had I known I was meeting, quite literally, the man of my dreams *and* that he'd have to have sex with me… I can't imagine how big of a fool I'd have made of myself. I was too astonished to say or do anything excessively stupid, right, darling?"

"You were lovely, and you quite literally fell for me right from the start," he said and laughed when she rolled her eyes.

"Aye, he's not wrong. I fell on my ass!" she said and told them the story.

They laughed and talked until it was time for them to go, though only after Emily and Deborah insisted on helping clear the table. They were sorry to say goodbye, but Emily promised to have them over to their flat very soon. Erin sent them home with a generous portion of lasagna, and they waved as the two women walked to their car, then they shut the door on the cold winter day.

"That was fun," she said.

"Aye, and I agree with Deborah; your lasagna is awfully good," David said and kissed the top of her head.

They headed toward the dining room to begin cleaning up, and Erin looked up at him. "Why were you late when they arrived? You seemed a bit flustered."

David let out a short laugh, and his face turned a bit red. "Ach, I uh, stopped up the toilet. I had to use the plunger, and it took a while."

"Ah, Prince David and your royal scepter!" She laughed and then exclaimed, "Shoot! Be right back." When she returned to the kitchen, the table was cleared, and David looked at her compassionately. "Almost didn't make it that time!"

"Ach, darling, et'll be over soon. Have a seat, and I'll hand you the dishes to dry."

Chapter Fifty-One

THE FIRST OF FEBRUARY

The first day of February dawned bright and mild. Erin was accustomed to February being bitterly cold, but it was expected to hit about thirty degrees Fahrenheit that day. She was happy about that, though she longed for a bit of warmth to make the last few weeks of her pregnancy a bit more pleasant.

"Do yeh fancy comin' to the set with me today, love?" David asked as he was getting ready that morning.

"I'd like to, but I have to pee every five minutes, so I should probably stay home," she said, resigned to her current lot in life.

"I'm thinkin' et may be a short day, so watch for me tae come home early," he said.

Erin hadn't quite gotten out of bed yet; she was procrastinating, sitting on the edge of their mattress. Everything took effort; the novelty had worn off completely, and she wanted it to be over. She had two due dates and didn't know which one to go by. However, since one was for February tenth, she decided to hope for it.

I can wait ten days, she thought, and remembered saying that same thing to David when they'd parted after their first treatment week in New Orleans. Her eyes filled with tears at the memory. Crying and being overly emotional had been the norm for her over the last week. She attributed it to hormones and tried to hide it from David, but this hit her hard. "Ten days," she said out loud, and David popped his head out of the bathroom.

"What did you say, darling?" he asked and then saw the tears on her face. "Oh, my love, what's the matter?"

It was the umpteenth time he'd had to ask the question that year, and she felt utterly sick of herself as he sat next to her. "I'm sorry I'm such a baby lately! It's silly, but I just realized it's ten days until my first due date. I was thinking about New Orleans and how—"

"We could wait ten days," he finished for her, then held her as she cried. "I love yer sentimental side, darling. Why don't yeh join me today? I think et would be good for you tae get out of the house for a few hours."

She looked into his big brown eyes. "Do you really want me there?" she asked. "I don't want to be in the way."

"I always want yeh there, especially now. I worry about yeh when we're apart. We're set tae film indoors today."

She looked up at his beautiful face. "Alright, I'll be ready in a few minutes… that is if you'll help me up?"

David had the next day off, being Sunday, and Erin went with him every day the next week. After that, she wasn't up to it, so he made sure someone watched his mobile like a hawk while the cameras were rolling. February tenth came and went without a single contraction, and the next three days went likewise. When he got home on February fourteenth, she was getting angry. He could tell by the tissues overflowing every garbage bin that she'd cried most of the day, so he held her and tried his best to comfort her.

Kitty had come to help her just after their lunch with Emily and Deborah, but she'd had to return to London earlier that week. Thus, it was up to Erin to cook and clean, and even with David doing most of it, it was proving too much for her. "I'm too old for this! I want it to be over! I can't move, I can't sleep, I have to pee *all the time*," she said as she cried on his shoulder.

"Aye, I ken et, darling. It'll be soon, I'm sure," he said, just as he had every night for a week. "I'm lookin' forward tae collecting the children tonight, aren't you?" He knew how much she loved spending time with them and hoped it would cheer her up.

"Yes," she said simply. "I want to see them, but I'm just so worn out. I'm sorry, but it's hard to get excited about anything right now."

"Ach, I understand, darling." He kissed the top of her head and then stood. He went to his dresser and took something from the top drawer. "I've something for yeh," he said and handed her a greeting card.

"But what's this for?" she asked.

"Just open et, love," he said.

———

She opened the red envelope and saw two old people holding hands on the front of the card. It read, 'Grow old with me?' She opened it, read the long poem, and then gasped when she read, 'Happy Valentine's Day, Love David.' "Oh, David! I forgot all about Valentine's Day! I'm the worst wife ever! I don't have anything for you!" she said and sobbed, feeling gutted.

"Ach, darling! Dinnae cry! Do you really think I need for yeh tae buy me anathin' when I've got you for ma own tae come home to evera day? Just give us a kiss, love, and tell me yeh love me; that's all I need from you... oh, and tae make love tae yeh would be nice, as well."

Erin lifted her tear-soaked face and kissed him. "I do love you, David, more than anything," she said, then her eyes welled up with tears again. "I want to make love to you, but I'm so tired. I don't know if I have the strength."

"How about I call Dr. Jill in the mornin' and find out what she'll have yeh do. Perhaps we should drive intae London tonight?" he said.

"Oh, yes! Let's do that! Maybe Francie will feed me something better than I'm able to make in this state! That would be amazing!" she said, feeling hopeful for the first time in weeks.

"I'll send her a message, though yeh may have tae wait until tomorrow for yer feast, being such short notice. We can order takeaway if that will suffice?"

David had the next three months off from filming and was relieved to be able to stay by his wife's side, especially now that the birth of their child was past due. He packed some clothes for Erin and didn't bother with much for himself, as he had plenty to wear at their house. He loaded the Range Rover he'd bought to drive to and from work and to pick up the children on their exeat weekends. It had plenty of room for everyone, their luggage, and the new bairn when it arrived.

Next, he helped Erin get to the vehicle. Once she was settled in, he locked up the cottage since they'd be gone for at least a month, maybe two, and headed to the boarding school. It usually took an hour to get there, but because they had to stop for Erin to use the toilet, it took a bit longer.

Chapter Fifty-Two

DOUBTFUL MOTIVES

As soon as they arrived at Puncknowle, Erin went inside the dormitories to use the bathroom while David loaded the children and their bags into the SUV. She didn't care if people stared or whispered about her; she had no choice if she didn't want to have an accident on the way back to London. "Hello, Mrs. Elliott," one of the aides said as she waddled into the building. "Any day now, hmm?" she said sympathetically.

"Yes, and it can't come soon enough," Erin replied.

When she was outside again, she saw a blonde woman speaking with David. She didn't appear to be flirting, so she used some techniques she'd read about in an article on how to keep from being jealous about something out of both her and David's control.

As she got closer, she saw that David seemed leery of the woman and was doing all he could to stay far away from her, which made her grateful. "Hello," Erin said as she reached David's side.

"Oh, hello. I was just asking your husband for the best route to find the M3 from here," she said, as though she had no idea who David was, which Erin doubted very much.

"Okay, then I'll let him finish," she said calmly. Ignoring the urge to stay put, she walked to the passenger door of their vehicle and got in. She couldn't put on her seatbelt, so she waited, trying hard not to watch them in the rear-view mirror. She had to learn to trust, and it had to start right then.

Needing a distraction, she asked the children if they'd heard any good jokes, hoping for a laugh. That was one of the coping exercises she'd read about. "I have one," Rosie said.

"Go on then," Erin said.

"What did the snowman say to the other snowman?"

"Gosh, I don't know."

"Do you smell carrots?" she said, earning a few snickers from her siblings and a smile from her.

"I've one as well," Charlie said. "How does Darth Vader like his toast?"

Erin felt like the answer was obvious, but she couldn't think of it. "Tell me."

"On the dark side, of course!" he said, and that time everyone laughed.

"Well done, Charlie!" Peter said.

"Yes, that was really clever," Erin said just as David came to her door and opened it.

"How're yeh feeling, love?" he asked, genuinely caring.

"Better, now I'm with you again," she said, "I love you so much!"

"Ach, I love yeh more!" he countered, and Erin didn't doubt he believed it.

"Let's go home," she said. He kissed her after he helped her buckle the seatbelt since she could no longer see the plug end of the buckle to do it herself.

Once she was ready to go, David got in and buckled up. "She was a bit dense; I had to tell her three times and show her where to go on her mobile maps app," he said, obviously more annoyed than interested in the woman.

"Everyone can't be as brilliant as I am, right, children?" she asked, and they smiled.

"Right," Rosie and Charlie said at the same time, then Peter agreed as well. Dan wasn't paying attention and sat staring out the window.

Yeah, sure! Not knowing how to get to the M3? That's clever. Erin thought but was able to keep herself from imagining anything worse.

They were off, though it took quite a while to get out of the car park, as everyone was trying to leave at the same time. Eventually, they made it through the tiny village roads to the B roads, which were far too narrow and winding. Before long, they were on the M3, heading northeast to London. They sang along with the satellite radio and laughed for most of the ride home. Erin had a sudden burst of energy and felt better than she had in a long time.

They stopped at a petrol station so she could use the loo twice. Each time, David had to help her out of the car, but they laughed about it. Finally, they made it to town, following the now familiar streets to their home, and parked next to his neglected motorbike. Her cheeks were rosy with the cold, and she was smiling as they went in through the back door of the sunroom.

As she stepped inside, a beam of lamplight hit her face, and David stopped to stare at her. "Ach, Erin, ye're glowin'! Ye've never been so bonnie!" he said.

They made their way through the house to the main staircase, which led to the bedrooms. Everyone carried their own suitcases or bags, except David, who was carrying both his and Erin's. As they reached the bottom of the stairs, the door opened, and in walked Kitty and Francie, each holding a bag of groceries.

David turned and saw them. "Allow me to help," he said to Francie and set his and Erin's bags on the step. "Peter, please help Kitty." Peter did as he was told while the rest of the children continued to their rooms. Both women said thank you, and Francie went straight to the kitchen, with David and Peter following like puppies.

——

"'Ellow, mum," Kitty said cheerfully. "Do ya need 'elp wif anyfing?"

Erin smiled at her. "I only need one thing, Kitty," she said and wrapped her arms around her in a tight hug.

Kitty was caught off guard but knew to expect the (pleasantly) unexpected from her, so she went along with it, hugging her back.

"I feel so good! I've got so much energy!" she exclaimed and then let her go.

I've seen this b'fore. I reckon she'll 'ave the baby in the next day or two. Kitty thought, but she wasn't going to say anything; she'd keep a close watch on things though. "I'm glad to 'ear it, mum," she said happily. David and Peter returned, and she watched as the three of them climbed the stairs. Then she made her way to the kitchen to see if Francie needed any help.

——

When David and Erin reached their room, they stopped and thanked Peter, who continued up the second flight of stairs to his room. After they walked in, Erin waited until David closed the door, then wrapped her arms around him. "I love you, David Elliott! I'm so excited to be back, and I can't wait to see our baby," she said.

Her excitement was contagious, and David grinned. "I love yeh as well, hen," he said.

Erin's eyes grew wide suddenly, and she pushed herself away from him. "Holy Moses, we need a nursery! Why didn't I think of that earlier?" she said. "Must be because we were in Dorset and not living here."

David had an odd expression cross his face. "I, uh, have a confession to make," he said. "I've been hidin' somethin' from yeh, and I hope yeh can forgive me."

Erin furrowed her brows, not wanting anything to ruin how good she was feeling just then. "Alright, out with it," she said and saw him smile. "I know that smile; what is it?"

"Well… the true reason Kitty left a bit early was tae help me clear out the guest room. Follow me," he said, leading her out of their room and down the hall to the spare room door. He opened it, and Erin gasped. "I didn't choose much, as I knew ye'd want tae make et yer own, but I managed tae have the basics installed. I hope yeh like et, darling."

She looked around her. All the furnishings had been removed, and the room was nearly bare. On one wall was a crib and changing table stocked with diapers, wipes, and creams. Everything was in place, ready to be used. Then she saw a big, comfortable-looking chair with a large, crescent-shaped nursing pillow lying on it. "Oh, David, it's perfect! I can't wait to make it a space filled with love and beautiful memories," she said.

Until then, that room had been a reminder of Susannah's evilness, but all of that was gone, erased, and washed away. She moved the pillow and sat in her new chair; it was comfortable and rocked. David then showed her how it was also a recliner, not the loud, clunky kind; this one was electric. She sat while he pushed a button, and the leg rest slid silently up, then back down.

"Thank you so much, darling," she said and patted the cushion next to her. The chair was so big, both of them could fit on it if they squeezed a bit.

"Stand up," he said and sat in her place. He then pulled her onto his lap and held her. "Ach, this is nice, ma love. I intend tae hold yeh like this as often as I can once the bairn has come."

"I look forward to it," she said and relaxed in his embrace.

That night, Erin dreamed that the blonde woman from the school was driving a vehicle she was in. David was trying to give her directions, but she turned the opposite way he told her to more often than she got it right. Then, she was sitting in the farthest back seat on a school bus and wanted to tell him that the woman was doing it on purpose, to sit next to him for as long as she could. When she opened her mouth, the radio suddenly came on, and no one would have heard her.

She woke feeling frustrated and sat on the edge of the bed, breathing a bit heavily. Once her breathing was back to normal, she lay down again, not wanting to tell David, but he was awake and asked her what was wrong. "Nothing, go back to sleep."

"I ken there's somethin' wrong, Erin; please spit et out," he said.

Sighing in exasperation, she said, "Fine, but it's not that big of a deal. It wasn't like the one on our honeymoon, but I had a weird dream, that's all." She told him what she'd dreamed, and he took her hand in his.

"I see where this is leadin', so I'll tell yeh now that I'm in no way attracted tae her. Not even a wee bit; if anathin' she makes me nervous and on ma guard, so dinnae worry, a'right?" he said, clearly trying to nip it in the bud before she got herself all worked up about it.

"Okay. I really am trying to learn to trust, and it's not that I don't trust you, exactly; I don't trust them, the women. I've never known a man, until you, who can control his eyes, so it's hard to believe that any man can. Wait, I take that back. As far as I know, my dad can... at least I've never seen him looking around," she said.

"Aye, I understand, and I reckon I dinnae trust them either."

"Thank you for... putting my mind at ease; that's just what I need you to do sometimes. I love you."

Chapter Fifty-Three

FEAR FACTOR

The next day, February fifteenth, went pretty fast. Erin, Rosie, and Charlie discussed ideas on what they could do to decorate the nursery, and at lunch, they talked more about what to name the baby when it arrived. They threw around quite a few good ones but never came to a concrete decision.

Daniel seemed oblivious to Erin's precarious state, but Peter was clearly on high alert. He was often found hovering near her as if waiting for a task or errand to fulfill. Finally, she asked him to sit with her on the office sofa, which, at that moment, was the most comfortable place for her.

The young man jumped to attention and nearly sprang to her side, eager to help. "Yes, Mum, what do you need?" he asked.

"I don't need anything, my sweet boy. I just want to put your mind at ease."

"What do you mean?" he asked, and she couldn't tell if he was serious or not.

"Well, you haven't left my side all day. I thoroughly enjoy your company, but I just want to know what's happening in your mind to make you do that?"

He shrugged his shoulders and cocked his head to the side as if trying to understand his actions as well. "I'm not sure if I'm honest. I reckon it just seems as though you might... pop at any second," he said and then laughed at the imagery it evoked. "I can't say what I think I'll accomplish by staying by your side except to keep you from overexerting yourself. If you'd rather I buggered off, I can."

She took his hand and then put her head on his shoulder, feeling such love and gratitude toward him. Tears threatened to fall down her cheeks, so she stayed quiet and still for a while, collecting herself internally before she said anything. "I truly wish I could express just how much that means to me, Peter. Thank you for being so thoughtful and considerate of me. I think, at this point, a little overexertion would be welcome if it meant this whole ordeal would finally be done."

"Yeah, not to be cheeky, but you do seem a bit knackered from it. I can't wait to meet him or her. I'm quite chuffed about it, really. Are you... oh, never mind," he said and seemed embarrassed.

"Go on and ask, whatever it is."

"It's a daft question, I reckon, but are you nervous?"

"You mean about giving birth? Terrified, but I'm trying not to think about it. I'm focusing on the lovely pain meds they'll give me to make it easier," she said and laughed.

Just then Daniel darted into the room holding a green toy soldier wearing a thin, plastic parachute. He began running in circles, trying to get the chute to catch the wind and open up, but all he was accomplishing was making a lot of noise. "Look, Erin, look! It really works, and when I throw him, he lands safely, like the real Paras!" He threw the figure across the room, nearly hitting the windowpane. Instead of landing softly on the floor, it hit the casing, and one of its little green legs flew off, hitting Peter's ear pretty hard.

"Oi! Give it a rest, Dan!" Peter said, and when his little brother didn't listen, he stood and took him by the earlobe, extracting a high-pitched yelp from the boy. "I said to give it a rest! Give Mum a bit of peace for once!"

"Oww! Leave off, Peter! You're not my dad or Nanny! What gives you the right—"

"Boys! Please stop," Erin said, both amused and wishing for a bit of quiet, as Peter had said. Dan picked up his toy and found the leg on the floor, next to the armrest of the couch. He looked so sad that her heart went out to him. "Let me see it, Dan," she said and took it out of his small, dirty hands. "What did you get into? Your hands are filthy! Ugh, never mind." She looked at the amputated leg and sighed. "Dan, I think it's beyond repair; I'm sorry."

Dan frowned and then looked up at her with a glint in his eyes. "It's no matter, Mummy, he'll become one of my wounded Tommies! He's not the first and won't be the last, I reckon." He rushed up to her, making her think he'd ram into her belly. Instead, he grabbed his soldier, its leg, and gently kissed her cheek, though he really had to stretch to reach it. He did it carefully enough that he didn't hurt her, and she was relieved.

As soon as he was gone, she smiled up at Peter and began to laugh. "Well, there's never a dull moment when Daniel Elliott is in the house, right?"

Peter had seemed quite angry, but when he saw her laughing, his frown became a smile, and he joined her on the sofa again. "He's a rascal, but even I must admit that he can be charming when the mood hits him. I'm only glad nothing was broken by his antics… this time."

After supper, they played a few rounds of Go Fish, then the children went upstairs to get ready for bed. David helped his wife up the stairs, and it was slow going. Erin decided to read their bedtime story from the comfort of her new nursing chair with the children seated on the floor in front of her.

When the chapters were read, each of her new children stood to kiss her and say goodnight, then they trooped upstairs, and David helped to tuck them in. She woke to David standing before her smiling. "Oh! I didn't realize I'd fallen asleep. Help me up, husband," she said and reached out her hands.

"Yes, my darling wife," he said and heaved her upright. He looked down at her and placed his hand on her neck, his fingers running through her long, brown and grey hair. There was something that felt more intense than usual, and she melted as he bent down to kiss her. "Come with me."

He pulled her by the hand into their bedroom and locked the door behind them. His gaze was penetrating and gave her butterflies in her stomach. In one short step, he was face to face with her again, and when he moved her hand to the front of his trousers, she gasped. "Oh, David! I need you!"

"And ye'll have me, but first things, first."

She allowed him to remove her top and ugly, enormous bra, then he pulled down her elastic-waisted stretchy pants and underwear all in one go.

Next, he took off his clothes, throwing them across the room in his excitement. She hadn't seen him that eager and passionate for a long time, and she could hardly stand the anticipation. "Please," she whispered, but he gently covered her mouth with his hand.

"Patience, ma love, now please lay on yer back," he said and pointed to their bed.

She heaved herself onto the mattress, and as soon as she was lying still, he buried his face into the folds between her legs, making her gasp and moan. It felt so good but laying on her back was beginning to get uncomfortable. "David... I need to move, please," she said.

He lifted his head and smiled at her, looking well-pleased with himself. "A'right, I have an idea." He helped her to stand and then pulled the Queen Ann chair out of the closet. He stood in front of it and pulled her toward him. He began kissing her face and neck, making her giggle, then he sat and kissed her belly. "Turn around," he said, and when she did, he pulled her to him by the hips. "Sit on me."

"I'll break this beautiful chair, David! Are you serious?"

"Aye, and ye'll not break et, trust me."

She gingerly lowered herself onto his lap and felt his hard cock enter her. The pulsing deep inside her began right away and built up again as he helped her rock back and forth as she rode him. "This is so nice!" she said and heard him moan.

"Aye! Ye're sae sexy, and I wish I could last all night, but..." He began pulling her by the hips, making her rock faster over his erection until she felt him shudder and groan deeply. "I'm sorry, love; I wanted tae last for you," he said as they continued moving for a few moments longer.

"Honestly, I was losing steam, but that was the best sex we've had in a long time! Thank you so much; it really was amazing!"

"Ye're welcome, and now I'm cream crackered! What do you say we go to sleep early tonight?"

"I say that's a great idea," she said as she stood and headed to the bathroom.

Chapter Fifty-Four

UNTO US A WEE CHILD IS BORN

February sixteenth promised to be a nice day; the high temperature in London was meant to be fifty degrees Fahrenheit or ten degrees Celsius, which was a heat wave compared to what Erin was used to. She hadn't slept well that night; her mind wouldn't shut down, thinking about all the things she could do in the nursery to make it special. Then, when she finally did fall asleep, back pain kept waking her, and she couldn't get comfortable.

David was already up, and she could hear the shower running. She thought of joining him but decided to stay in bed for a few more minutes instead. She managed to doze on and off, but the pain in her back would wake her up before she could get into a deep, restful sleep.

She examined her husband as he stepped into the bedroom, naked and looking delicious. He began picking up his clothes from the night before, and she watched him. Their clothing was scattered around the room after their throes of passion the night before. That is, as much passion as you can have when you're the size of a small house!

She rolled to her side and sat on the edge of the bed. Reluctantly, she heaved herself into a standing position, and water poured out of her onto the floor. She gasped and said, "David," trying not to panic.

"Aye?" he said and looked at her.

"My water broke!"

"A'right, let's not panic," he said and walked over to her.

"Easy for you to say! Please get a towel or something." She took a step, and more water ran down her legs. David hurried to the bathroom and returned, carrying half a dozen large bath towels, making her laugh. "Thank you, darling," she said, not wanting to tease him for his slight overkill.

"Are yeh havin' contractions?" he asked, and she stood still, not knowing what they felt like.

"I… don't know. I don't think—Oh! Ooooh!" she said, feeling a hard cramping come from the middle of her body. "Yes," she whispered, trying to ignore just how much it hurt. She'd been terrified of this part. The thought of labor and everything it entailed had been pushed to the back of her mind hundreds of times in the past few months, but she could no longer do that. *This is only the start; how much worse can it get?*

She'd seen signs for Lamaze classes but couldn't fathom feeling comfortable with half a dozen couples trying not to stare at David. Then, when one of David's fellow actors mentioned a class geared toward celebrities, she couldn't imagine all of them staring at her. Now she regretted that decision.

"Oh! Oww! Oh, it hurts so bad! I'm so scared, David!" she said after another strong one hit her. David had been getting dressed and looked at his watch.

"That was only six minutes!" he said. "We need tae get yeh tae hospital right now." He picked up his mobile and dialed 999, knowing it would take a long time for an ambulance to get there in the morning traffic. "Ma wife has begun labor… Aye… six minutes. Aye, verra strong." he said to the emergency operator on the other end of the line. He told them their address and hung up but continued to do something on his phone, which annoyed Erin.

"What are you doing? We need to go!" she barked and then felt bad. "I'm sorry."

"Et's a'right, now let's put some clothing on yeh." He helped her on with a stretchy dress, then Kitty appeared.

She started flying around the room, gathering things like her pre-packed overnight bag. "I'll just be a moment," she said.

"Hurry up! We need to get downstairs!" she snapped and was mortified. "I'm so sorr—" she began, but another contraction took her words away.

"Ach, darling, breathe… look at me and breathe," David said, then he and Kitty led her slowly to the staircase. It was slow-going as she eased herself down each step, and they had to stop at the bottom one for another strong contraction. "Five minutes." The fear in his voice was plain. "Kitty, have yeh ever delivered a bairn?"

"Well, sir, I've assisted in one, so I know what ta do until the ambulance arrives, I reckon."

David blew out a long slow breath, apparently feeling a bit relieved at that news. "Silver linings, eh?"

"I need to sit or… lie down," Erin said, and David led her to the sitting room. "Hold me!" she nearly yelled as another one hit her hard. She cried through it, holding David tightly. He stroked her hair and whispered soft shushing noises to her, waiting for it to pass.

"Yer doin' well, darling; it'll be over before yeh know et."

"Where's that goddamn ambulance?" she said impatiently. She didn't want to snap at him, so she tried to focus it all on something else. The pain was like nothing she'd ever experienced before, and she didn't think it was supposed to be going so fast.

Sitting on the sofa was uncomfortable and so was lying down, so she stood, leaning on David. "Be back in a tick," Kitty said and ran out of the room.

"David! If this is gonna happen here, I want it to be in your office; that room calms me down," Erin said suddenly.

"A'right," he said and supported her as they turned toward the door.

"Ahh! Ohh! Oh, that hurts!" she cried with the next contraction.

"Four minutes," he said.

"A'right, dinnae worry!" they heard Francie's thick Scottish accent say as she bustled into the room with an armful of towels and hot water. "Ah've done thes b'fore, dear."

"We were goin' tae move tae ma study," David told her, and she gave a short nod of approval.

"Aye, et's more comfortable, ah reckon."

"Th—ank you… Fran—" Erin began through her sobs, but another one hit her and kept her from finishing.

"A'right now, Erin, love, jest breathe and listen tae ma voice. Ye're gonnae be fine, dear." When the worst was over, they both helped her to the office. They brought her to the sofa and gently laid her down. "Lie on yer back sae ah can examine how far ye've progressed. Francie gently pulled Erin's underwear off, then dipped her hands into the scalding water and gently checked Erin's dilation with her fingers, barking out commands like an army captain.

"Now, David, clear away the rugs and spread the towels on the floor. Move yer desk chair against the wall, so et cannae move back. Now set yerself ontae et, and when ah tell yeh, hauld out yer arms like so." She held her arms out zombie style, making Erin laugh in spite of herself.

She lay on her side, trying to relax, and watched as he did everything she said like an obedient child. She half expected him to say, "Yes, ma'am," and salute after each order was given.

Francie helped her breathe through two more contractions while on the sofa, then took her hand. "Ye're fully dilated, dear, sae let's move yeh intae position." She helped Erin up and then over to David, having her stand, facing away from him. "Now, at yer next contraction, squat, and allow David tae hauld yeh up, but dinnae push until ah've said yeh may, and et'll be a'right."

Erin stood in front of her husband, and he wrapped his arms lightly around her belly. He laid his head against her back, and she placed her hands over his, enjoying the embrace while she could, which wasn't long, as another one came with full force. "Oh, God!" she said as she squatted, and David held her under her arms.

"A'right, now, jest let gravity do et's job, dear. Try tae relax and breathe," Francie said. Kitty was pacing nearby, biting her nails as if waiting for someone to tell her to do something. "Kitty, ah believe ah hear the children. Please gie them their breakfast, then bring our Erin a cup of ice chips and a cool, wet flannel."

"I... forgot about... the chil—" Erin began and had to stop with the pain. She tried to stay quiet so the children wouldn't be scared, but she couldn't and let out a very loud noise, something between a groan and a scream.

"A'right, Erin, yeh may push on yer next contraction," Francie said, and then the room was suddenly filled with people. The ambulance had finally arrived, and one of the paramedics was trying to take over, but Erin was having none of it.

"Leave her be! I want her to do it!" she demanded. "Unless you don't want to," she said to Francie as an afterthought.

448

"Aye, ah willnae leave yeh, love. Jest relax, and let yer body work; et knows what tae do, even if yeh don't.

Erin's eyes grew large, and she felt like she would burst or rip open from stem to stern. "Oh, Francie, it hurts! What should I do?"

"Dinnae fear, love, the head is crownin' now. Next one, yeh need tae push hard. David, ah reckon yer tired, but yeh must hold her up." He nodded, wide-eyed; his exhaustion showed plainly, but he didn't complain.

"I love you, David! Thank you for... helping—Oh, Fuck! Fuck! Oh!" she said, and let out another loud moan and screamed, pushing with all her might. She felt as though it wasn't helping until the head was out, and she could relax, but for only a moment. "Oh! No! Not yet, let me breathe!" Another scream, another hard, painful push, and the baby slipped out, landing safely in the towel Francie was holding in place.

"Et's a girl!" she said, tears rolling down her sweat-drenched face. Everyone cheered at first, but then the room became utterly silent. Not a noise was heard until Erin was finally able to breathe again and gasped, bawling from the stress of it all. Francie held the child up and smacked her rear end just enough so that she should start to cry. Nothing happened, so she put her mouth over its nose, gently sucked, clearing her airway, then spat into a towel.

The baby screamed, and the sound filled the room. Everyone cheered, but Erin wasn't finished yet. "Now comes the placenta, love," Francie said as she took a blanket one of the paramedics handed her and wrapped the baby in it. "Thes willnae hurt as much, but ye'll feel et." Erin nodded and felt another contraction. She wanted to lie down and be done. "Go on and push, dear."

Erin bore down one last time, though she was exhausted, and David's arms were digging into her sides. The placenta came out, landing on a towel underneath her. "Where's my baby?" she said, wanting with everything inside her to hold it.

"Dinnae worry, dear, they're cuttin' the cord now. Yeh did sae well, Erin! I'm sae verra proud of yeh." Francie's eyes were gushing tears as she held her employer's hand. "The paramedics have brought in a gurney, dear; let's get yeh ontae et. Yeh dinnae wannae soil the sofa."

David's arms were about to give out, but he gave one last heave, and Erin was standing. Several EMTs were there to help her, and she was finally able to get comfortable. "Here you are, Erin," one of the EMTs said and handed her their new baby girl.

"Oh, look at her, David, isn't she beautiful!" she said, touching her face, and felt her breasts start to gush when the baby began to cry again.

"She's the most beautiful thing I've ever seen!" he said as Erin tried to lift her dress so she could nurse her.

"Oh! Help me, please! I need to feed her, or I'll burst!" she said, feeling her milk running down her front. David and one of the EMTs managed to help her, and then came the challenge of getting the baby to latch on. They had a few false starts, but then all of a sudden, they figured it out.

There were people everywhere, and before she knew it, she was being rolled out into the hallway. "Wait! Stop! Let me finish this! Our children are out there, and I want them to see their new sister before we do anything else. You are not going to rush us and ruin it for me!" The EMTs pushed the bed back into the room and waited for her to finish feeding the baby while David watched them and cried.

"Ye're pure braw, Erin! I dinnae ken how yeh did et," he said and kissed his wife, then his new daughter.

When she was finished feeding and burping the baby, she covered back up, and they allowed the children to come in. They were all timid, except Dan, who came right up and looked into the baby's face. "Is it a boy or girl?" he asked.

"Et's a girl, Dan," David said.

Daniel frowned. "What's her name?" he asked.

David and Erin looked at each other and nodded. "Juniper Annis Elliott," Erin said and took David's hand.

Dan frowned again and tilted his head to the side as though looking intently at a piece of fine art hanging in a museum. Then, he slowly nodded and smiled his big, beautiful smile that made his dimples show. "I like it! I think it fits! I hate when babies have the wrong name," he said sincerely.

"I'm glad you approve!" David said, expertly hiding the laugh threatening to burst forth from him at any moment. The rest of the children weren't so bold. Charlie and Rosie came up to them together, holding hands as if for support. "Come close, and meet yer new sister Juniper," David said.

They stepped up and smiled at their dad, then at Erin. One of the baby's hands came free from her wrappings and flailed out. Rosie couldn't help herself and reached out to hold it. One of the EMTs stepped forward to stop her, but Erin shot him an angry look. Rosie saw the EMT and let go suddenly, as though she thought she'd get reprimanded. "I'm sorry!" she said timidly. "I did wash my hands though."

"You come right over and hold her hand, darling. It's okay," Erin said and smiled at her.

"She's beautiful, Mummy!" Rosie said, but they heard Dan in the background contradict her.

"She looks like a big pruney frog to me," he said, and Peter shook his head at him.

"Dan! That's rude!" he said as he waited for his turn.

Charlie touched the fuzz on top of her head and started laughing. "She's ginger!" he said and continued laughing as though it was the funniest joke he'd ever heard. Erin looked at David and laughed a bit as well.

"I'm mighty partial to gingers!" she said, repeating what she'd said at her parent's house that summer.

"Aye, and so am I," David said, smiling. "Dinnae be shy, Peter, she willnae bite yeh."

Peter smiled and stepped around the bed, as Juniper still had Rosie's finger in a death grip. "She is beautiful, Dad. I also like her name. We can call her Junie, can't we?" he asked, and David nodded. "Good, I like that." He gently put his finger against the tiny palm of her other hand, which had come free of the blankets, and she grabbed on tightly. He looked wide-eyed at Rosie, who was feeling the same thing, and then at Erin. "Wow! You're strong, little sprout!" He then looked up at the people who'd come with the ambulance. "Shouldn't you go now? I don't want anything bad to happen because you didn't go to hospital on time."

"Don't worry, darling boy," Erin said softly. "Everything is alright." Peter smiled at her and spontaneously bent down to kiss her cheek, then he kissed Junie's. When he stood upright again, she noticed he was blushing. "Thank you, Peter, you are a sweet thing. Alright, we can go now. Children, come here, please. I'm sorry if you were scared before you came in here; birth is a lot harder than I ever imagined it would be. I love you all, and I'll see you in a day or so, alright? Please behave for Kitty and Francie, okay?" she said, and they all nodded.

"We love you too," Rosie said as she was rolled out, covered in a heavy blanket against the cold February day.

Chapter Fifty-Five

LEARNING CURVE

David, Erin, and Juniper stayed at the hospital overnight, and Dr. Jill told them that everything looked perfect for both Erin and the baby. She was told to take it easy and not do any heavy lifting or strenuous activities. As for treatments, they were limited to point of ejaculation only.

It seemed plain to them, but there was still the question of paternity. For peace of mind, a test was done on David to ensure that Juniper was his child, not Todd's. They were told to expect the results within three to five days.

On Monday afternoon, they hired a car, having purchased a car seat from the gift shop. It was no easy task trying to figure out, first, how to buckle Juniper into the car seat and second, how to install the seat into the hired car. They finally managed the task and made it home to an excited household.

When they came into the house, Kitty and Francie stayed back until Erin called them to her. She told them the infant was *far* too heavy and cumbersome for her, so she asked them both to take turns holding Juniper while she got settled on the comfortable tan leather sofa in David's office. The two women cooed and fussed over the baby until the children appeared, then they stood to the side and watched the family as if on standby, waiting to be asked to do something… anything.

The children were over the moon, doting on both the baby and Erin. Daniel, whom they were assured had *just* washed his hands, sat on the couch next to Erin and was allowed to hold his new sister. He showed her his dimples as he smiled, and laughed at the funny faces she made while filling her diaper.

In true new father spirit, David laid her out on the changing pad that was in the diaper bag. Charlie handed him a fresh diaper, and Rosie held the baby wipes as he unsnapped her onesie and then unfastened the tabs that held the diaper on. When he pulled down the front of it, the whole room seemed about to gag, and Dan plugged his nose.

Junie was kicking her legs, so Erin suggested he hold them up, but everyone was so noisy with their complaining and grossing out about the smell that he didn't hear her. She was about to get on the floor to help him when Kitty stepped in and took over. In the blink of an eye, Junie was wiped clean, the soiled wipes were wrapped securely inside the old diaper, the new diaper was on, and the onesie was snapped shut again. She lifted the baby and handed her to David, who looked relieved.

"Thank you, Kitty! I reckon there's a learning curve for changing poo diapers," he said. "Now, who wants to hold her next?"

The next hour was spent passing Juniper around the room until she began to fuss. Erin asked the children to turn away while she started feeding her. David laid a receiving blanket over her and the baby, then they were allowed to turn back around. When Peter saw her, he blushed bright red and pretended he was engrossed with the book titles on the shelf nearest him.

After being fed and burped, it was nap time for both Junie and Erin. David carried the baby as they ascended the stairs to the nursery. He laid the sleeping girl in the crib, making sure she was safe, then he and Erin went to their room and got into bed. "I couldn't be more happy, darling," David said, but she was already asleep.

Erin woke to the baby wailing, though it didn't last long. She sat up, wishing for another hour of sleep, and smiled as David carried Juniper into their room. There was something so vulnerable about him at that moment; any guard he normally put up was disarmed, and the way he looked at his newest child made her catch her breath.

"Another poo diaper, that's all," he said and touched his pointer finger to her tiny nose. "Isn't that right, Junie, ma love? That's all et was. Ma Losh, but ye're lovely." He looked up at Erin then and smiled. "Ach, and you are as well, ma dearest. I can't believe how much she looks like the both of us; et's startling, innit?"

"Aye, it is. I just hope she grows up to be tall and lanky, like you," she said and took her daughter out of his outstretched arms. "Hello, Junie baby! I just love you so much! Yes, mummy does." David sat beside her on the bed and kissed her cheek. "Did Daddy change your yucky poo diaper all by himself? What a clever boy he is! What's that? It took him a really long time and your bottom got a bit chilly! Aww, my poor wee lassie! Dinnae fash, he'll get faster at it before long, I reckon."

"Aye, I reckon so. I just wanna stare at her! She's sae bonnie!"

"Well then, take her and stare all you wish while I use the loo," she said, handing him the tiny bundle of blankets, and then stood. As she washed her hands, her stomach started growling. "I'm starving, David—" she began, but he wasn't in the room any longer. She found him in the hallway with Rosie and Charlie, who were smiling as they interacted with their new sister.

"Oh, Mummy!" Rosie said. "She smiled at me just now!"

"No, Rosie, she smiled at me," Charlie said.

"Ach, I believe ye're mistaken; I clearly remember her smilin' at me," David said with a grin.

"Well, what's not to smile at? I mean you're all lovely to gaze upon, why wouldn't she smile whilst doing so?" Erin said and stepped up to the baby, who was awake and looking around her. "Hello, baby girl, I don't know about you, but Mummy is starving! Why don't we ask Daddy to carry you downstairs, hmm?"

"But Mummy, Daddy is just here!" Rosie said.

"Oh, right, I didn't think of that. David?"

"Aye," he said, revealing a very amused smile.

"Would you be so kind as to transport our little Juniper downstairs so that we might dine?" He gave her a confused look, and she laughed. "I don't know why I'm talking like that; just in a silly mood, I guess."

When the foursome entered the dining room, Erin was surprised to see a wicker bassinet standing in the corner of the room. She looked at David, but he shrugged. Rosie and Charlie began to giggle softly, so she turned to them with her eyebrow raised. Before she could say anything, Kitty entered the room, and they watched her whole head, from her neck to the tips of her earlobes become red.

"Aww, sorry, mum, sir, I din't know you was in 'ere! I… well, I wan'ed it ta be a surprise, like. It were mine, ya see, from when I were a babe. I 'ope it's not too presumptuous of me to—"

"Oh, Kitty! Kitty, it's lovely, simply lovely!" Erin said and walked over to it, touching the flounces and frills of the lining which was made from the most luxurious white and cream-colored silks and velvet.

"Me mum's the one what made the bedding and the like. I fink she's outdone 'erself on it if I might be so bold as to say so, mum," Kitty said, somehow looking both timid and proud at the same time. "Said she'd be honored, for yous ta 'ave it as a gift for your wee babe. Oh, and the inner bedding is washable, mind, she asked me ta mention 'at specifically."

"It's stunning, Kitty," Erin said and went to her, giving her a full embrace. "It means so much to me that it was yours, as well! Please give your mum a hug and tell her how grateful I am." She kissed her housekeeper's cheek and then looked at her husband. "Isn't it delicious, David?"

"Aye! Brilliant! Please thank yer mum for me as well, Kitty," he said and gently laid Juniper in it.

"Aww, and it rocks, as well," Kitty said and rushed over to it, pulling a pin with a brown knob out from one of the stands at the side. The little cradle was then free to sway, so David gently pushed it. The five of them stood around the bassinet and watched Junie's eyes try to keep up with the moving figures before her.

"Goh, isn't that stonking!" Daniel said very loudly when he entered the room. The sudden noise startled the baby, and she began to cry, which made Erin's milk drop and begin leaking, soaking her in seconds.

"Daniel! You're going to have to learn to keep your voice down!" David said with a quiet intensity.

"Shi—I mean… good night nurse, I need to feed her now. I'll take her into the study," Erin said. She lifted the baby and rushed out of the room.

———

"Well done, Dan!" Charlie said crossly.

"Aye, now take yer seat and be quiet, please," David said and followed his wife. He entered his office and closed the door behind him. Erin was sitting on the sofa, her top bunched up on the floor, clearly sopping wet. "Oh, darling, how can I help?" He could see she was in distress and most likely near tears. It seemed the baby wasn't latching on and was wailing at the top of her lungs.

"I don't know!" she snapped, having to raise her voice to be heard. "She won't drink! Come on now, Junie, baby, here you go," she said, holding up her breast and coaxing the child to begin suckling.

"Perhaps she's not hungry now; she was fed only about an hour and a half ago," he offered.

"I'm… completely drenched, David," she said, beginning to cry. "Please find me a towel or two."

"A'right, darling," he said and left the room, meeting Kitty coming out of the dining room.

"Aww, sir, what's the mat'er?" she said, clearly seeing his distress.

"Ach, Kitty, we need towels. Erin's havin' trouble nursing Juniper."

"I'm on it, sir! You go on and tend to Mrs. Elliott now," she said and hurried off toward the kitchen.

"Thank—" he began, but she was already gone. When he returned to the study, he found two frustrated females. Erin was crying, and so was Junie. "Allow me to take her, darling," he said, and she nearly flung the baby into his arms.

"I'm no good at this! I'm a terrible mother! I'm so angry at her right now I wanna—" she began, but there was a gentle knock on the door, and Kitty came in, holding two soft, clean towels and a clean bra and shirt. "Oh, Kitty! I don't know what I'm doing!" Erin wailed as David bounced and rocked his daughter.

He also didn't know what to do, so he tried everything he could think of. Rocking and bouncing weren't helping, so he moved her onto his chest and began gently patting her little back. After a few moments, a substantial belch emerged from the infant, and she stopped crying. There was finally a moment of peace in the room, and they all sighed with relief.

Juniper remained a bit fussy, making upset faces as she began rooting around on David's shirt. "I believe she's ready for supper now, love," he said and gave her back to Erin. It took a few minutes, but between the three of them, she finally began to nurse.

"I'm gonna need some extra-super-duper nursing pads if that's gonna happen every time she cries," Erin said. "I was instantly drenched! It's so embarrassing and gross and uncomfortable!"

"Aye, we'll find some for yeh. Are yeh alright, love? Yeh look sae bonnie feeding her, I must say!"

"Yes, I'm better now. I'm sorry I snapped at you," she said, and he saw tears fill her big brown eyes."

"Never mind that; I understand."

Just then, her belly growled loudly, and she groaned. "I'm so hungry; I wish she'd hurry up. The house smells so good, and I know that Francie is waiting supper for me," she said, and several tears fell down her face.

"Never you mind 'at, mum. I'll explain everyfing to 'ole Francie, and she'll understand," Kitty said and smiled down at her, then she smiled up at David. "I agree wif you, sir, she does look bonnie. Now, can I get ya anyfing else, mum, sir?"

"No, Kitty, you've done splendidly, thank you," David said.

When they finally entered the dining room, the atmosphere wasn't overly peaceful. Dan's face was red, and he was sitting with his arms crossed, glowering at Peter, whose face was also red. Charlie looked annoyed, and Rosie looked a bit frightened. "What's all this?" David said as Erin laid a sleeping Juniper in the bassinet.

Daniel was about to speak, but Erin put her finger to her lips for him to be quiet. "Peter, please tell us what's going on," she said calmly and sat wearily in her chair.

"It's alright, Mum, I've handled it," he said and glared at his brother.

"Dan was being a right doughnut, and Peter put him in his place," Charlie said.

"But I'm hungry! Why must *we* wait for—"

"Shut it!" Peter said with authority.

Erin was exhausted and just needed to eat supper. Dealing with a hungry eleven-year-old wasn't something she wanted to deal with. "Well, we're here now, so let's tuck in," she said. "Thank you, Peter. Rosie, darling, would you please run and tell Kitty—"

Just then, Kitty came in carrying a tureen of soup and began ladling it into the bowls at each setting. "Sorry it took so long, sir, mum, I were—"

"Never mind, Kitty, it's a'right," David said and gave her a weary smile.

The rest of the evening found the children enthralled with Juniper. Erin sat back, watching them bond with both the baby and their father, and it warmed her heart. The last thing she remembered was hearing Peter laugh, followed by David, before being startled awake by a crying infant.

Her milk dropped, and again, she was soaked through. "Holy Moses, this needs to stop!" she said and asked the children to turn away so she could feed her. There was a definite learning curve she and Junie would need to master, and it took a while for things to begin working smoothly.

Once again, David had to find Kitty and ask her to bring them towels while he ran upstairs to find a dry bra and top. David was still gone when Kitty appeared with several hand towels and began helping her. It didn't take long for the children to decide to leave after that, so when David returned, she was sitting alone, draped, and tucked with towels, crying. "This isn't fun, David," she said softly.

"Ach, ma darling, it'll become easier soon," he said, holding out the only bra he could find.

"That one doesn't fit me anymore but thank you for trying." Junie was finished nursing then, so she began burping her methodically. "I want to continue breastfeeding her, David, but I don't know if I can like this. Is it normal to have a tsunami every time she cries? What if we're in public when it happens? I feel so selfish, but this is... too much."

"Aye, I can see that it is. We'll ask the nurse at the postnatal appointment what can be done about et. Now allow me to take her, and we'll get you upstairs. I'm sure ye'll feel better in the morning."

"That appointment is six weeks from now!" she said and sighed. "I'll call the doctor tomorrow; I need to sleep. Thank you for trying to comfort me. I love you." She put the dry top over the towels and followed David upstairs. He laid Junie in her crib, then helped Erin get into her pajamas and into bed. The last thing she remembered was wanting to tell him how much she loved and needed him, but as soon as he covered her with the duvet, she was out.

———

It was up to David to tuck his children in at bedtime that night. He tried to answer their questions and help them understand what was happening. He urged them to be patient and understanding with Erin and Juniper and assured them that things would go back to normal before they knew it.

When they were all settled, he stepped into the nursery on his way to the bedroom to check on Junie and look at her again. "Ach, ye're bonnie, ma darling. Sleep tight," he whispered and then headed to bed. Erin didn't move when he crawled in next to her and said, "Ye're the love of ma life, and I'm thankful for yeh. Sweet dreams."

Chapter Fifty-Six

SLEEP DEPRIVED

Erin sat up in bed, gasping, and felt like a zombie. Juniper was screaming in the other room, so she stood, teetering a bit as she tried to clear her foggy mind. She waddled to the nursery and turned on the overhead light, wishing she hadn't. *I need a small lamp in here!* she thought as she picked Juniper up. Her diaper was wet, so she quickly changed her, then got settled in her new chair, using the nursing pillow to help support the baby.

When Junie finally latched on, she felt the draw of milk being pulled from her breast. It wasn't altogether unpleasant, and she relaxed with the rhythm of it. She dozed on and off until her right side was emptied and the baby began to fuss, then she put her on her shoulder to burp her.

The whole ordeal wouldn't have been quite so bad if it just took a bit less time. It was at least five minutes before she let out a burp, which doesn't seem so bad until you're sleep deprived. She switched sides, wishing she was in her nice comfortable bed, asleep next to her nice comfortable husband.

She woke to the baby being lifted out of her arms. David was burping her, and she smiled at the lovely scene. "I woke tae use the loo, and you weren't there, so I thought tae check on yeh," he said softly. Junie let out a nice loud burp, then he laid her in her crib. Next, he turned to Erin and helped her up.

"Thank you. I'm gonna need you so much if I'm going to survive this," she said and leaned on him as they went back to bed.

It felt like she'd been asleep for about fifteen minutes when Erin was wrenched from her dreams again by the baby crying. Using every bit of willpower she had, she got up and repeated the routine, though this time,

David didn't come to check on her. She woke with a snort, sitting in the nursing chair with Juniper asleep in her arms.

The morning sunshine was pouring through the window, bathing the floor in a long rectangle of light. Her body was stiff and sore as she moved the pillow and stood. She laid Junie in her crib, changed her dirty diaper, and since she was awake and happy, she played with her little toes. "Good morning, Junie baby," she said and then heard the children coming down the stairs for breakfast. She was wearing a nightgown but not a bra, so she quickly shut the door as they walked past.

"Good morning," she heard David say to them, and they returned his greeting. The nursery door opened, and he stepped into the room smiling. He looked so joyful it made her heart ache. "Ach, yeh look sae bonnie this mornin', darling."

"Wow, I think you should see the optometrist, David! You must've gone blind during the night!" she said and accepted the kiss he offered her.

Ignoring her, he turned to Juniper and lifted her in the air, laughing at the surprised look on her face. "And yeh look bonnie as well, ma wee girl." He cradled the baby, then turned to Erin again, giving her another kiss. "Yeh ken, I might *almost* be willin' tae say that the torment we've gone through up till now has been worth et just to have this time with ma family."

"Aye… almost," she said and put her arm around his waist. "I'm so glad everything is looking up now. I need a rest from all the stress. I just hope she'll get into a better schedule soon; I also need sleep."

"Are yeh hungry?"

"That's a silly question! I'll get dressed and meet you downstairs, okay?"

"Aye, and I'll take ma wee Junie down with me," he said, speaking to the baby.

Once she was dressed, and her teeth and hair brushed, Erin went downstairs for breakfast. The children greeted her with, "Good morning."

"Good morning, children," she said, and as she sat in her chair, David passed a section of his newspaper to her.

"Look what I found," he said.

She scanned the page and saw an article with their names in it.

Bundle of Joy or Future Delivery?

David Elliott and his new wife, Erin, have delivered a baby girl, or that is the rumour. They are keeping tight-lipped about the matter. We wish them the best of luck.

"Yeah, right," she said. "At least there isn't a photo of me looking like a walrus this time."

Daniel suddenly began coughing, choking, and laughing at the same time. It took quite a while of Charlie pounding on his back for him to explain himself. "Goh, Erin! That was brilliant!"

"Okay, what exactly was brilliant?" she asked, feeling like she'd missed something.

"A walrus! You said you looked like a walrus! All you need is a beard!" he said and snorted as he laughed.

"Dan! Shut it, would you?" Peter said hotly. "She didn't say she looked like one, but that there wasn't a photo of her looking like one."

His brother's rebuke did nothing to diminish his laughter; if anything, it seemed to make him laugh even harder, until she saw the corners of Rosie's and Charlie's mouths begin to turn up in amusement. Before long, everyone but her, David, and Peter were laughing hysterically. "A'right, now, that's enough," David tried, but it didn't help. Apparently, they all had the giggles, and as she looked at her husband and eldest son, she couldn't help but smile.

"Okay, I admit it was funny," she said and poured a much-needed cup of hot, rich tea, followed by a splash of cream and plenty of sugar.

"ORK, ORK, ORK," Dan said and pulled his arms up tight to his body while clapping his hands.

Rosie spat out her milk onto her plate, and Charlie laughed so hard he began coughing. "Ha, ha, ha, very funny, Daniel. Now eat your breakfast before I ask Kitty to take your plate away," Erin said with a knowing grin.

"Yes, Mum," he said, sobering up quite a bit, though he couldn't hide his dimples as he smiled at Rosie and Charlie.

Later that day, the mail contained the results of the paternity test. David hurried to find Erin, who was in the study, before opening it. "Oh, David, I'm so nervous!" she said, staring at the envelope in his hand.

"Not as nervous as I am, I assure you," he said and held it out to her.

"You do it and tell me what it says."

He furrowed his brows and sat next to her on the leather sofa. "Ach, et shouldn't be so nerve-wracking; we ken she's mine."

"Yes, we do. Maybe it's just the thought of what if. Here, I'll do it," she said and took it from him. The envelope ripping sounded louder than it should, and when she pulled out the folded paper, her hand trembled. "Well, I guess we should just rip the band-aid off, right?

"Right," he whispered.

She slowly unfolded the official-looking page and began reading out loud. "*Dear Mr. and Mrs. Elliott, Please find enclosed the results of your—*" She stopped speaking as she scanned the page then she let out a long breath.

"What? Go on and tell me already!"

"Read for yourself." She handed him the page and pointed to the place he should start.

"*The test reveals that David P. Elliott's DNA matches 99.91% with the DNA of Juniper A. Elliott. This result is sufficient to be certain of his parentage,*" he read and then closed his eyes. He laid the hand holding the letter on his lap and was motionless.

"David?"

He opened his eyes, and she watched as tears fell down his cheeks. "Thank God," he said softly and kissed her for a long time.

"Aye, thank God," she repeated.

That week went by in a blur. On Saturday, the kids had to start packing for school. Erin knew they were double-minded about going back. She'd heard Dan complaining about not sleeping very well because he'd heard the baby crying, but no one said anything to her about it.

She was sad they'd be gone, but in a small way, she was glad for the break. Junie was up two or three times each night, so she had to take naps when she could to catch up on sleep. It was difficult to not feel guilty about being too tired to spend as much quality time as she wanted with them while they were home.

David, on the other hand, had been able to spend as much time as he wanted with them. She'd never seen him so happy and fulfilled. When she was awake, he was always on hand to help with Junie and tried to think of things to do as a family, like playing cards or board games. When she was napping, he often took the older children to the park while Kitty kept an eye on Juniper.

On Sunday morning, after the rush of last-minute packing, they loaded up the SUV. The children hugged and kissed Erin and Junie several times, then David drove them to the train station. The house was suddenly too quiet, and Erin cried, knowing how much she'd miss them.

"Aww, what is it, mum?" Kitty said when she found her sitting on the stairs, head in her hands.

"It's silly, but I miss them already. I thought I'd be glad for the peace, but—"

"Aww, 'at's not silly, mum. They're a fine lot, they are, and I'm sure they'll miss you as well. Anaway, they've an exeat in two weeks' time, so you'll 'ardly know they're gone 'afore they're back, makin' a ruckus," she said sweetly.

"I know you're right, and thanks for the pep talk, but I feel like I'm in a whirlwind right now. Everything is going so fast. I want things to slow down, and at the same time, I want it to go faster, so Junie grows out of this waking every two hours nonsense. Why can't time just do what you want when you want it to?"

"Aww, mum, I know just what ya mean. Why don't you go up and 'ave a nice long shower? You'll feel bet'er after, don't ya fink? If Junie starts ta fuss, I'll pacify 'er till you're done."

465

"Okay, Kitty, I'm sure you're right," she said and hugged her friend and housekeeper.

Erin was about to turn off the shower when David stepped into the tub behind her. "Mind if I join yeh?" he asked and bent to kiss her shoulder.

"Mmm, I don't mind at all," she said and leaned back as he wrapped his arms around her. She could feel his excitement against her, and she gasped when he positioned his growing cock between her legs. "Oh, David, I want you so bad! I wish you could press me against the wall and pound me hard!"

"Ach, I wish I could do that as well." He gently thrust himself over her folds but didn't penetrate. The doctor had warned them that sex had to be point of ejaculation only for six weeks. It had only been one, and the thought of five more was disheartening. "Turn around."

She turned to face him, and he placed his hand between her legs and began stimulating her clitoris with his fingers. He turned her slightly to the side, allowing the warm water to wash over her erect nipples, then flow over his hand and rush down her legs. "Oh, yes, that feels so good!" She tried to grab his cock, wanting to stroke it, but he shook his head.

"You first, love," he said and leaned down to kiss her.

He knew what he was doing, circling her most sensitive spot round and round, taking his time and not rushing until she felt the delicious build-up that brought her to a fulfilling climax. She felt her body release, flexing and contracting with each continued touch of her husband's fingertips.

With her eyes closed, she stood, breathing hard, allowing the sensation to flow through her until it was finished, then she rested her forehead on his bicep. "Le Potage, David, that was so good. Now I need a nap or a cigarette," she said and laughed gently.

"Aye, and after my turn, we shall have a wee kip if our daughter will allow et." He took her forearm and pulled it to his slightly flaccid cock.

"Aww, the poor wee thing needs some help, I think," she said and crouched before him, but the water began pouring over her head, and she couldn't breathe. "Turn the showerhead, please." He moved it and then moaned when her lips touched the end of his shaft.

"Ach! Et won't be *wee* for long, love."

She parted her lips and wrapped them over his already full erection, sliding them over him. The sounds he made, gasping and panting, filled her with the desire to satisfy him. When her legs got tired in that position, she stood, with his help, and put a bit of her soap onto her hand. He gasped loudly when she took hold of him and began slowly stroking it. "Do you like that then?" she asked rhetorically.

"Ma Losh, Erin!" he said and had to catch his breath. "Ye're sae good at that. That's it, love—Almost there—There—" He placed his arm out to steady himself on the tiled shower wall and then took hold of her hand to stop her. "Thank you, darling. Et may not be *as* good as the real thing, but et's still bloody fantastic."

"Yeah, it is. I reckon it'll do for another five weeks, but no longer," she said with a laugh as she stepped out of the tub and grabbed her towel.

"Absolutely no longer!"

Chapter Fifty-Seven

NEW BAIRN AT OWLGATE

When Juniper Elliott was nearly three weeks old, the children came home on an exeat from school, so they decided to visit the family at Owlgate for the weekend. Miraculously, Junie didn't cry at all on the airplane. She waited until they got into David's mother's SUV that Roger had picked them up in to start wailing at the top of her lungs, wanting to be fed.

"David! Please help me. I need to feed her now, or I'll be soaked through!" Erin said in a slight panic. She could already feel her milk saturating her breast pads and began to unfasten her top and nursing bra.

David got Juniper out of the car seat, which wasn't easy since she was flailing her arms as her piercing screams filled the air. Dan was covering his ears with the palms of his hands, and everyone else was covering their eyes or looking away.

"I'm sorry, everyone," Erin nearly yelled to be heard over Junie's dreadful pleas for food. Finally, she latched on, and everyone breathed a sigh of relief when the vehicle was quiet. "Go ahead, Roger, just watch traffic, okay?" She knew it would take a while to feed her, and she was getting cold with her wet bra and damp shirt.

David lovingly covered her with a receiving blanket but peeked under it a few times. "Ach, I feel something so indescribably rich and deep inside ma verra soul at the sight of you feeding our child," he whispered in her ear.

They were soon at Owlgate, where Tilly was waiting to open and close the gate for them. "Well, that's convenient! You need to keep her around!" Erin teased Roger since he didn't need to go through the routine and trouble of doing it himself.

"Aye, she's handy tae have on standby," he said, smiling at her in the rearview mirror.

With David's help, she'd been able to switch sides halfway there, so Juniper was now sound asleep, though Erin still needed to get herself covered back up.

The children exited the SUV as soon as the doors were unlocked, and she sighed. "Breastfeeding is a real pain in the butt!" she said, feeling stressed and chilled. "I'm gonna be homebound for months! It's too much work to go out unless it's important."

"Ach, but et's so bonnie tae see yeh doin' et," David said as he bundled the baby up, then stepped out onto the driveway.

"I'm glad *you* enjoy it," she said with a hint of sarcasm and put her shirt back down. She then took his offered hand and allowed him to help her out as well.

"Ooooh! I can't wait to see her!" Tilly said as she hurried toward them and grabbed the diaper bag while Roger began hauling the luggage to the door.

"She's bonnie, but she certainly has a set of pipes on her!" Roger said.

"That's for sure!" Erin agreed.

They walked into the light, lovely foyer and could finally relax. There was a cheerful fire in the small fireplace, and the dogs were away, chasing Dan. By the sound of it, they were already upstairs.

"Ach, Losh, but et's good tae see yeh," Annis said and hugged David, then she stepped up to Erin, who was holding the tiny bundle of blankets.

Her mother-in-law's face read like an open book, and Erin laughed. "Ach, you're not fooling anyone. I know you're not interested in me; you want to see your new granddaughter," she said and began unwrapping her like she was peeling an onion, handing the blankets to David as she went.

"Yeh ken I love you, dear." Annis let out a squeal of delight when she was handed the sleeping newborn. "Ma Losh, she's ginger!" she exclaimed and patted down a fluffy orange cowlick on her little head.

Millie entered the room and didn't even bother with the pretense of greeting anyone but Juniper. "Ach, Erin, she looks like you," the aging woman said as her eyes filled with tears.

"I need to change into something dry, so you go ahead and get your fill. I'll be back in a few—"

"No need tae rush, dear," Annis said, rocking and gazing lovingly at the baby in her arms.

"I won't then. You'll know if she needs anything; the whole street will know. David, will you please come up and help me? Oh, and bring the white tube of cream from the diaper bag."

———

David smiled at his mother and her partner Millie, the woman who'd been his nanny. "Aye, right behind yeh," he said. His mother looked at him and smiled as Millie cooed and made little clicking noises. He rooted around in the bag but couldn't find a tube of cream, so he wisely took out a diaper and a package of wipes. He handed them to Millie, then took the whole bag upstairs with him.

"I'm sorry, I should've told you where it was," she said when he entered the room with a sheepish grin. She unzipped a side pocket, pulled out a tube of ointment, and began massaging it into her nipples. He could see they were red and irritated.

"That looks painful," he said, scrunching up his face in imagined discomfort.

"It's not bad now, but I've gotta remember to use this stuff every time I feed her, or it'll be brutal."

"Mum and Millie are in heaven," he said as he opened their bags and began unpacking.

"Aye, I'm so glad we were able to come up for the weekend. I need a rest," she said and finished getting dressed.

"I'm glad I'm here to help yeh, love. I can't imagine what a single mother would do. You need four hands far too often to do it alone."

"I'm thankful I have you. I'm also glad your days on the set are usually short and that you'll be on hiatus soon. I'm also thankful that our baby will have the fresh ocean air instead of the polluted London smog filling her wee lungs for her first few months."

"Erin?" he said softly and gave her a knowing smile. "Do yeh reckon we could—I mean, I could give yeh a wee treatment? If I do as the doctor said and not penetrate yeh deeply?"

Erin smiled at him and unbuttoned her slacks with the elastic band at the back. "I'd really like that, but can I suck on you first?"

David began breathing heavily and nodded, then he went into the bathroom to find some towels. "I'd really like that."

Half an hour later, after taking their time and being very gentle, they were dressed again. "Thank you, darling. I don't want to hurt yeh, but I desire yeh so badly… verra often, more than ever, in fact."

"Probably sympathy hormones," she said.

"Is that a thing?" he asked, his curiosity piqued.

"Prolly not. I made it up," she said with a laugh, "but it could be."

Erin was allowed to rest the whole day, which her body really needed. Not being able to have regular treatments was keeping her just on the edge of exhaustion all the time, and the only way to heal was to rest. The more she tried to do, the slower her recovery would be.

There were plenty of people able and willing to care for Juniper there. The only thing she was really needed for was feeding her, which seemed to be falling exactly on Millie's schedule. At supper, everyone got to eat at the table while Erin fed the baby, sitting on the sofa. Everyone was nearly finished by the time she was able to join them. The same thing happened with breakfast and lunch the next day as well.

After lunch on the second day they were there, she decided to take a nap. When she came downstairs, she heard David in a heated discussion with his mum. "I don't want tae go; I dinnae care what they've done for us. I dinnae want to think on the reason they became involved in our lives at all," David was saying.

"David, you must understand; if yeh don't go, they may see et as a spurn, and you don't want them tae realize they suddenly haven't enough room for him anamore, do yeh?"

"They wouldn't do that... would they?" she heard him say.

As she got to the doorway, she saw him pacing and running his fingers through his hair. She stepped into the sitting room and said, "Room for whom?"

David looked at his mother and then walked over to Erin. "Hello, love, did yeh sleep well?" he said, clearly trying to sound cheerful.

She looked at him, then at Annis. "Room for whom?" she asked again. She was about to walk over to the couch but froze, suddenly realizing whom they were most likely talking about. "Bran? Is this about him? But I thought you'd given them a sizable donation to have him... taken away, Ann?" She shivered and felt a cold sweat break out on the back of her neck.

"I did, dear, tae take him, but keepin' him there may be quite a different kettle of fish," she said.

"There's a gala dinner tae raise funds for Thistledown in a few months, and we've been invited to attend, but I dinnae want tae go!" David said adamantly.

She went to the sofa and sat next to Annis. "But... what if they *do* let him go, David?" she asked, not liking the idea of that one bit. "Who knows what he'll do to get back at everyone for putting him in there?"

Annis took her hand and patted it. "She's right, David. Surely you can acquiesce this time?" she said.

"I'll think on et," he said and left the room.

Erin sighed, and Annis stood, helping her to stand. "You must try to convince him, dear; he'll listen tae you."

"I'll try," Erin said and followed him outside to the back patio.

He looked at her solemnly, then took her by the hand and led her back into the house. She followed him up the backstairs and into his room where Junie was sleeping, and he shut the door firmly behind them. "Erin... there's somethin' else."

"I'm not surprised with the way you're acting."

"Aye, well, I'm fairly certain there will be people at this event who… who were in the photos you found. I would prefer tae avoid them if possible," he said quietly.

"I understand, but which is worse, spending the evening with people who don't know you've seen the pictures, pictures you're not even in, or potentially allowing Bran to be released?" she asked.

"That's an impossibly hard decision," he said thoughtfully and began biting his nails.

Clearly there was more he wanted to say, but he was hesitating. She looked into his eyes and cocked her head to the side. "Alright, what else? I know that look, David Elliot; there's something more, and I want to know what it is," she demanded, and he sighed.

"Yeh ken those people were friends with or knew Susannah, right?" he said, plainly trying to choose his words wisely.

"I can imagine they did, and?"

"They'll not take tae yeh verra quickly, if at all, and I just don't want yeh tae have a bad experience."

Erin touched his face. "I'll survive, I'm sure."

"Aye, yeh will, but yeh may be missin' a limb or two," he said with a smile.

"Would you prefer I didn't go?" she asked, wondering if that was what he meant.

"What? I'll not go without yeh! Oh no, we're in this together or not at all."

"I suppose it's fancy dress?" she said, dreading the thought of finding an outfit that looked even slightly decent on her.

"Fancy dress? Et's not a costume party if that's what you mean. It's a black-tie, formal event. Ye'll be expected tae wear a gown."

"That's what I meant, but an actual *gown*? Good night nurse," she groaned, "that won't be fun at all, but it won't keep me away."

"So… ye're willin' tae go, even if people are ill-mannered and uncivil to yeh?" he asked.

"Well, I don't see a choice. I say we go and try to enjoy ourselves. If anyone is overly rude, I'll just have a little chat with Oscar," she said, smiling.

473

"I can't believe ye've met him! He's the stuff of legend, yeh ken. Not many people can say they've actually been face tae face with him," David said, shaking his head.

"Aye, and they can't say he's kissed their hand, either then, can they?" She offered up the hand he'd kissed as evidence. "I have witnesses to prove it."

"Ach, I reckon et's settled then, though I'm not looking forward to et."

"But on the bright side, you'll have a chance to meet the man, the legend himself, right?" she said and hugged him around the middle.

"Aye, silver linings."

That day, David joined Erin in eating late as she fed Juniper, helping her to feel less ostracized, which really helped a lot. Her hormones were still on a rollercoaster, and the slightest thing could sometimes set her off. She spoke to Annis about finding a gown for the gala and decided she should wait to start searching. Her body would most likely change a lot in the next few months, and putting it off would be less stressful.

That evening, Annis handed out gifts, including a tiny, hooded snowsuit with fur around the face that made Junie look like a pink elf. It was way too big, even though it said it was a size 'newborn.' She'd made tiny baby booties out of the softest yarn, and Erin joked that she wanted a big pair for herself. She also got them a baby carrier that could be used like a sling or converted into a front-facing backpack.

Millie made several little burp rags and bibs with delightful embroidery on them. She made Erin promise to use them after she'd said they were too elegant and beautiful for everyday use.

Tilly had found a stuffed *Future Explorations* time travel device that squeaked when you squeezed it. She and Erin had fun throwing it to each other, though it would occasionally end up bouncing off David's head, back, or arm. Roger gave her a gyroscope, which Charlie and Rosie found interesting when he showed them what it did.

On Sunday morning, mealtime went a bit more smoothly, as Junie was hungry half an hour before breakfast, but then they had to leave. The children had to return to school, so as soon as the morning meal was done, David, Roger, and the children began loading the SUV for their trip back home. Erin had the luxury of spending a few more minutes with her new mother-in-law and Millie.

It was hard saying goodbye, harder than usual, but they promised to visit again as soon as possible. There were lots of hugs, kisses, and tears as everyone got into the SUV that morning. For some reason, the emotions started affecting Rosie, and she cried all the way to the airport. Junie, on the other hand, slept for the whole flight and didn't cry once.

Soon they were home, but for just long enough to eat lunch, then pack any last-minute school things. Poor Rosie shed quite a few more tears when they had to say goodbye to Erin and her new baby sister. The boys were sad, but they didn't cry at all. Finally, it was time for David to deliver them to the station and see them safely onto their train headed south to Dorset.

———

When he returned to the house, David was tired and climbed the stairs, longing to be with his wife again. He found her asleep in the nursery on the chair he'd bought her. Junie was asleep as well, propped up by the pillow, so she wouldn't fall out of Erin's arms.

Erin had obviously fallen asleep while feeding her since her breast was bare, and Junie was only a few centimeters away from it. He lifted his daughter and laid her over his shoulder to burp her. It took a long time as he gently patted her back and bounced her before a decent size belch freed itself from the infant's belly.

"Well done, you," he whispered and laid her on her back in the crib, as he'd been taught, then covered her with a light blanket. He watched his baby girl squirm for just a moment, ready to pick her up at the slightest grumble, but she didn't complain and fell back to sleep right away.

"Well done *you*," he heard from across the room. "You'll be an old pro in no time," Erin said, holding out her arms for him to help her up.

"Aye, et took an awfully long time to burp her though," he said as they looked down at their child with their arms around each other.

"You've gotta be tough; she can take it."

"Ach, I can't bring maself tae beat ma daughter."

"You're not beating her, you're helping her. Honestly, darling, it feels good to her, and the sooner the better," she said and then chuckled as Junie smiled in her sleep. "Look at her, David! Have you ever seen anything so beautiful?"

He didn't say anything, so she looked up at him. He'd shifted his gaze to her and smiled warmly. "Only when I look at you, Erin."

"Come make love to me, okay?"

"I'd like that," he said, and they left the room, keeping the door open a crack.

Chapter Fifty-Eight

A LATE WINTER STROLL

On March tenth, twenty-three days after Juniper Elliott was born, the weather became unseasonably warm. Longing to get out of the house, David and Erin decided to go for a walk using the sling carrier Annis had given them. David insisted on carrying her, declaring that she'd carried her for over nine months, and it was his turn. They laughed as they tried to figure out how to get the sling onto him and then how to get the baby into it once it was on.

Hoping to avoid the few remaining paparazzo who'd camped outside their house, they took their chances, David wearing a ball cap and dark sunglasses as they walked out the back door. However, as they made their way to the park, they noticed a few men taking photos of them. They didn't mind too much as Junie was so small, she wasn't visible outside her carrier, and they were far too happy to care, as long as they kept their distance.

They held hands and kissed openly, loving the freedom they had now that they were married. "I can't believe this weather!" David said. "You must've brought et with yeh from America."

"Ha! Not likely! It's…" she began and took out her cell phone to check the weather in Wisconsin. "…negative four degrees Fahrenheit in Green Bay right now! What would that be in Celsius?"

David did some quick math. "That's negative twenty. A'right, I take et back; I'm glad we're not there!" he said as a man approached them, staying back far enough not to be intrusive.

"May I take a photo for the papers, Mr. and Mrs. Elliott?" he asked politely, so David agreed. They smiled but didn't take Juniper out of the sling. "Thank you! I see *you're* wearin' the sling, David."

"Aye. Ma wife has carried the baby quite long enough. Et's my turn now."

"Good on you, mate! Cheers," the man said and then left them alone.

They made it to a nearby park they'd surprisingly never been to before and strolled around it, hand in hand, taking their time. Erin found a pretty pink rock that sparkled when the sun hit it and asked David to put it in his pocket. At one point, they sat on a bench in the sun and discussed their hopes for the future.

When the sun decided to hide behind a large clump of clouds, they decided to head home. On the way there, Junie's pacifier fell out of the sling and hit the pavement. David replaced the dirty one with a clean one he'd thought to put in his pocket on the way out, feeling quite chuffed at how prepared he'd been.

When they arrived home, it was time for lunch. Since Junie was sleeping, he kept the sling on at the table, so they could eat together in peace. She started fussing just at the end of the meal, so he carried her upstairs. When Erin was ready, he managed to get her out of the contraption, though it was more difficult than it should have been.

He sat on the floor near her feet, watching his wife and newborn daughter bonding. His heart felt so full it almost hurt at the sight. There was something so beautiful about the scene that he couldn't speak, though he tried unsuccessfully in his mind to put it into words.

Erin's eyes were droopy as he beheld her, and when Junie was done nursing, she yawned so hard that he saw her eyes become teary. When he yawned in response, she laughed as she burped the baby, then handed his daughter to him.

"Ach, ma wee bairn, I can't tell yeh just how much I love yeh! I'm beside maself, knowin' I'll be able tae raise yeh in the way I wanted to do for yer brothers and sister. I'll finally be the 'da I've always wanted tae be for yeh," he whispered and lay her in the crib.

"I'm so happy, David. I feel like things are finally getting better and we'll be able to move on," Erin said softly as they stood side by side, watching their baby girl.

Chapter Fifty-Nine

CLIVE GETS HIS WAY

Juniper Elliott was just twenty-three days old when David and Erin were upstairs watching their little girl sleep after their walk in the park. They heard a knock on the door, then a loud commotion coming from downstairs. Kitty was yelling, telling whomever it was that they couldn't come in, though, from the sound of things, they were undeterred.

They rushed down the stairs to find out what was happening and saw Detective Chief Superintendent, Clive Dawson, walk from the entryway toward the kitchen. "What's goin' on?" David asked as he and Erin followed him, but Clive told two of the four officers he'd brought with him to hold him.

"I'm arresting you for—" He turned and looked Erin up and down; she was angry, and her face was flushed. Stepping closer, he gently touched her cheek. "You couldn't be more different from Susannah, could you?" he said to her, then looked at David. "I imagine she's good at something, though, isn't she, Elliott?" He brought his face up close to Erin's as if he were going to kiss her, and David started straining to get free from the men holding him.

"Leave her be! There's no need tae—" he began, but then Clive did kiss her, or tried to, though she turned her head and his lips landed on her cheek.

With one large hand, he grabbed a chunk of hair at the back of her head and pulled hard, making her reveal her soft, vulnerable, ivory neck to him. He put his face up to it and took a deep breath. "That's nice!" he said, and David writhed, trying to free himself. Clive began nibbling her earlobe before progressing to her neck and sucking on it while she fought to push him away.

She could see David struggling with all his might, so much so that to keep their hold on him the young policemen were forced to brace themselves. In one swift movement, Clive yanked her hair so hard and unexpectedly that he was able to whip her around and pin her face down over the breakfast table. *Of course I had to wear a skirt today, didn't I?* she thought, her mind racing. He reached under her skirt and touched her over her panties. *What should I do?*

"Don't you dare touch my wife!" David yelled, straining to be free from the men holding him.

Erin was struggling as well, not making it easy for him. He placed his hand on her head, pushing hard while holding a chunk of her hair, then unzipped his fly. "No! Don't!" she screamed as he tried to get his cock out of his slacks with one hand. *Oh, God! Where's Kitty?* she thought, not sure if she wanted her to be a witness to his brutality or safely hiding in another room.

"Hold her!" Clive barked at the two other men he'd brought with him. The men did as they were told, spreading her arms out to each side of her.

David was screaming, and Erin felt dissociated with the scene, as though she were looking down on the madness, but she herself was calm. Suddenly, it dawned on her that there was no way he was going to rape her; she was still bleeding. He must've felt the heavy-duty menstrual pad she was wearing when he touched her.

Instantly she understood that his goal was to get a reaction from David, to get him to do something so he could arrest him. She wanted to tell David, to warn him, but her words would've been drowned out by the chaos and yelling. Clive then acted as though he'd pulled himself out and was preparing to rape her, but he actually hadn't done that at all. She thought she should try to scream, but it felt strange since she knew he wasn't going to follow through. All she could do was wait as it unfolded.

It was then that David finally accomplished whatever he'd been set up to do, though Erin didn't see what it was. Clive stepped away from her, leaving her pinned down by the men, her skirt flung onto her back, and her underwear still all the way up. She heard him zip his trousers, then he barked, "Let her go." When they released her, she stood and turned to look at David.

The scene felt like it was moving in slow motion as she watched the evil man grin at her husband and finish the charge he'd started earlier, "…assault of an emergency worker... with intent to resist arrest," he said quietly, as though he'd won the battle and was rubbing it in. "Restrain him."

Erin didn't know how serious the offense was, but she knew they'd been manipulated and that it couldn't be legal. David had been impelled into a crime, but who could prove it? Surely none of the men standing in that room would say anything. All she could do was stare in horror as they put handcuffs on her husband and read him his rights, not that he actually had any rights in that situation.

"David! Don't say anything! I'll call your lawyer—What's his name?" He stared wide-eyed at her, fear written all over him, then Junie began to cry. "I love you, David!" Erin said as they led him out of the house, down the five steps to the gate, out to the sidewalk, and into the waiting squad car with a blue and yellow checkerboard pattern on it.

ACKNOWLEDGEMENTS

I'd like to thank:

Karen Rathburn, Linda Utrie, Colleen Bucholtz, and Scott Boede for being my beta readers.

Marni MacRae, for being my editor and for just being awesome! I raise my glass to you—*Slàinte mhath!* Here's to Scotland... perhaps next year.

Rehman, for the cover!

My family, friends, and fans of my books for your support and enthusiasm.

And finally, to my mother, who passed away before this book was ready to be published. I know you did your best to be a good mommy with everything you were delt in life, and I will love you forever and always!